THE NIGHTMARE FROM WORLD'S END

ROBERT J. STAVA

SEVERED PRESS
HOBART

THE NIGHTMARE FROM WORLD'S END

ISBN: 978-1-925493-87-0

This book is dedicated to wife, Tomiko,
who continues to inspire my imagination, and to Michael Crichton:
this one is all your fault.

"I only know that sometimes we are lucky enough to know that our lives have been changed, to discard the old, embrace the new, and run headlong down an immutable course ... ."

Jacques Cousteau

INTRODUCTION: UPDATE FROM THE HUDSONVALLEY

I'm so glad you came back! Sure, I know it's been a while, but not too long I hope. The folks in Wyvern Falls have been busy as ever since that last bit of business (and boy it got a little nasty, didn't it?) involving that Crowley guy and his Golden Dawn Cult cronies. I can tell you I haven't cracked open my deck of 'Toth' Tarot Cards since; it's been relegated to an upper, dusty shelf in the library where it can collect more dust just as long as it wants.

As I sit here in my library typing this out, it's a cool, rainy November morning out there. We managed to get through the blitz of Halloween festivities (and I swear they ship in truckloads of kids from other countries to target our street – it's like the Invasion of Normandy, with an army of little monsters) this region is known for and right now that fearsome Turkey Day is still a week into the future, so there's still time to double-up on the exercise routine and hide the bathroom scale.

So here I am with my warm, padded Japanese house-vest – courtesy of my Japanese in-laws - and a steaming cup of fresh coffee. It's cozy here in this room, with its books and ship models, fireplace and framed pictures. Yes, our family dog Max is next to my feet, a malamute dozing on his back in that peculiar way malamute's do, and though the cat is busy terrorizing one of the upstairs bedrooms, it's relatively quiet here; a bastion of comfort on a cold autumn morning.

A place one could sit and write forever.

And yet my gaze keeps straying out the window and down the street … a street that looks suspiciously like any number of ones you might find yourself strolling on in Wyvern Falls. And I know that at some point this morning, I'm going to have to shuck the PJ's, get properly dressed, saddle up the dog, and get out there to see what's happening.

Because the truth is that mysterious village isn't that far away from my own, or any number of doorsteps the world over for that matter. You'd be surprised at what you can find out there just beyond those front steps, and who … or *what* … you might just run into. Like that gigantic crate I discovered one day washed up on the shores of the Hudson right after that hurricane … the one that seemed to rock ever so slightly when I approached it.

So, what do you say? Up for a little stroll? I for one am dying to find out what all that commotion is about and where the hell all those police cars are heading …

-R.J.S.

PRELUDE:

It was two days after Hurricane Cassandra swept the area that late August that the three kids found the crate along the shoreline, though perhaps *crate* didn't quite accurately describe it.

For starters, it was *massive*.

And old.

It was Jeremy Caldwell who spotted it first.

Caldwell, a small ten-year-old kid with buck teeth and a 'Bieber' haircut, had been out exploring the outer shoreline of Raadsel point with his two pals, Domingo Vasquez and Curtis Jackson. The hurricane had been a *wicked cool* event in 'Jeremese' for these kids (none of whose houses were within the flood plain), and they'd biked out to the point late that morning to see what treasures the storm surge may have left along their section of the Hudson River shoreline. They'd actually seen the motor boat left washed up on the Metro North tracks and had heard rumors of all sorts of stuff being found from lost wallets, booze crates, and even dead bodies.

At first thought, it was looking as though their 'Hudson Explorers Club Official Salvage Expedition' (as Caldwell titled it) was going to yield little more than smashed coolers, some rubber hosing, and a sodden sweatshirt. They'd parked their bikes near the old abandoned swimming pool complex and taken the footpath through the bramble and trees to the shore. When they'd first emerged, they'd stumbled across a young scruffy-looking photographer – an artsy-looking type from Peekskill – setting up a tripod to photograph a young woman against a complex jumble of huge trees that had washed up. The guy looked like he had an expensive camera, but while attractive in a hip 'coffee house' sort of way, the girl was a long way shy of a Victoria's Secret model (in the three boy's estimation), so they didn't pay much attention.

The storm surge had receded and the tide was out, so they were able to pick their way along the outer shoreline of the point where it curved around, all the way to Murderer's Creek if one went far enough.

Overhead, a few gulls winged through the washed-out skies and the river was still muddied by run-off (and God knows what else). The shore was a mess of slime-covered rocks, shells – mostly bleached-out oysters

– and all sorts of debris. There was all manner of trees and logs, chunks of flotation pieces from local marinas, tangled ropes and fishing lines and various garbage, but nothing looking of much value until Jeremy skirted around one enormous pile of tree roots and spotted the crate.

"Holy crap!" he'd yelled. "Guys!"

A moment later, the two other boys caught up with him, expecting to see a shipwreck or something.

Curtis Jackson, a lanky black kid who had the studied look of a future banker or lawyer, pulled up short and scratched his head. Domingo, who was muscular and a rising star on the fifth-grade wrestling team, bumped into him.

What the—?" Curtis said, adjusting his glasses.

Jeremy stood with his hands-on hips, looking at the object that was perhaps a few dozen yards further down the shoreline to the north.

A huge crate.

Even at a distance, it was clear that whatever it was, based on the amount of seaweed and discolored timbers, it had been until recently underwater.

Perhaps forty feet long by eight wide and five high, it was constructed of massive 4x4 timbers in a complex array that resembled not so much a crate as a ridiculously heavy duty *cage*.

The kids worked their way to it and stood, marveling.

The crate was still partially in the water but had been thrust up and left on the beach as if by some massive unseen hand.

"What do you think it is?" Domingo asked, blinking.

"Fuck if I know!" Jeremy said, in a tone that also said, '*but stupendously fucking awesome!*'

The thing looked old, ancient actually, and gave off a rank fishy stench tinged with brine.

"Maybe it's some sort of lost sea treasure!" Jeremy offered, stepping up and trying to peer in the heavy and thick array of beams. Whatever it was, it still looked solid enough to withstand a hundred hurricanes.

Domingo and Curtis seemed less entranced. Domingo looked a little suspicious, as he was of anything not fitting into a textbook definition of the world. Curtis was distinctly uneasy. He wasn't sure what, but something about the crate *scared* him.

It seemed to give off an aura of something with inherent menace, like a dangerous trap waiting to be sprung.

That was ridiculous of course, but …

"Guys, maybe we should just keep going," he suggested, a nervous edge creeping into his voice, "I bet there's more cool things up the beach." But even as he said it, he knew it was a lost cause, as were most his suggestions with his friend. Jeremy was already trying to climb on top of the thing.

"Gimme a leg up, bro!" Jeremy said to Domingo, who complied by interlacing his hands palms up.

A moment later, Jeremy was standing on top of the crate, struggling to keep his balance. He held his fist high up in the air, a triumphant explorer dressed in cargo shorts, an Iron Man T-shirt, and sneakers.

"Yoweee!" he yelled. "I hereby claim this treasure in th—"

Suddenly with a groan, the crate shifted and Jeremy's feet slid out from under him on the algae and slime-covered wood. He landed with a smacking *thud* on his right arm that made the other two boys wince.

But then he bounced back up with his usual bravado.

"Fine, I'm fine!" He grinned, even though his arm went momentarily numb.

Curtis saw blood dripping out where the forearm had been cut on some barnacles. "Dude, maybe you should get down, that thing is dangerous. And you cut yourself – check out your arm."

Jeremy looked at it and made an exaggerated face, "Oh God, I'm dead – I'm dead!" followed by ridiculous gagging sounds. Then he jumped down next to his friends, turned around, and making his best 'Walking Dead' zombie face (which wasn't very good) lurched towards Curtis and began to drool. "Brains ... brains ...!"

"Knock it off, twerp!" Curtis said, backing away. Now he definitely wanted to get out of here. He could have sworn he'd heard something large shift inside a moment before the crate moved.

Something *heavy* and *squishy*.

That couldn't be possible of course. Whatever this thing was, it looked like it had been sitting underwater a long, *long* time. Plus, he noticed there were traces of writing on the side, barely legible. It looked like it said 'Edmund Wood' though the first two letters were hardly there at all. *Why was that name familiar? Something he'd once heard in his history class ... sort of ... it had been a field trip to West Point when ...*

"Guys, check this out!" Jeremy cut in. He'd already moved on to the end of the crate where he was standing tiptoe on a large boulder and peering into the crisscrossed beams. There was no getting around the fact that the crate was oddly constructed, *super-reinforced* one might even say.

What the heck was this thing for? Curtis wondered.

Jeremy was peering into the crate where it appeared there was a wider space. The beams had been constructed like a haphazard jigsaw puzzle and the mix of crisscrossed shadows made perception tricky ... but for a second, he swore he saw something, a *glistening* something, move inside. He had an impression of an eye the size of a dinner plate ... but then it was gone. But the stench was nearly overwhelming. Dead muck and fishes, the gagging brackish smell of living things long buried deep underwater.

He swore he heard what could be described as a *'sclorking'* sound ... and then he saw what looked like a shiny disc, like a coin. He reached in carefully.

"Hey dudes, I think I—" he said then stopped when something wet and powerful, like a slimy rope, caressed his forearm. He looked in and was shocked to see a sort of thick blackish-green tentacle probing inside the space, as if tasting his arm. "What the ...?" he managed to get out, when with lightning speed the tentacle seized his arm like a vise. Even as he looked on with dawning horror, at least a dozen other tentacles appeared – of various sizes – accompanied by an unmistakable slithering/sucking sound.

Domingo was standing closest to him, looking up as his friend was suddenly yanked *into* the crate with a sickening *crack* as the side of his head impacted the beam above his arm. A slack look of dumb terror registered on Jeremy's face, then there was a dry pop as his neck broke and incredibly, his entire body was yanked into the smaller space in a flurry of splintering wood and (it took a moment for Domingo and Curtis to consider this) the hideous snaps of his bones breaking.

The crate was now shuddering and shaking. The two friends looked on in horror as for the moment, the only remaining visible part of Jeremy – his sneakered foot – was sticking out of the side. Then, with a wet pop, it too disappeared, followed by a horrible crunching and wet *gobbling* sound.

The timbers groaned and splintered. Something massive shifted and expanded within the crate.

Domingo had just turned to his friend, mouth quivering in terror when, what looked like a thick rope whipped through the air. It made a whickered, slippery sound, and Curtis registered it was a snake-like appendage ending in curved black claws as it latched onto his friend's head, punching through the skin like a spread of pneumatic nails. Domingo let out a strangled 'ungh!" then was yanked backwards through the air, landing in a sickening pile near the side of the crate. Then it appeared as if a *branch* of tentacles erupted out of the side of the crate (with splinters of flying wood), seizing his friend, and ripping him to pieces in seconds.

Curtis felt like his feet were paralyzed as he stood shaking and shivering. "No-no-no-no," he started babbling, unaware of the spray of blood across his glasses and faces.

More groans and cracks of timbers breaking. Whatever was inside was growing. And breaking free.

Curtis barely noted his bladder letting go and the tears streaming down his cheeks – he had never come anywhere close in his ten years on earth to experiencing the shattering wave of terror that was enveloping him now, of being an insignificant tidbit in the lethal proximity of something so giant, terrifying ... and *hungry*.

The last things he remembered before the blackness eclipsed him was the sound of wood exploding and the sun way, way up high, at the end of disappearing dark tunnel ...

Down the beach, the photographer, whose name was Cal Deinhardt, thought he heard a scream and sounds of timbers snapping followed by what sounded like a huge object landing in the water.

The girl, Emma Richards, a freshman at PACE in Tarrytown and someone whose pants he was contemplating getting into by helping her with some amateur 'modeling' shots, looked around nervously.

"What was that?" she asked. She had finely drawn, natural 'blue-blood' looks that certainly had potential for a successful modeling career, which she was still on the fence about. She thought Cal was kind of cute but though older, perhaps a little beneath her. Despite his claims of being a top-notch photographer, he did work at Angela's coffee shop after all...

Cal looked around. "Dunno. Stay here a second."

He stepped around the tripod and camera and walked up the beach a bit, half-annoyed and half-concerned.

Dumb kids, he thought.

He walked about twenty yards or so until he saw the giant crate way down on the beach, but no sign of them. There was a large pattern of ripples as if something – say the size of a whale – had entered the water near there.

But that was ridiculous, of course.

"Hmm," he said. He had a troubled look on his brow but wasn't sure what bothered him.

Maybe I'll go check that out later. Got to take these shots while the sun is still right though ...

He turned back to finish up his shoot.

1. NEVER ARGUE WITH A WOMAN WITH A BIG KNIFE ...

John Easton was walking his dog near the cabins out at Raadsel Point when he first saw her.

Who was walking who was a topic of some conjecture as the animal – a hundred and fifty-pound Caucasian Mountain dog called *Rovsky* – looked powerful enough to pull a freight train. Rovsky looked like a mad scientist's idea of a grizzly bear crossed with a werewolf. The bear effect was heightened by the fact that he had no ears, or rather ragged tufts where the flaps had been badly clipped. Since the dog had adopted him (rather than the other way around), Easton had no idea what the story was regarding that, though strangely Rovsky seemed to enjoy getting what Easton called 'stub-rubs'. It wouldn't have been much of a stretch to picture him in an Alaskan stream catching salmon in mid-air, or perhaps lying by the hearth of some medieval castle where joints of lamb were tossed over armored shoulders. Here out on one of the most popular camping and hiking destinations in the vicinity of Wyvern Falls, however, he was more apt to result in panicked calls to the Park Rangers or State Police. Hence the leash.

At least it was mid-September – which meant the worst of the summer crowds were gone, although the RV trailer park area further north would be occupied right through to December. Being a weekday, it was relatively quiet.

Easton, a lean man in his early forties with the rugged looks one associated with Daniel Craig or Steve McQueen, had no particular agenda that day other than to get out and enjoy the weather. He had just wrapped up a busy four weeks cracking a weapons smuggling case in Newburgh that involved both a local politician's kid and some unscrupulous army brats, one whose father was a respected West Point officer. Easton was in a unique position as a private detective. Technically, he was still a CID Detective with the Royal Turks and Caicos Police Department – albeit on indefinite unpaid leave – so he maintained some clout with official local channels despite being a member of a foreign police force.

Plus, he had established a reputation for being discreet. And playing fair.

In this last case, he had been hired by the politician – a County Executive – to smoke out which of the army brats was fingering his son;

a critical point after one of the guns he had apparently bought was used previously in a double homicide.

He'd uploaded the photos and his report to the politician's attorney the night before via a secure file transfer service he preferred, had a stiff drink, and called it a night.

With nothing on his plate for the next few days, he decided to take a little walk.

It was a calm day out on the Point, though that would be going by the board in a week and a half when the yearly 'GreenWaters' festival arrived the weekend of the twentieth, the anniversary of the Raadsel Point recreational area being officially commissioned as a New York State Park. It was also the anniversary of the official launch date of the GreenWater movement, led by (a now) aging folk singer named Paul Travers. Flyers and posters had been showing up everywhere in the village for weeks now, along with frequent plugs on the daily Wyvern Falls web-blast.

But that was in the future.

For Easton and Rovsky, at the moment, there was nothing more than the simple pleasure of a warm late summer morning, the sky that clear flawless blue one only seems to see in September in the northeast.

Dressed in a pair of jeans, casual walking sneakers, and a grey windbreaker with 'Montauk' stitched on the left breast, he felt relaxed and alive. A slight breeze ruffled his wiry blond hair and his gray-blue eyes – the color which his mother always said was picked straight from the ocean off their native Cornwall – were calm and relaxed for a change.

They had come out to the clearing area where there were a cluster of rustic cabins. The park rented them out over the summer months at a nominal fee, though an occasional stalwart camper could be found this time of year. Rovsky was eyeing a gaggle of Canadian geese grazing on the far side (which were watching the big dog nervously) when a Jeep Grand Cherokee pulled up abruptly, barely a few yards away from them.

The door flew open and Easton caught a glimpse of a remarkable woman.

His first impression was that she was of medium height with long straight black hair, dark flinty-looking eyes and strong cheekbones, and what he would describe as a striking, almost *bitchy* looking face. *Definitely American Indian, between the features and the coppery hue of her skin,* he noted, sizing her up. She seemed to cut a nice figure, though she was dressed purely for outdoor work; old jeans, banged-up Timberline work boots, a T-top under a faded Levi jacket, and a Seattle

Mariners bill-cap. She had some sort of necklace made from a leather thong but what really drew his eye was the enormous Bowie knife in a hand-tooled sheath on one hip and what looked like an antique ivory-handled government issue .45 on the other.

She looked exotic, definitely armed, and dangerous.

She glanced at him, arching one eyebrow slightly at Rovsky, then turned around, and slinging an oversized knapsack over one shoulder, walked the dozen or so steps to the cabin.

A moment later, the door banged shut, and he heard some rummaging around inside.

Easton looked down at Rovsky, who rolled his eyes back up at him.

He was about to turn and continue on his walk when the door banged open again and the woman returned, this time heading around to the back of the Jeep to get a what looked like a large box filled with groceries.

"Need a hand?" Easton offered without thinking.

She came around from the back of the truck and looked him up and down as if seeing him for the first time. It wasn't a particularly friendly look.

Easton was surprised when she said, "Sure. Grab a box."

He dropped the leash and grabbed a box out of the Jeep and followed her in. Rovsky ambled after him and started sniffing around.

The inside of the cabin was spartan but quaint with its knotty yellow pine paneling, plank flooring, and dusty lace curtains. There was a small threadbare living area with a banged-up table, a mismatched plaid sofa and chairs, and a built-in bookcase with a few dog-eared paperbacks in it. Easton was surprised to see this cabin had a brick fireplace with a rough-hewn oak mantel above as he'd noted from the metal chimneys, all the others had Franklin stoves. To the right was a kitchenette that might have been last upgraded in the nineteen-seventies, with its wood veneer cabinets and white Formica countertops. To the back was a short hallway that led off to what looked like a couple small bedrooms and a bathroom. There was a dated white refrigerator and a working stove at least, a couple farmer's style pendant lights with metal shields and on two of walls a few faded framed prints of wilderness scenes including one Kodachrome of the exterior of Cortlandt Manor that might have been shot in the 1940's.

The air smelt musty and vaguely of Pine-Sol.

"Sorry, he's a bit of a snoop," Easton offered.

The woman was putting away groceries into one of two wood cabinets. "What kind of dog is that?" she asked without turning around.

"Well, I'm not a hundred percent sure he's actually a 'dog' per se, but there are those of the opinion he's a Caucasian Mountain dog."

That got a slight laugh. She turned around and glanced at him again.

"*Na Lënu Òk Nèl Mwekaneyëma ...*" she said, slowly enunciating the words. The cadences were strange, but not unpleasing, to Easton.

'Sorry?" he said.

"It's an old story my mother used to tell ... 'A man and his dog ... '"

Easton looked at the gun at her hip. "You always walk around armed like that?" he asked, changing the topic.

She looked him in the eye. He noticed she had dark lashes that made her look like she was wearing mascara even though she wasn't. She looked pointedly at his left armpit where his Beretta was holstered.

"At least I don't conceal what I'm carrying." She had a strong voice.

Easton chuckled, "*Touché.*" He put out his hand. "I'm John Easton by the way. *Detective* John Easton."

She took his hand and shook it firmly. "Sarah Ramhorne," she answered, "*Doctor* Sarah Ramhorne."

There was a brief moment as their hands touched that Easton felt an odd premonition. Almost as if—

She pulled her hand back quickly then gave him a wary, but slightly puzzled look.

"Have we met before?" she asked.

Easton crossed his arms and leaned against the wall. "Not that I'm aware of. Did I ever arrest you?" he joked.

She shot him a hard look.

Oops, he thought.

"I doubt it. So do the police always send out a welcoming committee like you?"

Easton smiled. "No, nothing like that. I'm a private detective, locally that is. Though technically I'm still a Detective Superintendent with Royal Turk and Caicos Police Force, Criminal Investigation Department."

"Sounds like you're a long way from home, Double-Detective Easton."

"Right. Well, it's complicated."

"I'm sure it is," she said dismissively.

Easton felt disappointed. He had an inexplicable urge to try and make things well, though he wasn't sure why – he'd just met her.

Oh come off it mate, he heard a voice in his head that sounded suspiciously like an old UK Detective friend of his in CID named Nightingale, *she's a hot ticket.*

He tried a different tack. "So what brings a doctor to stay in our fine accommodations here at the Point?"

She looked around. "I'd much rather be here than some antiseptic hotel with bad artwork on the walls. But since you ask, I'm here on a grant courtesy of the National Museum of the American Indian to research some new findings in the area. These days, I'm employed by the American Museum of Natural History."

"Do they always send out their researchers heavily armed?"

That got a little smile at least. "It's licensed. I sometimes run into some dangerous animals – and creepy people in some of the places I go. You'd be surprised. Last month, I got attacked by a rabid coyote while tracing an unusual petroglyph up in the Catskills. Took three bullets to drop him."

"Yikes."

"Yes, *yikes*."

"Well, my mother always told me 'never argue with a woman with a big knife.' I guess that goes for guns as well."

"It's a good thing to listen to your mother."

"So what kind of 'findings' are you finding out here, if you don't mind my asking?"

She paused and looked up at the ceiling, then back at him. "Investigating some caves on the far side of the point where some petroglyphs have been discovered. There may be a connection to later religious ceremonies held in the large palisade that used to stand up on the high ground of the Point here – that wonderful spot the, shall we say *non-Indians*, turned into a parking lot?"

"It's a popular Yankee past-time," Easton said, raising a brow. "Or not. Come to think of it, they recently found King Richard the Third buried under a parking lot back in England, so I guess my own countrymen shouldn't talk."

Sarah smiled as she leaned against the counter and put her hands in her back pockets. Easton decided he liked that smile. It had fine laugh-lines accenting it on either side.

"So I heard," she said. "I also heard he looked a lot like Quentin Tarantino."

"Dead ringer. In fact, Tarantino has already started his version of it starring himself – with vampires and chainsaws, of course."

Sarah tilted her head, managing to look simultaneously amused and incredulous. "Really."

"Well … perhaps maybe." Easton noticed Rovsky had gotten over to the stove and had apparently discovered something of interest underneath it. He had started sniffing it with big snorting *huffs*. Easton sensed he'd managed to get things back on a better track with this woman, though she was starting to look impatient. Which meant it was time to go.

"Well, I'm sure you have plenty of work to do. Welcome to Wyvern Falls by the way." He stepped over and grabbed Rovsky's leash. He stopped at the door. "At the risk of making a horse's ass out of myself, which *tribe* are you from?"

For a moment, he wasn't sure if she was appalled or about to burst out laughing. She covered her mouth with her hand and shaking her head looked away so he decided it was the latter. But surprisingly, she answered.

"*Wappinger* and *Mohican* on my father's side. *Lenape* on my mother's. Though there's Irish and German in there too. But I can trace my family to *Weskanane* who was a big Sachem around here in his day, and relatives who fought with Daniel Nimham under Washington. Not very many of us left though."

Easton considered this. In his few years here, he couldn't recall meeting any local Indians, ever. It never struck him as odd, until now.

"Well, nice meeting you. But a word of advice …"

She gave him a narrow 'not-in-the-mood-for-advice' look.

"… just be extra careful poking around in the caves around here."

"Really?" she said again, skeptically.

"Really. Trust me on that. You never know what you might find. Come on, pal," he said, giving a jerk on Rovsky's leash.

Without waiting for a response, Easton stepped out onto the front porch. There was still a whole beautiful day ahead of him.

2. NORTH OF THE TAPPAN ZEE BRIDGE ...

At 9:30 am on a Tuesday morning, Ben Reinhardt was resting his arms on the back rail of the *Thomas Jefferson*, the cutter used by the National Oceanic and Atmospheric Administration for various projects up and down the U.S. coastlines and for the past month, the Hudson River. As part of their current assignment, they were slowly making their way up the river just north of the Tappan Zee Bridge construction zone, mapping the river bottom using the latest side-scan sonar system.

Ben was a stocky man in his mid-twenties with curly blond hair and a perpetually bored expression that was highly deceptive. Born and raised in Boston, he'd graduated near the top of his graduate class from Columbia in Marine Biology a year previous and wrangled a job with the NOAA after a successful internship. His real interest was in marine ecology and paleontology, but it was his minor in GIS and cartographic systems that landed him his current job which, while about as exciting as watching paint dry, at least paid a measly salary. Which was better than most of his friends were doing.

He had already calculated that at his current salary he would be able to pay off his student loans in just over six-hundred and forty years.

Up in the pilot cabin, Tom Connolly, a veteran pilot on the Hudson (and a NOAA stalwart) for over thirty years called down, "How's it looking, college boy?"

Ben checked the tension on the cable that was dragging the tow sled underwater behind them. On it was the side-scan sonar unit they had been using to map the river bottom. The unit had been acting erratically since they'd collided with an underwater tree the day before, but at least they hadn't lost it.

Might be better if we had, he thought, *damn thing is acting like it's half-fried*.

"*Excellenté!*" he shouted back.

It was tedious work, mapping this section of the river. They essentially had to work a 'mowing the lawn' pattern: back and forth, back and forth. Further north and further south was where all the cool stuff was – shipwrecks, sunken barges, even the odd vehicle, especially when you got to the East River. There was a story he'd heard that back in the day when the mob used to dump all their vehicles there was one police diver who would tell his partner, "Go to the Chevy, make a left, and if you come to the Dodge, you've gone too far."

Here, the most exciting thing was the occasional floating log or a sunken pier.

He headed into the main control room where two other NOAA scientists were going over the data from the earlier scans and took a sip from his coffee, looking out at the shore. *Be nice to have a little cottage there ...*

He just happened to glance down when he saw it; a huge elongated blur on the workstation monitors.

The shape looked vaguely like a gigantic fat squid.

"What the ...?"

Then it was gone.

No fucking way.

"Uh guys, you might want to take a look at this ..."

3. RAADSEL POINT.

"I'm telling you this will be totally cool. And fucking hilarious. We'll make millions when this gets out!"

The speaker was a spindly waif of a girl named Jennie Roderick, a twenty-year-old archeology student at the State University at New Paltz with a classic Emo/Goth look; asymmetrical black-dyed hair moussed in a look that implied it had been frozen in the middle of a tornado. Dressed in black, multi-zippered clothes that apparently had been vacu-formed to her body, she also sported a copious number of piercings and ink that suggested she'd made some tattoo parlor owner a very happy camper.

Her boyfriend was a likable lug named John Barringer. He had the broad shoulders and narrow hips of a naturally born athlete; a career path that had been aborted by a bad leg fracture in his mid-teens from a motorcycle accident that had left him a partial cripple. On rainy days, he still walked with a cane.

Barringer was good-looking in an open-faced, 'Royal Mounted Police' sort-of-way (he was in fact originally from Alberta, Canada), and while a reasonably intelligent sort, he had a bit of a 'passive giant' air about him. He was also a student at New Paltz – majoring in Fine Arts – and had picked up a part-time summer job as a framer at 'The Art Mill,' a custom print and frame store occupying the old upper mill near the Highgate Bridge in Wyvern Falls. He usually could be found driving an old 1949 Indian motorcycle that had been in the family for generations. It was a battered Model 249 'Super Scout' with a 440cc engine which, while in dire need of a restoration, was one of the things Jennie loved about him: in her mind, it echoed Barringer himself who also seemed (emotionally) in bad need of restoration as well.

The only thing she hated was having to wear that stupid motorcycle helmet which wreaked havoc with her hairdo.

Always a bit of a schemer, it was Jennie who had cooked up this little plan while she'd been working a summer internship at the Wyvern Falls Historical Society (which had at least earned her three credits). It had been just before the two of them dropped out for the semester, landing a shabby apartment in the Riverfront district partially subsidized by Jennie's estranged dad. It was the combination of a text message from her father threatening to pull the plug on her finances and a summer-long addiction to re-runs of 'Explorers of the Ancient Universe' on cable that had seeded the plan, which had first dawned on her one day while in the process of drearily cataloguing the contents of some thirty boxes of Indian artifacts in the basement of the Historical Society.

There were more than twenty-five thousand artifacts in the collection which had been the yield of a series of digs spanning six years out at Raadsel Point back in the 1980's, and while an Archeologists' treasure trove, it was more akin to a lot of rocks taking up space in the basement.

Jennie had been sorting through one sagging box of pendant-like rocks referred to by some as 'portable petroglyphs' when she'd spotted one that vaguely suggested an alien-like being to her. Scratching her head, she was struck by a wild idea; an idea that began to take on a level of expediency when she caught word that a certain Indian Anthropologist would be arriving in September to conduct a study of some of the petroglyph sites out on the point.

That night over reheated takeout (courtesy of Shin Kee's over on South Hudson), she'd laid out three of the rocks she'd 'borrowed' from the collection on their coffee table.

"Won't you get in trouble for this?" Barringer asked through a mouthful of *#27 Salted Pepper Squid*. The fried rice paste coating had gone soggy overnight and the squid rubbery; Barringer looked like a cow chewing cud as he talked.

"I seriously doubt it," Jennie replied, "No one's really interested in this stuff. They already have four display cases of Indian artifacts at the Society – they only agreed to store this entire collection back when the Archeology Group thought they were going to lose their building out on Raadsel Point. Now it's just sitting in the basement collecting dust. All I did was take the page out of the log-book these items were listed on. It'll be years before anyone realizes they're missing. If ever. And now that I'll be working there part-time this fall, I'll be in a primo position to figure a way to get these to … where they need to go."

"Ah, yeah. And where is that again?"

"Don't you worry about that, my darling, I have a couple ideas. It's a matter of the right plan and opportunity presenting itself." She raised her hands like claws. "I'm like a cat … ready to pounce!"

Barringer blinked couple times, trying to process this. "Uh Jen, isn't this like, *unethical*?"

Jennie gave him one of her milder 'give-me-a-break' looks. "What's *unethical*, hon, is you and I starving the rest of the way through college and beyond, especially when we get nailed with the tab from those wonderful student loans."

She laid out a bunch of other odd-shaped rocks and stones she'd lifted from the collection. "But since you're the *artiste*, I need your help. It's called 'dinging' (here, she took up two of the stones and demonstrated), you use this stone as a chisel and the other as a hammer and you incise the shape. You can practice first on some ordinary stones I collected. We just tweak the petroglyph to look more like aliens and spaceships, make a few innocent inquiries on a few targeted blog sites, and let people's imaginations do the rest ..."

It had taken two weeks to doctor the petroglyphs to Jennie's satisfaction, and another two days to fake the weathering and patina properly. Jennie figured it would take months or longer – maybe even years – to figure out the stones had been altered, by which time they would be traveling across Europe or deep in the Australian Outback where she'd always fantasized traveling to.

With a flush bank account of course.

The following night, they snuck off to the cave where the Raadsel Petroglyphs were and set about carefully staging the doctored stones amongst a bunch others she'd lifted that were untouched. She'd only been to a few live dig-sites during her schooling, but had augmented her education with a bunch of methods not found on the school curriculum (but found easily enough on the internet) on faking archeology sites and what to avoid.

However, Jennie never stopped to consider while staging her find what might actually be lying *underneath* the 'discovery' she was cooking up ...

4. ANOTHER NIGHT AT MOONEY'S

"So is she hot?" Jim Franks asked.

Easton took a sip off his glass of single malt – it was a twelve-year-old Aberlour – and gave his friend a direct look. "Yeah, she's easy on the eyes you might say."

Franks took a pull off his bottle of Pilsner. Pretty soon, he'd be shifting over to fall beers but for now, with the weather still balmy, he still preferred the light taste of the Pilsners.

It was a busy Wednesday night at Mooney's Bar & Grill, one of the most popular (and oldest) watering holes in Wyvern Falls. Located on Main Street, it was nestled in with a row of buildings that had gone up in the eighteen seventies and eighties. The bar, originally called 'Horseheads Tavern' when it first opened in the year 1900, was an eclectic mix of new and old. Pat Mooney, the silver-haired (and silver-tongued) Irishman who'd owned it for the past thirty years was adamant about maintaining its old world charm, but had made a few concessions in recent years to keep the place competitive with other popular establishments like the Peekskill Brewery or Keenan's in Ossining.

Despite that the bar itself, with its Art Nouveau-styled mirror and liquor shelf, still looked remarkably close to the hundred-year-old plus photos in the Wyvern Falls' Historical Society's archives. But the taps and bottles now included designer vodkas and a myriad of microbrewery beers that would have had the hard-faced men with their bowler hats and starched collars seen in those same photos scratching their heads in bewilderment. And the Wurlitzer Jukebox in the far corner and the wall-mounted flat screen television would have been considered products of science-fiction.

The TV – muted and pretty much resigned to broadcasting only Channel 12 Westchester –was more of a concession to the occasional lone drinkers to give them something to look at while the jukebox, with its oddball selection of everything from *Patsy Cline* to *Them Crooked Vultures*, ran more or less constantly. Pat claimed that he had nothing to do with what was on the selection and swore up and down that it spontaneously reprogrammed itself every so often (*'tis possessed, I tell you! It's magical!'*), though most of his regular patrons placed that assurance in the same camp as his tales of leprechauns and other Irish malarkey.

The real secret weapon in Mooney's arsenal, however, was his sister, Irene, who was responsible for the grill's killer menu which had chefs as far away as New York City trying to puzzle out its recipes. The soups alone were something to die for, and the rumor was everything was kept under lock & key in a recipe bible in a kitchen safe that even Pat wasn't privy to the combination of. Certainly every inquiry as to what went into this or that (always from newcomers who didn't know better) was met with stone-faced silence with perhaps a subtly raised brow and suggestion of a smile.

At the moment, the 'possessed' Wurlitzer was featuring Neil Young churning through the riffs of 'Cinnamon Girl' while Easton and Franks had both just finished up bowls of Irene's 'Hudson Clam Chowder,' the ingredients which she was predictably tight-lipped on.

Franks, an almost too good-looking man in his early thirties with penetrating green eyes and straight black hair, mixed boyish charm and a deadpan sense of humor in equal amounts. Despite possessing an easy-going charisma that drew people to him naturally, he was intensely loyal and like a brother to Easton. The two of them had met years before over the disaster at the Van Eyckmann's estate when Franks had found Easton, bloodied and battered, staggering down Route 9B and lucky to be alive. Something had connected right then and they wound up being best friends ever since.

But Franks had been worried about Easton for some time now.

It had been just over a year since the terrifying events surrounding Alexander Crowley and the Temple of the New Order of the Golden Dawn in which Easton's ex-girlfriend Vivienne and her child had died horribly, and it was clear that in the aftermath part of his friend had simply shut down.

There was nothing clear-cut about it; in fact, there were all sorts of messy loose ends. At the time, Easton had moved on to what appeared to be an inspired relationship with a local dance teacher (and ex-soloist with New York City Ballet) named Olivia Hernandez when in the midst of a series of unraveling events Vivienne – who had disappeared two years previous – had suddenly shown up beaten and naked on Easton's doorstep.

As far as Franks knew, that had been the end of Easton's relationship with Olivia then and there, but he had never gotten any details. Any effort to get Easton to talk about it had run into a stone wall. There had been no leads through the grapevine from Olivia either – as far as anyone knew, she simply clammed up and went on with her life as if they had never dated.

That by itself wasn't any direct cause for concern, it was the fact that Easton hadn't demonstrated interest in *anyone* since. Increasingly, it was the way he was acting like he was emotionally cooling off out in the woods – as in *Siberian forest* woods – that had Franks worried.

When Franks had announced his October wedding date with Karen Evershaw and asked Easton to be his best man, the Englishman had simply responded, "Of course, it would be my pleasure," with all the enthusiasm of a British butler offering to assist with a tea service. Karen was equally concerned but equally wary of meddling. She still felt partly responsible for his current state – she had originally set up Vivienne with Easton in the first place.

So when word started getting around town about some sharp-looking archaeologist from the city researching some drawings uncovered out at the point, Franks secretly hoped it might give Easton some spark of interest. She had even got a little blurb in the Wyvern Falls Gazette. Along with the requisite blurry and badly cropped photo.

But there was a more serious angle to consider as well. The cave where the Indian pictographs had been discovered were around five-hundred yards from where the underground grotto – and gateway of sorts – that had been destroyed the previous year. And while the more watchful eyes in the village were fairly positive that abomination had been sealed up for good, it was a prudent idea to keep tabs on anything going on in the area.

Just in case.

Easton had thought so too when Franks, along with the village's head librarian Tucker Brooks, had brought it up recently. So his walk out to the Point earlier wasn't entirely accidental.

Pat Mooney sauntered over and cleared their soup bowls, a white bar towel draped over his left shoulder. Easton sometimes wondered if it was part of some obscure bartender's dress code: when behind the bar, Pat always had that towel somewhere on his person, either tucked in his apron, draped over his forearm or shoulder.

Maybe it's his lucky Irish towel, he thought.

"Easy on the eyes, you say?" Franks said, breaking into his thoughts of lucky towels.

"Quite," Easton agreed.

"Striking looks, great cheekbones, piercing eyes … long black hair?"

Easton took a long draw off his scotch. "Yes, quite a hot ticket. In a savage kind of way."

Franks grinned. "Aha. And she has fine laugh-lines around the mouth?"

"Yes, come to think of it."

Suddenly, Easton grew wary. Franks was up to something.

Placing the tumbler on the bar, he leaned back and laced his fingers together. "Why do you ask?" he said, already suspecting the answer.

Franks wagged his bottle of beer. "Because she's standing right behind you."

Easton half-turned and found himself looking up into Sarah Ramhorne's face. He couldn't tell if she was amused or about to slap him across the face. He had a hunch it was the latter.

"… in a '*savage kind of way?*'" she said, glaring at him.

Easton tried to stifle a grin. "Yes, well … er, it's a *British* term implying 'impressive.' As in 'smashing,' 'brilliant': '*savage*'."

"It's true," Franks interjected.

Sarah's flat-eyed look went back and forth between both men, ninety-nine and a half percent sure she was getting her leg pulled. It was Pat Mooney who came to the rescue. He must have overheard most of the exchange but how he produced the bottle of eighteen-year-old Highland Park so fast Easton would never know, only that suddenly he was there with it along with one of his more mischievous grins.

"Johnny, I've a fine bottle here I've been wanting your opinion on, a real *savage* whiskey from the Orkney's as it were!" he said, putting on his most charming Irish lilt. Then he put on a dramatic pause, as if seeing Sarah for the first time. "Oh, ah, aren't you a sight for sore eyes! If there was ever a prettier lass I've seen in these parts, I've certainly forgotten her face now! Now what can I get you?"

Sarah looked like she wasn't quite buying Pat Mooney's pitch either, but she also looked like she *didn't mind* not buying it either. Easton felt a little jealous. He knew Pat could be a hard-nosed bastard when he wanted, but he could equally charm the pants off a woman as well.

"I'll have a shot of your best Kentucky Bourbon. And a Dos Equis ale on the side. With a wedge of lime."

Pat raised his eyebrows and raised the wattage on his smile with them. "A fine choice, and a lady after my own heart …"

Franks glanced at Sarah and said, "Wow, he's really laying it on thick tonight. If you're not careful, you'll have his wife down here chasing you out the door!"

Sarah stood between them, hands in pockets. Easton noted she'd changed into a pair of tight black jeans, cowboy boots that looked like they'd been knocked around quite a bit, and an open-necked black silk shirt and doeskin jacket. It was an eclectic look that mixed with her coppery complexion suggested a distinct *otherness* that immediately set her apart from anyone else in the room. She looked like a visitor from another country. Which struck him as ironic.

If she was aware of it, she didn't show it, a quality Easton readily admired. So did Franks, if the expression on his face was any indication.

Easton stood up and offered his seat, which she declined.

"This is my friend, Jim Franks," he said.

Franks stood up and shook her hand. It was a firm, dry shake. "At your service."

"Doctor Sarah Ramhorne," she answered, a smile lightening her face.

Easton realized she had a fair amount of charm herself, when she chose to use it. He also decided he'd never seen such dark – and intense – eyes on someone before. Like chips of flint.

Her bourbon and beer arrived a moment later.

"Welcome to Wyvern Falls," he said, raising his scotch. Glasses clinked. Sarah downed her shot in one gulp, then chased it with the beer.

"So what brings you out to this fine establishment this evening?" Easton asked.

She flashed him a grin of even, very white teeth. *"You do*, Detective."

Easton looked taken aback. "Er, *really?*" he said.

She seemed to enjoy his discomfort, looking him in the eye and waiting a moment before continuing. "Yes, *really*. I was speaking with one of the Park Rangers today – Jack Vance – and he mentioned you could introduce me to someone in your Historical Society to assist with some research ... yes?"

Easton was a little thrown by her directness. *No roundabout approaches with this one*, he thought.

"Ah, well, Wes Fowler is the president. He's also the captain on our police department. And then Tucker Brooks, our head librarian, he's the vice president. But it's a little late for office hours," he added dryly.

Sarah took a pull off her beer. "I had a busy day. And I figured I might as well find out what passes for night-life in this town."

"Well, for the over twenty-five crowd, this is it. There's a few clubs in the waterfront district, or if you're into cheap beers at sleazy dives with lounge bands and hookers, there's always Carlotta's," Franks offered.

"Sounds delightful, but I think I'll pass," she said dismissively. She turned her gaze on Easton. "Is that the kind of place do you prefer, Detective?"

Easton suddenly became aware of her nearness. And also that she smelled of cedar and … *oranges? Mint?* Something natural and exotic. He couldn't quite place it. He also wasn't sure what he thought of her. There was a certain challenging arrogance and over-confidence to her demeanor that put him on edge. For a moment, he wondered if she might be a lesbian – he had a vague sense she didn't like men much.

Or perhaps just *white* men …

"No. I'm quite alright with good scotch served by silver-tongued Irishmen," he replied.

"So I see. I would have figured you for the 'shaken, not stirred' martini type. I don't suppose you have an Aston Martin out front?"

Easton was getting the sense everything was a sparring match with this woman. He could almost see the swords clacking in the air between them.

"Close. It's a Maserati."

"Impressive," she said, taking another pull off her beer, "I didn't realize the private detective business was so lucrative here in Westchester. There must be a lot of bored rich housewives around here."

Easton bristled. "Oh yes, *thousands*," he said.

Franks cut in, "Are you from around here?"

She gave him an amused glance. "There hasn't been a Native American from 'around here' since the early eighteen hundreds."

"Really?" Franks was always undaunted around women. "You haven't met 'Crazy Jack' yet, apparently."

That earned him a second flat-eyed look. "*Crazy Jack?* You must be joking."

"No joke. He's the last surviving Indian around here – I believe – of the Sestaqua tribe."

This time, it was Sarah who stifled a laugh. "Then someone's pulling *your* leg. There are no Sestaqua Indians left – they disappeared in the late sixteen hundreds. And if there were, they certainly wouldn't be named 'Crazy Jack.' That'd be … sort of a ridiculous name for an Indian to use … no, the Sestaqua are long gone."

Franks smiled and shrugged. "How do you know?"

Sarah gave him a cold look. "Because my ancestors *were* from around here. Long before your kind showed up. And 'Crazy Jack' is just an old folktale."

Franks was still undaunted. "Hey, don't look at me – I just migrated here four years ago. Drawn here by legends of abundant gold and rich housewives. So where *did* you grow up?"

"The Tonawanda Reservation outside of Buffalo. But we also frequently visited relatives on the Stockbridge Munsee reservation in Wisconsin and the Lenape reservation in Oklahoma. My father became an attorney for the reservations so we traveled a lot. We have family everywhere – most of the Hudson Valley Indian tribes fractured as they were forced out west. Though I'm told I also have relatives on the Shinnecock reservation out on Long Island. The second one – out in the swamp. The first one was turned into a golf course."

"Did I tell you how much I hate golf?" Franks answered, making a face.

"Nasty bit of business," Easton cut in, "and unfortunately not the first nor last in the history of the human race."

Sarah turned to him, her expression somewhere between angry and puzzled. Then she surprised him again by taking a different tack. "Well, I've got an early morning. Can you make introductions the Historical Society for me, tomorrow, *Detective* Easton?"

"I've got a busy day myself," he responded. "I'm afraid—"

"—No, he doesn't," Franks cut him off before Sarah could react. "He'll pick you up at ten."

Sarah drained her beer. "Glad to hear it. See you then." She started to leave and then, tilting her head, turned back and leaned over put her lips to Easton's ear.

"Oh, and I'm not a *lesbian*," she whispered.

Then she was gone, leaving him with a slight blush and confused expression.

The next thing he was aware of was Franks smacking him on the shoulder. "Nice," he said admiringly. "She's a *pistol* alright."

Easton blinked and rubbed his forehead. "Right. A pistol. Thanks."

Franks laughed. "Sorry, pal, I had to pull you off Grump Mountain. Besides, she likes you."

"What on earth are you talking about?" Easton said, looking annoyed.

"John, you're a great friend. And a great cop. But you really don't know jack-shit about women."

"To hell I don't," he answered. "I think she was just looking for an opportunity to bury a hatchet in my head."

5. RAADSEL POINT, CORTLANDT PICNIC AREA, 2PM, FRIDAY.

"Daddy, Daddy, the ducks are disappearing!" Katie Carson yelled.

A sandy-haired seven-year-old with a dimpled smile and a mischievous face that seemed tailor made for having her cheeks pinched by adults, Katie had been standing near one of the concrete-topped sea barriers that reinforced the outer shoreline of Raadsel Point in the various areas where erosion was an issue.

It was a balmy day with a low string of puffy cumulus clouds loitering over the river and only a trace of a breeze ruffled the treetops.

Katie should have been in school, but she was out for a few days because of something she called a 'stripped throat,' which according to her parents meant she had to take these big pills and stay away from the other kids. Her dad, Kevin Carson, was a contract electrician who'd just ended a long-term assignment at a new mall up near Beacon. After kicking around a few options, he'd decided to pack up his family and camper for a few days R&R at the Raadsel Point campgrounds. After lunch, her mom had announced her immediate goal was to stretch out in the hammock with her Kindle and earphones for a little 'me time' while Katie and her dad biked over to the picnic area for a little sightseeing.

That had developed into her dad getting preoccupied with a large 'Bald Eagle' kite while Druthers, their Golden Retriever, ran manic laps and barked furiously. Fortunately, there was no-one there to be upset – the nearest people were a couple of young fishermen a couple hundred yards away to the south.

Katie had grown bored with watching her dad wrestling with the kite after twenty minutes and had wandered over to the barrier to throw random bread crumbs to the Mallard ducks that were idling around in the nearly perfectly still river. She made a point of being very careful (a studiously behaved little girl was Katie) and to stay *behind* the barrier because her father had told her the river was *deep and dangerous* for little kids.

Especially this spot, where past a narrow underwater shelf along the shore was a drop-off to a deeper channel of the river.

After she had run out of breadcrumbs, she had made up a game on the spot of naming the ducks after her friends at school that she was missing terribly, though there were a total of eight ducks and she only had five *forreal* friends, so two teachers and her school principal had found their way into the mix.

She'd turned away (for only an instant it seemed) to admonish Druthers, who had now decided barking and chasing a bumblebee around a nearby bush was the focal point of the universe for the moment, and when she turned back, she was surprised to see there were fewer ducks.

Her brow knitted comically as if this new development made her mad somehow, and she began counting ducks again.

Seven.

She looked up and around, but there was nothing in the air but a bored seagull looping lazy-eights in the distance.

Katie put her hands over her eyes and counted to ten, thinking she could *wish* the missing eighth duck back into existence.

When she opened her hands in the classic 'peekaboo' gesture, there were only six.

Now her face scrunched up in frustration as she tried to process this impossible development, convinced the ducks were playing some sort of trick on her.

She turned around and called out to her daddy (who had all but given up the kite exercise with the uncooperative wind conditions) and then, hearing a watery 'plop' sound wheeled back again only to see that *all* the ducks were now gone, every single one including the one she'd named Lara MacDonald, her 'bestest' friend.

Now, despite the pouty 'o' her mouth had formed, she was mad.

Stupid duckies, she thought, *where did you go?*

Her dad walked over to her, the plastic eagle kite tucked under his arm. Druthers had either lost the bee or it had wandered out of his limited attention span (probably the latter) and had come wagging up to the two of them, panting from his exertions.

"What's up, Sugarpop?" Kevin Carson asked, using his pet name for his daughter.

A tall, bland-faced man in his mid-thirties going prematurely gray and working on developing a small beer gut, Carson was an easy-going guy who liked his football on Sundays, was a die-hard Yankee's fan, and drove a five-year-old Dodge Ram that did double duty towing his camper-trailer.

He was also a man who seriously loved only two things in life – his wife and his daughter.

Katie's face took on an almost comically adult seriousness. "Now *all* the duckies are gone!" she said to her father, as if he were the child and somehow responsible for this development.

"They are!?" her dad said, with mock disbelief. "Well, where did they all go?"

"They just went bye-bye. There were eight before!"

Kevin Carson scratched his head, trying to figure this one. He vaguely recalled seeing some ducks in the water when they'd first arrived but he'd gotten distracted with all the business with the new kite, an oversized one they'd paid too much money for over at White's Pharmacy.

Probably flew off, he thought.

Though that didn't seem quite right. For starters, the sky was clear of birds, second, even a kid from Sausalito (where he'd grown up) knew that ducks raised up a fuss when they took off. Third, nary was a duck to be seen paddling up or down the river.

Though there were a couple feathers floating on the surface of the water.

His thoughts were interrupted by Druthers, who bounded up to the concrete cap running along the top of the barrier and began firing off a series of barks at the water.

'Druthers!" Katie admonished. She started towards the dog but her dad motioned her to stay back.

"Stay put, Sugarpop," he said, stepping up onto the cap and shielding his eyes with his hand. It did look like there was an extensive disturbance in the water, despite the lack of wind.

Must be the current, he thought. Though he'd lived in the area only a few years – they'd moved to the east coast to be closer to his wife Judy's parents after her dad had been diagnosed with the Big C the year before – he'd gone on a Striper fishing charter up the river with his neighbors the previous spring. He recalled the skipper talking about the rogue currents of the Hudson River: "Sure, it may look safe on the surface but underneath all sorts of stuff can be going on – the river'll bite you like a bitch if you're not careful – current'll pull you right under, as even a few police divers could testify … if they were alive that is."

Carson thought the skipper – a salty-looking guy with skin like beaten leather, half his teeth missing, and a stub of an unlit cigar sticking out of one side of his mouth – might have been yanking his chain just a little bit, but his neighbor Steve Driscoll had backed him up. "Oh, it can be dangerous alright. Divers hate it. And the visibility sucks."

Looking down into it Carson could see why. Opaque and murky, it was all but impossible to know *what* could be going on under the surface.

He turned around and looked at Katie. "It's just the current, Hon—" he began, then faltered as Katie began to scream.

He had time to register the smell – it was awful, as if something fishy and long dead had been vomited up from the bottom of the ocean – before a long black tentacle as thick as his forearm looped almost gracefully around his ankle.

He looked down, perplexed. He was staggered as a dozen of variably sized tentacles followed suit, snaking around his legs and torso.

Then just like that, he wasn't there, like the duckies.

Druthers was barking furiously and Katie kept screaming. One moment, her dad had been standing there, oblivious to the undulating black cables that appeared in the air behind him, then he was *gone*.

She ran up to grab the dog but before she could, he bunched up and leapt into the water after her father.

"Druthers … no!!" she screamed.

Terrified, Katie ran up to the cap and looked over. Druthers was dog-paddling furiously in the water, barking and thrashing about. But not for long.

His barking ended with a brief yelp as he was yanked under by some powerful force.

Katie's scream tapered off into shocked silence, tears streaming down her face.

No, Daddy *and* Druthers were both *gone*.

A series of bubbles broke the surface, then diluted crimson smear began to appear and drift with the current …

6. RAADSEL POINT, CORTLANDT PICNIC AREA, 2:14PM, FRIDAY

Two hundred yards south of where Katie Carson was crying two young men, Jan Deavers and Al Dipola, were having a slow day with the fish.

In fairness, they were having a slow week in what had been an abysmally slow year, at least employment-wise, hence their presence along the Raadsel Point shoreline on an early Friday afternoon.

Twenty-year-old Jan hadn't worked a job since being laid off as a driver at Brandreth Industries back in July, and when not collecting his weekly unemployment check, he split his time judiciously between watching online porn, reality TV shows, and fishing. He still lived at home with his dad at a ramshackle Sears Roebuck bungalow over on Rittenhouse that had been teetering on foreclosure for years.

For his part, the twenty-one-year-old Al was at least soon to be employed – he was due to start a job for the Wyvern Falls Department of Public Works the following Monday (after a six-month employment hiatus) and was enjoying his last Friday off for the foreseeable future by enjoying a little fishing with his high-school bud along with a few Coors Lights and a couple of frozen burgers on the public charcoal grill they'd fired up.

Both young men were still in that preternatural phase of lean bodies, zero body fat and hyper-stamina before the inevitable effects of their staple diet of cigarettes, beer, and bad food had yet to kick in. But while their ambitions didn't seem to entail much outside their localized existence, they weren't particularly bad kids either.

Both wouldn't have hesitated to help out if they'd heard Katie's screams.

It's arguable it wouldn't have made much difference if they had, but despite the lightness of the breeze, they were still quite a ways downwind, and regardless, Al had brought along his boom box which at that moment was cranking out – ironically – the Buzzcocks' classic 'Something's Gone Wrong Again.'

Jan was just sauntering over to his rod where it was wedged near the concrete cap when to his amazement, it began to bend, the line paying out with a high-pitched whizzing sound.

"Shit!" he said, taking a last drag off his cigarette before flicking it away towards the water and reaching over to grab the pole. Just as he did, it snapped through the air, the reel clipping the side of his face as the pole described a tumbling arc through the air before disappearing twenty yards away into the river with a splash.

Al, who had been studiously rolling a joint while sitting spread-eagled atop one of the rough-shod wooden park benches jumped up, dropping his baggy and rolling papers as the other two poles they had set followed the first in quick succession. It was almost as if a giant underwater hand had systematically grabbed and yanked each rod into the river.

"Fuck!" Jan said, rubbing his smarting cheek. "Did you see that shit!?"

Al stepped up beside him, hands on hips. Under his bill cap, his narrow features took on a puzzled look, which deepened as he saw a disturbance in the water. Behind them on the boom box, Pete Shelley was warbling in his high-pitched Manchester accent that 'nothing ever happens to people like us' when the thing that was in the river rose to the surface.

Jan was interrupted mid-gawk as one cable-like appendage whipped out of the water and looped around his thigh. He barely managed a, 'What the fu—?" before he found himself yanked headlong into the spray of glistening tentacles breaking the surface.

Al was trying to process what his eyes were trying to tell him and failing miserably. He caught a glimpse of a giant, elongated greenish-black body with a shovel-shaped head and huge, saucer-like eyes and mesmerized, could only cough up the eloquent statement: 'Fuck you, motherfucker!" before his feet finally got the message from his (pot-addled) brain and he jumped backwards.

He made it five steps before another elongated tentacle – this one ending with an array of glistening, pearlescent hooks – sailed through the air and caught him around the head. Al's last image as he was catapulted backwards towards the river was the ground disappearing away under his feet (*look, Ma, I'm flying!*) before his world was eclipsed by the overwhelming dead fish smell, and the crunching snaps of his facial bones breaking.

Then blackness.

7. ONE FOR THE BOOKS ...

Lieutenant Raymond Sanchez was not having one of his better days.

The first indicator all was not going to be rosy in the World of Raymond was the call from his mother that morning telling him the results from his younger sister's tests were in, confirming that she would have to go on dialysis.

Twenty-seven, two kids, and her kidneys were failing.

He'd stopped to visit her and her husband and so started his shift an hour late.

Then, to add another curveball his girlfriend – Detective Eckhart – was acting squirrely after finding out her ex-husband Hal was coming back to town for the upcoming GreenWater's festival. Sanchez had never actually met him. Hal had dropped out of a corporate gig at IBM to pursue a film career (his one and only film had bombed spectacularly) and was now apparently heading some sort of sustainable bamboo farming venture while living out of a commune north of Peekskill.

The new waitress at Xeno's had screwed up Sanchez's take-out order at lunch (he'd wound up with a Gyro wrap *with* onions instead of a Chicken Souvlaki Salad *without*), and then, just as the afternoon was looking to quiet down, a frantic call had come in from some camper over at Raadsel Point about her missing husband and dog that her hysterical daughter claimed had been eaten up by a giant sea monster.

I could think of a few people I wouldn't mind getting eaten up by a sea monster, Sanchez had mused, *starting with a guy named Hal.*

The popular consensus around the Wyvern Falls Police Department (and the village as well) was that Ray Sanchez was quite the ladies' man. Thirty years old and blessed with a boxer's physique, if a roomful of ladies were presented with a group photo of the 60-odd members of the village police department and were told 'Tall, Dark, and Handsome,' all fingers would be instantly pointing at him.

The truth of Ray Sanchez was far more complex of course, starting with his girlfriend of more than two years, Detective Katrina Eckhart. For starters, Katrina was divorced and twelve years older than him. Second, though she was blessed with good genes and looked ten years younger than her forty-two years, she wasn't exactly the drop dead gorgeous knock-out type one might have presumed to be hanging on the lieutenant's shoulder. Eckhart was a somewhat short, blonde-haired woman with searching brown eyes and a trim figure that suggested a self-contained, low-maintenance woman.

Along with a large fan-club of jealous-eyed woman in the area, Sanchez' mother and sister hated her, or at least went out of their way to make her feel unwelcome. The why's and how's had never been explicitly spelled out – but it was clear it was something along the lines of being considered unworthy of such a fine man. Only Sanchez' older brother Gustav seemed to accept her, though he seemed to have that approach with everyone.

But what Ray Sanchez saw in Katrina Eckhart was a subject of mystery (and nasty beauty parlor gossip) around the town that had many people stumped. And while they kept their relationship on the Q.T., it was even more telling how many people tried to ignore it altogether, as if by not acknowledging it would make it not so.

That had been the early (and failed) strategy of Sanchez' mother and sister.

The closest anyone had come to an explanation was when one of Sanchez' colleagues on the force came right out and asked, "What do you see in that woman anyhow?" over beers one night. Sanchez had looked at him pointedly, shrugged, and responded, "She *gets* me. Plus she's a cop."

That's all he would say on the matter.

A fifteen-year veteran of the Wyvern Falls Police Force, Eckhart had gravitated naturally towards the position of the Child Services Detective. Though childless herself, she had a natural aptitude and empathetic demeanor that quickly put kids at ease. But her best asset was her inviting features; looking into Detective Eckhart's face was like looking at a warm, sunny day, one that reminded you that the darkness would always pass and bluer skies were on the horizon.

Which was no doubt a clue to Sanchez' attraction to her.

Although the whole department was (by now) well aware of their relationship, and their almost amusing level of discretion in how they showed it, Chief Hendricks often sent them out together because they worked so well as a team when it came to any situations involving kids.

Which was why the two of them found themselves that Friday afternoon in one of the Police Department's SUV's driving out towards the campgrounds on Raadsel Point.

Raadsel Point was a roughly mile-long peninsula that jutted out into the Hudson River in the shape of a flattened (or as some fanciful legends claimed, 'Wyvern-shaped') wing extending southward. To the north where it curved back into the main shoreline, it was marked by a deep waterway known as 'Murderer's Creek' while to the south the point itself delineated the three-quarter mile wide basin that was Raadsel Bay. The eastern shore of the bay formed the upper part of the Wyvern Falls waterfront which included the Raadsel Bay Yacht Club and Condominiums, north of there was the single access road that crossed Wyvern Falls' Creek via a low concrete bridge (which had replaced the steel truss one that collapsed back in 1981) and led out past the carnival grounds and into the camping grounds and cabin areas.

"Thai or Japanese?" Sanchez asked as they passed the empty carnival grounds. The clock on the dash had just registered 3pm.

"Hmm. Not sold. Italian?" Eckhart responded.

Like most couples over time, they had developed their own verbal shorthand – and routines – that could be expressed with minimal words and gestures.

Sanchez scrunched his lips. "Riverboat?"

That was their favorite waterfront restaurant, a casual place that served excellent martinis. It also implied dining out versus eating in.

"It's Friday," she said, meaning; *It'll be jammed.*

"There's always *Ray's.*"

That was a standing joke response – Eckhart tended to be a bit of a health-food nut and hated pizza. 'The Original Ray's' was a recent transplant from the city (where there was no shortage of claims on that name) over on Main Street. Eckhart probably wouldn't go in there even if it was a call for a robbery in progress. She'd probably cheer them on.

Further discussion on solving the evening's dinner dilemma, however, was put on hold as they pulled up to camper location #17 where an obviously hysterical woman was already running out to greet them, her sobbing daughter in her arms.

It took a good five minutes to calm her down to a state collected enough to get a few critical facts out of her and true to their reputation, Sanchez and Eckhart handled their job with calm and authoritative precision. They first had to get them back inside the camper and away from the other campers standing around gawking (it never failed to prick Sanchez' irritation at how often people would stand around staring without offering any sort of assistance to someone in obvious distress).

Sanchez took Arlene Carson's statement while Eckhart focused on the daughter, talking quietly to the girl until she could get a cohesive narrative out her. Sanchez always marveled at how she did it; it was some elusive combination of her soothing voice, concerned eyes and, 'I'll take care of everything' demeanor that convinced even the most hysterical kids (and parents) that awful as any current situation was, somehow there was hope still flickering at the end of the dark tunnel and that it was reachable. Perhaps not today, or tomorrow, but at some point.

"… and did you get a good look at the sea monster?" Eckhart asked, in a tone that suggested sea monsters were common as oysters here along the Hudson. She kept the questions on an objectified level, avoiding references that might prove upsetting.

Katie unclenched the hem of her dress where she had been bunching it. "No … it was hiding in the water … but it had big long black arms … *icky* arms … "

Sanchez had to stifle a laugh as an absurd memory popped into his head – an old Monty Python episode he'd caught late one night: "*it was a giant spine-tingling electric penguin with tentacles!*"

"It had icky arms …" Eckhart repeated, dutifully writing in her notebook.

"Lots and lots of them!" Then she started to cry again.

After taking the statements, Eckhart was able to quickly recruit an elderly couple two trailers away who were retired schoolteachers to stay with the mother and daughter while they drove out to the spot where the incident occurred. Eckhart had an expert ability to profile reliable assistants from a group of civilians with uncanny accuracy, often with just a glance and often without even being aware of it.

"What do you think?" she asked as they stood by the barrier cap.

Sanchez was squatting on his haunches and rubbing his chin, looking at the muddied shoe and paw-prints on the concrete and frowning. Nearby were the crumpled remains of the large American eagle kite. The story they suggested wasn't promising.

"Do you think he …?" Eckhart asked.

Sanchez shook his head. "What I think is that we need to get the police launch up here with a couple divers. Whatever happened here, I think it's safe to say we have a man and a dog somewhere in the water. Tide is still coming in so most likely they'd be upriver by this point."

He also noticed a few smears of greenish-black substance across the cap. He dabbed his fingers and sniffed, then made a face.

Eckhart squatted near him. "What is it?"

"No idea. Smells like something dead and rotting from the water was dragged across here … or maybe a rope that's been underwater a long time?" He stood up and pulling out a smartphone snapped a few photos.

Then he sniffed again and turned towards the south. In the distance, he spotted the grill stand with smoke coming out of it. He also noted the fishing coolers along with the lack of fishing rods or anyone manning them.

Sanchez didn't like that one bit.

"Come on, Detective," he said. "Something's up."

"This is one for the books."

Sanchez had examined the coolers, the marks in the dirt and the charred remains of the burgers left on the grill.

"This doesn't make any sense," Eckhart agreed.

"No, it doesn't. Whoever was here left a cooler half-filled with fish, food cooking on the grill, took their poles and …"

"…And left their cigarettes," Eckhart finished for him, picking up the nearly full pack of American Spirits on the picnic table. "How much does a pack of these go for these days?"

"Too much to just leave lying around, I'd say," Sanchez said. He was looking a set of marks on the concrete cap that looked identical to the ones where the girl's father had disappeared. The brackish smelling slime was half-dried in the sun. He produced a zip-top evidence bag out from one of the cases on his duty belt and took a small sample.

"Ray?"

"Yes?"

"Can you come here a second?"

Sanchez stepped over gingerly to where Eckhart was crouching a dozen feet away.

"Does that look like blood to you?"

He crouched next to her, looking at a spatter of maroon-colored drops on the half-dead tufts of grass.

Another evidence bag appeared. The whole thing was beginning to feel *hinky* to him. Like that whole business a couple years ago with the bizarre ventriloquist's workshop (nearby in fact) and mutilated bodies … this was different of course, but similar in its essential *wrongness*.

Dad vanishes along with family dog.

Fisherman (or *fishermen*, if the multiple pole marks were an indication).

The kite.

The cigarettes.

The girl's statement … *sea monster … with lots of arms*?

Sure thing, Ray, common problem around here this time of year – sea monster migratory patterns and all – and don't forget to include the

UFOs and little bug-eyed green men in your report. All those inconvenient abductions ...

That last thought troubled him though ... something about the ...

Eckhart looked nervous. He didn't realize at first that it was because *he* looked nervous, and she'd never seen him that way. It was an uncomfortable off-guard moment for him – for reasons he couldn't even articulate to himself, Sanchez didn't like letting his guard down on the job even in front of his partner (and lover). Off-duty was another story. Especially in those 'pillow-talk' moments late in the evening after one of their marathon sex sessions. But out here, with his uniform on, badge and gun visible in public, he was *Lieutenant* Sanchez.

He shook his head and smiled to regain his composure. "I think it's time we called in for some back-up. Let's get this area taped off and go talk with the girl again." He stepped up to Eckhart and looked her in the eye.

"And whatever the hell is going on here, we'll get to the bottom of it," he added, sounding considerably more confident than he felt.

8. ARTIFACTS ...

The Jeep Grand Cherokee eased to a stop in the semi-circular drive of the Gothic Revival mansion known as the 'Havell House' on South Hudson Avenue.

A complex-looking two-story structure with numerous gabled dormers and steepled towers, bay windows and a steep slate-shingled roof, it featured numerous details such as bracketed cornices, flared eaves and was unique amongst all the buildings in Wyvern Falls in that it was built out of stucco-faced concrete block. Commissioned by a relative of one of the area's most revered painters in 1872, it was such an innovative approach to home building at the time that special carpenters had to be brought over from England where the technique had originated.

Due to the solidness of the construction, even after a hundred and forty years the entire house was perfectly level, with all its floors and walls as true as the day they were laid. In recent years, the exterior had been painted an understated greyish-tan with white trim while the yard and garden were still as meticulously maintained as they had with the original owners.

The house had the enigmatic air of a secret kept in plain sight – while many in the area passed it daily, only the truly curious ever stopped to photograph it and few knew of its mixed history of ghosts, murders, and adulterer's and bootleggers.

Regardless, prestigious house - with its colorful history - was now owned and maintained by the Wyvern Falls Historical Society, having been sold to the society in 1996 by a Havell descendant for the princely sum of one dollar.

It was certainly the envy of Historical Societies throughout Westchester County.

Even Sarah Ramhorne looked impressed.

"Nice set up," she said to Easton, sitting in the passenger seat.

"It really is quite something," Easton agreed. "Wait until you see the inside."

Easton had been sitting on his front porch finishing up his second cup of coffee that morning when Sarah pulled up in front of his house at nine-thirty.

Rovsky had been sitting on the front steps surveying the neighborhood (Easton had noted for some time that the dog was only comfortable when he was at a vantage point where he could keep watch over his surroundings) and let out a single deep throated 'woof!' that threatened to flatten the grass on the front lawn when he saw who their visitor was.

"Morning," Easton had said, uncrossing his feet from the porch rail and standing up. "I thought I was supposed to be picking *you* up."

Sarah had walked up to the front steps and paused, hands on hips and studying Rovsky dubiously.

"I'm not in the habit of waiting for men to do things," she'd responded, "besides, I was already in town getting some supplies." Then she looked closely at the dog as if seeing him for the first time.

"Where's his ears?" she'd asked – the first question everyone asked.

Easton had walked over to the top of the stairs with his coffee in one hand and looked around nonchalantly. "Good question, we've looking all over for them this morning. If you find a pair, let me know."

He still didn't know what to make out of her – she seemed to irritate and attract him in equal measure. But she did manage to look good no matter what she was wearing. On this morning, that involved a faded denim shirt and jeans, the scuffed cowboy boots and a black cowboy hat with a snakeskin band.

She'd given him an annoyed look, not bothering to respond to what was obviously a ridiculous response, then made an odd gesture with her hand in front of Rovsky's nose that made him tilt his head curiously. Then he'd craned his massive head forward and licked her palm.

"Old Indian trick?" he'd asked.

Sarah had snorted. "No, just something I saw on TV once. I guess it really works." She'd looked up at the house. "Early twenties Craftsman?"

"Nineteen fifteen actually, bought it fully loaded with period furniture." The place had been something of a coup – Easton had purchased it from a guy named Edwards a few years back whose father had purchased right after World War I. It hadn't been a happy situation – the father had been obsessed with hunting down an enemy German pilot during the war, an obsession that had haunted him to his grave. His son, upon reaching retirement age himself, made no bones about not having any sentimental attachments to the place and had all but walked away from it.

"You have an interest in old houses?" Easton had asked, curious.

"Actually, I originally majored in architecture ..." Sarah had answered. She'd looked like she had a few additional things to say on that topic but then decided against it.

Sarah opened the hatch door to the Jeep and handed Easton a knapsack while she grabbed a leather folio. The bag was incredibly heavy.

"What are you carrying in here – bricks?" East asked.

"No, it's just the White Man's burden." She surprised him with a quick smile. "It's a joke. *Kipling*?"

"Right. Got it."

"It's rocks, actually. Some very interesting ones in fact."

Easton set the sack down, and instead of ringing the doorbell, opted to use the massive iron doorknocker in the shape of a snarling lion's head. The heavy oak front door looked solid enough to stop a tank.

"Igor should be here any moment," he quipped.

After a minute, there came the sound of a heavy locks turning from inside, and with heavy creak, the door opened. Standing inside was a tall, lanky man with close-cropped grey hair and long features. He was dressed in a polo shirt and jeans with sneakers and could have easily passed for a dad at little-league baseball game, except for his hard gray eyes.

"Hey, John," the man said, a half-smile on his face.

"Hello, Wes," Easton replied. "This is Doctor Sarah Ramhorne, the archeologist who's been working out at the Point. Sarah, Wes Fowler, captain on our police department and president of our Historical Society."

"A pleasure, a real pleasure," Fowler said, offering his hand. His firm but laconic demeanor had a way of putting people on their guard and at ease simultaneously. But what immediately came through about him was his sincerity. Even when he was pulling your leg, which he could do with a poker-player's face as Easton had discovered on more than one occasion.

"Come in, come in," Fowler added, motioning them in to the mahogany-paneled foyer. It was an impressive space with its polished Sing-Sing marble floor, spiraling staircase with a sweeping balustrade and diffuse light coming in through a roundel window on the second floor. The foyer was the base floor for the central tower of the house and had been designed for maximum visual effect.

To one side was a massive grandfather clock that intimated time was as immutable and fixed as the Victorian era in which it was built. To the other was a Gothic-looking bench and coat rack with a long bevel-cut mirror whose patina suggested any number of spirits might be lurking within its depths. Next to the clock hung a magnificent 1843 oil painting by Robert Havell Jr. titled 'View of the Hudson River over Raadsel Point.' Along the wall of the staircase hung a series of Victorian portraits of stern (and very unhappy) looking people dating back to the 18th century. If the consensus of expressions were any indication, the past wasn't much of a fun time to be sitting around in.

Easton's quip wasn't far off the mark – it wouldn't have been unexpected to see a hunched-back manservant with a leering eye ushering them into the space, perhaps to be greeted by an aristocratic-looking mad doctor along the lines of the late British actor Peter Cushing.

Instead, their casually dressed police captain ushered them to a study in the back of the house that had been converted into the main office for the Historical Society.

It was a low-ceilinged room that seemed to condense the Victorian/Gothic theme of the rest of the house into its cozy space; square-paneled wainscoting with hand-painted wallpaper of assorted leaves against a mustard background above, arched stained-glass windows and a heavy stone-hearth fireplace that seemed too large for its surroundings. Built-in bookcases lined three of the walls and against the other was a set of wooden file cabinets. Dominating the space was a broad oak desk with a banker's lamp and a red leather cushioned swivel chair. The room had a formal-but-messy look that might be described as 'antique casual.'

Fowler sat himself behind the desk and clearing stacks of papers and folders, put his feet up and leaned back.

"Care to have a seat?" he asked, indicating a couple antique cane chairs to the side.

"No thanks," Sarah responded. Setting down the leather folio, she walked over to one of the bookcases where a bunch of artifacts were casually laid out on top including some projectile heads and a human skull.

First, she picked up one of the flint spearheads and examined it. "Local?"

"Place called Ravenhead, near here. That was from an excavation from eighty-three to eighty-seven. Some of the artifacts go back as much as sixty-five hundred years."

"This is unusual, it's fluted," she said, looking at the concave depression running the length of the spearhead, "and it's a continuous grove, done in one shot. Whoever made this was a master."

"That's what I've been told," Fowler responded, resting his chin on his hand.

She picked up the skull next.

"That's '*Makkitotosimew*'," Fowler said, nodding at her.

Sarah gave him a narrow look. For a concerned moment, Easton thought she was going to throw the skull at the captain or maybe even bean him over the head with it. Easton cocked his head and raised his eyebrows as Sarah turned her gaze to him.

"That's an Indian name for *big tits*," she said, turning the skull around in her hand. "Only there's a problem ..."

"... with her tits?" Easton cut in, unable to resist. For a moment, it looked like *he* was the one about to get beaned. But despite her murderous look, Sarah couldn't stop a hint of a smile tugging at the edge of her lips. Fowler was shaking his head and covering his eyes with his hand.

"No, I'm sure her tits were fine." Now she did look annoyed. "The problem is this isn't an *Indian* skull. It belongs to a Caucasian woman."

Fowler dropped his hand as if to wipe the grin off his face.

Then he fessed up, "Well, when we first dug it up thirty years ago, we thought it *was* an Indian woman, and that was the story we told for many years. And you can see the cleft in the back of the skull where she was killed from behind with a hatchet. Then one day I told that story to a couple of American Indian Archeologists from Stockbridge and couldn't figure out why they grew real quiet that morning. It wasn't until they were leaving one pulled me aside and told me the same thing, and he had already ball-parked it as being only a hundred and fifty years old."

"I'm not quite sure I follow," Easton admitted.

Fowler looked at him. "We bungled a crime scene without knowing it. Back in the middle eighteen-hundreds, some farmer probably decided to off his wife, and after planting an axe in her skull, he inadvertently buried her in with a bunch of Indian artifacts ..."

"Oops."

"Oops is right. We narrowed it down to a few culprits, but we'd already excavated and processed the site so any other evidence was destroyed ... believe it or not, it happens."

Sarah shuddered and placed the skull back on the shelf.

"My apologies, Doctor," Fowler hastily added. "It's a bit of an old joke around here. So what is it you wanted to see me about? John said you had some questions about some artifacts you've located in a cave out on the point."

Sarah was smart enough to know Fowler had been testing her. But instead of saying anything, she went over and picked up the knack sack from which she produced three large flat rocks and a series of small rounded ones. She placed them on the desk in front of the captain, who dropped his feet and leaned forward in anticipation. Easton was curious as well, but for other reasons.

"Ever seen anything like this before?"

Fowler's eyes went wide as he looked over the rocks, and the petroglyphs carved into them. "Nope. Can't say I ever have." Then he looked up at her. "Is this some kind of a hoax?"

9 … AND ALIENS?

"That's exactly what I wanted to ask *you*. Please tell me someone around here isn't trying to pull a stupid practical joke," Sarah said.

Fowler examined each of the rocks for a moment, turning them this way and that in his large hands, then after setting them down leaned back, tapping his fingers together. If he was insulted by the implied accusation, then he didn't show it. "Well, I've seen all sorts of portable petroglyphs in the past. But I can't say anything quite like I'm seeing here. Where exactly did you find these?"

Sarah stared at him, measuring his sincerity. "In the floor of the cave, not far from the newly discovered petroglyphs and pictographs."

"Newly discovered …?" Easton cut in. He had taken a seat in one of the thick-cushioned black cane chairs with legs crossed, English fashion.

Sarah leaned against the fireplace mantel and crossing her arms, looked at Easton. "What's commonly called the 'Raadsel Petroglyph' has been well known since it was first discovered in a shallow cave at the northwest part of the point in the late seventeen hundreds. It's been dated to the Early Woodland Period around 2800 to 3000 B.P. Its purpose has been the subject of some debate but it's generally believed to have been a kind of ceremonial or visionary art. After the hurricane last year the tidal surge collapsed the back of the cave, revealing a secondary area with additional petroglyphs and pictographs no one had any idea existed."

"Sorry if I came a little late to this party, but what exactly are 'petroglyphs'?" Easton asked. As a (British) detective, few things irked him more than finding himself in the midst of a conversation whose key terms he wasn't clear on.

"Petroglyphs are incised carvings, John," Fowler interrupted, "usually cut into the rock using stone – or later metal – chisels. Pictographs are, as you may surmise, painted images." He glanced at Sarah. "Sorry, continue."

Sarah's right hand absently touched her chin and she looked left into space before focusing back on Easton. "A couple of hikers stumbled across the new drawings this past spring, and at some point, your captain here got wind of it and the museum was notified, which ultimately brought me here."

Easton was intrigued. He had a general awareness, like many people in the area, that Native Indians had called the Hudson Valley home until being bought out, forced out, or killed by the Europeans, but never placed any particular significance to Raadsel Point, at least not of the sort that would perk the interest of a major museum.

"So just what *does* bring you here?"

"Raadsel Point was a very significant location for the local tribes," she replied, again looking him straight in the eye (Easton was beginning to find her intense way of looking that way at him both a little unnerving and intriguing), "with major settlements there going back as much as eight thousand years. Plus, it was the site of an important native 'castle' – at the plateau northeast of the campground was one of the largest palisaded forts in the lower Hudson. Remnants of it still existed well into the eighteen hundreds. And the southern tip – where the British later built the fort – was a major meeting ground for local sachems."

"Sachems?" Easton asked. All at once, he was aware they seemed to be communicating on two simultaneous but separate levels; on one she was speaking to him conversationally – in the measured and confident tones of someone who enjoys imparting a part of her own ethnic history. On the other level, it felt like an unspoken dialogue was taking place, an invisible (perhaps intimate) space where subtle signals were coming and going at the speed of thought. Was it just his imagination or did her pupils dilate when she spoke to him? For a split second, he had an overwhelmingly crazy urge to jump up, run over, and grab her in his arms and kiss her passionately on the mouth …

"… Chief," Fowler was saying.

"Eh?" Easton said, snapping to attention.

Fowler gave him a dry look as if he knew exactly what Easton had been thinking. "Sachem is another word for chief," he repeated.

Easton was aware Sarah had a trace of a smile tugging at the side of her mouth. *Damn the woman!* he thought. *Why in the hell does she have to be so … so …?*

"So is there *anything* else do you want to ask me?" she said in a challenging tone.

Fowler's eyes were going back and forth between the two of them with amusement. Easton, an old hand at the reflexive 'redirect' from his years a policeman, uncrossed his legs and reached over to pick up one of the flat rocks. "Yes. So what makes you think these are some sort of hoax?"

Was that a look of disappointment in her eye?

She stepped over to him and traced the image inscribed into the rocks' smooth surface with her forefinger. There was a moment when she briefly touched the top of his thumb. Somehow, it felt agonizingly erotic.

Easton tried to remember the last time he had sex, and at the moment, he found he couldn't. He focused on the images on the stone instead. It showed a bunch of primitive-looking figures with v-shaped heads dancing around what looked like a kind of monster underwater. The monster looked like a sort of four-legged reptile with big jaws, like an alligator with over-sized feet or flippers. Over the top of the figures heads were three oval-shapes with a line of dots across them. Each had a tiny figure emerging from the side, as if suggesting a pilot or passenger.

The first thing it made him think of was aliens and UFOs.

Sarah was pointing to monster in the water however.

"There's an old Lenape legend about a sea monster – the *Maxa'xak* – but I've never seen one depicted like this." She looked up at Fowler. "Have you, Captain?"

Fowler shook his head. "Can't say I have. But I'm strictly an amateur on the subject."

Easton knew Fowler was anything but – if there was anyone more knowledgeable about local history (and that included natives), he was yet to have met them. Even Tucker Brooks, with his encyclopedic knowledge of just about everything, was known to defer to him on the subject.

"The body looks almost right. But the flippers? It looks like someone was trying to depict a sea dinosaur, actually a sea *reptile*. Like a mosasaur."

"I'm afraid I'm not familiar with them. And perhaps for the better," Easton quipped.

"They were some of the largest marine predators ever," Sarah added. "But they died out around 99 million years ago. Which is an obvious problem in itself, but not the only one."

"What's the other?" Easton noticed once again how her voice had an unusual timber to it that only Native Americans seemed to possess, though she spoke with the articulation of college professor. He wondered how long it had taken her to master it or if she'd taken language lessons. If the American colleges were even remotely similar to those in England, she would have had a hard time getting professors to take her seriously with a native accent.

"Well, there's a few, actually," Sarah was saying. "First, the flippers. I'll have to take these back to the lab for a full forensic analysis, but in examining them, I get the impression – and this is hardly scientific – that they may have been added. You develop a sense for these things after a while. And the 'flying saucer' figures overhead don't fit contextually either."

"What do you mean?"

"Well, the *drawing* style looks correct. But the position and spatial relationship is all wrong with the rest of the petroglyph. It suggests they were added later. Either as an afterthought, or deliberately."

"A hoax, in other words," Easton offered.

"Yes, a hoax."

Easton looked at the rock closely, turning it this way and that. The lines and images all looked consistently the same to him, even to his detective's eyes. "I wouldn't have a clue," he admitted.

Sarah took the rock from Easton. "Don't feel bad. Neither would most trained archeologists," she said. "Because I'm pretty sure it's an altered original, and whoever did it was good. It'll take a multi-tiered approach of Cation-ratio dating and AMC14C dating which looks at weathering rind organics. Also, we'll have to analyze rock varnish microlaminations to really sort this one out, if you know what I mean ..." She trailed off as Easton's eyes began to take on a glazed-over look.

Easton sensed she was toying with him, but only a little. He also had a hunch that being both a Native American *and* a woman, she would have had an uphill battle proving herself in academic circles, even in the 21st century. Still, he couldn't resist responding, "Absolutely. I was just about to suggest analyzing the rock varnish ... er, laminations and such." *Wow, bet that's a real icebreaker at parties*, he thought.

That earned him a flat look from Sarah.

Fowler leaned forward, his chair creaking loudly in the cozy study. "Well, I'd love to have a look at the site, if it won't interfere with your studies. What do you want to do with these samples?"

Sarah considered this a moment. "I could truck these back to the museum myself. Or ... actually, do you have a FedEx here in town?"

Fowler thought a moment. He was certainly interested in checking out the site – he hadn't been to that particular area since the incident with the three kids the previous fall. And then there was the strange business that happened yesterday with the father and dog and the two missing fishermen ... Fowler thought it might be a good idea to have a casual look around while he was out there ...

"Sure, he said. "We have a postal/copy center over at Avalon Mall that handles FedEx, UPS, and USPS, and they're actually really reliable. But I'll tell you what. Why don't you box these up here, I'll have my assistant run them over, and the three of us can go grab some lunch and head over to the point so I can see where these came from? How does that strike you? John, you have a little time to spare?"

Sarah rubbed her chin with her thumb and forefinger. As a general rule, she preferred working alone or if part of a team, at least a team of professionals. She had mixed feelings about inviting a town police captain-playing-amateur historian to poke around a site she was working on ... but on the other hand, the idea of lugging what might turn out to be a bunch of doctored petroglyphs down to the city and back (particularly considering she had to wrap up her research by the following weekend when the place would be over-run by the GreenWater's festival), and besides ... there was something about this John Easton ...

"Okay," she said. "You're on. But I'll want to pack these myself."

"Excellent," Fowler said, nodding. He picked up the receiver off the desk phone next to him. Easton was surprised to see it was one of the old-fashioned kind with a cord. Fowler punched a button.

"Hi Jennie, could you come up to my office? And bring a bunch of medium and small FedEx boxes with packing materials with you ..."

10. BY THE WORD OF THE GREAT SPIRIT ...

The Indian known as 'Crazy Jack' opened his eyes suddenly, looking at the cracked ceiling of the bedroom. He could still hear the echo of the voice that sounded like it had spoken directly into his ear: "*Kpëntaihëna hèch?*"

Did you hear us?

Yes, I heard.

From his makeshift bed, Jack stared at the ceiling unblinking. He hadn't heard the voices in some time, but now he was hearing them quite often. He didn't care much for those voices. They usually meant unpleasant work.

The building he currently called home was an abandoned store/house out on The Old Post Road that had originally been built as a dry goods store back in the mid-1800's when the road had been a major trade route connecting the Falls to the highland towns. That had been superseded by Route 131 and the Post Road, like so many once critical-but-now-forgotten byways across America, had become a neglected footnote relegated to old historical maps and old-timers reminisces.

The store's last active incarnation had been as a gun shop in the 1940s and 50s before being abandoned altogether around the time Kennedy was sworn into office. Then, like so many dilapidated buildings, it managed to fall out of ownership until it became the structural equivalent of a local homeless person; a soiled, vagrant eyesore no one wanted to actually do anything about.

Set back in the woods on a low rise that overlooked the road, the building had been painted a dull dark brown at some point. With moss-caked roof, soaped-up storefront, and remnants of yellowed lace curtains behind its windows, it suggested a slightly crazy old aunt who should have been shuffled off to the retirement home years ago.

For Crazy Jack, however, it was as good a spot to hang his hat as any. And there was something more than that – he sensed the house wanted him there. When he'd first stumbled into the place ten years previous (through the open back door), he had found in the mess of a kitchen at the back an old colonial-looking table with a single chair, and before the chair had been resting the tarnished key to the premises as if placed there for him.

There was no electricity of course, but the old Franklin stove worked just fine in the fall and winter, and if any locals were aware he was squatting in their neighborhood, they apparently didn't mind. Or perhaps the house dimmed his presence.

He had a hunch that was the case.

He'd found a few kerosene lanterns in the basement and together with odd bits of furniture, an old iron bed fitted with a surprisingly decent mattress he'd rescued from someone's curb years previous, it became a rough, but crudely comfortable home.

He didn't mind the squirrels in the attic nor the birds in the eaves and most importantly, the rent was cheap and he had a dry roof over his head. There had only been a couple incidents of intruders over the years, the most recent four years previous when a wandering homeless man had broken in and tried to rifle through his meager belongings one night.

Crazy Jack had caught him in the doorway upstairs. The six-inch Bowie knife the intruder had suddenly found at his throat had convinced him to seek his fortunes elsewhere.

On the few occasions kids would come by and poke around, Crazy Jack would disappear into the old closet in the basement until they left.

He hadn't always been known as 'Crazy Jack.' The actual name he had been born with was Solomon Jack Wackemane, but that was a name no one had called him that in many, many years, and not since he was released from Mohansic State Hospital.

It had been the voices that he had first started hearing as a teenager that had gotten him into trouble, voices claiming to be the twelve dead Sestaqua ancestors once buried out on Raadsel Point; a place he had only heard about in his youth. Sometimes, their clamor made him crazy, leading to violent outbursts. In his later tweens, he wound up hospitalized twice. Matters took decidedly more serious turn with the college student he had killed one night in 1979, outside a bar in Dayton, Ohio. Crazy Jack had only been passing through, having picked up a few weeks of carpentry work for a local contractor. He'd had been drinking that night and there had been a cute half-Creek young woman he'd met at the bar. Sometime later, the student, a pug-faced jock with dark curly hair and a blocky physique, showed up and made it clear he liked her better, and Crazy Jack not at all. After they were both thrown out, the fight had resumed in the parking lot and the last thing Crazy Jack remembered of that night was the kid leaning against a rust bucket of a Volkswagen, staring in shock at the blood running through his hands where Crazy Jack's knife had pierced his guts.

Later at the trial, it came out the kid had died right there still standing.

Crazy Jack testified (truthfully) that he had been drinking to silence the voices in his head and through the auspices of a semi-competent public defender, had wound up making a ten-year circuit of mental hospitals before he was finally released.

Still, the ghost of the young man he'd killed followed him everywhere.

And the voices, the ones that claimed to be his dead ancestors, hadn't stopped.

Increasingly, however, these days it was hard to remember what parts of his life really happened and those which he imagined, or dreamt, as they all seemed to blend sometimes. There were snatches of life growing up on the reservation – more like torn shreds of recollections that occasionally fluttered past his mind's eye. It had been a hard life, a life of battered poverty and bleak options.

And sometimes he would dream of his mother.

He could still see her face; sad and kind, a network of lines and creases mapped across it; etched by the uncertainties and the tragic reality of a once proud tribe facing a diminishing future. There had been a time, ages ago when every tribe in the area had its own distinct language, ethnicity and sometimes even myths. Few people outside of dedicated anthropologists and archeologists had any concept of the cultural train wreck Europeans had brought upon the American Indians or the magnitude of what had been lost, particularly in the Hudson Valley. James Fenmore Cooper's 'The Last of the Mohicans' had brought some notoriety to that particular tribe in the north despite his rambling and sometimes confused narrative, a fantasy further exasperated by the Hollywood remake in the 90's which featured absurdly romanticized actors prancing about in curiously spotless clothes.

Weckquaesgeck, Kitchawank, Mahican, Wappinger, Sint-Sinck, Munsee, Lenape.

Tribes and sub-tribes whose languages were as radically different as French was to Chinese, natives who once filled the shores of the Hudson but who by this twenty-first century had been mostly relegated to dusty old maps, mid-western reservations, and the occasional grade-school assignment.

Crazy Jack finally blinked and sat up looking sideways. Outside in the trees, the light had taken on the amber hues of early evening and somewhere a night bird began its first, earnest announcements.

The ghost of the young man he had murdered was no longer standing in the corner of the room, suggested in the shadows that always seemed to gather there, though Crazy Jack knew he'd return. He always did.

But the voices had a mission for him today, and he wasn't going to accomplish much counting cracks in the plaster.

Hours later, Crazy Jack stood in front of the display case in the second-floor Indian artifacts room of the Wyvern Falls Historical Society, dressed in an old denim shirt and jeans along with his trademark cowboy hat. There was a silent expectancy in the air, the telltale odor of old artifacts waiting too many years in un-air-conditioned rooms for something to happen. In this particular one, thousands of years of artifacts, some that dated back long before the pyramids of Egypt were built.

Breaking in had been surprisingly simple. For starters, when the ADT alarm system had been installed eight years previous, no one had considered the possibility of gaining access through the attic gable windows, which could be entered by scaling a two-story drainpipe at the back of the building.

Amongst Crazy Jack's many talents – despite being sixty years old – was discreetly getting into places most people couldn't.

In the center of the antique glass case was an oversized horn. Nearly three feet long, it resembled a steer horn (if that steer had been, say, the size of an elephant) and was curiously covered with both incised and painted images and symbols, along with the remains of a leather harness crafted by unknown hands in a lost, forgotten age.

The Horn of Skarreh.

The currently accepted theory was that it was from a species of extinct prehistoric Giant Bison, though no one had yet to make head nor tail of meanings of the images on it. But Crazy Jack knew better because the voices had told him; this was the surviving Horn of the Last Witch Buffalo.

It had been a gift to the Sestaqua by the Wyandot during the former's migration to the east nearly five thousand years previous, part of a prophecy that was yet to be fulfilled. Part of the legend of the Witch Buffalo was that when the last one was slain by the Wyandot it was from its blood that sprang cranberries, which was why we have them today. But the horn itself had another purpose according the twelve ancestors Crazy Jack was saddled with.

It could summon a great monster to do battle with other monsters.

The cacophony of glass being shattered in the quiet room sounded both like an offence and a release.

Crazy Jack used the metal base of his Bowie knife to knock aside the larger pieces and carefully extract the horn. He might have just as easily pried the case open, but a symbolic gesture had been on order. With the closed windows and the lack of any resident homes nearby, it was unlikely anyone had heard, however.

The horn was surprisingly light for such a large object, though it was hollow after all. Tucking the horn under one arm, Jack pulled out from his shirt a dog-eared manila folder he had taken from the downstairs office earlier and laid it in the display case where the horn had been. On top of it, he placed a slim book had taken from the library/reading room down the hall.

The folder contained a rare copy of type-written notes by one of Jacques Cousteau's crew from an unusual expedition off the west coast of Africa in 1954. Wes Fowler had found the folder jammed at the back one of the file cabinets a few weeks earlier by accident – he had pulled out the drawer only to discover it had apparently somehow fallen in there, probably decades previous, long before he had become associated with the society. He'd only had time for a cursory glance and after a mental note to get back to it left it in one of the many stacks occupying his desk.

The book was a monograph dated from 1904. It contained the account of a sailor who had survived the wreck of the Edmund Wood that same year up in that narrow and most dangerous stretch of the Hudson River known as 'World's End.'

10. "… CLEARLY EVIDENCE OF ANCIENT ASTRONAUTS!"

Guillamo Del Tesler was in a slump.

After riding a momentary burst in fame (but not exactly fortunes), the self-ascribed 'Ancient Astronaut Theorist' and editor of the 'Star Colony: The Monthly Journal on Ancient Alien Civilizations' was shocked at finding himself with little to do. Along with his mentor Otto Wierling (who with film-maker Heinrich Hessler had co/authored the controversial 'Codex of the Gods' and 'Explorers of the Ancient Universe'), he had been prominently seen in recent a rash of 'documentaries' on the History Channel and had reveled in the sudden flux in interviews, fan letters and phone calls.

There were those of his detractors who asserted the increased lunacy of his claims were growing in direct proportion to his increasingly weirdly sculpted hairdo and that the so-called 'documentaries' were seriously undermining the credibility of History Channel. But in an age where the intelligence of what had once been the vanguards of cultural programming had apparently devolved to imbecilic levels, their complaints – if ratings were any indication – were falling on deaf ears.

These days, America was in love with the lives of infantile housewives, infantile celebrities, infantile back-woods people, and anyone else who could be cajoled into appearing on TV and shamelessly acting like idiots; but apparently, their interest in Colonization by Ancient Beings only went so far.

Del Tesler, whose birth name was Ron Schmensky, had been a second-year student majoring in Animal Husbandry at Cornell when he had fully converted to the gospel of Ancient Alienism ten years previous. He had first stumbled across the subject through an interview with Otto Wierling in The Fortean Times he'd found perusing the student bookstore. Oblivious to the magazine's tongue-and-cheek slant, what Wierling had said had made perfect sense to the impressionable Schmensky, and he'd quickly shifted his focus from animal mating studies to devouring all available media on what was *clearly* evidence of ancient visitations by alien beings.

His super-strict parents back in Deer Park, Long Island had been less than impressed and cut off funding after Ron announced he was dropping out of school to pursue what he described as his 'life's calling.' Ron's response was to legally change his name, grow his naturally wavy black hair out and start producing his first magazine, a shoe-string publication titled 'I, Alien.' Three years later, Ron – now Guillamo Del Tesler (a named derived from a distant relative on his mother's side of the family) – managed to land a gig as an editor working for Wierling's various publications and the rest as they say, was history.

His parents, first generation immigrants from Albania, had been horrified.

Del Tesler, however, was having the time of his life.

A stocky man now in his early thirties who had mastered the ability to arch either eyebrow independently to emphasize his points, Del Tesler combined affable charm, disarming sincerity, and a keen sense of humor that went a long ways to ingratiating him with others well past his average looks. Wierling, who came off as a slightly deranged, eccentric old Kraut, immediately recognized the value in having the boyishly enthusiastic Del Tesler as a spokesperson in his organization; Del Tesler was photogenic, engaging, and had the rare knack of making his critics appear petty and mean-spirited. In short, he was good for ratings. And donations.

Even so, for the past few months, things hadn't been going all that great.

Sure, 'Star Colony' magazine and affiliated products sales were holding steady, but despite the high visibility of the cable shows, the financial compensation was meager and well short of the cash cow both Del Tesler and Wierling had envisioned. Despite the recent upswing, Wierling's fortunes had been in steady decline since its crest back in the late 1970's and early 1980's when his then controversial theories had made him a regular on talk shows and covers of such publications as *Omni* and *Discover* shortly after 'Codex of the Gods' was released in theaters as an indie documentary.

While Del Tesler had a huge following on Twitter and on Facebook, inevitably sparked numerous replies in his blog, and had an established fan base, none of that had so far translated into a lucrative living.

And while he wholeheartedly believed in what he preached, he was growing increasingly tired of the growing lunatic fringe he was attracting. People who presented *clear, compelling evidence* of Ancient Astronauts (like Wierling) he embraced. People who clearly were out of their minds – and probably their meds – were a different matter. One thing had become abundantly obvious after the latest shows on the History Channel: there was no shortage of bat-shit fucking crazy people out there.

Like the insane woman who called at 2am the previous night and left a message so long it had filled up the entire capacity of the machine about how the CIA was following her, monitoring her every word and breath, and how Del Tesler would understand and would he contact her parents after the aliens took her away for medical experiments … followed by a rambling interlude where she described in explicit detail what naughty things she would like him to do to her (while handcuffed to the bed) before they did.

Del Tesler had to admit as he sat there re-listening to it over coffee in his Park Slope garden apartment that morning that he was more than a little turned on by it, despite the fact the caller was *clearly* out of her mind. Her girlish voice brought up a fantasy image of a petite, nerdy librarian-type in a Catholic schoolgirl uniform, though he knew enough from recent experiences it was more likely she was an overweight fifty-something who had forgotten to take her anti-psychotics again.

Regardless, it had to go. The crazy broad had filled up the entire ten minutes of message memory with her insane babble. *Too bad I can't transfer it*, he thought, *maybe I could sell it to a talk show or something.*

He pressed the delete button on the message machine and sat back.

The apartment, a modest one bedroom in a privately owned Brownstone on President Street, was an amazing deal he had scored through the local co-op years back when he was a nobody. It was even on the same block as actor/director John Turturro, whom he had finally run into just a month previous (Turturro had given him a wide-eyed look, then turned and all but sprinted in the opposite direction). Del Tesler's bedroom was in the back and opened into an adjoining room/office with exposed brick and a door into a small backyard patio.

The place looked like a deranged college dorm in the aftermath of a hurricane. Take-out food containers, life-sized alien and Sci-Fi props, beer and soda cans lay scattered amongst overflowing bookcases, 70s furniture (including a bean-bag chair), an oversized flat-screen with an Xbox Kinect system and framed photos of everything from the great pyramids to aerial shots of the Nazca lines in Peru. Only Del Tesler's workspace was, oddly, preternaturally neat with its hi-tech glass-and-metal desk, stainless steel phone system unit, and sleek Mac workstation.

It was like an island of order in a sea of chaos.

Next to the computer screen was a small stand with Del Tesler's private obsession: a Hohner Blues Harmonica, Key of C.

Del Tesler sat in front of his computer and was contemplating whether to give into the urge to go play Far Cry 5 for a few hours or get back onto writing his new book, which was puttering along miserably, when the phone rang.

It was a 914 number.

He put the unit on speaker and stood up, nibbling his right knuckle absentmindedly.

"Hello?"

"Hi. Mister Del Tesler?" It was a young woman's voice.

"That's me."

"Jennie Roderick. From the Wyvern Falls Historical Society? We spoke the other day?"

"Yes." Del Tesler's eyes brightened.

"Those objects I mentioned? I have them."

"Excellent!" Del Tesler picked up the phone and automatically switching back to normal handset mode as he walked back into the front of the apartment and began to talk.

If he hadn't stepped away, he might have seen a minor breaking story on his CNN feed about a young, pretty librarian in Manhattan who'd gone missing that morning, from inside her locked apartment.

It was followed by a report of strange lights seen over Central Park.

11. RAADSEL POINT, 4:15AM, MONDAY.

At the southern tip of Raadsel Point, which jutted out into the Hudson River not unlike the trailing tip of say, a Wyvern's wing, were the remains of a simple Revolutionary War era fort that had been sited on the rise there. The fort itself had been constructed atop a *midden* of discarded oyster shells built up over thousands of years by the local Indians; essentially, it was built on an old Indian garbage dump.

To the lee side of the fort a precipitous trail wound down to the strip of loose rocks and gravel at the base of the point – remains of a geological dump left by the receding glacier some 15,000 years ago – where the occasional intrepid fishermen would show up at low tide to test their meddle where the currents from the bay wrangled with those of the river itself.

Fishing-wise, it was a lucrative (if dangerous) spot, and also, like the fort above, a very scenic one, affording panoramic views of the river and valley. On clearer days, one could make out the skyline of Manhattan way to the south.

However, on this particular morning, just before the break of dawn, only a lone figure could be seen there, standing up to his knees in the freezing waters. The tide was at its lowest and the turbulence minimal, but even so, it was a precarious position, particularly for an older man.

Crazy Jack stood with the massive horn cradled in his arms. His face was inscrutable in the dim light, almost meditative. To his left, a few random lights twinkled across Raadsel Bay, to his right across the river the Palisades yet slumbered in darkness. The sky was a blaze of stars and only a few wisps of clouds scudded overhead. The quarter moon had just set under the horizon.

Except for the clothing, Crazy Jack could have easily passed for a ghost of one of his ancestors. Those of them that hadn't been lost to the decimating effects smallpox and ethnic cleansing brought on by the early settlers (in particular Kieft, that particularly inept and vindictive Dutch Governor) had trickled out of the area and joined the exodus to the west hundreds of years previous.

Except for the Sestaqua.

Nobody to this day knew what happened to them. Except, perhaps, Crazy Jack.

What was patently clear to him, however, was what he had been instructed to do by those voices haunting him, whether real or imagined.

He found himself humming a half-forgotten song his mother had taught him, a mournful and bittersweet tune about the *Mahicantuck* – the river that flows both ways. Then he paused to let his internal energies coalesce. After a moment, he lowered the base end of the horn into the water and placing his lips over the pinhole at the tip, began to blow.

A curious, muffled sound echoed off into the currents, not unlike the call of a whale. A *summoning* call.

Three times.

Crazy Jack stood the horn trailing in the water, and putting the mouthpiece to his ear, listened.

He might have imagined it, but he could have sworn that from across the miles and vast aeons of time, something answered.

And closer by, in the murky, unlit depths of the river, something else – a *massive* something else – quivered and recoiled.

Some miles away aboard the *Thomas Jefferson*, Ben Reinhardt was startled out of his sleep in his chair by the monitoring station in the control room. The underwater mics had picked up what sounded like a whale's distress call from somewhere *up* the river, which was strange. Although a rare occurrence, whales had been known to venture up the Hudson, but none much past New York harbor in recent years.

Reinhardt made a note in the log, and after listening for another twenty minutes and not hearing anything further, decided to wait until a more civilized hour in the morning when fortified with a good cup of java, he'd review the recorded data.

Over on Irving Avenue, John Easton was sitting in his kitchen with a mug of steaming Sumatra coffee and a bowl of Greek yogurt (with fresh blueberries), listening to the latest *Toby Foster at Breakfast* podcast on BBC Radio 4 when his phone rang.

He knew the number right away even without the caller ID: Police Chief Roy Hendricks.

"Hi, Roy," Easton said. "You're on the job bright and early. Yearly performance reviews?"

From the other end of the line, Hendricks chuckled. A sharp-eyed ex-state trooper in his late fifties, he'd gone after the police chief position to spend more time with his two daughters after his wife had died some five years previous. The girls were now in college, but being a life-long appointment, Hendricks wasn't going anywhere anytime soon, which now that he'd settled into this particular river village's routines, it suited him just fine.

"Nothing so exciting," he answered. "But nonetheless strange. There was a break-in at the Historical Society last night."

Easton perked up. Although Wyvern Falls seemed to have a disproportionate amount of strange things going on, a hotbed of crime it was not. Most of what Hendricks' sixty-one member police force dealt with on a daily basis involved incidents of the stray pet and domestic dispute variety, punctuated by the occasional accident (although there had been quite a bit excitement with that local cult business the year before). Breaking and entering was such a rare occurrence it was pretty much an anomaly.

The Historical Society? In his four years of living in Wyvern Falls, that was a first.

"What was taken?" he asked.

"Well now, that's just the thing, John. It appears something was stolen *and* returned. Along with that, whoever did it apparently left a message for *you*."

"For *me?* What on earth do you mean?"

"Captain Fowler can fill you in if you wouldn't mind swinging over there. He's there now in fact."

It didn't sound like a question to Easton. Something was up. He swirled the last of his coffee around in his mug, one wary eye on Rovsky who was sitting a foot away and fixedly staring at the bowl of yogurt as if he could will it closer. Easton couldn't figure out for the life of him what made the dog crave it so much. *Dairy addiction?*

"I don't mean to suggest she's involved in anyway," Hendricks said after a pause, "but I was hoping you might be able to ring up your friend Doctor Ramhorne and see if she could shed any light on the matter."

Easton's jaw tightened. It sounded like that was *exactly* what Hendricks might be suggesting. "I don't understand," he relied circumspectly.

"Well, the artifact that was stolen and returned, it was an *Indian* artifact."

Sarah met him in the driveway of the Historical Society around eight-thirty. This time, she looked more the part of the archeologist with cuffed Khaki shorts, work boots and a clean white denim shirt with the sleeves rolled up. Her hair was pulled back in a heavy braid. Easton couldn't deny wondering again what she might be like in bed. This morning there was a hint of something more desirable and it took him a moment to peg why – she had put on some light make-up, including a pale lip gloss.

For him?

"Hi," she said, walking up to him by his SUV. She eyed him with a challenging glance. "I got here as soon as I could."

After a little freshen-up, he thought. *But why do I get the feeling she's constantly testing me?*

Easton was more on the casual side this morning with faded jeans and a black knit short-sleeve shirt, along with his usual blue-grey 'wet-suit' style windbreaker.

"You look a little dressed up for this hour," he said. When she responded with a wry look, he added, "Thanks for coming by this early."

"I'm usually up by 5am. This is *late* for me. So what's the story with this Indian artifact business?"

Easton stood with his hands splayed on his hips, a hold-over habit from his full-time CID days when he wanted to appear casual yet make sure the badge on his belt was displayed. These days, the Detective Superintendent badge spent most of its time in a drawer in his desk back home. The New York State Private Detective's license was in his wallet, however.

"Right, well that's what we're here to find out."

"One of our local 'Sanitation Executives' spotted it early this morning as they were driving by," Captain Fowler said. The three of them were back in main the office of the Historical Society, this time sitting around the desk where the large horn now rested.

"Where was it?" Easton asked.

"Someone left it standing on end on the step before the front doorway. A little hard to miss."

"Some sort of practical joke?"

Fowler made a dismissive gesture with his right hand. "Beats me. You get people doing all sorts of whacked-out things at my job, but I can't really figure this one. Someone snuck in here in the middle of night, liberates an oversized artifact from one of our display cases, dips it in water – probably the river – then returns it. What does that suggest to you, John?"

"Water?"

"The open end was still wet inside."

"Then I'd say someone around here is willing to go to great lengths to blow bubbles," Easton said dryly. That got a short laugh out of Fowler. "Seriously though, do you have any security cameras? Alarm system?"

"Just ADT on the first and second floors. The Historical Society's operating budget isn't exactly flush. It looks like whoever did it accessed an attic window. They'd need to be a professional cat burglar to get to it though."

Easton pondered this. "At least you got it back. And nothing else was taken?"

"Nope."

"So somebody – a very *able* somebody – sneaks in here in the middle of the night, steals a specific artifact, presumably for a specific purpose, uses it, then returns it, leaving it in a location where its sure to be spotted."

"That's about the cut of it," Fowler agreed.

"Any fingerprints?"

"I did a quick dusting. It looks like the perpetrator wore gloves. If this was a more serious crime, I'd be a little more thorough, but calling the crime lab boys on this would have the whole department busting on me 'til Christmas. I'd probably get gift-wrapped steer horns from Charlie Manson, horn-handled magnifying lenses from Sherlock Holmes ... you know how these guys work."

Easton nodded. "Yeah." He glanced over at Sarah, then the horn. "Sarah, what do you think? Any idea who or why someone would nick this thing?"

Sarah stood up and picking it up, looked it over. "I don't recognize the symbols, but I'd say this is definitely ceremonial and very old. It's not only a horn, but I would say it was meant to be used as one, which is very unusual. I've seen them used as powder horns, or as part of a ceremonial headdress, but never like this. Nor have I ever heard about such a thing, even as a myth. You say it's Wyandot?"

"That's what I understand," Fowler answered. "It's been in our collection since the 1870s." He handed her a yellowed typewritten page.

"The Horn of the Last Witch Buffalo, also known as the *Horn of Skarreh*," she read. "That myth I *do* know about. One of the twin brothers in certain Indian creation myths. In the Wyandot stories, it's actually spelled 'Skä'rĕh.' He was the evil one." Sarah paused, surprised to see both men studying her with rapt attention. "Do you really want to hear this? It's Huron-Wyandot myth, not Mahican or Wappinger or Lenape for that matter, though we do both share an almost identical Witch Buffalo legend. In the Lenape version, it's *Witch Mastodons* though."

Fowler spoke first. "Absolutely. It's not like we have professional Native Indian archeologist's giving us the low down here every week. Let's hear it."

Sarah handed the paper back to Fowler and sat down. "Have you heard of 'The Woman who fell down from Heaven'? No? She's the Wyandot version of the Earth Goddess. Well, it's like this; she had twin sons, *Tsē'sĕh-howngk'* and *Tä'wĕ-skä'rōōngk*. It's easier to refer to them by the diminutive form of their names, *Sē'stä* and *Skä'rĕh*. The Good one and the Evil one. That's a whole telling in itself, but you only need to be concerned with is *Skä'rĕh*. Always a lot of trouble that one. Being gods, they got up to making all sorts of things and as you can probably guess, all of *Skä'rĕh's* creations were highly unpleasant. Among the monsters he made were the Witch Buffalo. They had long horns on their heads and tusks longer than those of any elephant, and had thick hides covered with coarse black hair. They had magic power too of course, and all the animals and Indians were terrified of them."

"Anyhow, as the story goes, there was this large spring – so large you could barely see across it and so clear you could see a pebble at the bottom of it. Some said the brothers were born there, others that *Sē'stä* created it, but regardless, all the animals cherished and drank from it until the Witch Buffaloes showed up and started terrorizing everyone. Finally, the animals had enough of this and went to the Indians and asked for their help. The Indians went to the Little People of the forest and got them to lend a hand, along with Heno the Thunder God, who wielded thunder and lightning."

"A huge battle followed, with *Sē'sta* and *Ska'rĕh* watching from the mountains on either side. By the time the sun began to set, all but one of the Witch Buffalo was slain, and seeing how things were going, he decided to hightail it out of there. So using his magic power, he leapt – clear over the Ohio River and with another leap into the far north where it is always winter. He's there to this day, the Keeper of the North Wind."

"Anyhow, the dead Witch Buffalo disappeared into the ground and where their blood dried up was found a bunch of red berries which were good to eat, which is how we got cranberries – the only good thing to come out of the Witch Buffalo." She sat back with a ghost of a smile on her lips, crossing her arms. "And that is the end of that one."

Easton was impressed. It was as if Sarah had transformed into a whole other person as she went into storytelling mode, even speaking in a different cadence that evoked something timeless and ancient. It wasn't a far stretch to imagine sitting around some campfire a millennia ago, listening to that voice speak instead of here in a paneled office in the 21st century.

"Where'd you learn to tell stories like that?" he asked.

"My great aunt, Nora Thompson Dean. She was one of the best," Sarah answered.

"So how would it be this horn is from the last Witch Buffalo, if he's alive and well and living somewhere up along the North Pole?" Easton added.

Sarah gave him a flat, sideways look. "Not everything needs to make cold, logical sense. Although at a glance, I'd say that looks suspiciously like a Giant Bison horn."

"That's what we thought," Fowler cut in, leaning forward and tapping it. "But the test the Natural History Museum did on it years back was inconclusive. But the question in my mind is, if this is a horn – evil brothers aside – is what would it be used for? Or more importantly, what might someone *think* it should be used for?"

"To ring up a Witch Buffalo?" Easton offered.

That earned him a second flat look from Sarah. "Perhaps a river monster?" she said turning to Fowler.

"A … what?" he said back, unable to keep the incredulous look off his face.

Sarah shrugged. "You were fishing for an explanation. There are several stories about river monsters created by *Skä'rĕh*. Serpents, and things called 'Hookies.' Perhaps that's what your thief was looking to do."

Fowler thought about it. It was ridiculous of course, but something about the idea made him uneasy. Particularly in light of the recent disappearances out at Raadsel Point. But even suspending disbelief, why summon something that had already shown up? It didn't make any sense. He decided to put that on the shelf for the moment and move on.

"Well, something to consider. And thanks for your insights. But there's an additional twist." Leaning back, he pulled out and dropped a manila folder and a slim, antique-looking book on the desk next to the horn. "Our considerate thief left this out," he looked Easton in the eye. "Specifically for you."

12. A STRANGE MESSAGE ...

"I just don't get it," Easton said again, shaking his head. Fowler had explained how the folder and book had been left in place of the horn in the shattered display case, along with a yellow Post-it note on top that said 'For John Easton' written in simple block letters.

The book was a slim cloth-bound volume in dark-green with faded gold lettering that read: 'Being an Account of the Last Voyage of the Edmund Wood.' At a glance, it appeared to be a privately produced account of the final voyage of that particular ship, which foundered and sank in 1904 at the deepest part of the Hudson River up at the entrance of the Hudson Highlands sometimes referred to as 'World's End.'

The account was apparently told by the only survivor of the wreck, an able seaman named Jonas Forsythe.

The manila folder contained fifty-odd typewritten pages, single-spaced, of various notes by a man named Pierre Tailliez who was a crewman on an early – and apparently unknown – Jacques Cousteau expedition around the Mediterranean and West Coast of Africa in 1954. It looked like a mimeographed copy and still gave off that faint sweet chemical smell that made Easton think of his earliest school years. Specifically, those dreadful 'pop quizzes.'

"Any ideas why someone would address these to you?"

"None," Easton replied. "I've never heard or seen of either of these things before in my life. Where did they come from?"

Fowler steepled his fingers and tapped his fingers together. "Well, that's kind of the weird part, as if none of this was weird; the book is from our library upstairs – it has our stamp on the back page – though I don't recall having seen it before. And the folder was just discovered a couple weeks ago by fluke. I was having trouble closing one of the file cabinet drawers one day and found it jammed at the back. It must have fallen out years ago. I've been meaning to sit down and read it thoroughly but just hadn't gotten around to it." He glanced at his watch then at Easton. "Tell you what ... look those over and tell me what you think. Maybe you can make sense out of it."

Sensing this was their cue to leave, Easton and Sarah stood up. Easton tucked the book and envelope under his arm. As he shook hands with Fowler, the captain added one more thing.

"Oh, and John?"

"Yes?"

"I believe a lot of things in life are just plain coincidences, but I have a hunch this one isn't: last year when there was that incident with the three kids out at the Point? Do you recall?"

"Vaguely. Two disappeared. The survivor was so traumatized he was committed to the Psychiatric Ward at Philipseburg."

"Yeah ... well, there was one other detail we didn't make public."

"Which was ...?"

"At the location where it all happened at the shoreline, there was a crate. A *huge* crate. It must have been dislodged and washed up from the depths of the river by the hurricane. But – and this is even yet weirder – it was a relic from an old shipwreck."

"Come again?" Easton cocked his head.

"Ready for this? It was from the wreck of a ship called the *Edmund Wood*."

13. "ARE YOU ASKING ME OUT?"

Out in the drive, Easton turned to Sarah.

"What do you think?" he asked.

"I'm beginning to think this is one seriously strange town," she answered.

"Oh, it is at that." He looked up at the sky where a red-tailed hawk was drifting around the thermals, feeling a little nervous at what he was about to ask next. There was no way around it so he just said it. "You like Mexican food?"

She responded with a careful look. "I've been known to eat it once in a blue moon."

His eyes met hers. "There's a decent place down the road on 9B called 'Quetzalcoatl.' Pretty authentic, run by real Mexicans, actually. How about catching dinner there to tonight?"

Her teeth looked very strong and white as she flashed him a smile. "Are you asking me out on a date, white man?"

"I think that's what I just did."

The smile widened. She seemed genuinely amused. "Okay then. You're on."

"I'll pick you up around eight."

At just about the same time Easton had finally decided to ask Sarah Ramhorne out, a Jet Ski race was going on just past the Point.

Brad Tyrell and 'Dicky' Lawrence had decided to take advantage of the mild weather and have a little fun on the Hudson, said fun in the form of Tyrell's two brand new 'personal watercraft' courtesy of Kawasaki Heavy Industries Motorcycle & Engine. Said fun also included two waitresses Tyrell had cajoled into joining them, Carol Innes and Bev Carlyle, one on each Jet Ski.

Tyrell was a twenty-eight-year-old restaurant owner from Bedford while Lawrence was an old high-school chum who worked at a local cycle shop owned by his dad. The restaurant – an upscale eatery in Chappaqua called 'Sherwood Manor' – was really an occupational hobby Tyrell's father had set up to give his oldest son something to do. Tyrell's primary ambition in life, in spite of having two kids and the kind of wife who looks great at all those dinners at the country club, was simply to party, party, and then party some more. The fact that he had woken up 'early' this particular Monday was a remarkable achievement in and of itself. His usual timetable involved waking up around noon, detoxing with a sauna and swim before ambling over to the restaurant somewhere between five and seven pm.

Lawrence fared a little better – he actually *worked* at the cycle shop (Pro-Rider, over on North Hudson) as a sales manager and it was his dad who had sold Tyrell the two Jet Ski's they were currently zipping up the Hudson on.

The waitresses both worked the dinner shift at Sherwood and it hadn't taken much in the way of convincing to get them involved for the days outing. Carol Innes, a flashy twenty-two-year-old brunette who was long on looks (and a little short on brains) had made it clear since being hired a couple months previous she had the hot's for Tyrell, along with pretty much anything falling under the category 'Lets Party'- a phrase she could actually say in three different languages. Bev Carlyle, a gangly blonde whom she'd met through the restaurant, ran pretty much along the same stripe.

It had been Tyrell's idea of course. Pretty much everything they did were his ideas and typically were of the last moment 'Dude-we-gotta-do-this-today' variety, of which Tyrell – master of all things adventure & alcohol (and recreational drugs) – was king. In this case, the idea for the day's outing had come up around 10pm the previous night while hanging out at the restaurant's bar after closing. Lawrence had swung by for a nightcap and had found Tyrell at the bar in the company of both young ladies. Being a slow Sunday, he'd let the bartender off early and decided a little socializing with the employees was in order.

Typically, any adventure would be commenced by a few brews and perhaps a joint or two. Today, however, it had only taken him a single beer to get fired up and out to the Raadsel Bay Yacht Club. Tyrell, a dark-haired guy with rugged looks slowly going to seed (along with the beginnings of a pot-belly where his six-pack abs once proudly resided) had led them out on the water and through a series of fishtailing antics before getting bored, despite numerous hoots and yells from their passengers. Then he'd struck on the idea of Lawrence and him doing a race down the river.

They'd idled to a burbling stop just past the tip of the point when he'd turned to Lawrence – a sandy-haired guy with a receding chin and loopy smile – and flashing a big grin snapped his goggles back into place and announced, "Hey … got it! Dude, let's do a race. From the mid-channel buoy to say … just past Teller's Landing on the opposite shore? Loser buys drinks at the Clubhouse!"

Which meant *Lawrence was buying drinks*. Tyrell never let him win anymore – not since the restaurant started seriously losing money and besides, Lawrence just didn't have an aggressive 'win-at-all-costs' gene in his body. Lawrence's path in life seemed to be pretty much whichever one everyone else told him to go on.

"Yeah ... sure ... cool!" he said, checking his life vest. He half turned to Bev, who was straddled behind him with her arms around his waist. "I mean, is that cool with you?"

"Sure!" Bev said. She was having the time of her life. She'd never been on a Jet Ski before.

It was a clear, warm, late summer day. The river was empty of traffic (except for a large yacht lazily tacking a couple miles downriver), the water barely had a ripple in it, and the sun suggested a day that could stretch on forever.

What could go wrong?

"One-two-four *go!*" Tyrell yelled, gunning his throttle. Both Kawasaki Jet Ski Ultra LX's shot forward, leaving identical rooster-tails of water arcing out behind them. Tyrell immediately took the lead. In that sense, he was either reckless, fearless or stupid (or all three depending on your viewpoint); the Tyrells of the world always pushing everything immediately to the max whether it involved women, alcohol, or throttles. Especially throttles.

Lawrence, on the other hand, belonged to the Hesitators Tribe of the human race, always erring on the side of caution, never quite pushing it all the way. Each in their own fashion served a function.

With the throttles opened up, the Jet Ski flew down the river at a heady fifty-five miles per hour, the four-stroke 1498cc engines letting out a throaty roar. Tyrell continued to lead the way, angling towards Tellers Landing on the opposite shore where the Palisade cliffs jutted up a good two to three hundred feet in the air. From the seat behind him, Carol whooped and hollered, interjecting the occasional '*Oh yeah!*' and '*Whoooie!*'

They'd barely covered half a mile, however, when disaster struck.

It happened too fast to process, but Lawrence's initial thought was that Tyrell must have hit a submerged log or something. One minute, the restaurateur was hunkered down a good forty feet ahead, the next he and Carol were separated from his personal watercraft and doing end over end cartwheels across the surface of the river while the Jet Ski did an ungainly spin and tumble.

Lawrence meanwhile chopped his throttle and veered off into a wide loop.

"Brad!? Brad!?" he yelled. Behind him, Bev gripped him silently, her face a study in shock.

Tyrell had ended up apparently unconscious, floating along in his black and electric blue life-vest, head lolling and mouth agape. The large tribal tattoo on his right shoulder glistened in the late morning sunlight.

Carol floated a few yards away, blinking and stunned. The left side of her face was numb and the fifty-mile-an-hour tumble across the water had left her feeling like she'd been bitch-slapped by a sheet of linoleum, but aside from a hot throb of what was probably a sprained neck, she felt more or less intact.

"Brad!" Lawrence screamed again, panic edging into his voice. He had just begun maneuvering his Jet Ski in closer, however, when Tyrell's eyes snapped open and spitting water he said, "*Cowabunga!*" and started laughing hysterically.

Lawrence leaned forward on the handlebars of the Jet Ski and shook his head. "Jesus fucking Christ man, I can't believe you. Fuckin-a."

Tyrell, despite his legs and arms feeling like they'd been bent the wrong way around a barrel – or perhaps because of it – snapped his neck to one side then the other and said, "Shit man, you *know* I'm Mister Indestructible. Hey Carol, how are – Carol?"

Carol was still floating a few yards away, but her face was now contorted in a rictus of pain, her eyes bulging to the bursting point. Gagging sounds came out of her mouth. Then a curtain of blood erupted and gushed over her lips as her eyelids began to flutter.

"What the –?" Tyrell said, cutting himself off as the waitress suddenly disappeared under as if yanked by an unseen hand beneath the waves. That had them remaining there speechless for about the space of twenty seconds, which was when the surface of the river erupted into foaming chaos.

The thrashing massive greenish-black tentacles seemed like some spectacular Hollywood special effect, though there was nothing fake about the one over-sized tentacle that broke the surface gripping the remains of Carol Innes. It appeared as if some giant predator had bitten off her head and her entire left arm and shoulder. One perfect breast was flopping out of the torn lifejacket. Three sets of eyes went wide in horror, and it was Tyrell who managed to get his scream out first.

As if they'd been listening, the other tentacles zeroed right in on him. Almost playfully.

Lawrence didn't hesitate a second. He gunned the throttle and shot off in the other direction so abruptly Bev lost her grip and tumbled right off.

He never looked back as he sped back toward the yacht club, grateful that the roar of the Jet Ski's engine obscured the combined pleading cries that quickly turned into hideous gurgling and the gunshot snaps of bones being broken.

14. IT LOOKS LIKE WE HAVE A PROBLEM ...

"Jesus H. Christ on a stick, Wes," Police Chief Roy Hendricks said.

Hendricks was in his office at the Wyvern Falls Police Station; that stalwart Depression-era building located at the corner of Van Wyck Avenue and Hanson Place.

The police chief's office was as austere and trim as the man whose job was to occupy it. On one wall hung a large antique map of Wyvern Falls, on the other a framed print of one of Havell's classic Hudson Valley paintings from early 1832 with its glorious evening lighting and lush rural idealism. Next to it was hung an original autographed photograph of football legend Jim Thorpe and behind him, in an almost humorous contrast to the police chief's stern face with its steel-grey, hooded eyes, was a bookshelf filled with assorted stuffed animals and toys; gifts from his quiet fan club of local kids he was involved with through various community organizations.

It had a way of throwing his staff off. At the moment, Lieutenant Sanchez, seated between Captain Fowler and Detective Eckhart, found his eyes wandering between the police chief and the kid-sized Big Bird propped up on the shelf behind.

Fowler had his tall, lanky frame bent into a chair that seemed a size too small for him, one leg crossed with his hand on the ankle. He hadn't been openly thrilled about having to deliver this latest report, especially on the same week as the GreenWaters Festival was scheduled to begin. Coupled with the other three missing people (and one dog), it was already shaping up to be a mess of a Monday and all indications were that the forecast for Tuesday and probably the rest of the week wasn't looking any better.

"So we have only one survivor from this latest boating – sorry, Jet Ski – accident on the river?" Hendricks continued. He was sitting with his left fist covered by his right hand, eyes locked onto his captain but giving away little of what might be going on in the mind operating behind them. Although his staff had never known him to gamble (actually there was a time in his twenties when he had, and after it had gotten him into a serious bit of trouble, he had sworn off it for good), he could readily put on a poker player's face; blank and inscrutable.

"That's correct, Chief." Although Fowler and Hendricks were good friends, they always used proper titles when subordinates were present. "Bill Lawrence's son. They sent him home under heavy sedation, after he gave us a fairly incoherent statement about a 'giant sea monster' gobbling up his friends." Fowlers palms open gesture reflected what his opinion on that claim was. "We recovered the other Jet Ski, no sign of the three people yet. Lieutenant Maynard is out there now with the divers dragging the area just as you ordered, but with the tide coming in, it's too dangerous to dive. It is *odd* there's not any sign of them – all three had on life jackets supposedly. But stranger things have happened."

"What's your take?" Hendricks asked.

Fowler's foot went up and down a few times. "It may just be a tragic boating accident. Hitting say, a log, at that high of a speed can cause you all sorts of problems. We have a few witnesses from along the waterfront, but being the accident happened on the far side of the river, they couldn't provide much info aside from all agreeing that *something* happened. Richard Lawrence did have alcohol in his system and he all but reeked of marijuana, so it's very likely that was a contributing factor. The way these kids race up and down the river and given the percentage of underwater obstacles scattered around the river, it was only a matter of time before something like this occurred. Cripes, there's submerged rocks all along the shores. Sometimes you get waterlogged trees just under the surface. You can't see them until you're right on top of them. At fifty miles an hour, that's not a lot of wiggle room. And you know how it is with guys like Tyrell – their antics have them with one foot in the grave and the other on a banana peel."

"But we also have two young ladies involved."

"Uh-uh, that too," Fowler agreed, knowing the police chief was undoubtedly thinking about his own two daughters who were nearly the same age as the missing waitresses. "I know Tyrell's dad is breathing hard on your neck on this one …"

Hendricks made a slight nod. Both men knew it was messier than that. Senior Tyrell was also bullying them not to reveal the fact that his son's missing passenger wasn't someone other than the young Mrs. Tyrell. *Goddamn rich kids*, he thought, *do they ever have any real idea how much trouble they cause?*

"So we have enough to stick to the alcohol/underwater obstacle story?"

"Unless you want me to put out an APB for a sea monster," Fowler answered with a grin.

Hendricks snorted and was about to respond when Sanchez cut in, "Excuse me, Chief? Sorry to interrupt, but there may be something to that …"

"Relating to the other cases on the Point?" The chief's eyes zeroed in on the lieutenant.

"Exactly."

"Talk to me."

"Well, there's nothing conclusive yet, but that evidence we reported finding at the site of the disappearances? That slimy substance found left behind on the concrete bulwarks?" He took the 9x12 envelope he had been holding in his hands and leaning forward placed it in front of the police chief. "Those are the results from the Marine Biology Lab in Woods Hole, Massachusetts, which was where Columbia sent them to. They faxed us back directly."

Hendricks hesitated, as if debating whether he might really want to see the results or not. Something in Sanchez' tone suggested the latter. Unfortunately, he had no choice.

A few minutes later he dropped the folder and contents on his desk.

"The summary said, 'Mitochondrial DNA is of unknown species, but is similar to the prehistoric class of *cephalopoda*, which includes squid, cuttlefish, and octopi.' So that's it, we have giant cuttlefish eating up parents and dogs along our shores?"

"Cuttlefish are a form of mollusks, Chief; it may well be we have a giant killer clam in our local waters," Fowler offered.

"Even worse," Hendricks sighed. "Probably seeking revenge on our local firemen for all those years of clam bakes at the carnival." Seeing the mortified expression on Detective Eckhart's face, he cleared his throat and rubbed his jaw. "Well, bad jokes aside, Lieutenant, what does this *realistically* suggest?"

Sanchez shrugged. "I have no idea, Chief. That's why I invited someone who might." He stood up and motioned towards the pebbled glass door dividing the chief's office from his secretary's where the ever intimidating and fearsome Beatrice Voight sat guarding the entrance like a middle-aged, thick-waisted Cerberus with sculpted gray hair.

"May I?" the lieutenant asked.

Hendricks responded with a curt nod.

A moment later, Sanchez was ushering in a young, good-looking man with curly blond hair, dressed in a T-shirt, old jeans, and a pair of Docksiders. Hendricks wondered if this was some sort of joke – the kid looked barely out of college.

"Chief, I'd like you to meet Ben Reinhardt."

After introductions had been made and Reinhardt's credentials with the NOAA established, the oceanographer gave a brief summary of his findings. As fate would have it when Sanchez first spoke with the lab at Columbia his contact there – a career graduate student named Theresa he'd dated once or twice – informed him that one of their boy wonders happened to be right in the area doing research.

"They've got him on some droll GIS mapping assignment," she'd offered helpfully. "A waste, really. He's a hot-ticket marine paleontologist, recently graduated top of his class. And he's twiddling his thumbs right down the river from you, probably bored out of his skull. I'll give you his cell. I'm sure he'd jump at the opportunity. Speaking of which, haven't seen *you* around in a while, *Raymond* …"

Sanchez had cut her off with a, 'Gotta go; emergency call on another line' (which was actually Detective Eckhart giving him one of her better eagle-eyed stares from the next desk over), and an hour later, he was down at the Metro North Station picking up Reinhardt.

"Whatever left that residue at your, er crime scene, is certainly scientifically significant. *Extremely* significant." Reinhardt wished he'd had more time to pull some materials together; instead, he'd have to make do with the police station's laptop, which was hopelessly antiquated. It was that or pass around his smartphone.

"As I told your lieutenant, the lab analysis indicated that the sample was from an unknown species, closely related to *cephalopoda*, but different. The mitochondrial DNA suggests something prehistoric in nature and based on the measurements of the marks from the crime scene, quite large."

"Quite large?" Hendricks asked. "As in how 'quite large'?"

Reinhardt had his closed fist to his mouth, something he did frequently when thinking. "Extrapolating from known species? Fifty to sixty feet perhaps."

"*Fifty … or sixty feet!?*" Hendricks responded while leaning forward, drawing out each word in disbelief. Fowler let out a low whistle.

"Sounds like a sea monster to me," Detective Eckhart put in, speaking up for the first time.

Hendricks sat back, dropping a pencil he'd picked up at some point on his desk. He looked up at the ceiling fan spinning lazily overhead as if seeking inspiration, then back at Reinhardt. "I'm having a little difficulty with all this, Reinhardt. For starters, even if it were a given such things exist, why would a prehistoric cuttlefish just show up on the shores of the Hudson River – Raadsel Point specifically – out of the blue? This isn't the Marianas Trench or the coast of Africa. We simply don't have extinct species popping up around here like some kind of dinosaur hotspot. And I would think that if something of this magnitude did there would be other, clear collaborating evidence - say a major drop in fish populations, multiple sightings, etc. So my question to you is; what other explanations do we have?" From the tone of his voice, it was clear that Hendricks had just about his fill of 'giant cuttlefish' talk. If nothing else, he was a severe pragmatist. Particularly when he had a growing list of missing persons on his hands.

Reinhardt looked nonplussed. "Other explanations?" he said.

"Yes. Such as a prank or practical joke. What would it take to stage something like this?"

Reinhardt shook his head and blinked as if unable to comprehend the question. "Well, you'd have to locate some sort of rare or unknown species ... then fabricate marks to suggest a much larger creature, then have enough knowledge to stage the scene convincingly ... it would be extremely difficult ..."

"Give it some thought then," Hendricks said, cutting him off. He looked around at each of his three officers in turn. "And that goes for the rest of you as well. We've got several very upset families out there right now – including the Tyrells – breathing down my neck. I am not going back to them with 'shucks, it looks like a big ol' sea monster gobbled up your loved ones' as a response. Especially on the eve of a major local festival that like it or not generates massive revenues for our village. That alone is suspicious timing. I want facts, evidence, and every possibility looked at, starting with who would gain the most if the GreenWater Festival were deep-sixed. Am I making myself clear?"

From the stung looks on their faces, it appeared he was.

Fowler hung back a moment while the rest stood up and filed out.

Hendricks waited until the room was empty. "I'm a little surprised at you, Wes. You should know better."

Fowler rubbed the back of his neck with his hand. Sarah Ramhorne's Indian story about sea monsters ... and the business with the horn resurfaced in his thoughts.

"I do know better, Roy, and I apologize. I know Tyrell and that suit he pays a few hundred an hour are jumping all over you. But all my instincts are telling me this isn't a hoax. I don't feel good about this at all."

Hendricks looked off into space. The pencil was back in his hand, tapping slowly away at the desktop. "Then give me something I can work with, Wes. *Quickly.*"

In the hallway outside the chief's office, Fowler found Reinhardt in an animated discussion with Lieutenant Sanchez and Detective Eckhart.

"... I don't think he gets it," Reinhardt was saying. "This is the real deal! The MBL people at Woods Hole were all but jumping out of their underwear! This huge! As in *major scientific breakthrough huge*. Like when they found that live coelacanth off Africa ..."

"You didn't tell them where the samples came from, right?" Fowler cut in.

"No, of course not," Reinhardt answered.

"And that's how it'll stay for the moment, understood? As Lieutenant Sanchez explained earlier, its evidence in a crime scene that involves several missing people ... very possibly *dead* missing people, yes? Any information that gets leaked in such an ongoing investigation would be dealt with to the maximum extent of the law. Do you follow?"

"I follow," Reinhardt said, looking like a sullen schoolboy. "Look, I can try and wrangle some time to look into this, but I need a boat."

"What about the 'Thomas Jefferson?'" Sanchez asked.

"No. That'll never happen short of a Federal Emergency," Reinhardt replied. "The allocation plan for each ship is worked out for the entire year and has to be signed off by a battery of NOAA officers – right now she's booked on a god-awful river mapping assignment. The Gordon Gunter would be ideal, but she's down in the Gulf of Mexico right now." Reinhardt scratched his head. "You know, I've been messing around with this new phase differencing bathymetric sonar unit we've been evaluating ... this one is fairly portable. I could even make do with a boat that's small and mobile."

Sanchez looked at Fowler. "The police launch is already tied up sweeping the river. But we have that Zodiac SRR ...?"

15. THE TROUBLE ALWAYS STARTS WITH TEQUILA ...

Located to the south of the village, about a quarter mile past the Citgo station owned by a Vietnamese guy named Chu Loc and his family, Quetzalcoatl's had all the trappings of an upscale south-of-the-border eatery. Owned by Francisco Morelos, the restaurant looked like a cozy *hacienda* with its tile roofs, weathered timber and stucco walls, abundant planters (overflowing with lush plants and palms), and acres of imported Spanish tile. The rooms were also generously decorated with antique knick-knacks and old paintings from Mexico, heavy furniture that suggested Spanish Colonial origins and large ceiling fans that turned lazily even in winter.

The staff were all strictly *Mexicanos* including the top-notch Mariachi band that worked the floor every night including Sundays. To the generally wealthy clientele (mostly the kind that drove Lexus's or Mercedes and lived in sprawling houses with expansive lawns), Morelos was a throwback to another era, a vaguely better era reminiscent of well-groomed and obeisant Mexican restaurant owners that favored big smiles, impeccable manners, and pencil-thin moustaches. To the observant few and to those who knew him directly, it was all a very shrewd and calculated act, right down to bow and hand kiss invariably bestowed on female customers. Behind the façade, Morelos was a strict and often abusive boss, driving his staff with an iron hand and sharp tongue though not without some measure of fairness; at Quetzalcoatl's, those who worked hard were at least paid well. Although few of his fellow Mexicans could afford the prices on the printed menu, he discreetly made available a secondary menu that kept a fair number of Latin Americans populating the tables to maintain an appearance of authenticity so that his wealthier patrons could tell their (also wealthy) friends as much.

For the most part, it all worked though, and Quetzalcoatl's was a very profitable restaurant and an enjoyable meal if one didn't scratch the surface too hard. Oddly, the one real wildcard in the whole picture was Francisco Morelos' wife.

Ana Maria Rivera Morelos was crazier than a bag of bouncing coconuts.

Though she fancied herself a tragically misunderstood artist, she was more in the neighborhood of delusional nut case with a chronic habit of straying off her meds. All this was abundantly clear – 'crystal clear' in one seriously delusional celebrity's parlance – to those who chose to look. What was uncanny, however, was those who chose not to, and that group included her husband along with most of the staff at Quetzalcoatl's.

The clues were hidden in plain sight as they say. Whether it was the bizarre 'animal pen' just visible at the back of the building with its plastic lawn creatures painted in all variety of psychedelic colors or the random delivery trucks showing up with curious supplies (like the time she ordered two dozen rolls of raw duck canvas imported all the way from a specialist art supplier in Italy). More interesting for the patrons of Quetzalcoatl were the occasional nights she would show up at the front bar in anything from a slinky cocktail dress to paint (presumably) stained bib overalls. At least twice, she had snuck in completely naked and tried to order a dry martini from the bartender before Mister Morelos, with suave efficiency, materialized and after draping his dinner jacket over her shoulders, quietly whisked her off through the kitchen and thence to their apartment upstairs.

The rumor was he kept a special locked and windowless room for those occasions.

Much of this Easton related to Sarah in quiet tones while they enjoyed a quiet dinner at a table near the massive stone fireplace at the back of the main dining room.

They had already worked through the irresistible stone bowl of guacamole (prepared fresh at the table) and an appetizer of reasonably good *Ceviche de Camarones*; the shrimp was a little over-marinated with lime juice (in Easton's opinion it all but pickled the dish) but the cilantro, jalapeños, and onions were fresh. Easton was warily pecking at the sizzling iron skillet of Steak *Fajitas* he'd ordered while Sarah was going at her Chicken Tomales Mixtecos with gusto.

Next to his entrée was a half-empty glass of 12-year-old Macallan – neat – while Sarah had gone with a tall and exotic looking glass of Sangria.

Sarah certainly looked striking. When Easton had picked her up earlier, he'd been pleasantly surprised when she'd opened the screen door in a fitted Spanish-looking black cotton dress that flared out from the waist down in sculpted folds. She had also been sporting high-strapped sandals, a silver necklace with earrings of silver and – to Easton's further surprise – set with amber. The entire combination was exotic, and Easton had to say, pretty hot. She'd pulled her hair back into a French twist with a hair clip, and despite wearing little make-up aside from some pale lipstick and a hint of eye-shadow (that he could tell, that is), she looked as smart as any woman getting out of a cab at Lincoln Center down in the city that evening.

After a bit of a debate about his wardrobe earlier, he'd opted to go dress casual himself – a tailored black Armani blazer with an open-necked white dress shirt, narrow tan slacks, and Italian shoes. Despite feeling over-dressed (he'd finally decided: *a date is a date, screw it*), he'd grabbed the keys to the Maserati and hoped for the best.

"How are your *tamales*?" Easton asked, managing to roll a few steak strips into a wrap along with a generous help of guacamole, refried beans, and sour cream without giving himself third-degree burns.

"Delicious," Sarah said through a mouthful. Easton noticed she tended to cover her mouth with her hand when she chewed.

There were many things Easton was skilled at. Improvising a *fajita* roll was not one of them. He made a gallant try but gave up after one bite resulted in half the contents spilling back onto his plate. He opted for a safer approach using his fork and knife.

"So tell me, *Detective* John Easton, how is it you came to 'Wyvern Falls'? It's such an odd place, this village."

Easton put his knife and fork down and took a pull off his scotch. "Well, it's a bit of complicated story involving a very wealthy and very naughty Dutchman who turned out to be a real pain in the arse to a lot of people."

Sarah took another bite of her dinner. "Really?" she said. "What did you have to do?"

Easton half-smiled. "Well … I wound up having to run him through with a sword."

Sarah almost choked on her tamale. After she finally managed to swallow it and wash it down with a gulp of Sangria, she looked at him earnestly.

"You're not joking."

"No, I'm afraid I'm not," Easton admitted.

"You can do that? And not be in jail?"

"Well, apparently so. Shut him up for good. But like I said, it's a bit complicated."

"You *killed* him?"

"Er, yes. But you have to understand, he'd done a lot of awful things to a lot of people over a long period of time. He got the easy end of the deal, believe me. But it's not the kind of thing I care to discuss while eating. So I'll tell you what, you tell me your story first, and I'll finish mine over a nightcap at the bar. Deal?"

Sarah gave him a long look while her finger traveled around the rim of her glass. "Okay then. A deal." She paused to collect herself and clear her throat. "So, many snows ago when I was a girl ... I'm just kidding. It's really not that exciting a story. But here it is ..."

Compared to the poverty on the reservation, her family was relatively well off, but relative to how people lived outside the reservation, that wasn't saying much. As she'd told Jim Franks before, she'd been born on the reservation in Tonawanda, New York. She'd originally grown up in a 1940's farmhouse on Skye Road that had belonged to her grandparents. Her father had left the reservation to get his law degree at the University of Buffalo, and after a brief stint with the U.S. Attorney's Office in Western New York, he became an advocate with the Bureau of Indian Affairs which led to a fair amount of travel, including the opportunity to track down distant relatives, which was one of his personal hobbies.

Some relatives from the Munsee side were located at the Stockbridge reservation in Wisconsin, others including her great Aunt Nora Thompson Dean, were near Bartlesville, Oklahoma.

"She was a great storyteller," Sarah said. "Though I was very little when she passed. But we still have many of her books. She was pure blood Delaware – from the Lenape (that's my mother's side) who used to live on the west bank of the Hudson River hundreds of years ago – and was really big on preserving the old traditions. Yes, your surprise is written on your face; most of the Indians who lived in this area before the Europeans were shoved off to the mid-west."

"That's another story though. So, my father's side were descended from the Wappinger and Mahicans that originally lived in this area. In fact, the Indian name for the Hudson River was '*Mahicannituck*,' a Mahican word which translated loosely means 'The River that Flows Two Ways'."

"Really?" Easton replied, after ordering a second round of drinks from their waiter. "I'd heard it was a tidal basin, but I didn't know that." It was clear to him she enjoyed talking about her background without soapboxing about it; he got the sense that she didn't talk about herself all that often. "So – I'm sorry – are the *Mahicans* the same as the Mohicans as in 'The Last of' ...?"

Sarah let out a knowing laugh. "Well ... yes. In fairness, most of the names you hear today are only European approximations of the original Indian names. Or complete mispronunciations that simply stuck. For example, the 'Iroquois' never referred to themselves as such; their original name was *Ongwe-oweh* or 'Men of Men.' Later, they became *Haudenosaunee* or 'People of the Long House.' The name *Iroquois* came from the French trying to pronounce *Hirokoa*, which was what the Wyandotte – Iroquois enemies – called them. It actually means 'real adders'; because tribes like the lower Hudson ones feared them as much as deadly snakes. And being a French name its pronounced 'Ear-o-kwah', not 'Ear-o-coy' most U.S. schools teach. You'll find a lot of Indian names have many different spellings. It gets complicated."

"So how did you get from Tonawanda to New York City?" Easton prompted, taking a sip of his scotch.

"Well, it was a long walk I can tell you." After seeing Easton's brow go up, she added, "I'm *kidding*. Actually, I ended up going to the University of Pennsylvania where I majored first in architecture, then anthropology, then switched to archaeology for my masters at Columbia. Focusing on American Indian history, of course."

"Sounds like you picked up your father's interest in the family tree," Easton said.

An intensely sad expression suddenly stole over Sarah's face.

"What?" Easton asked, realizing he already knew the answer. "Talk to me."

At first, he didn't think she would.

"It happened when I was nineteen," she began. "I was home from college and that summer my father was around a lot – there was some legal dispute going on with the ownership rights of the turtle museum up in Niagara Falls that year – and it was a Friday night. He was walking back from a late meeting with the elders. It was a hit and run. The sheriff later determined the driver was probably intoxicated based on the skid marks all up and down the road. It wasn't that far from our house – Council House Road. Someone ran him down and left him dying in the weeds while we sat on the front porch less than a mile away. We thought he was just staying late and swapping stories with his friends – he did that sometimes – so it wasn't until after midnight we began to wonder. By the time they found him, he was dead. The irony was that he didn't drink himself."

Easton was sitting back with his hands clasped in front of him, studying Sarah with a measured look. "Did they catch the driver?"

Sarah dabbed at her eye with her napkin. "No, though we were pretty sure who it was. Being a government employee, you would have thought they would have gone to great lengths to find the man responsible – but they didn't. My father had enemies too. Some on the reservation resented the fact he had left and come back, especially making decent money from the government that had stolen so much from our people."

"But you said he was an advocate for American Indian rights?"

"Yes. And he did a lot of good things. But certain people didn't see it that way. They only saw a man whose family had what they didn't, and they hated him for it. We suspected those same people helped protect the man who killed my father."

Easton considered this. "Well, for what it's worth, I'm truly sorry. It's a terrible thing to lose someone that way."

"I suppose you've seen a lot of that in your line of work."

Easton nodded. "A bit. But you never really get used to it."

Sarah took a long drink of her Sangria. "I loved my father very much. He was so proud of his family ... and his history. We actually had a relative who fought in the Revolutionary War if you can believe that. He fought alongside a great Wappinger Sachem named Daniel Nimham, who served under Washington and died in the Battle of Kingsbridge at what is now Van Cortlandt Park in the Bronx, in 1778. They fought bravely, but the British nearly slaughtered the whole unit. After the war, the families petitioned to get their lands back for their service but were denied. It's always the same story. But my father was working on all sorts of things like that – he was trying to re-petition the government the year he died. A lot of things died with him."

"How about the rest of your family?" Easton asked, trying to shift the topic.

"My mother is still alive. She lives in Niagara Falls now. And I have a younger brother. He's now an officer with the Genesee County Sheriff's Office ... and that's pretty much it."

"Pretty much it?"

"Without the messy details. So tell me something about yourself. The word about town was that you were a big shot detective down in the Caribbean?"

Easton shook his head and chuckled. "Who on earth told you that?"

She flashed him a mischievous smile then leaning forward and crossing her arms looked him in the eye. "A little bird. But tell me. Did you run around chasing bad guys with swords there too?"

That got an outright laugh from Easton. "Not usually," he replied. "They issue us guns, but we try not to use them."

There was a pause while the dishes were cleared and Easton ordered them coffee after they both declined dessert.

Easton sat back. He wasn't comfortable talking about himself, but at the same time, he was struck how nice it was to be sharing a dinner with

– no denying it – a woman he found himself increasingly attracted to. *Christ how long has it been*, he thought, *a year?*

Longer.

Since that whole disaster with Crowley. And the cave … and Vivienne … and of course Olivia. The latter he had only seen a few times over the past year, where she would invariably 'unsee' him in that fierce way only certain temperamental Latino woman seem capable of.

Easton took a sip of the coffee – which tasted strong enough to curl his chest hair – and cleared his thoughts as he savored the rich aroma. He'd spent enough nights with the ghosts of his past this previous year …

"I was a detective superintendent with the Royal Turk and Caicos Police Department," he heard himself saying. "Actually I still am, technically. I'm on indefinite unpaid leave – it's a loophole that leaves the door open. But I wound up here after I had to take time off after a rather messy case back there involving a Ponzi scheme artist and some trigger-happy drug-lords … and, well, found myself staying. That was over three years ago."

"Would you go back?"

Easton rubbed his chin. It was a question he dodged with himself repeatedly. "I'm not sure. Probably not. That last case there ended badly and there was a lot of resentment over it. At least where my balance book sits. But it more and more it seems more like a part of my life that has fallen irrevocably into the past. Still, there's certain advantages to keeping that door open. Official privileges you might say."

"And you grew up there?"

"No … no. I grew up in Falmouth, England. That's on the southwest coast in a region known as Cornwall. Seafaring town. But a few years after graduating from the academy, an opportunity came up in Grand Turk and Caicos and I took it. Chance to go someplace different, fresh start – that sort of thing. But the Hudson Valley is my adopted home now … and I have to say I quite like it here."

Sarah rested her chin on her hand and looked across the room where the Mariachi band was serenading an elderly black couple that might have been in their sixties. The husband had sharp, almost angry features, while the wife had a calming, serene look that only certain people who managed to land on the better side after a long hard life seemed to have. Despite the husband's scowl, there was no mistaking the tender way he held her hand in his as the music briskly filled the air around them.

"Hmmm," she said. "Sometimes I wish … " She seemed to catch herself, then turned her gaze back to Easton. "I've never been to the Caribbean. Or to England. Though I did get to Italy and to Egypt back when I was in college. But I'm kind of dull that way – I work all the time."

Easton thought she might be selling herself short but refrained from saying anything. All in all, the date seemed to be doing pretty good, but he still wasn't sure which way it was going. For a fleeting moment, though, sitting here after an excellent dinner, a few drinks with a very attractive woman with a wistful look on her face and the upbeat music in the background, he felt like he wouldn't mind staying just like this for a long time.

"How about a night cap?" she asked him.

"Sorry?" Easton shook himself out of his reverie.

"Over at the bar? I really feel like a stiff drink."

"Of course," he said, motioning to their waiter and pulling out his wallet.

Five minutes later, they were sitting at the bar, which was mostly empty. Outside, a heavy rain came down as a storm front moved through the Hudson Valley.

"Looks like we're not going anywhere for a little bit," Easton observed.

Sarah nodded and turned to the bartender named Rico, an overly handsome man who Easton always thought looked like a Central American version of George Chakiris from West Side Story.

"Two shots of tequila," she told him, "the Herradura Tequila Anejo."

"My pleasure," Rico said, flashing unnaturally white teeth. Seconds later, two of the better snifters materialized on the bar before them.

That was how the second part of the night started.

Easton woke up with a searing headache, convinced someone had driven a rail spike through his forehead. The sunlight coming through his bedroom window seemed to be aimed directly through his blinking eyes to the back of his skull where it was trying to burn its way out. Somewhere downstairs, the phone was ringing, and Rovsky stood in the doorway with a look that suggested he'd been waiting all morning for Easton to take him out.

It took Easton a slow moment to realize he was completely naked, then a slightly less slower moment to register the naked body tangled up in the sheets next to him.

Bloody Hell, he thought, *what in the hell happened here?*

Through the twist of sheets, he could see a lithe figure, surprisingly firm and without a trace of body fat.

The form next to him let out a muffled groan and turned around. A bleary eye peeked out from underneath one of his pillows.

"Hi," Sarah said in a small voice.

"Hi back," he replied. She reached out with her finger and traced the tip of his nose. A vague smile played across his lips in spite of what was no doubt going to be a massive hangover. His brow furrowed as he tried to think – a monumental task that seemed to require a ridiculous amount of energy. Just when he considered the possibility he might never be able to form a complete thought in his head it all began to come back to him…

The rain had been hammering outside the windows by the bar with the force of a monsoon. After the third round of tequila, they'd taken a fourth (along with a couple beer chasers) over to a table out on the small enclosed porch just off the bar. The porch had been empty, as if reserved just for them.

At some point, the conversation had drifted into more intimate territory, as did their seats in the cool dampness of the room. Black iron sconces with amber glass lent the space a cozy flavor. Rain curtained down the picture window that overlooked Route 9B, distorting the occasional intrepid driver who crept by well below the speed limit. It was a good night to be indoors.

Easton couldn't remember much about what he'd said, although he vaguely recalled spilling the story about his traumatic childhood experience when a friend of his – Gerry Holdsender – had accidentally blown himself up playing around with a scale brass display cannon and Easton, who had been watching along with his best friend that day, had run away like a coward and left him to die alone. Sarah hadn't been fazed when he mentioned the part his limited psychic ability had played, nor had she said anything when he talked about his guilt over not acting on the premonition he'd had beforehand. She did, however, touch her fingers to his during the end of the story.

At another point, Sarah confessed her anger and frustration – particularly as an undergrad – at being dismissed by many of her professors (and peers) for being both an American Indian and too attractive. Half the guys she met feigned interest in her intellect under the guise of trying to get in her pants, the rest went to absurd lengths to ingratiate themselves by claiming kinship ('Did I tell you I'm one-quarter Cherokee?' 'Hey, you know my great-grandfather was Native American too', etc.) to the point where apparently, half the male population of the school had 'native blood' and thus 'understood' her. That included one archeology professor who had tried to 'understand her' through a little groping on one Pre-Clovis dig in Pennsylvania. His clumsy (and insulting) actions had come to a quick stop when the business end of Sarah's Bowie knife had appeared under his chin. She quietly withdrew from his course the next day.

"It got far worse after ridiculous Hollywood movies like 'Dances with Wolves' and 'Last of the Mohicans'," she'd said unsparingly. "Films made by ignorant white people to make them feel better about themselves and tragedy they put upon the American Indian …"

Columbia University and its dizzying diversity of people had been a refreshing change for her. Nobody in New York City seemed to give a crap where you were from or how hard you'd had it, only what you could do in the moment ("Yeah, you're an Indian. So? I'm from fucking Brooklyn. *Top that*."). For the first time in her life, she found out what it was like to be Sarah Ramhorne, college student, not *Sarah Ramhorne, American Indian College Student*. There was still the occasional dolt with the Indian Squaw Fantasy that hit on her, but by and large, she met people who took her at face value.

Easton had followed up with, "Well, did I happen to tell you my mother was one-quarter –" before being cut off a mock-angry look from Sarah as she grabbed his ear and gave it a warning twist.

"I was going to say 'Scottish'," Easton had finished, wincing.

Then to his surprise, she'd leaned forward and said in his ear, "Do you remember that first time we met? When you showed up at the cabin?" (To which he nodded) "I felt this intense urge to kiss you. It scared me."

At that moment, Easton, despite being aware he was quite intoxicated (or perhaps because of it), was also keenly aware of how close she was to him. In fact, she'd somehow managed to put both her legs over his. She let go of his ear and placed one cool hand on the back of his neck. Easton looked her in the eye and had enough presence of mind to savor that enticing moment when you fully realize you are about to kiss someone for the first time, the awareness that everything in your world that follows will be forever changed.

She pulled him in and kissed him first. He was surprised to find she was quite an erotic kisser.

They didn't stop for a long time.

Easton blinked. Things had taken on a fragmented quality after that. At some point the rain had stopped, and the bartender was noisily clearing his throat in the doorway. Not very smartly, they'd stumbled their way to Easton's car, which he'd driven home at half the speed limit.

He remembered saying something completely illogical like, 'I have to go home to walk the dog … or dog the walk, so you'll just have to come with me … " and from there, they'd wound up on the living room couch, making out as if they were a couple of high school students whose parents were finally out of the house.

He had a tantalizingly incomplete scrap of Sarah standing in front of him and slowly stripping out of her dress and underwear, a wild look in her eyes (which were locked onto his the whole time) as she loosened her hair. Half of it hung in her face, the rest in a crazy whirlwind around her head. And he remembered her gasp when grabbing her firmly by the buttocks he pulled her up onto the couch and began to kiss her between the legs, gently at first, and noting how her pubic area was surprisingly small and dense. Then they were upstairs in bed, the breeze through the open window plucking at the curtains while she straddled him on top, nails digging into his shoulders.

It was arguably the most quietly intense sex he'd ever had.

Except for the part where she'd screamed at the end.

Now what? he thought. At least the tequila had been top shelf. The headache was a refined one at least, not the rough bludgeoning kind one got from cheap liquor.

Sarah's fingers went to his jawline, then down to his chest. They moved over to his side where there was the scar from a gunshot wound, then after loitering a moment, they continued on down to his groin where he was already growing stiff.

It went on like that for a good two minutes, her fingers caressing him this way and that. Then she pulled the sheets away and smiling, eased herself on top of him and without any hesitation put one breast before his mouth. Her nipple was large, dark, and undeniably erect.

Guess that answers that question, he thought.

From the doorway came a heavy thud and sigh as Rovsky dropped to the floor, having resigned himself to a delayed breakfast.

"How do you like your eggs?" Sarah asked, having commandeered the kitchen.

Easton was sitting at the table with a very black cup of coffee. Rovsky lay on the floor nearby, eyes zeroed in on the archeologist like she was the focal point of the known universe. His previous experience had demonstrated the 'Woman + Kitchen = Food' equation to work well in his favor.

Sarah was wearing Easton's black terry cloth bathrobe with the sleeves rolled back, and the way she half-turned to him, head inclined and spatula poised in the air made him think of a couple lines from an old Tom Waits song, 'Invitation to the Blues':

... howyougonnalikethem ... over medium or scrambled?
Anyways the only way, be careful not to gamble ...

Surprisingly though – hangover aside – he felt calm with the whole situation and something about Sarah's posture echoed the same. When he'd first come downstairs, he'd stood in the doorway and shook his head. A woman standing in front of the stove. The mixed aromas of food cooking. The dog lying on the floor looking up expectantly. There was an inescapable sense of déjà vu about the scene, it was almost as if she had always cooked him breakfast like this and always would.

"Over easy," he said finally.

The two of them sat at the round kitchen table – a rustic farmer's antique made of yellow pine – studying at each other like two chess players contemplating their next moves. The kitchen was one of the few rooms he'd had remodeled after buying the house three years previous. The floors had been stripped, re-stained in dark teak and polyurethaned in semi-gloss, the metal cabinets installed sometime in the 1950's replaced with solid Georgia Pine. The linoleum countertops were now dark granite and the stainless-steel appliances completed the picture; comfortable and stylish.

"What are you thinking?" Sarah asked, studying him over the rim of the coffee mug she held up in both hands.

He was thinking about his current caseload, which had grown light, and whether he could stall on the one he'd been hired to investigate the previous week involving some thefts from wealthy homes around Bedford Hills. It was beginning to look more and more like a bunch of bored rich kids from the very same neighborhoods were involved and Easton was already regretting taking the job. He decided he could blow it off for a day or two at least.

"I'm thinking you're looking quite fine in that old bathrobe of mine."

"I bet you say that to all the girls," she countered.

Easton wasn't sure if she was joking or not.

"Only most of them," he replied.

Sarah put down the mug and walking over to where Easton was sitting and looked down at him quietly for a moment. The robe slid off and dropped to the floor as she stood before him, uninhibited by her nakedness. There was something primal about her he found intoxicating. She took his chin in one hand and tilted his head up.

"If you haven't figured it out already, I'm not 'most' of them."

"Obviously not," he agreed. Then he pulled her down onto his lap.

She resisted at first, as if teasing him. Then she took charge.

16. OKEANOS EXPLORER CONTROL ROOM, 225 MILES ESE OF NEW YORK HARBOR

"Keep it at 20 percent thrust," the man's voice said through the headset.

"Copy that," the young woman responded, trying to keep the girlish excitement out of her voice.

"Advance point three … is your descent locked in?"

"I'm locked in at 31."

"Okay. Someone increase the range on the sonars. Can you bring up the tether cam in monitor 3?" the man said, addressing the video engineer sitting next to him. "It's labeled 'ROV 4' on my panel for some reason…"

"Standby," the younger man's voice said. A moment later, one of the larger wall monitors that had been blank suddenly came to life. Mounted about twenty feet up from the umbilical tether line that connected the ROV to the ship, this camera gave a top-down overview of the descent. At the moment, the 'Deep Discoverer' – the primary ROV or 'Remote Operated Vehicle' they were using on this dive – appeared to be floating against a sea of blue. Only the random bits of ocean detritus and plankton zooming past gave any indication of motion.

"Afternoon front row," cut in a second woman's voice.

"Afternoon back row," came the response.

In the darkened control room officially known as the 'ROV mapping/operations office,' the ongoing dialogue through the headsets of the personnel had the measured, relaxed inflections of people accustomed to speaking frequently, clearly and unselfconsciously with each other and to themselves. Partly this was a required skill, partly experience. All dives were recorded and broadcast through live video feed directly to the NOAA public internet site as well as directly to five landside control rooms; speaking articulately and minding one's 'P's' and 'Q's' was absolutely mandatory.

Located just aft of the center of the ship on the 'fcsl' deck, the control room faced the stern of the ship as you entered. To the immediate left was a chart table and a row of three seats with keyboards and a bank of five rack-mounted HD TV monitors before them. In front was the ROV operator's desk with its battery of wall monitors, ROV control stations, and a large digital clock with a red LED readout. With its dark grey soundproof panels, black carpet, and dark furniture, the room had a crowded, hi-tech flavor that suggested more of a cozy downtown production studio than the cutting-edge oceanographic operations center it was.

"… check the relays … comms look good," the older man was saying, "Sonars are now up to 140."

"When we have bottom, I'd like to check the white balance on the pilot cam," the video engineer added.

"Wait … Bridge, can you repeat that?" the woman in the second row cut in. Then addressing the people in front of her, "We have something on sonar thirty-five meters to port … can we get a lock …?"

The pilot cam on the ROV swiveled sideways in time to see what the approaching object was.

"… Oh my God," the young girl exclaimed.

The following day in the control room of the NOAA vessel *Okeanos Explorer*, things had finally calmed down somewhat.

Commissioned in 2008, the ship was the first of its kind in the NOAA fleet; a fully outfitted vessel whose sole purpose was the exploration and discovery of the world's oceans. At 224' long, the ship had ample space to accommodate its crew of 18 in addition to 19 mission personal. With two ROV's, two 22' EX1 Rescue craft, the latest in multibeam echo sounder systems (a Kongsberg Maritime EM302 capable of acquiring 3-dimensional high-resolution mapping data to a 1cm resolution), various experimental sub-bottom profilers, a 16-foot 'golf ball' VSAT system mounted behind the pilot house capable of sending high-resolution data feeds simultaneously to five the Exploration Command Centers located throughout the United States, a single beam echo sounder as well as a battery of meteorological and oceanographic profiling equipment, the *Okeanos Explorer* essentially combined the best in all available ocean research equipment in the world.

It was in short, a twenty-first-century oceanographer's wet dream.

Currently positioned close to a hundred miles off course from where it was supposed to be going through shake-down exercises on its Northeast U.S. expedition, days before the *Okeanos* had instead found itself diverted to the wreck site of a previously unknown – and unaccounted for – WWII German U-boat. Normally, the *Okeanos* would be feeding live video through its uplink and updating its GPS coordinates in real-time. Instead, a blanket story that the ship's data systems had been hacked and were being de-bugged had been issued, along with the statement that all operations had been 'temporarily suspended.'

Even the ships exploration team – led by none other than the legendary Doctor Robert Ballard himself – were perplexed (and miffed) at the cagey level of secrecy that had come down through NOAA administration regarding this new mission. Their new orders involved the assessment and feasibility of recovery of materials from the wreck, which they had been told was a Type XXI submarine dispatched near the end of the war that apparently contained a valuable (and apparently highly sensitive) cargo. No further information had been provided, other than that all data was to be uploaded via a separate uplink with an ultra-high-level encryption code.

Ballard, who was now director of the newly created Center for Ocean Exploration at the University of Rhode Island's Graduate School of Oceanography – the same man who had discovered the wrecks of the *Titanic* and *Bismark* – certainly understood the need for discretion in certain situations, but secretly he sensed something a little odd about this particular case.

The wreck of the German sub had been discovered by accident in a canyon at a depth of 3,215 meters by the *SSN-794 New York* – a recently launched Virginia-class U.S. Navy sub out on its own shakedown cruise in the western Atlantic. The hatches of the German sub were open, leading to speculation on whether any crew had remained with her when she sunk, but it had been on the fourth ROV dive on the second day that something completely unexpected momentarily sidetracked the mission.

They'd spotted a giant squid.

The ROV 'Deep Discoverer' had been descending past 2000 meters when the creature appeared out of nowhere. Being a routine descent at that point, it so happened that Kate Christian – a graduate student from the University of Florida – was getting some training time at the controls for a few minutes when the stunning creature glided into view perhaps fifty meters away. One of the more seasoned crew, Operations Coordinator Art Cameron, had been sitting at the navigation console next to her talking over his shoulder at ROV Operations Manager Jackie Arkos when Christian had gasped.

" ... Oh my God ..." Christian had said, and suddenly all six people in the dark control room were staring awestruck at the bank of monitors before them.

It was the first living giant squid witnessed in its natural habitat since the breakthrough footage captured off the coast of Japan in 2012, and the first ever seen in the Atlantic.

To her credit, Christian had maintained a steady hand at the controls when the squid first appeared like some sort of giant ghostly torpedo, its tentacles closed up tight. Later on, they would decide it must have been attracted to the multi-colored lights in the experimental 'disco dome' atop the ROV, but for the moment, it was all they could do except stare with jaws open at this unexpected apparition.

"Are you getting this?" Cameron had whispered into his headset to Ballard, who was with the captain up on the bridge.

"Copy that," came the quiet response.

The squid altered its course and suddenly came at the ROV camera, its tentacles opening up in a dramatic splayed pattern, causing everyone to instinctively flinch. There were a few collective gasps.

Then just like that, it was gone.

It was the following day – Tuesday – that the squid re-appeared during the third dive.

The over-sized digital clock in the control room was reading 01:52:23 when the wide beam sonar picked up the giant cephalopod approaching. This time, it was a veteran pilot and diver named Walter Pickman running the ROV. Art Cameron was again at the nav station while in the back row Arkos, Ballard, and a marine biologist named Steve Hooper from the Woods Hole Oceanographic Institute were watching the dive.

Although the primary mission was still to assess the U-boat wreck, they'd been given leeway to collect any data on the squid. Hooper had helped rig a multicolored dome light for the ROV he'd jury-rigged that was intended to mimic the flashing bioluminescent pattern of a jellyfish in distress – essentially a jellyfish's burglar alarm. While the giant squid didn't eat jellyfish itself, it was known to go after the predators that did. Nothing had come of the earlier dives, but now they'd hit pay dirt.

The team was riveted to the monitors as the giant squid tried to puzzle out this new bait when something bizarre happened.

The view frame of the pilot cam was all but filled up with undulating tentacles when suddenly the whole ROV and camera lurched sickeningly to one side. There was a burst of bubbles and black ink as the camera was jerked violently again, this way and that, before being spun sideways and released. Moments later, a grisly chunk of torn tentacle floated into view, accompanied by a viscous tendril of blue blood. Then the Deep Discoverer's screens went dark.

"What the heck?" someone in the control room said.

There was a mad scramble until it was determined that while Deep Discoverer's camera was off-line, the ROV was still operational. It took

Ballard a few minutes to sort out what had happened. Whatever had pulled the hit-and-run attack on the squid was the size of a sperm whale – the squid's natural predator – but had approached much faster than any whale was known to swim. This attacker had hit its prey at nearly twice the speed of a panicked whale.

It took a bit of scrubbing back and forth through the two video feeds to reveal clues as to what had occurred and even then it was inconclusive.

"What is it?" Ballard asked excitedly, all but squeezing Hooper aside at the workstation. In one monitor, emerging out of the murk of squid blood and ink in frame-by-frame slow motion was a terrifying set of teeth.

The tether cam revealed something even more interesting – a giant undulating shape that accelerated into the light.

"Uh-uh, no way. This is *not* possible," Hooper said, his head shaking in quick short movements

The blurred image of the creature looked like a sort of nightmarish sea monster, as if someone had taken a giant alligator head, stuck it on a whale's torso, and added a giant eel as a tail. Even at a glance, based on the scale of the ROV visible in the tether cam, it was clear the monster was eighteen to twenty meters in length.

"Jesu–" Hooper slipped before Ballard clamped a hand over the marine biologist's mouth. "I mean, 'Yikes'," Hooper continued once his mouth was free.

"What is it?" Ballard said, asking the obvious.

"What it *looks* like is a *Tylosaurus proriger*, the largest of all mosasaurs. But there's no ... no way."

"A *sea dinosaur*?" Arkos asked from over Hooper's other shoulder.

"From the Late Cretaceous Period," Ballard added. "One of the deadliest ocean predators that ever existed."

Hooper seemed exasperated. "But that can't be here ... now. It's been extinct for millions of years. There's no way something this large could have survived undetected. It doesn't add up."

"Lots of things don't add up in the ocean," Ballard responded. "You of all people should know that."

"Yeah," Hooper snorted. "But this isn't finding mutated worms around volcanic sea vents. This is like finding a T-rex has been running around in the woods behind your house. There's simply no way ... and they didn't get this big. Ten, maybe twelve meters tops. They screwed it up in that TV show ..." He trailed off, then narrowed his eyes and looked his companions on either side. "Ah. I get it. This is a practical joke. Good one, guys. Set up a feed with doctored footage." He leaned back and laughed, slapping his thighs with both hands for emphasis. "This is rich. Bust the new guys' chops. Wow. I mean it looks good, real good. 3D model from 'Walking with Dinosaurs'? Yep, you really had me going there ..."

Ballard was ignoring him, focusing on the image on the screen. He managed to look amused, amazed, and fascinated all at the same time.

"This isn't a joke, Hooper," he said absently, "This isn't a joke at all..."

17. THE WRECK OF THE EDMUND WOOD

Easton decided the Bedford Hills case could wait.

Actually, after everything that had happened over the previous twenty-four hours with Sarah Ramhorne, he'd decided the entire universe could wait for that matter.

Sitting that Tuesday evening in his overstuffed leather club chair, a glass of 14-year-old Auchentoshan Signatory Vintage Single Malt resting on the side table next to him and a light rain misting up the windows of his living room, Easton was feeling extremely mellow and relaxed.

It was a cool enough night that he'd laid a fire in the fieldstone fireplace. The television was off and in the background the stereo was set to a local classical station. The melancholy strains of Debussy's 'Clair de lune' wandered quietly through the room, a fitting backdrop to Easton's present mood.

He tried to sort through his feelings without much success. Partly, he was wiped out after the past twenty-four hours. The hangover was all but gone and the scotch ('A little hair of the dog that bit you ...' as his friend Jim Franks would say) had smoothed out most the edges of his thoughts for the time being. Even so, he felt like he'd just stepped out of a tornado.

He wondered what Sarah was thinking right at the moment.

Don't be a sap, old man. And don't get sloppy. She was probably just looking for a little roll in the hay.

Which is just fine, he decided. Especially given the disastrous way his last couple of relationships had ended.

He brushed aside those thoughts before they could devolve toward self-pity and instead opened the monograph Fowler had given him – the one relating the doomed final voyage of the Edmund Wood. The pages were yellowed but in surprisingly good condition – it had the look of a book that had been filed up on a shelf long ago and subsequently forgotten. Even Fowler, who had an encyclopedic knowledge of the Hudson River region, had never heard of the wreck before.

Easton took another sip of scotch, let it settle around his mouth a bit, then started reading:

The Final Voyage and Shipwreck of the Edmund G. Wood
1903-1904

As related by Joshua Singleton, Third Engineer and only known
survivor
Authored by Benjamin Winthrop
American Oceanographic Institute Press
City of Hudson, New York
1905

The opening pages described how on the morning following a particularly rough Nor'easter that swept through the region on October 16, 1904, a man was spotted wandering around stark naked on a small island near Highland Falls on the stretch of river known as 'World's End' by a passing fisherman.

The man was found to be in a semi-delirious state and it took some time for the authorities in nearby Garrison to sort out a coherent narrative of what turned out to be a truly bizarre – and in their estimate highly improbable – tale involving an expedition in the Mediterranean, a sea monster, and a clandestine arrangement involving, supposedly, none other than Prince Albert I of Monaco and Cornelius Vanderbilt III.

Described as 'a short man in his early thirties, broad of chest, of dark blond hair and heavy moustache,' the main identified himself as Joshua Singleton, a third engineer who had signed on with the *Edmund G. Wood* in Boston a year previous.

According to Singleton, the *Edmund G. Wood*, a 5600-ton merchant vessel out of Baltimore, had been diverted from its return from a cargo run in the Eastern Mediterranean to meet up with the *Princess Alice* – Prince Albert of Monaco's research yacht – in the Ionian Sea just off the southwest coast of Greece. Singleton was short on particulars, stating that he only knew that the *Princess Alice* had somehow captured some mysterious creature a week or so previous and had contrived to cage it in an 'enormous wooden crate' which they'd floated alongside the yacht. There was an 'air of unusual secrecy' about what was going on, though the rumors amongst the crew suggested that Cornelius Vanderbilt III – one of the *Edmund G. Woods* owners – had made some private sort of arrangement for them to take the specimen up to the newly established Oceanographic Institute in the City of Hudson for safekeeping until the Prince of Monaco could complete his own *Musée Océanographique de Monaco*, which was under the first stages of construction atop the cliffs overlooking the harbor.

The crate was enormous. 'Large enough to hold a whale' in Singleton's words, and it was clear from the get-go there was no conceivable way the *Princess Alice* could take it on board with her cluttered deck space and small cranes.

As to what the nature of the specimen was, they were never told other than it was a previously undiscovered marine creature that had become tangled in the nets off the coast of Greece near the Calypso Deep, that deepest part of the Mediterranean basin also known as the "Hellenic Trench.'

It took the better part of a day to hoist the unwieldy crate onto the deck of the *Edmund Wood* and secure it; by the end of the third watch, they were underway and steaming at full power towards Gibraltar and the Atlantic. That night speculation was rampant in the forecastle about its contents and ultimate destination ...

Easton paused to refill his scotch and settling back in his chair, picked up the narrative where the Singleton was getting interviewed by the local constable in Garrison, identified as 'R.M. Dalton':

"What led you to believe it was in some sort of fashion a 'sea monster'," Dalton asked.

"Well, for starters the smell – it was something fearful, dead, and brackish – and the sounds coming out of the crate – no whale ever made such a noise! *Slithering* sounds. And a wet ... chittering or clicking," Singleton claimed. "We were told to water it down with the deck hoses three times a day to keep whatever it was inside damp, though no one seemed to know if this was sufficient to keep it alive or not. Either way, it was done from a distance."

"Had you much previous experience with captured whales, or such?" Dalton countered.

"None whatsoever. But Reese did. He was the old man on the crew and a Bedford whaler from way back. And on his word, it was no whale we had with us on that cursed crate."

"And what happened to Reese?"

"Dead. With the rest of them. Went down with the ship. God, I wish I'd never seen ..."

"But the nature of the cargo ... that was never indicated?"

"No, it weren't. I was with the carpenter – a Swede by the name of Pilkvist – when he confronted the first mate a day into the Atlantic. A stony-eyed look was all we got for our trouble; 'Just mind your business and keep your traps shut.' The first mate told 'im, 'and watch your step around our cargo – it's not safe.' He had the look of a man inclined to add a thing or two to that but couldn't, and that was that."

"So aside from odd smells and noises, was there any other evidence regarding what was in the crate?"

"Well … there was what the bosun o'erheard during his night watch by the captain's cabin window a fortnight later …"

"… Mark my words, we shall yet find that there's the devil to pay when this is over," came the first mate's voice through the porthole. "This cargo is a sinister business, to be sure."

Captain Conrad, whose words were always spoken in tones as compact and brusk as was his appearance, took a moment before responding. "*Bosh*, Mister Wait. It's just another cargo. A marine specimen, as it were."

"'Just another cargo' you say? That's why we'll be receiving a handsome bonus pay at the end of this voyage?"

"We're being paid for our discretion and expediency, not to stand about wringing our skirts like old superstitious women."

There was another pause while one of them prepared and lit a pipe. Shortly after, a cloud of tobacco smoke writhed through the porthole.

There was the sound of knuckles rapping on wood. "And you're not the least bit curious about our cargo?" the first mate finally said.

"No."

"Hah, the set of your jaw says otherwise, Captain."

"Never mind the set of my jaw, Mister Wait."

"Hmm. Another spot of your brandy?"

"Serve yourself."

Another pause, a clink of glass then the first mate spoke up again. "The rumor is it's a sea monster, like Typhon – from the Greek myth – that will doom us all to a –"

"Nonsense!" said the captain in a harsh tone, cutting him off. "It's nothing more than a mutant strain of cephalopod, a rare scientific discovery."

"Aha! So you did know!" Wait countered, pleased his trick had worked. "Have you seen it?"

"Blast your eyes, Wait, and not another word on the matter or I'll have you in irons for the duration! Damn you and the brandy …"

"So, even by hearsay, there was a scientific explanation to all this," Dalton said.

"Ough, aye. 'Scientific explanation' you say. You weren't there, were you? Well, there was nothing scientific about what was in that giant crate…"

"Yes, I'm sure," Dalton continued. "So for the record, tell me again what happened the night before last, the night the *Edmund G. Wood* foundered and sank."

"Hmmm. We knew it was coming. By the time we entered the Hudson River, the first part of the voyage seemed lost in a haze – nothing more than a gossamer suspicion of a previous existence. But as we passed Tarrytown and then Sing-Sing, we all felt it – something bad was soon to happen. I was in the bridge with the captain and first mate when the bosun turned to them and said; 'We're going to catch it this time, the barometer is tumbling down like anything, Captain.' But you didn't need a barometer to see the thunderheads rolling out of the east like the wrath of Zeus, blotting out the stars while the howling wind pulled catspaws off the waves …

"No sooner did we pass Anthony's Nose, however, than we found ourselves in the fight for our lives. The waves were kicking up something fierce and sheets of rain pounded our decks; the ship began to roll like an old boot. The bridge became like a half-tide rock awash on the coast, the water boiling up and streaming over, and then I saw it. One of the crew – a young man by the name of Crenshaw – had slid across the deck and found himself clinging to that damned crate for life, when a tentacle, thicker than any Burmese python, slithered out and wrapped itself around his torso like so. We could hear his screams and snapping bones even above the din of the storm. I swear to you his eyes popped out of his sockets like exploding grapes, his pitiful cries muffled by curtains of blood and gore ejecting from his mouth. It was Greeley who tried to save him – quick with an axe he found God-knows-where – chopped that tentacle off in four blows. Too late for Crenshaw, the poor soul, he was washed over by the next wave, but we had other matters to concern ourselves with. Just then right off to port we saw the cliffs – may have been West Point – appear out of the gloom and the captain put the helm hard over. We might have even made it, but for that cursed cage. All sorts of tentacles erupted out of every crack and crevice and the whole thing shifted, the thing within chittering in rage – but damned the Gods, it caused the ship to roll to port, into the rocks as it turned out. There was a teeth-snapping jolt that knocked nearly all of us to the deck (except the captain, who gripped that wheel like it held closed the Gates of Hades) and the terrible sound of the hull plates being punched, then we knew we were done for. When I looked out again, the decks were swept clean ('cept for that cursed cage), rails were bent and the weather cloths burst and where the port lifeboats were gone already; empty davits leaning empty into the blackness. The ship gave a sickening lurch and slid to starboard while our insidious cargo rocked and shuddered on the deck. The lines held though – our men had secured it well enough – but you could almost feel the thing's fury. Typhon. That's what we called it by then.

"Another able seaman tried to scrabble past after popping out of the forecastle, it may have been the cook but I couldn't tell, and I saw another of those damned tentacles snag his leg and snap it in two like a dry twig. There wasn't time to dwell on it though. The captain was yelling at us to abandon ship, and I found myself clambering down the starboard side of the bridge in my sea boots and oilskin coat, desperately trying to make my way to one of the lifeboats there. Somewhere in route, I realized I had grabbed a life preserver – one of the smaller round ones – and hooked my arm through it to the shoulder. Screams and salt water filled my mouth. When I got to the main deck, 'twas a mess. The closest boat was hanging by one line and smashing itself to bits against the hull; from the other davit, a pulley and an iron-bound block were capering in the air, and it was that block that did me in – or saved me – as it were.

"The ship lurched again and hesitated as if clinging to the rocks for dear life, terrified of the pull and deep of that racing abyss we call 'World's End,' then all I was seeing were stars as the flying block connected with my head, hurling me out into the seething waters of the Hudson.

"I thought I was done for. Certainly, the ship was. Screams and groans of man and metal, and that damned chittering – I swore I could hear that cursed thing as well – then with terrifying swiftness, the *Edmund G. Wood* slid and rolled under to its watery grave, the storm raging on like the Devil's wrath while I resigned myself to die. That last thing I saw of that poor ship was a glimpse of Captain Conrad through the windows of the bridge. He was screaming; though whether in fear or fury, I'll never know. Perhaps both.

"Things were a-jumble after that. I managed to shed my clothes while hanging to that preserver for dear life, the current pulling and tugging me every which way. At one point, I would have sworn I felt one of Typhon's tentacles plucking at my feet, but of course that was impossible – it had gone down with the ship and as you know – that is the deepest part of the Hudson.

"I must have blacked out for a time, though I do remember struggling and being tossed about like a cork, until by the grace of God in the wee hours I found myself washed up along the shore, naked as a jay-bird and delirious with exposure and half-drowned from salt-water. I was in the grips of a fever and only vaguely recall walking about and babbling all manner of nonsense when that fisherman found me, and here I am."

"Yes. And with a remarkable story," replied Dalton. "But with nothing more but your word on it. Unfortunately, Mister Singleton, all hands went down with the ship. You were the only survivor."

Easton sat back and drained the scotch. *A remarkable story indeed.* But was any of it true?

There didn't seem to be any question the book itself was authentic. But Constable Dalton's account (Easton made a mental note to have Fowler check if there was any additional information on the man through the Historical Society) had sounded skeptical to the point of being rude. The remainder of the book covered the drab details of the constable's follow-up investigation, which turned up little else. The only other evidence of the event was the life preserver with *Edmund G. Wood* stamped on it – he was unable to locate any witnesses to collaborate that the ship had sunk off World's End, though perhaps not surprising given the ferocity of the storm and certainly not the first unreported ship to disappear in these waters. It had been confirmed the *Edmund G. Wood* had sailed out of Boston six weeks previous and was a week overdue to its next scheduled port of call, which was Liverpool, but no evidence that it had instead sailed to New York.

Nor would there be, Easton mused, *unless it actually stopped in the harbor.*

He knew even from cursory research that a hundred years back, New York's harbors and rivers were jammed with shipping traffic. And not like today with all our micro-surveillance security and satellite cameras documenting everything. One more merchant steaming up the Hudson – particularly on a stormy day – wouldn't have necessarily drawn any additional attention.

Riding that line of thinking was another set of questions bothering him; who had left out the book to be deliberately discovered, and for what purpose? And even more curious; how would they have known this particular book was in the Historical Society library?

The last question might be the key, he thought. It hadn't been placed – the end page had been stamped along with the date of entry – August 1905. In theory, anyone could have seen it, though the amount of dust accumulated along the top of the book indicated it hadn't been moved or opened in years, which suggested that somebody had known it was there for a quite some time.

Then there was the folder with typewritten notes.

Easton took a break to refill his drink and stoke the logs in the fireplace before sitting back in his chair again, this time with a folder open in his lap. It was getting late – just past 11:30pm – but his curiosity was piqued. He wanted answers.

"Report of Portuguese Trawler Attacked By Alleged 'Sea Monster' off the coast of Senegal, May 10th, 1954, as related to Pierre Tailliez, Oceanographer, Calypso: 1954 French Oceanographic Campaign (FOC)," he read.

Tailliez was crewing with Cousteau on one of the early FOC exploration missions off North and West Africa when they'd received a distress call from a local fishing vessel. The ship, a 75' trawler named *Nuno Tristão* had been pulling in its nets that morning when things went haywire. Most of the story came through the one member of the fishing crew who spoke French, and the story he gave Tailliez was no less fanciful than that of the *Edmund Wood*, though completely different.

According to the crewman, it had all started out routine until something huge became entangled in the nets, seizing up the winches and causing the ship to list dangerously to port. The immediate assumption was that it was a whale, though the violence of the thrashing – which bent the mast before snapping the boom of the fishing derrick attached to it completely off – was nothing like any whale they'd ever encountered. Two of the fishermen standing next to it were seriously injured.

Right after that, the waters alongside the ship began to boil and froth as whatever leviathan of the deep they'd captured grew even more agitated. One of the older hands, a veteran fisherman named Paolo, had clambered up and out onto the derrick in an effort to cut away the net lines – it was beginning to look like the ship was in danger of capsizing – when the monster revealed itself and breached the surface.

It was terrifying.

The fisherman being interviewed claimed the head of the thing was a good 'six or seven feet in length, long and narrow, like a gigantic alligators head; grayish green-colored with a pale underbelly and a mouth filled with savage-looking teeth. Fixing the horrified men on board with one baleful eye, its jaws snapped open as it shot out of the water and closed on the helpless Paolo like a trap. The old man's screams had been brief, but the hideous snapping of bones in the brief moments before he was swallowed whole would haunt the fisherman for the rest of his years.

Though the nets were cut away (or chewed off), the creature circled the trawler for the next hour or so, occasionally slamming into the hull and keeping the entire crew in terror despite attempts to get underway. At one point, the rudder had been damaged and the trawler was left to turn lazy circles. But by the time the *Calypso* arrived on the scene, there had been no sign of the monster for a couple hours. Both Cousteau and Tailliez had donned their scuba gear, which the Portuguese crew found fascinating, and did a couple of short dives around both vessels, but found no sign of the creature other than a few dented hull plates with deep scratches on them.

While it was clear to Cousteau's crew *something* had happened, they were clearly skeptical that it was some sort of giant sea monster, and in Tailliez' notes was speculation that it might have been an enraged great white shark or killer whale. "Perhaps," the notes read, "these terrified fishermen, sober and hardworking men as they may be, let their minds alter details to what their eyes saw in some effort to come to terms with the tragedy that occurred."

One thing was curious; the fisherman Tailliez interviewed refused to return to his ship and insisted on sailing back with Cousteau's crew. After assistance from the *Calypso*'s engineers, the rudder was repaired and the *Nuno Tristão* was able to get underway again. However, that evening they lost radio contact with her during a squall.

The Portuguese trawler was never seen again.

Easton set the papers aside and let out a slow yawn. Despite the cozy confines of his house, he could vividly imagine the ill-fated events unfolding somewhere out in the Atlantic all those years ago, shuddering at the thought of such a creature – any creature – hurtling out of the ocean's depths and swallowing a man alive. It touched on our most deep-seated fears.

Spielberg knew exactly what he was doing all those years ago when he filmed 'Jaws,' despite all the over-the-top dialogue and now dated-looking (and problematic) villain, he thought. But something else was nagging him as well. The Portuguese fisherman who had survived – he had identified himself as 'Raymundo Dimas.' He knew that name from around the neighborhood.

It was the same name as Luis Dimas' grandfather, the old retired stonemason. It was a stretch, but even so, Easton made a mental note to follow up the next day.

He took another sip of the scotch and rubbed his eyes. It was hard to make any sense of it all. Two completely different accounts. Of two different sea monsters. One in 1904, the other in 1954. The only connecting evidence between the two that he could think of offhand was Jacques Cousteau and the Prince of Monaco; according to the first account, the creature captured by Prince Albert was handed off to the Hudson Oceanographic Institute because his own Musée Océanographique wasn't finished at the time – nor would it for another twelve years, long after the *Edmund Wood* and its cargo were doomed to the bottom of World's End. Easton, who had visited the museum in Monaco once years ago, knew that Jacques Cousteau had become its director in 1959, only five years after the incident off West Africa.

It may mean something. Or it may mean nothing at all, he mused. *But then how does is all tie into what's been happening out at Raadsel Point ... and why now? And who on earth put these two items out for him specifically?*

It was maddening. More information only led to more questions. He shook his head and decided to let it go until the morning. Instead, his thoughts drifted over to Sarah and what she might be doing right at that moment. It had been one wild roll in the hay alright, though he knew better than to try to make it into anything more than just that.

Still, part of him had an urge to call her, just for the hell of it.

He held up the glass of scotch and giving it a swirl, peered into its amber depths.

Just then the phone rang.

"Hello?"

There was a pause, and for one strange moment, Easton had this irrational fear he might hear a voice on the other end from the grave, like his old friend Gerry Holdsender. Instead, there was muffled sound like someone adjusting their hold on the other end, then her voice spoke softly in his ear, "*Hè.*"

Easton relaxed in his chair. "Hey back."

"I was thinking about you. Sorry to call so late."

"No problem." Her voice sounded sleepy. And sexy. That particular timber and cadence to her voice that was unmistakably American Indian was growing on him – it was quite distinct. He found her slow and steady way of speaking inherently calming.

"What are you doing right now?"

"Oh, reading up on giant sea monsters. How about yourself?"

"I was listening to the rain."

Easton sipped his scotch and half-tilted his head. There was something prodding and playful in her delivery that kept a smile tugging at the corners of his mouth. "And what was the rain telling you?" he asked.

"It was telling me I should call a certain Englishman to tell him to stop reading about sea monsters and come over and warm up my bed."

"Really?"

"Really."

"That's quite fascinating. The rain in this neck of the woods was telling me you should be *here* warming up *my* bed."

She laughed quietly on the other end. "Hmm. Sounds like the rain can't get its story straight. What are we to do about this?"

For a moment, Easton turned this over in his head. He couldn't deny he was feeling mellow and relaxed and that the prospect of heading out on a cold rainy night didn't appeal to his over-forty side. On the other hand, she sounded close and quite desirable over the phone and he could swear her scent was lingering in the air around him. It was one of those things that never ceased to amaze him; how two people could go from being complete strangers into a conspiracy of intimacy at the drop of a hat.

And right back to being strangers again. Don't forget that, pal, the cynic in him piped up.

Aloud, he said something that came out half-muffled as he set down his drink, fumbling the phone.

"What was that?" she asked.

"I was telling Rovsky to pack his travel bag; I'm taking him on a late night field trip."

That got him another soft laugh. "I'll leave the porch light on then … *Alàpsi wëntaxa*," she said, then hung up.

18. 'OSSIE'

It was on Thursday that week that Whelma Fitzpatick, a part-time receptionist at the Open Door Mission in Wyvern Falls, found herself having lunch along the village waterfront. The rainy weather earlier in the week had given way into a couple balmy days as if this part of the Hudson Valley had decided to hold off on autumn for a little bit longer. Also, being her third consecutive week of being sober, Whelma had decided to treat herself to a take-out lunch from Slate's Deli which included today's soup special – Pasta Fagioli – and some of their fabulous lasagna, with a small side salad in a token nod for nutrition's sake. Though she couldn't afford to go there often, she adored the way the Latin American guy who worked there, Antonio, always gave her a quick smile and a wink and said, "an excellent choice!" no matter what she selected. She had a hunch she could walk in and ask for stale Twinkies and he would still say, "An excellent choice!"

At forty-seven and tipping the scales at nearly two-hundred and eight pounds, Whelma knew she should be minding her calories and get back on a diet again, but the summer had been a difficult one with her daughter Jeanie getting knocked up again by that good-for-nothing career Food Stamp collector, Larry, (adding another mouth to the three they already couldn't afford) and her 25-year-old son Tommy moving back home after losing his cashier job at Staples.

All that was set aside for the moment, however, while Whelma took a little 'time out' for herself and enjoyed her lunch. It was a cloudless day with a moderate breeze, and she'd staked out a bench along the public park just south of the Raadsel Bay Yacht Club, next to the sidewalk above the large rocks that formed the bank of the river there. A seagull she had decided to call 'Frederick' was standing impatiently to one side, shifting back and forth on its webbed feet while waiting for scraps. Out on the water, a gaggle of Canadian geese seemed to be aimlessly paddling about.

The sun felt good on her forehead. Though not an attractive woman – she'd inherited her mother's broad Hungarian features – her face had an expression approaching Zen-like serenity as she sipped her soup and basked. She'd just finished all the bits of carrot first when all of a sudden she was jarred out of her reverie by the Klaxon jangle of her cell phone.

Never one to miss a call, *any* call (including ones from those pesky telemarketers), Whelma expertly set aside lunch and was pleased to see it was her sister Laurie, who ran a tchotchke shop in Cold Springs. One of their running jokes was that Laurie was the one 'Professional Tchotchkeologist' in the family.

"Hi, Whelma," her younger sister all-but-yelled out of the phone. "I'm having *yet* another terrible day, what is it with kids these days? Aaron just dropped out of school again and …" the conversation went on for about two minutes about her pot-addled son before switching tracks without any segue into a rant on The Affordable Healthcare Act which apparently was on a personal mission to keep making her lose her coverage, but about five words into the second topic, Whelma abruptly stopped listening.

Her brain was too busy trying to process what her eyes were transmitting, and failing miserably.

About twenty yards out where the channel was – and where the gaggle of geese was a split second before – an apparition out of a horror movie had erupted from the surface of the river like some sort of nightmare whale breaching. Except this whale had the head of a prehistoric reptile; a long gaping jaw lined with curved, wicked-looking teeth that swallowed up all ten geese in one gulp. Whatever it was, its momentum carried it at least a dozen feet out of the water, enough so that Whelma had time to observe the glistening paddle-like fins, the dark green and blue pattern of is skin, and one ferocious-looking eye, then, with a sort of spinning shake, the monster slammed into the water.

Whelma Fitzpatrick's mouth formed a gaping O of shock while still holding the phone to her ear, not even registering the object that arced through the air and ricocheted off the bench next to her – a severed goose head that left a delicate spray of blood and gore.

Her sister's voice continued complaining unabated through the cell phone for another moment before catching that something was amiss.

"Whelma, wait, what did you *just* say?" Laurie Fitzpatrick asked, obviously annoyed.

Whelma, who along with her sister had been born and raised in nearby Ossining, absently repeated the only word that formed in her mind.

'*Ossie*,' she said, before collapsing in a dead faint.

Within an hour, a new legend was born.

19. 'SUCH A DANGEROUS THING ... "

It was a short while after, in the parking lot along the strip of beach on Raadsel Bay, Lieutenant Sanchez and Detective Eckhart were leaning against the hood of their squad SUV eating Souvlaki wraps when something truly strange happened.

At first, it all just seemed a normal afternoon. Sanchez and Eckhart were idly watching a handful of kite-surfer's racing back and forth across the bay. The three men and a woman out on the water were a fairly tame bunch doing nothing extreme; just a few lazy forward and backward loops and rolls. Mostly they just were cutting back and forth, their crescent-shaped kites dancing high above. A fourth man, with the unusual name of Jeevers Rainey, was standing next to Sanchez and explaining the mechanics of how they worked the air currents. After his own Ocean Rodeo 'Diablo' kite had been damaged earlier (after knocking him along the rocks at the far end of the beach and bruising his shins badly), Jeevers had taken it upon himself chill out a little bit. He shortly found himself chatting it up with the two cops, oblivious to the fact he was interrupting their lunch. Nearly as tall as Sanchez, Jeevers had a scraggly beard and the odd combination of his wetsuit and signature 19th-century hat (with blue-tinted spectacles) suggested an aging steampunk veteran out for a little water sporting.

"You see, Officer Dude, when you're in a Chicken Loop, you have to extend your arms like so ..." Jeevers was explaining, his arms out to his sides, when Sanchez stopped listening. He'd been absently noting the floating log out on the water and wondering if it might prove to be a hazard to one of the approaching kite-surfers when curiously, it just disappeared, as if yanked underwater.

The kite-surfer, a cut-looking man with long curly brown hair had just executed two tight loops and was in the process of landing when with no warning, a giant monster's head erupted out of the water, clamping down on the lower half of the man's body in its jaws.

Following Sanchez' gaze, Jeevers ongoing commentary (he seemed to never stop talking) went from, "Ooh-hoo! Nice one!" to, "Oh shit, dude, that is so not good."

The two police looked on in shock as the kite-surfer screamed and disappeared in a tangle of lines and spraying blood, then came a thundering splash as whatever it was – to Sanchez it looked like a giant alligator of sorts – went under again with its prey. A second male kite-surfer who had been cutting along the water right behind the first, observed this and adjusted his course obliquely with a snap of his hips. For a moment, it looked like he was free and clear. Then a massive serpentine tail, with glistening scales and dorsal fin on the top, broke the surface and with a whipping motion cut through the air.

All three observers on the beach distinctly heard both of the man's legs snap. Then he was carried away by a surge of wind in his kite, dragged tumbling and screaming towards the yacht basin.

Sanchez tossed what was left of his wrap and ran to the water's edge, waving his arms and yelling at the remaining two kite-surfers who had been heading in the opposite direction and oblivious to the horrible tableau behind them.

"Get out of the water! Now!" Sanchez yelled at the top of his lungs. Eckhart, whose best attention-getting tool in her arsenal was a piercing two-fingered whistle that could snap a dog's ears up from a mile away, joined her partner and began repeating the loudest one she knew how – the one with both pinkies in her mouth.

The female surfer – a short, stocky-looking woman – looked over to them first, her look of annoyance visible even at a distance. With a dismissive shake of her head, she executed a neat half loop through the air and began heading in the opposite direction. It didn't take her long to put together two facts; that two fellow surfers had vanished (except for the collapsed kite from one floating in the water) and all the yelling and whistling coming from the shore. Then her eyes went wide as she registered something massive just under the surface approaching her.

Her reflexes were good. No sooner did the monster's six-foot head breach the water – twisting as it did – then she adjusted her kite to catch more wind for a jump, tucking her legs and board up as she did so.

She almost made it.

For a split second, she thought she had. There was a jarring thump and searing pain in one foot as she arced up into the air. Then, as she continued her ascent, she glanced down to see the remains of her board spinning away in various directions and a jagged stump where her left foot used to be. The last thing she saw before she fainted was a glistening, twisting shape of the creature corkscrewing back underwater; a fifty-foot-long monster with paddle-like flippers and a savage-looking head.

Behind her, the last kite-surfer came about just in time to see his partner land back into the water in a helpless jumble, lines and kite tangling. He had been dating the woman, a personal trainer/yoga instructor named Terrie Conners, barely a month. Then he saw the huge head of her attacker break the surface and start heading towards him and all thoughts of Miss Conners and her possible fate evaporated.

What happened next was almost amusing. Almost. Instinctively reacting like his partner, this last kite-surfer – an auto-mechanic named Dale – veered towards the yacht club and executed a 'huge jump' as the wind caught his kite and plucked him into the sky. His luck was a little better – as the monsters head broke the surface and snapped its tremendous jaws upon (for a moment as he peed in his wetsuit, Dale's entire world was filled with rows of wicked-looking teeth and a glistening pink maw that looked as big as a sewer pipe), then came a 'thump!' as the bottom of his board bounced off the thing's snout and flew free and clear.

It was a good jump. He landed after clearing forty feet and began zooming away to the southeast toward where the yacht club – and a passed-out woman on a park bench –were. He wasn't focused on that, however; Dale was looking back in horror at the thing that twisted about and dove underwater with a sinuous grace. Whatever this monster was, it was coming right after him.

The pressing question was, of course, how fast was it?

Dale had no idea. At least he was moving at a good clip, perhaps twenty-five or thirty miles an hour. He kept squinting and looking back, trying to get any indication of his pursuer's location while keeping his shaking legs as steady as possible.

He didn't see the channel buoy until it was too late.

"Ouch squared!" Jeevers said. He couldn't make out the details from this distance, but he knew the visible part of the channel buoy was a four-foot-high steel superstructure solid enough to withstand an impact from smaller craft at least. Dale slammed into fast enough to knock it askew before another gust yanked his flailing body up and over and across the docks of the Raadsel Bay Yacht Club where it eventually became tangled around the flag mast on the front lawn.

None of this Lieutenant Sanchez nor Detective Eckhart witnessed. Sanchez was already on the radio to the dispatcher phoning for backup, multiple ambulances and the National Guard if they were available, the U.S. Navy or anything armed with depth charges if they weren't. Eckhart had grabbed anything resembling life-saving equipment and had waded up to her knees in the water, trying to determine if any of the kite-surfers were still alive. She'd spent summers as a teen as a lifesaver and was still an excellent swimmer, but the million dollar question didn't involve her rescue ability but what may or not be still out there in the bay.

The woman was floating out there but not moving. There was no sign of the two other men other than the folded remains of one kite.

Sanchez waded out to his partner and grabbed her firmly by the arm. "Don't," he said, as if reading her thoughts.

Tears were streaming down Eckhart's face. "What the hell just happened, Ray?" she said with a sob. "Just what in the hell was that thing!?"

"I don't know, I really don't," Sanchez said quietly, his eyes scanning every which way for any sign of the thing. For one of the first times in his life, he was truly terrified. One of his secret fears, one that he realized he'd mostly forgotten about until now, was of large dangerous things lurking underwater coming to devour him. He'd never told anyone including Eckhart – even in their more intimate moments – and he'd half-laughed at it until know. A stupid childhood thing. *Watching too many Saturday monster movies, Raymond*, his mother would have said. Once when he'd been six, his father had wrangled a free ferry ride to Haverstraw and Sanchez had started screaming hysterically like a baby, convinced if they did a giant sea monster would rise up out of the depths and eat all of them.

That's ridiculous, his father had said, furious, *there's no such thing sea monsters. Stop being a cry baby!*

That's what they always say in the movie, little Raymond had thought. *Just before they all die.*

And here he had just witnessed it with his own eyes. Four people. A giant ... what in God's name was it? It looked like a dinosaur of sorts, like the one he'd seen on that BBC series a few years back ... 'Swimming with the Dinosaurs.' Except that had been all computer graphics and special effects.

Standing there knee deep in the water, he managed to project his usual calm, careful demeanor on the outside while inside his guts were doing flip-flops.

Its jaws alone had been enormous, at least four feet long.

He knew Katrina Eckhart well enough to know every fiber in her body was telling her to get out there and help. Just as he knew whatever was out there was *still* out there.

Behind him, Jeevers sat down cross-legged in the sand, shaking his head. Across the water came the first wailing alarm (and distinctive '*Skonk!*') from the village's municipal building summoning the volunteer fire department, accompanied shortly by the sirens of the first police cars to mobilize. Flashing lights came from the marina as the police launch emerged and headed straight toward them.

"You can't do this!"

Mayor Ray Santos was shaking his head rapidly in disbelief. A stocky, immaculately dressed and almost obsessively groomed man in his late thirties, Mayor Santos had glided his way through three terms already largely on the merit of his obeisant charm and 'teddy bear' demeanor. Little which was in evidence as he paced back and forth across Police Chief Hendricks' office, wringing his hands.

"As a matter of fact, I can, and will," Hendricks countered. "Four people died today, and presumably three more this past week. Until we get to the bottom of this, I can't have anyone near the water. I'm closing down the GreenWaters Festival this year, Ray."

The mayor winced at the words 'closing' and 'GreenWaters Festival,' as if the police chief had physically struck him. The yearly music and crafts festival organized by local Hudson River activists had snowballed in stature from a sort of low-key 'Folkie/Hippy-fest' back in the 1970s to major money-making venture drawing top talent and $75 per head gate prices. The September date apparently started when an aging hippy named Arnie Paulson waded out into the shallows off Raadsel Point one day in 1976 with a sign that read 'No More PCBs!' and stood there in protest for thirty hours, garnering local and even some national news. A less charitable version of events had it he was high as a kite and had meant to write 'No More PCP's' (which had claimed the life of his best friend earlier that week) but had gotten confused.

"We could just scale it back … put up security fences to keep people away from the water? Wouldn't that—?"

"No," Hendricks said, tapping his forefinger once on his desktop for emphasis. "Ray, I'm not risking a single person's life for the sake of the festival."

The mayor kept shaking his head, refusing to accept this changing course of events. Crammed into the office with them was Captain Fowler, Lieutenant Sanchez, Detective Eckhart and the Village Manager, Joan Whitman. Whitman, a silver-haired woman whose once pretty looks had been marred by a thirty-year martini habit, had surprised everyone by actually showing up sober. Next to her stood Steve Weathers, a heavy-set black man who was the recreation supervisor and in charge of all the parks.

"Ray, you do remember that festival is a major revenue source for our town *and* village. Major as in capital 'M.' The permits alone … no … no we cannot just return them their money. You understand we're still in the midst of a recession … do you have any idea the impact this would have on our finances? Any at all?"

"Thought you said everything's just rosy, with our Aa2 Bond rating and all?" Captain Fowler cut in, referring to the glowingly optimistic 'Letter from the Mayor' on the village website that was the source of ongoing jokes in the police department. Fowler made no bones about his low opinion of the mayor, or anyone on the village board for that matter.

The mayor gave him a withering look.

Hendricks, who had learned the value of honing his diplomatic streak over the years, spoke up. "Ray, I know full well the impact on the village finances. This is not a decision I'm making hastily, or without considering the consequences. Cripes, you know me better than that."

The mayor still kept shaking his head. "No. You can't do this. There has to be another solution. Call in the Coast Guard, set up nets and perimeters, put in some overtime and catch this thing, whatever it takes … do whatever it takes … " He repeated the last line as if to himself, the first signs of hysteria creeping into his voice.

"Ray. My first and foremost duty is the safety and welfare of this village, and the people in it. And anyone who passes through it as well. I'm not negotiating with you on this. My decision is final. *No festival.*"

"No!" the mayor shouted, throwing his hands up in the air, "You, you cannot do this! Do your job and catch this thing, whatever it is! If it even exists!"

"My officers saw it. We don't know exactly what it is yet, but it exists." Even Hendricks was having difficulty in using the term 'sea monster.'

The mayor swung on him. "Really? You don't seem to be able to get your stories straight! First, they tell you it's a … a cephalopod, some mutant oversized squid thingy with tentacles, now it's some sort of giant sea dinosaur … what'll it be tomorrow, a giant lobster with fangs? Seems like your officers have overactive imaginations."

"Four people are dead, Ray. The fire department is still hosing down what's left of that guy who wound up marrying the yacht club's flagpole. I'm not budging on this."

"Then you better start thinking of a way to!" the mayor screamed. Then he dropped his hands to his sides and regained some of his composure. "This isn't over," he added in a threatening tone. "I'm calling the board together. We're going to override you on this." Without waiting for a response, he turned on his heel and, motioning for Whitman and Weathers to follow him, stormed out of the room.

"Someone had a little too much coffee with his *Arepas* this morning," Fowler commented, after the door slammed close.

"Can he really do that? Override you?" Sanchez asked.

"No, he can't do that," Hendricks replied, leaning back in his chair. "He'll come around to it." *At least I hope he does*, he thought. Privately, he wasn't so sure. Mayor Santos had a track record as a slippery customer, particularly when he wanted his way on something. And Hendricks had never seen him so upset, or actually shout like that. Something else was going on here.

"Captain, set up a checkpoint by the entrance to the Point, and no one goes in or out without my explicit say so? Okay?" Fowler nodded and he turned to Sanchez and Eckhart. "The mayor did have a point. I'm hearing two different stories as well. What the hell is going on?"

Sanchez looked stung. He knew the police chief thought highly of him – to the point of treating him like a son sometimes – and it pained him to be sounding like a fool in front of the man he looked up to.

"Chief, the evidence we found earlier this week was exactly what we described. But what the detective here and I saw today was something completely different. It was, it was … "

"It looked like a dinosaur," Eckhart finally spoke up. "It was a sort of sea dinosaur – there's just no other way to describe it. The head must have been six feet long."

"Six feet long," Hendricks said, sounding skeptical. "You're sure about that? Could it have been some sort of oversized sturgeon? There's been rumors of them getting as big as fifteen feet long."

"It swallowed an entire man in a single bite. Three of us witnessed it," Sanchez replied. "And it came half out of the water. Large flippers, a long sinuous tail – I'd estimate the thing was at least fifty feet long. Easy. It wasn't any sturgeon, Chief. "

"You understand, Lieutenant, why I might be having a hard time with all this?"

Sanchez nodded, "Absolutely, Chief. *I'm* having a hard time all this. It's almost as if … no … that'd be crazy."

Hendricks looked at him steadily a moment, as if weighing whether to press him for more information. Instead, he asked, "What about that marine biologist kid? Rhinebeck, er, Rhinehard … whatever his name was. Can he shed any light on this?"

"*Reinhardt*," Sanchez corrected. "I'll contact him as soon as we get out of here. Last I heard, he'd gone back down to the city today to sign out a new experimental side-scan sonar he was helping develop. I was going to help him take it out our launch tomorrow and test it out."

Hendricks' finger was tapping the desk again. "Well, tomorrow may be too late. See if he can get it out on the water tonight. We need to find out what in the hell we're dealing with, and I've just landed myself in a shit-storm by canceling the festival. I'm going to have to give a press conference tomorrow explaining myself and I need facts, or I'll just be making a horse's ass out of myself. Are we clear?"

"On it," Sanchez said, standing up.

"Get to work."

As the detective and lieutenant started to leave, Hendricks added, "Lieutenant, Detective?"

"Yes?" they both said at once, standing by the open door.

"I realize I'm putting a lot of pressure on both of you, but for God's sakes, be careful. I don't want anyone else getting hurt."

Outside in the parking lot, Sanchez sat in the driver's seat, head back and staring at the ceiling of the Police Department's Ford Bronco. Next to him, Detective Eckhart looked at him worriedly, her hand on his.

"My God, what a day," she said.

Sanchez barked out a laugh. "Yeah. You could say that again."

"My God what a day," she repeated.

Sanchez looked at her, then clasped her hand in his. Their relationship was more or less an open secret in the department and had it proven to be any issue, Hendricks would have assigned them separately, but the truth was they worked exceptionally well together so he let it go. Despite his reputation as a ladies' man, Sanchez was completely devoted to Eckhart. Though she was twelve years his senior – or partly *because* of it – he found a strength and calmness in her that was like an anchor in a stormy sea.

Even today, despite the horrors of what they'd witnessed earlier, she'd kept her cool, in a way no other woman he'd ever known would have done. Her eyes looked terribly sad, but she was holding it together. It was one of the many things he admired about her.

There hadn't been any further sign of the sea monster when the launch had arrived. One of the officers had taken down Jeevers statement, then helped him collect his gear and sent him home. Only three bodies had been completely accounted for. The kite surfer with the broken legs had drowned, the one who eventually married the flagpole in front of the yacht club was unquestionably dead on the spot (his head had been pulverized beyond recognition courtesy of the channel buoy), and the woman had died of shock and blood loss. Of the fourth kite-surfer, as so far only his arm had been recovered, he was presumed dead.

After cleaning up and changing into dry clothes, Sanchez and Eckhart had given their respective statements before being called up to the police chief's office to lay out what had happened directly.

Despite their spotless reputation on the department, Hendricks would have had more of a hard time accepting what they told him if it hadn't been for Jeevers Rainey's and then Whelma Fitzpatrick's corroborating statements. In most cases, eyewitness accounts tended to vary wildly. This was one of those rare times they all lined up together like a neat row of ducks. Jeevers seemed to take it all in like some sort of major cosmic but somehow unsurprising tragedy ("I'm telling you, this is all because of Indian Point. Nuclear waste, man! Fucking up the ecosystem bigtime!" he kept repeating). Whelma's statement had been given at the scene after she'd been treated for shock and given a sedative, neither which slowed her down very much. Before she'd walked through the front door of her house on Clairemont, she had gotten on the phone and along with her sister started blatting on her entire network about her terrifying encounter with 'Ossie.' Which after her third daiquiri, had taken on the epic proportions of a Hollywood movie. Or at least a front-page article for say, Us Weekly. Or FOX news.

"We should call Reinhardt," Eckhart prompted.

Sanchez sighed. What he really wanted more than anything was a long hot shower, then to slip into the sheets with the woman next to him for an even longer nap. After a little booty call, of course. But the day wasn't over yet.

"Yep. I'll do it right now."

Eckhart looked off into the distance. "Ray, what do you think is really going on here? Do you think we saw today is connected to the disappearances out on the Point?"

"Yes ... no ... Hell, I don't know," Sanchez replied, then: "Yes, I think they must be connected. But I'm pretty sure we're dealing with two separate problems."

"Two sea monsters?" She didn't sound surprised.

"Looks that way," he laughed. "Listen to us. Did you, in your wildest dreams, ever think you'd be in a squad car one day having this conversation?"

"Nope. I most certainly didn't."

Sanchez pulled her hand to his mouth and kissed the back of it. Then he picked up the radio mic.

20. "A GIRL HAS GOT TO MAKE A LIVING ... "

"Oh my God, I can't believe it ... he's actually coming!" Jennie Roderick said, jumping up and down and squeezing her fingers. She had met up with John during his lunch break that Thursday, picking up some sandwiches and heading over to one of their favorite spots, a park bench overlooking the falls not far from The Art Mill. It was a scenic spot on the north side of Wyvern Falls Creek (or 'Kill,' as it was officially called in Dutch) near the bridge. On the south side was the village proper. Toward the west, the creek wound through an equally scenic gorge where it went past the old water mill and emptied into Raadsel Bay.

The Falls were still pretty forceful from the runoff after the hurricane, and the heady aroma of water, wet dirt, and leaves wafted up and around them.

Barringer studied his ham and Swiss, then took a sizable bite which he chewed with the side of his mouth.

"Who is coming?" he asked.

"Duh. Guillamo Del Tesler, Mister Ancient Astronaut Theorist himself! He just texted me. This is so totally cool!"

"Huh," he grunted, feeling a pang of jealousy. Lately, everything Jennie talked about was *Guillamo this* and *Guillamo that* as if they were old friends. By contrast, he felt like he was being treated increasingly like a piece of furniture. Doctoring the rocks and selling them to the whacky alien guy had been one thing, but now he was *coming here*?

"He's bringing a small crew to shoot some footage. Apparently, in addition to the rocks we sent him, he's discovered 'additional, unequivocal evidence of ancient alien's here in the Hudson Valley.' He'll be here tomorrow morning! This is so awesome!"

Barringer took another bite of his sandwich. "And you don't see a problem with this?"

"With what, darling?" Jennie said distractedly as she texted.

"With the fact that we sold him doctored evidence and he's basing his actions on it?"

Jennie finished her message and looked up at him, annoyed. "Like *no*. I mean, what's your problem? *Everything's* fiction these days. The news. Our bank accounts. The so-called reasons we've been in three different wars this past decade ... and like our entire freaking stock market. *Hello*?"

And what, am I fiction too? he heard himself thinking. "Uh … okay," he said aloud. But Barringer was never one to overly dwell on things. Besides, she was still calling him *darling*. He always liked that. "So what's the plan?"

"He's driving up tomorrow morning and meeting his film crew here. He asked if I could be his local guide. Isn't this so exciting?"

Barringer felt his spirits sinking again. "But I have to work," he said dejectedly.

"I know that, silly. But I don't. Don't worry, this'll be great. Trust me on this!"

Yeah … great for who? he wondered.

"So, they pay you to come out here and collect rocks?" Easton said, looking around the cave. He was glad to see it was really more of an underground passageway and didn't lead anywhere other than in and out. After the whole nightmare with Simon Crowley and the Golden Dawn business a year previous, he'd developed a distinct aversion to caves … and the things that might be lurking around in them. This one was on the northwestern part of Raadsel Point where at some point in the distant past the river had carved out a narrow passage out of the rocky shoreline that rose there. The passage could be entered from either side and was perhaps no more than forty feet long, its floor covered in sand and loose gravel. Toward its middle was a raised, hollowed area that had been supposedly used for ceremonial purposes by the Indians, though probably in a limited away – there was perhaps enough space for a dozen people at most and that would be crowding it. It was in this area where one particularly large boulder had fractured off from the wall and been used as a palette for the Indian artists. The other walls had been the subject of more recent use – mostly graffiti by errant teenagers over the ensuing years – but surprisingly the area around the original Indian petroglyphs was untouched.

It was early Thursday afternoon and Easton had accepted Sarah's invitation to visit the site she was working on, unaware of the unfolding events on the bay to the south of them.

"Well, a girl has to earn a living," she answered, squatting near the boulder while idly prodding the gravel with a foldable hand shovel. The ground around it had a collapsible grid set up and nearby was a rucksack with various tools and camera equipment, a couple of battered wood-framed sieves and brushes. The entrances had yellow warning tape across them, but being public property, there was little to be done to secure the area, so any valuable equipment had to be carried in and out. Also, the cave was vulnerable to the elements – while the floor was a few feet above the high-tide line a flood tide could easily submerge it.

Easton was standing nearby, hands in pockets. A light breeze ruffled his windbreaker. "I could think of far less interesting ways to do it," he said.

She looked up with one eye narrowed as if trying to measure whether he was being sincere or sarcastic. Sometimes, he wasn't sure himself.

"I mean, er, well I have to say you're the first archaeologist I ever met," he added.

And the first one I've ever fallen for, as well.

It had been a frenzied two days, starting with his last-minute visit late Tuesday night. He was a little thrown at how easy and natural it had been, underscored by almost an entire year without any intimate female contact. That decision had been partly conscious; the last relationship he'd been involved with – with a thirty-something Hispanic woman named Olivia who ran a local ballet academy – had gone balls-up through the whole fiasco with the Sacred Dawn business he'd gotten tangled in the year before. So he'd decided to lay low in that department for a while. At the same time, being alone came naturally to him. Even as a kid, Easton was a reserved, loner sort, completely self-sufficient and not seeking others to validate himself.

But with the sinuous ease that he found himself slipping into (*did it qualify as a 'relationship' yet*, he wondered?), this latest situation wasn't just disconcerting, it was almost scary. Yet there was a flip side to this as well, as one of his more favorite Joseph Campbell quotes put it: "If you find yourself falling, then dive."

The whole thing could blow up on a dime, he kept reminding himself, *so just enjoy it.*

That went easy enough in theory, but the hell of it was, once you'd been intimate with someone after a long period of abstinence, you craved it like a junkie.

Sarah had been wearing a flannel nightgown when she'd greeted him at the door that night. Rovsky had ambled past her into the cabin and plunked himself on the floor in the main room as if he already owned the place while Easton, half-soaked, took off his cap and stood there, taking her in. There was something odd, elementally different about her that he found uniquely attractive; the square shoulders, strong features and her uncompromising directness were refreshing.

Though nearly as tall as he was, she'd stood up on tiptoe and kissed him first quickly, then a second time more passionately before pulling him inside. After fetching a towel from the bathroom, she'd dried his face, carefully taken off his jacket, and hung it. Then she'd removed his Beretta and shoulder holster and hung that on top of it. The room was toasty with the coals of an earlier fire in the hearth.

"What was it you said on the phone? Alupsee ...?" he'd asked.

"*Alàpsi wëntaxa*. It's an old, secret Indian phrase."

"It is?"

"No," she'd teased, "it just means 'hurry up and get your ass over here.'"

With a smile playing at the corners of her mouth, she'd slowly opened her robe, revealing her nakedness. Easton had stood there, savoring the moment, instantly aroused.

This time, their sex was much slower, as if by mutual agreement.

One of the last things Easton remembered before dozing off was the light dribble of rain on the roof, and a knot popping in the fireplace. The tiny bedroom barely had room for the double bed, and with the small yellow pine dresser wedged in next to it with its antique lamp, the room felt both musty yet strangely cozy; like an illicit liaison. The sheets were rough, but Sarah opened up her down sleeping bag as a comforter. He'd held off sleep a few minutes, acutely aware of Sarah's body wrapped tightly around his own, her warmth like a low-banked fire. He remembered catching the hint of cedar as he ran his fingers through her hair, just before he'd slid off into a dreamless abyss.

Wednesday went in a blur.

Easton had cancelled his appointments and talked Sarah into blowing off the day for a little sightseeing up the Hudson. There was a restaurant called The Greystone Inn situated atop the cliffs at the Hudson Highlands overlooking the river, with a scenic view of Bannerman's Castle to the north. The main structure of the restaurant was a converted lodge with a similarly rustic style as the Old Bear Mountain Inn on the other side of the river, but at a smaller scale.

Being mid-week and well before the fall colors would reach their peak, the place was fairly quiet and Easton had picked a table near the veranda with a panoramic view of the River Valley. It was cool enough to have a fire going in the fieldstone fireplace. The main dining room had an open-beamed ceiling with timber-and-stone walls decorated with old paintings and photographs of the region. An old moose head was mounted over the mantle.

Easton had ordered one of the special Autumn Ales while Sarah had gone with a glass of Pinot Grigio. At his suggestion, they'd shared a large bowl of French onion soup which was one of his favorite items on the menu; he still hadn't been able to tease out of the chef exactly which Swiss cheese they used, only it was the best he thought he'd ever tasted.

"Interesting place," Sarah had mused. "You said you know the owner?"

"Young Japanese gentlemen, believe it or not. He developed an interest in the history of the region and came into some money not so long ago, and this place happened to be on the market for a new owner and makeover at the time. Since then, it's become something of a local hotspot. I don't think there's anything bad on the menu."

Sarah had taken a sip from her glass and gazed out the picture windows. The first splashes of yellows and oranges were highlighting the trees on the opposite shore. It was a sunny afternoon with whorls and ribbons of cirrus clouds crisscrossing the sky.

She'd glanced down at the island with its ruined castle. "Looks like someone's fairytale went badly."

Easton was admiring the graceful line of her neck and decided the more he looked at her, the more beautiful she appeared, as if she was revealing herself to him in measured degrees. Yet at that moment, he saw something else as well, a sort of wistful sadness.

"Yes, that's Bannerman's Castle. Are you familiar with it?"

"Sort of. But tell me."

"Built by a Scotsman named Francis Bannerman in the early 1900s. Sort of an odd character, but very successful. Back in the latter 1800s, he bought up a lot of Spanish Civil War and Army surplus – guns, cannon, uniforms, eventually everything military – and made a fortune as the premier source for that sort of thing. Within a few years, Bannerman's became the largest Army surplus supplier in the world – there were claims he sold one South American country a battleship and allegedly supplied the Japanese for their victorious war against the Russians in 1905. The inventory they expanded to was stupendous – everything from stone-age weapons made by ancient Britons to Medieval crossbows, armor, Civil War artillery to WWI anti-aircraft guns. Looking for a twelve-inch howitzer mounted on a rail carriage? A 75mm all-purpose cannon to compliment your front-yard garden? Bannerman was your 'go-to' man. The main warehouse was down in New York City at 501 Broadway, but the castle there became his pet project, inspired by the castles of his native Scotland. He started building it in 1901 and kept adding to it until his death in 1918. It's actually two buildings; one was for his residence and the other was an armory."

Sarah had frowned. "What happened to it?"

"Well, I understand the armory blew up in 1920, and the rest was devastated in a 1969 fire. Now it's just ruins. Sort of a testament of one man's dreams gone from riches to dust."

"Sometimes that's not such a bad thing," she'd said, but didn't elaborate.

Just then their main courses had arrived, breaking the somber mood. After lunch, they'd walked out on the terrace to take in the views. A lone barge was making its way up the river. Just below them, a couple of red-tailed hawks were banking around on the thermals.

Sarah had leaned on the wooden rail, looking down at the sprawling vista of the Hudson River valley. "You like high places," she'd said, as if stating a fact.

Next to her, Easton was leaning on one elbow. "I'd never really thought about it. But yeah, it seems that way."

Then just as abruptly she turned and looked him directly in the eye. "I'm afraid, John," she'd said.

Easton didn't reply, but had simply raised his eyebrows. She'd glanced down as if embarrassed, then looked him in the eye again. He could sense her struggling for the proper words. "All of this. What's happening with the river ... with the future. With ... us."

Easton had studied her a moment, then nodded. "Well, I can't speak to the first two, but as to the third, I'm balls-out terrified myself."

Somehow, that seemed to amuse her. "Really?" she'd said, nudging in closer to him. Then after a pause added more seriously, "Tell me that you won't hurt me, John."

Easton was positive he would remember that moment for the rest of his life; the cool September breeze, the distant cry of the hawk, the sense of being in such proximity and intimacy with someone while standing on the precipice of such an enormous physical space, her breath warming his cheek.

He was acutely aware that she'd just opened herself up to him, laid down her defenses.

And in that split second, he knew instantly and unequivocally that he had fallen in love.

How in the hell did that happen? he'd wondered.

"I won't," he'd said quietly.

She'd leaned forward and brushed his lips with hers. "I want you," she whispered.

Easton let out a little smile. "Right here on the terrace?"

Sarah had glanced sideways back at the restaurant, realizing for the first time they had an audience. A retired-age couple was sitting at a table by the window watching them with identical yearning expressions. The waiter standing next to them was also gazing at Easton and Sarah with the linen napkin he had been folding bunched up in his hands, his customers forgotten.

"Well … perhaps you could take me somewhere a little more private." They'd spent the rest of the afternoon in Easton's bed.

Thursday morning, they'd grabbed breakfast at Xenos, the Greek diner/restaurant over on upper Main Street. A local institution, Xenos was practically its own tourist destination. It featured a faux 'Mediterranean Grotto' wall that was an odd amalgam of trickling fountains and pools, starfish, shells and sponges, and a ship model or two. Every so often, one of the owner's family or friends would come back from the home country with some tchotchke or trinket and it would get added to the décor. Consequently, on the ledge next to their table, they found themselves staring at a 15" figurine of Perseus that some wit had added a miniature fisherman's cap to as well as two tiny strips of electrical tape criss-crossed over the genitals.

Sarah was back in her khaki's and hiking boots again while Easton had gone for one of his 'casual outdoor' get ups; Levi's with a lightweight black turtleneck, a pair of black Chambray sneakers, and a grey windbreaker. Over the tall menu, he noticed Sarah smiling to herself. "What?" he'd asked.

"Oh, it's sort of stupid," she said, laying the menu down, "but the name of this restaurant – Xenos – makes me think of Heno. He's the God of Thunder in Wyandot and Iroquois mythology."

"Well, that would make a certain degree of sense," Easton had replied, nodding towards the open cook counter at the back of the dining area. Inside the kitchen was a giant of a man who looked like an angry Zero Mostel crammed into a Pillsbury Doughboy uniform. The cook was yelling at somebody while clouds of smoke erupted on either side. "That's one of the owners, Pashamou. He may be related."

Sarah had laughed. "Why does he yell everything three times?" she'd asked.

"I have no idea. It may be something they're taught in Greek cooking school."

Over lunch, Easton told Sarah about the *Edmund G. Wood* account and the papers from the Cousteau expedition. He'd half-expected her to break out laughing. Instead, she'd looked concerned.

"So there is *two* monsters," she'd said.

Easton had looked at her incredulously. "You're joking. You don't think those stories are true, do you? It's starting to look more and more to me like an elaborate hoax."

Sarah had shaken her head. "I don't think it is, John. Why don't you join me out at the point after this? There's something I think you should see …"

Easton had been idly looking at a spray-painted message – 'Lonely Dancers Rock The Roost!' – when Sarah began to dig away the sand and gravel at the base of the rock. "Last evening after you dropped me off, I ended up coming back here and digging around a bit. Something's been bothering me about these petroglyphs … a vague sense they were incomplete. That's when I discovered there's a second set of petroglyphs lower on the rock that were buried over time. At a calculated guess, I'd say hundreds of years ago the floor of this cave was a couple feet lower. I put the soil back because I don't want anyone to know about this yet." She pointed to a shovel leaning against the wall. "Can you grab that and give me a hand here? This is where things start to get a little weird."

Ten minutes later, Easton stepped back while Sarah washed off the rock face carefully with a bucket of water. Six inches below the original soil line, a whole new set of images were revealed.

It appeared to be a sequence of events that suggested a fantastic scenario to Easton, but he was wary of misinterpreting what could very likely be ambiguous images – he was all-too-familiar with the natural tendency to project meaning in these sorts of situations. From left to right, the images showed a series of triangle-headed stick people in a canoe battling what looked like a serpent/monster in the river. A middle image included a figure with what might have been a stylized horn and the third image what might have been a battle between two monsters. But how this related to the patterns and images above it was beyond him.

Leaning on the shovel, Easton said, "Well, I could tell you what it *looks* like to me. But this is really your area of expertise. So what am I looking at?"

Kneeling, Sarah traced her fingers over the images as if drawing additional insight by physical touch. "This first image shows a *Maxa'xak* – an evil river serpent – attacking these fishermen in a canoe. I've seen similar petroglyphs of these before – though nothing quite like this. These squiggly lines suggest something other than appendages … they might be tentacles. The some of the fisherman are attacking it with spears, but the flattened ones underneath indicate many have died. In the next grouping there's a shaman – he's the one with the spirit figure coming out of his head – performing some sort of dance or ritual. There's some barely visible lines connecting this to the main images on the rock above. They're all but completely eroded away towards the bottom. Now with this next set, the shaman is using a horn, and from these lines here, I'd guess it's extended underwater. See, it could easily pass for the Horn of Skarreh. Then we see a second monster with four fins attacking the first – a great battle. In the last order is restored and the fisherman are back on the river – the many canoes and fish indicate successful resolution and bounty." She stood up and ran her fingers to the main image which to Easton looked like a meaningless jumble of primitive images and geometric designs.

"See, originally these appeared as *Manëtuwàk*, spirits descended from the sun and a group of seven stars we call *Ansisktayèsàk*. And this here the big boat or *Xinkwi Mùxul* they arrived in. By itself, the top image suggests one thing; combined with the lower ones something else altogether."

"I'm not sure I follow," Easton confessed.

"Well, one interpretation could be that the seven spirits arrived from above in the big boat and gave the river people, who were besieged by an evil river monster, a magic horn to summon another monster to destroy the first one." Sarah shook her head as if embarrassed at the words she'd just spoken aloud.

Easton considered this. "But is it a literal depiction of events or a symbolic one?"

Sarah put her hands on her hips. "Who knows? It could be a historic record preserving a collective memory or visionary art used for ceremonies and rituals ... or it could be both. But don't you see how weird this all is?"

"Well, I'm afraid to break this to you, but weird is pretty much par for the course around here," he quipped. But he had an idea where this was all going. "The rocks you brought to the Historical Society ... the petroglyphs or something ..."

Sarah looked at him, "Exactly. They were faked – I'm almost positive of that. But this is the real thing. We'd have to do a detailed AMC 14C dating to verify it, but I'd be willing to bet my reputation these drawings are authentic. They were concealed *underneath* where the faked stones were. You don't find that a little ... *ironic*?"

Easton chuckled and shook his head. "Never say God doesn't have a sense of humor. But are we seriously having a discussion about aliens and magic horns and a couple of sea monsters? Here in the Hudson River?"

Sarah stepped over to him and gave him a challenging look. "Are we?"

"Do you believe in monsters?"

"Yes. And no. That serpent could just also be a sturgeon. They're prehistoric, they're scary-looking, and they've been known to get as large as twenty-seven feet long."

"But you don't really think that."

Sarah bit her lip. "No. Actually, I don't know what to think. Doctor Sarah Ramhorne doesn't believe in them, but Sarah Ramhorne, American Indian does."

"Well, then that's pretty funny."

"Funny?" He felt her tense up.

"Yes, *funny*. Because I *do* believe in monsters. Absolutely and positively. But this doesn't add up to me."

"Why not?"

Easton looked away. "Because of the timing. Why now? Why right on the eve of the GreenWater Festival? And why while you're here, just in time to find a bunch of doctored ... what did you call them? Portable petroglyphs?"

Sarah's eyes narrowed. "You don't think I ...?"

"No. Not you. But these aren't just random events here. I wouldn't be at all surprised if they were being orchestrated by human design. If only I could—"

Any further thoughts were interrupted as his smartphone began to buzz.

At some point, Easton had accepted his Droid as a necessary evil. But he still couldn't deny the urge to fling it as far as he could every time the damn thing rang. "Hello?"

"John?" The voice was breaking up, but he knew the number – Jim Franks.

"What's up, mate?" He took a few steps towards the southern entrance. The reception picked up slightly, but not much. Another single bar appeared on the phone.

"Where have you been, pal? Holed up in a cave somewhere?"

"You could say that. Are you at work?" Franks was the owner and creative behind a boutique digital design company down in Irvington called Kinetic Media Associates.

"Yeah, we're having fun trying to wrap up a website and rebranding campaign by end-of-business day tomorrow for an extremely neurotic architect. One who apparently has descended to us from the design heaven and is attempting to instruct us on the error of our ways. Sound familiar?"

Easton laughed. Franks alternately loved and hated his business and wasn't shy about unloading on his friend. He was pretty sure he knew who the client was; an Iranian ex-pat who was an amazing designer and also borderline insane. On more than one occasion, Franks had Easton practically on the floor laughing while recounting the man's ridiculously elaborate 'Archispeak' tirades. Phrases like, "articulate an ongoing texturalized dialogue" or "elaborating upon a contemporary conflation of contradictions," or as the client unbelievably once accused Franks: "Your web solution tends to unnecessarily problematize the dynamic structural articulation of my sophisticated design solution."

"Let me guess, the 'Terror of Tehran' again?"

"One and the same. This is the third time we've rebranded him this year. But that's not what I called to bend your ear about. Where *are* you, by the way?"

"Actually, *I am* standing in a cave. With Sarah Ramhorne."

There was a pause on the other end of the line while Franks let out a low chuckle. "So that's where you've been holing up. Karen was convinced you'd run off and joined the French Foreign Legion or something. Sarah, huh? First name basis, are you now? Tell me you've officially dropped out of League of Grumpy Monks and are back in action again."

"You might say that."

"Ah. To quote my good friends Bill and Ted: "Most Excellent!" So you've heard about the commotion in town?"

"What do you mean?"

"*Ossie.*"

Easton looked at the phone like he didn't recognize it. "Sorry?"

"It's all over the village. Wyvern Falls now officially has its very own sea monster, Ossie."

"What are you talking about?" Easton asked. *As if I didn't know.*

"Four kite surfers bought it about an hour ago, and there was a ringside witness – Whelma Fitzpatrick. For Christ sakes, pal, you're up there and I'm down here, and I'm the one filling *you* in on the news?"

Easton tried to think if he remembered any Whelma Fitzpatricks and came up empty. "Well, we've been at dig site here on the northwest shore of the point since breakfast. What's this about kite surfers?"

Franks told him.

"Ouch."

"Look, why don't you grab the good doctor and join us at my place for dinner tomorrow tonight? Fish on the grill. Karen's working on some top-secret salad but won't divulge details. What do you say?"

Easton covered the mouthpiece. "Would you like to join some friends for dinner Friday?" he asked Sarah. She shrugged. Then nodded.

"What time?" he asked Franks.

"Make it seven. The sedatives should have kicked in with my client by then."

"Should I bring a bottle?"

"You always pick a good one."

"No worries. See you then." Easton turned off the phone and clipped back onto his belt. Sarah had a distracted, concerned look. "Are you okay?"

"I'm okay," she said.

Easton wasn't convinced. This whole business wasn't sitting well with him either, for that matter. Sea monsters? Mystical horns? Indian legends? Now kite surfer's being attacked?

A minute later, his phone rang again. This time, it was the number of an attorney he knew from White Plains. Once in a while, she'd hook him up with a job – usually very lucrative ones. This one was for a judge she was friends with, whose wife he suspected was doing the mattress mambo with her tennis coach as well as treating her lover to a wardrobe overhaul that included Gucci shoes and monogrammed Louis Vuitton gym bags. Easton didn't usually take surveillance jobs – they tended to leave him feeling dirty and depressed – but figured he could sub it out to a local retired NYPD detective he knew. That would require drawing up a contract and a quick meeting, however.

He hung up the phone and looked at Sarah.

"I'm going to have to run out for a bit – that old 'earning a living' thing. I'll call you a little later?"

"Or you can just call me Sarah," she replied.

"How about I just call you 'I'm coming over to your place to spend the night'," he deadpanned back without missing a beat.

Sarah grinned. "It's a bit of a mouthful, but that'll work too."

21. 'A MAN CAN BE DESTROYED BUT NOT DEFEATED ... '

It was just after eight pm. when the *Artful Dodger*, a thirty-six foot Sportcraft Pesca owned and operated by Nick Lonnegan, eased out into the river from the Peekskill Marina with four customers and one crew despite the current safety advisory against overnight fishing charters up and down the river. Nick Lonnegan had been running fishing charters on the river for thirty years and for ten years before that had served in the Navy. Nothing short of a hurricane would keep him out of his business and probably not even that, if a client was willing to pay.

Though it was a bit early for the fall striped bass season, the four clients had shown up eager and with wallets ready, and Lonnegan was more than happy to oblige them. This group was up from north Jersey; a couple of software engineers from Samsung, a video editor from South Africa, and an older gentleman who appeared to be living out a Hemmingway fantasy with his trimmed white beard, Panama hat, and khakis.

Despite a light rain earlier in the evening, the river was calm and the falling high tide looked favorable for catching stripers. Lonnegan cased them out into the main channel then opened up the throttles as they veered north towards the Bear Mountain Bridge and World's End. Lonnegan, a crusty fifty-seven year old with greying curly hair, mutton chops and roughly half his teeth left, looked every inch the veteran river fisherman with his frayed bill cap and peacoat. A widower with little tolerance for sentimentality, he could often be found at Knickerbocker's waterfront tavern where he was known on more than one occasion to tell a fellow drinker, "I was born by the river, I live by the river, and Goddammit I'll die by the river, or *on* it if I can."

He also tended to be a spendthrift, except where his boat was concerned. The *Artful Dodger* was his pride and joy and he spared no expense on her equipment. Decked out with a Furuno Radar Lowrance GPS with Chart Plotter, a Garmin 720 Color Fish Finder and Raymarine VHF Radio, if there was one thing Nick Lonnegan had made a local name for himself for, it was delivering the goods when it came to his fishing charters. Some people claimed he could *smell* where the fish were even before he pulled out of the dock, but his real secret was really the

Garmin Fish Finder – the damn thing had cost him near a fortune but had paid itself off in spades. Between the 3D dimensional contour touch-screen display and depth plotter, he could pretty much put your live bait and hook right in front of whichever fish you wanted.

Tonight, however, Lonnegan sensed there was something off. Nothing he could put his finger to, partly it was due to a recent drop in the fishing population, partly it was just gut instinct after spending so many years making his living off the river. There had been a moment while staring at the Hemmingway wanna-be (a certain Chester Heiney, according to his AmEx) and his fellow would-be fishing heroes at the dock, noting their soft, uncalloused hands and bulging guts, when Lonnegan briefly considered flicking the credit card back at them and walking back to his battered pick-up. He could have turned the key and inside of five minutes be sitting at his favorite spot at the bar nursing a tall cool cold one. But, of course, he couldn't; his father Reggie Lonnegan didn't raise any sissy-pants in his family, and Nick wasn't about to turn a yellow stripe just on a hunch. Plus, he desperately needed the money. Although business had been better than the previous year, it was nowhere near what it had been before the recession, and now diesel fuel prices were creeping up again. Not to mention the notice he'd received the day before about school taxes going up. "Apparently for everyone else, the economy is just fucking dandy – time to squeeze us working folk again," he'd told his pal Fred at the Sunoco Station that morning.

So he'd taken Heiney's card and swiped it, put a crooked smile on his face, and welcomed them aboard.

The river *was* spookily quiet though. Normally, there'd be at least a couple other charters out on the water or maybe a barge or two. But rumors had been swirling up and down the Hudson this past week, then the advisory issued by the Wyvern Falls Police Department.

Well to fuck if some land-lubber cops are going to stop me from making a living, he thought as the boat passed under the shadow of the Bear Mountain Bridge, *lest they want to pop by the bank and plunk down my mortgage payment for me.*

Lonnegan cut the throttles and flicked on the Garmin mounted between the GPS tracker and VHS unit. He knew a nice spot towards the west shore that was usually a good starting point. Typically, this time of night, the stripers would be favoring the shallows. Sure enough, after a few minutes of idling along, he was able to spot the tell-tale grouping of fish, though they were in even shallower water than was usual. In fact, Lonnegan noted with a scowl, the whole shoreline seemed crowded, as if all the fish were avoiding the deeper water of the channel.

Lonnegan studied the monitor a moment, one gnarled finger tapping the stubble on his chin, then with a grunt turned and headed to the stern where the poles were set up. He let Dicky Juarez, his one crewman, demonstrate the routine of wetting ones hands, grabbing a handful of sand out of the bucket by the rail and working it over the palms so one could grab a live eel out of a second bucket and hook it, while Lonnegan himself walked them through casting their lines and securing the rods. The two software engineers had balked at baiting their hooks so Dicky handled it for them (without one of his usual smirks, even) and within five minutes all were set, lines trolling off the stern, Lonnegan sitting in his swivel seat with one eye on the Garmin.

It was looking good until the monitor began to beep.

"Ah, this reminds me of fishing off the Great Barrier Reef," Heiney was telling his colleagues, oblivious to the fact that nothing about the narrows of World's End remotely resembled the huge expanses off the coast of Australia. Heiney, a retired English teacher from Paramus who had actually never done any sort of deep-sea fishing other than an aborted fishing charter out of Point Pleasant four years previous had assiduously built himself up in their neighborhood as something of a daring adventurer and world traveler. His long summer absences from the neighborhood were in truth spent out at an old family cabin in the Poconos reading and re-reading his extensive collection of Hemmingway novels and paying one of his ex-students to Photoshop his picture into exotic backdrops downloaded from Flickr. These he would have printed as glossy 4x6's at the local CVS and either pass off at neighborhood BBQ's or have framed and scattered around the house, augmented by various keepsakes he claimed were 'picked up' in his travels (but which were in actuality purchased off of eBay or Amazon).

Bob Clarkson and Ted Osterling, the two software engineers who were in awe of their 'worldly' neighbor, had been talked into their current adventure a month before when Heiney had approached them with 'how about joining me for my annual Hudson River Fishing Charter next month?' That had been roughly fifteen minutes after Jerome Burke – the South African videographer - who with his girlfriend was hosting that particular Sunday BBQ – had pulled Heiney aside and outright accused him of being a fake. Burke didn't have any specific evidence to support this other than realizing a lot of Heiney's verbose tales never seemed to really add up. Heiney had hotly denied this (which only further convinced Burke that his neighbor was lying) and not long after an extended visit to the bathroom, Heiney brought up the fishing charter business.

And here they were.

Heiney had dropped the eel he was trying to bait three times before he finally asked for assistance, claiming his 'arthritis was acting up.' Not saying a word (but noting the squeamish look on his neighbor's face), Burke had plunged his hand in the sand pail, plucked the squirming eel off the deck and hooked it in practically one fluid motion. Heiney made a clumsy cast accompanied by an exaggerated wince while noting to himself in a grim tone, "A man can be destroyed but not defeated ..."

Clarkson and Osterling simply nodded at this apparent pearl of wisdom while Burke tried not to burst out laughing, thinking, *God, the old man is utterly shameless about stealing his idols' quotes* when the boat gave a sudden lurch.

"Hey, this isn't—!" Heiney managed to get out before Juarez' powerful brown hand caught his arm and stopped him from pitching over the stern rail. A second later, Lonnegan was there, gripping the rail and glaring at the water as if daring whatever had just struck them to show itself.

"Was that a log?" Clarkson asked at his side.

"No ... that wasn't no *log*," Lonnegan said through his (remaining) clenched teeth. He was focused on the area of water off the starboard quarter which was beginning to froth and seethe.

"What the hell is that?" someone else spoke up. The truth was, Lonnegan hadn't a clue. The fish finder had showed a massive object rocketing up from the depths that was now floating about five feet below the surface. But how anything that big could float in position in such a powerful current didn't make any sense. Without warning, something large shot out of the water and tumbled like an ungainly football to bounce and land on the back deck.

The group of men looked down, shocked, to see the severed head of a river sturgeon lying there, its gills still pulsing.

Then whatever was in the water began to move towards them.

Lonnegan reacted instantly. He hissed 'Shit!' and shoving past the men at the stern bolted to the skipper's chair and thumbed the ignition button. The turbo diesels began to turn over sluggishly as Lonnegan muttered urgently, "Come on, come on you bitch ..."

By the stern of the boat, the five men stood by the now-forgotten fishing rigs and gaped at the nightmare apparition emerging out of the water. The gigantic greenish-black head of the thing resembled the plated carapace of some sort of sea bug or isopod merged with a giant squid, if that squid had clusters of tentacles, many ending in an array of chitinous hooks.

Osterling had half-turned to Lonnegan and managed to say, "Uh, Captain, I think we should—" before one massive tentacle whipped through the air and plucked him out of the boat like a kind of hideous rodeo trick. His scream was lost in the roar of the diesels as the engines came to life, belching smoke out of the exhaust ports. Even as Lonnegan rammed the throttles forward, however, the thing latched onto the boat with what seemed like dozens of tentacles.

Juarez was instantly crushed against the rail while the sudden weight at the back of the boat caused the bow to angle up out of the water. Clarkson and Heiney tumbled over the stern and into the frothing mess, screaming, while Burke was able to leap to his left and grapple the side rail with both hands. The engines struggled against the tremendous additional weight as the screams were lost in the cacophony of metal and fiberglass groaning and snapping. Tentacles – some thick as a telephone pole – flicked and writhed through the air as the thing yanked the ship even further into its merciless grip. The engine screws must have torn into the thing's flesh as it let out an enraged buzzing/clicking sound and attacked the boat even more aggressively, ripping off whole pieces it. Heiney managed to haul himself up briefly onto what was now only a partially attached stern rail, and when Clarkson tried to grab onto him for help, the retired teacher kicked him away in a panic.

"Help me!" Clarkson screamed, even as two fat black tentacles wrapped around his torso and squeezed. Blood and gore ruptured out of his mouth, spraying Heiney, before his body was whisked out of sight. Heiney tried to pull himself up further into the boat, instead slashing his right forearm to the bone on a jagged piece of fiberglass where the hull had been fractured. Panicked and heart hammering with adrenaline, he made a valiant effort regardless, bringing one chubby leg up for traction until he realized with horror his foot was no longer attached to it. His lips were quivering in fear as it seemed to finally sink in that none of this was going to end well. Then there was a violent tug at his other leg, and he was screaming as his femur was torn out of the hip socket, enveloping him in a sheet of white agony. His screams were cut short as a thinner tentacle whipped through the air and plunged into his mouth, shredding esophagus and vocal chords as it shot all the way down into his stomach, rupturing it. The last thing he saw before his consciousness winked out was dinner plate-sized eye with its strange w-shaped iris, then his corpse was being chopped up by the scissoring beak of the thing's mouth.

The boat tilted even further up and Burke swung himself out over the side and jumped into the water, slapping aside a few tentacles in the process, his life vest taking several ragged slices. Lonnegan, meanwhile, found himself literally hanging off his swivel chair, his face set in a rictus of terror. He had enough time to consider reaching for the side drawer next to the seat where he always kept a loaded .44 magnum, but even as began to unclench the fingers of his right hand from the chair, he was snatched off by two tentacles thick as his legs. One wrapped around his waist, the other his chest, and with an awful rip twisted his body in two, spilling his insides across the sinking deck.

Burke was flailing in the water a few yards away, only his life vest keeping him afloat as the current threatened to drag him under, when something splashed into the water next to him. There was just enough light for him to register that it was Lonnegan, and for a crazy moment, he thought the skipper was there to help, then the body tipped and Burke saw that there was nothing left of the man from the ribcage down. Unable to control himself, he began vomiting in the water.

More cracking and groans followed as the *Artful Dodger* was pulled down to its watery grave, so violently that the suction drew Burke and the corpse of the skipper under and into the blackness ...

Miles away, Easton had dozed off on top of his bed, the book he had been reading – *The Italian Secretary* by Caleb Carr – cracked open across his chest. He had drifted into yet another variation on a recurring nightmare, this one where he and Sarah were on a yacht drifting down the Hudson. It was one of those classic 1930s ketches, with teak trim and brass porthole windows along the main cabin. In fact, the boat looked suspiciously like *Solomon's Seal*, the yacht owned by the late Harold Hilderman, the unscrupulous businessman who had been murdered up at Taron Hall.

Sarah was calmly explaining about the differences between various petroglyphs she'd studied but Easton wasn't listening; he was staring with growing horror at the tentacles monstrosity erupting out of the water behind her. In his head, he was screaming but his dream-self was simply sitting there, frozen, while Sarah rambled on oblivious to the monster about to attack them. He could smell it too – a cloying aroma of rotting fish and things long dead in the murky silt of the briny depths. Not until the writhing shadows of the giant tentacles blotted out the sunlight did she look up, then the world capsized in an explosion of snapping timbers and blood ...

Easton's eyelids fluttered as he woke up, half-knocking the book off his chest. For a disorientated moment, he looked wildly around the bedroom as if he'd never seen it before.

Slowly, however, the familiar elements re-asserted themselves; the arched mission-style footboard at the bottom of the bed, the 'six over one' grilles of the double windows opposite, the mellow glow from the antique mica-shaded lamp on the nightstand next to him. Despite being at the front of the house, it was a good bedroom for sleeping – spacious yet cozy, with rich oak woodwork and walls painted in a warm golden hue. Above the wide shaker dresser to his right was an oversized framed print of a 19th-century autumn morning scene of 'Raquette Lake in Adirondacks' by A.F. Tait – a gift from a recent job he'd helped out a local historian on. For a moment, it almost looked like the deer in the picture were moving … or perhaps it was something moving in the reflection off the glass … like a spectral figure dodging out of sight.

Easton rubbed his eyes and sat up in bed. He'd kicked off his shoes but was still fully dressed in jeans and a black denim shirt, and still had on his shoulder holster with the 92FS Beretta in it. Next to the lamp, the Naxa digital alarm clock read 10:17pm.

He was debating whether he should call Sarah when he realized someone was standing in the open doorway of the bedroom. At first, this didn't make any sense – Rovsky would have alerted him to anyone entering the house, and if it was a stranger, they wouldn't have gotten a foot into the premises before finding themselves in a very serious predicament. Someone had once told Easton that having a Ovcharka around the house was akin to having a loaded gun laying around – you'd better know exactly where it is at all times.

So who was this phantom visitor?

The hallway light was off and the figure looked more shadow than substance.

A ghost? A—?

The figure edged ever so slightly more into the light, revealing the decimated corpse of a black man dressed in a British police uniform. The uniform – the same dress one he had been buried in – was now stained with body fluids and sprouting several colorful colonies of mold. Even in this grossly decayed form, Easton recognized his close friend and fellow policeman from the Royal Turks and Caicos Islands Police Force: Constable Drex Pearson.

Pearson had been dead some four years now, gunned down in the fiasco of Easton's last official case there, but was apparently still up and about and making the rounds. The last time he had seen Pearson (or his ghost at least) was at the beginning of another near disaster, the one up at Van Eyckmann's estate – Taron Hall.

Easton's hand went subconsciously to his chest where Pearson's Saint Christopher's medallion hung from a leather thong under his shirt. That too had materialized – impossibly – while at Taron Hall. Just in time to save his skin as it were.

"Drex?" he asked.

"J-John," his dead friend answered in a garbled, somehow *wet* voice. Easton noticed that one of the eyes was opaque white, the other obscured by a spider web. He could just see the slender brown legs of the arachnid poised just inside. Pearson had taken a bullet through that eye, if memory served.

The blackened teeth continued to work. "J-John … you're running out of time … you'll have to let her go …"

Easton sat frozen. "What do you mean? Let *who* go?"

But even as he looked, the apparition of his friend was dissolving, losing form. But as it did, there was no missing the hissing echo of his last word drifting around the room, "S-S-Sarah …"

Easton leapt out of the bed. "Drex? Drex!?" he hissed.

Nothing.

Rattled, Easton headed quietly down the stairs in his socks. When he got to the bottom landing, he could see Rovsky stretched out on the wood floor, his legs twitching and little *huffs* coming from his jowls.

Guess I'm not the only one having bad dreams, he thought.

Minutes later, he was sitting in his overstuffed cigar chair, a tumbler of single malt scotch at his elbow, the wireless phone to his ear. Rovsky had awakened long enough to relocate himself near Easton's feet. The few lights on gave the room a moody, nostalgic atmosphere, accenting the oak ceiling beams and wainscoting. From speakers mounted in the built-in bookshelves surrounding the fieldstone fireplace the strains of Debussy's "La Mer: I. from Dawn Till Noon On the Sea" eased through the room. Above the mantel was a large framed print of 18th-century ship under full sail titled, "A Corvette in Passing Squall over Portsmouth."

"How are you doing?" he spoke into the phone.

"I'm good," came Sarah's sleepy voice from the other end. "Yes, I'm good," she repeated, as if to reassure herself of the fact. She sounded breathy and intimate. "How is my favorite English detective doing?"

Easton let that linger in his ear a moment before replying. "Just woke up. Dozed off while reading. I think I'm starting to become like my old man. I used to laugh at how he'd nod off reading a book by 9pm. Pretty soon, I'll just be shuffling about in only my boxer shorts and smelly leather slippers, hair standing up in tufts while muttering curses at the telly."

Sarah laughed on the other end, and for an aching moment, he wanted nothing more than to hold her, and feel her warmth.

"Well, maybe you'll find yourself stuck with a crazy old squaw in a bathrobe and worn-out moccasins, whacking you on the head with a wooden spoon and telling you to shut up."

That got one out of Easton in return. He took a healthy pull off the scotch and savored the mellow warmth diffusing through his chest.

The silence drew out a bit and then she asked, "Bad dreams again?"

"Yeah. And you?"

Another silence. Then: "Yes. Maybe you should bring me a bunch of those dream catcher thingies."

"Do they really work?" he asked.

"Well … only if you're an Ojibwe. But they also work well for separating white men from the green stuff in their wallets."

"Good to know," Easton said. "Well, I just wanted to check in." What he really wanted right then was to spend every waking second with her, but he wasn't about to say that.

"I'm glad you did. Are you free tomorrow?"

"I'll be in White Plains in the morning with a client, but the afternoon looks good."

"Maybe I can swing by early … before dinner?" Her voice grew quiet. "I have a little surprise for you."

"In that case, the afternoon is looking *really* good."

Sarah laughed. "I'll see you tomorrow, then. But John?"

"Yes?"

"Try and get some sleep. I think we're both going to need it … I think the hard part comes next."

Easton was puzzled. "What do you mean?"

"We'll know when we get there. Sweet dreams."

"You too."

He sat there a moment, aware that she hadn't hung up but was sitting quietly on the other end of the line. Then he added, "Good night, Sarah." And hung up.

He sat there staring into the quiet room, feeling elated, perplexed, and worried. It was several hours before he got back to bed.

22. "I DON'T THINK THEY WANTED TO HEAR THAT ... "

Friday morning arrived like so many in the Hudson River region this time of year; a clear cool morning with an occasional seagull or red-tailed hawk arcing through the sky; a subtle clarity in the atmosphere as if the world was offering up a good long look at this last image of summer before the whole stage was switched over to autumn.

Chief Hendricks called the press conference right at lunchtime so anyone involved in local businesses could attend. 'Press Conference' was a bit of a stretch – it wasn't like it was attended by the major news organizations and a huge crowd (though reporter Donna Hartley, Westchester News 12's latest acquisition was there) – but it was still a newsworthy event in a village like Wyvern Falls, where these days almost all pressing announcements were conveyed through web blasts these days.

Hendricks, however, knowing this was probably going to be the most unpopular announcement in his career as police chief to date, figured the best way to tackle it was head on and in person. One thing his father ingrained in him from an early age was that if you were going to say something that was going to piss a lot of people off, the only proper way to do it was to look them square in the eye as you did and then take what was coming.

This event, however, was certainly a first in village history; not only was he about to shut down the GreenWater Festival for the first time in its forty-odd years of being held, as an official, he was about to do it alone – Mayor Sanchez was nowhere in sight. Which in itself he found troubling.

Only Captain Fowler and Lieutenant Sanchez were at his side.

A portable podium with speakers had been set up in front of the red sandstone art deco building that was the police station, a building that harkened back to the dusty Depression-era days of FDR and Public Works Projects. The station itself had been designed by the eccentric architect (and long vanished) Frank Baum, who had been apparently obsessed with the justice theme of '*O Fortuna.*' Bronze disks and deco-esque eagles carried the motif across the façade.

Roughly fifty or so people had gathered on the steps of the station to hear the police chief's announcement – about a third local business people but the majority vendors and supporters of the GreenWater Festival.

At age fifty-five, Roy Hendricks looked just as trim and eagle-eyed as he had in his younger days as a New York State Trooper. A sharp-featured man with hooded, grey-blue eyes, he looked as ready and able to take the world down as ever, in a regulation choke-hold if necessary. Only the crow's feet gathered around those eyes, the slight tinge of gray around his temples, and the weathered counters of his face betrayed his age. He stood with his hands on his hips, facing the crowd defiantly.

After clearing his throat once and tapping the microphone, he jumped right in, "Folks, I'd like to thank you for coming here today to hear what, as many of you already know, is a difficult – and no doubt highly unpopular decision for me to announce … that is of course that in the interest of public safety, Raadsel Point will be closed until further notice. Unfortunately, that means with it the GreenWater Festival will be shut down with it this year, unless a more suitable, safer location can be –"

Here, the chief was cut off by a barrage of boos and hisses. Assorted catcalls were hurled at him – "*Fascist!*", "*Pigs!*" "*You have no legal right!*" – along with more colorful expletives. All which Hendricks bore with steely calm, like a tank that has to take a bunch of small-arms fire before it can continue.

He waited until the worst of it had died down then holding up one hand, continued, "Folks, this isn't a decision I've made lightly because I'm well aware of the importance, both culturally and financially to all of us here, but the fact is …"

Here, he was cut off by a bearded young man with scraggly hair and a 'Give Peace A Chance" T-shirt, "—Fact is *what*, man!?" he hissed. "You're leveraging this whole 'Ossie' business to suppress us? Fucking typical establishment bullshit!"

"Yeah, and where's the mayor? Why isn't he with you on this?" said a woman Hendricks recognized as Rita Conklin, the village 'cat lady' who made trouble at every weekly village hall meeting for lack of nothing better to do.

"He's afraid of a sea monster!" a reedy voice chimed in from the back.

"Look, three people are confirmed dead, four more are missing," Hendricks said loudly, enough to temporarily squash further outbreaks. "And that's three (and four) too many. You appointed me to protect this community, so that is exactly what I am doing. Now any questions? Make them legitimate."

"Maybe they were a bunch of Wall Streeters! Fuckers had it coming!" someone yelled.

Hendricks shook his head, both annoyed and amused. He pointed to Donna Hartley, who looked like she might have the only sensible question of the bunch.

"Chief Hendricks, can you comment on the rumors that there is a monster out in the river killing people?" she asked.

"Not with any certainty,' he shot back, thinking, *Christ almighty, I can't believe this is even a topic I'm addressing*, "but it's under investigation. If there is anything out there responsible for these deaths, it'll be dealt with. We're already consulting with a marine biologist on the matter. I'll be happy to share whatever we find, *when* find it." He pointed to a sandy-haired man he recognized as Jan Kruger, a local realtor.

"Is it true the Navy is sending up a cutter armed with a Seals team and depth charges to deal with this thing?" Kruger asked.

Hendricks gave him a *'you've got to be kidding'* look. "Not that I'm aware of. You need to knock off the Clancy novels, Jan. Next?"

"What about the kid they found last year out at the point – the one whose friends disappeared? I heard he's finally come out of his coma – can you comment on that?"

That one caught Hendricks by surprise. Curtis Jackson had been something of an unsolved mystery case for them since the boy was discovered by a photographer covered in blood and in a state of shock by the remains of a huge wooden crate washed up on Raadsel Point the year before. The doctors at Philipseburg Memorial said he was suffering from traumatic shock. By the time the police had arrived, some damned salvager had attempted to haul it onto a barge, but in its frail condition, it had disintegrated and broken up into the river, its evidence contaminated. Hendricks had been furious.

But Curtis Jackson out of his coma? The hospital should have contacted him immediately. He glanced down at his cell phone. Sure enough there *had* been a call, twenty-two minutes ago. He'd been in his office catching hell from the festival vendors and missed it. *But how had ...?* He glanced through the crowd to see who had asked the question, but only caught a small man with long grey hair walking away. Crazy Jack? What the hell would he know?

Hendricks looked back over the crowd and leaning into the mic said, "That'll be it for now. And we'll be contacting vendors and organizers directly to resolve refunds and our financial obligations. Until then, thanks for your cooperation and folks, *please* stay off the Point. I'm dead serious about this. Any violators will be arrested."

With that, he turned on his heel and went back through the main doors of the police station, chased by a few more catcalls and boos.

As they entered the main room with the dispatcher's desk, Lieutenant Sanchez said quietly to the chief, "I don't think they wanted to hear that…"

Hendricks shook his head in response and out of the side of his mouth replied, "Yeah, well I liked telling them that even less."

The first thing he was going to do back in his office was to call the hospital. Then he had to find out what in the hell the mayor had gotten up to.

23. OLD MAN DIMAS.

Easton was just about to turn onto Irving Avenue when he spotted Old Man Dimas. He was sitting out front of his son's house on the low wall by the sidewalk in his usual stiff-backed hands-on-knees pose, thick framed glasses gazing up at the heavens.

Easton pulled the car over and got out. It was only one-thirty and he had some time before Sarah came by to head out to dinner. In the meantime, he had a very important question for his neighbor.

Raymundo Dimas, or 'Rambo' as he preferred to be called – he'd seen the movie only once back in the 1980s but became enamored with the name – was something of a local character and curbstone philosopher as many in the neighborhood could testify. He was also the grandfather of Luis Dimas, whom Easton had helped out of a jam or two over the years. A short, barrel-chested man with abnormally long arms and hands and a spray of white hair that stood up like a surprised dandelion, Dimas had first arrived in America back in the 1970s after establishing himself as a stonemason back in Portugal. The story was that he got off the boat, took one long sniff of New York City air, and decided immediately to head north to Westchester where'd heard about a job opportunity in a quarry. As the tale went, he confused 'Wappinger Falls' with 'Wyvern Falls' and ended up in the wrong place, but upon getting directions straightened out by a fine-looking Portuguese woman named Eva, he decided to stick around and marry her. The rest, as they always say, was history.

Long since retired, Dimas kept himself busy around the household with odd fixer-upper projects and an outrageously overgrown garden. He and Eva lived in a separate basement apartment while his son's family lived upstairs.

Once in a while, Easton would stop by – usually while out walking Rovsky – and have a few words with the old man. The conversations were usually interesting and often half-speculative; 'Rambo' Dimas had a tendency to mash English and Portuguese together with perplexing results for people like Easton, though usually enough got through to get the gist of the matter.

"*Alô!*" Easton said, sitting himself down next to the old man. Dimas looked at him, eyes made enormous by the thick lenses, and nodded as if he'd expected Easton to be there all along. He had on an old pair of jeans and one of his faded blue flannel shirts, which he seemed to have a whole closet of.

"*Alô*," he replied, returning his gaze to the distant horizon. Easton knew to wait and let the old man speak. It was almost always worth it.

After the space of a few minutes while a car or two drove by and a cardinal made a circuit of the neighborhood, Dimas began by squeezing his kneecaps. "Jeesh," he said in his halting English, "You know … the secret to happiness? *No big secret.*" His scarred hands came up for emphasis as his shoulders bunched up into one of his professional shrugs. "We always want something better … a better lawn. A better woman. A better house. That thing over there, it always looks *better*. I say, *stop looking over there*." The hands patted the stone wall. "Look *here*. At what you already have. That's it."

Easton, leaning forward with his forearms on his legs, chuckled. "You may be onto something there, Rambo. Look, there's something I wanted to ask you about."

"Okay."

"Years ago, before you came to the U.S., did you by any chance work as a sailor?"

Both of Dimas' bushy eyebrows went up and Easton got a wary, sideways look.

"Why do you ask this?"

Because it's a small fucking world, mate, Easton wanted to say, *and no matter how much time or distance you think you put behind you, it always comes back around in one full circle and bites you in the ass.* He didn't need an answer to know the truth though, really. Nor the psychic flash that came along with Dimas' dilating pupils:

Fear … the smell of brine and ocean. Paolo – a wiry man, impossibly thin, known for his cat green eyes and white grin, now desperate, slashing furiously at the tangled lines with his knife. Time seems to slow down as the huge jaws of the thing breaches the ocean's surface, foaming seawater streaming away from those rows of wickedly curved teeth … stained, glistening: he clearly sees the dappled light and dark pattern of its reptilian skin and something even stranger; the lower jaw flexing as if attached by a secondary hinge, like a python. Dimas isn't even aware that he's screaming at the top of his lungs, his entire focus is on Paolo's head turning towards him as they lock eyes briefly … those bright green eyes that were always so mischievous, now filled with nothing but glassy, naked terror … a spray of water droplets … the whitish pink flesh of the cavernous inside of the monsters mouth … then a resounding 'kachump!' as the jaws snap shut, smashing bones, wood, and rigging alike. Bright red blood and seawater jetting in all directions, Paolo gone in a flash, except for the torn half of a hand cartwheeling through the air.

His friend. Paolo. Devoured in an instant. Like chum.

For a space, Dimas didn't say anything. He just sat there, eyes boring into Easton's and Easton saw it all; terror, horror, pain, misery and even anger; anger at bringing this all back from the dim recesses of memory.

All this time, I had no idea the terrible memories that lurked just below the surface, the nightmares that crept into his dreams at night ...

Easton drew back slightly, thrown by the intensity of emotions in the old man's face and feeling a sharp pang of guilt at being the instrument of them. But, of course, he really wasn't; it was whatever was lurking out there in the Hudson River that was the root of all this.

Now Easton knew for certain. Whatever was out there wasn't any hoax.

"*Nuno Tristão,*" he said.

Dimas' eyebrows went even higher, all the way to his white hairline it seemed. Then he looked away. Suddenly, he looked ten years older, his features sagging. A single tear worked its way down one seamed cheek. Easton felt terrible. In a way, he loved the old man like a surrogate grandfather, enjoyed their random meet-ups and casual conversations unfettered by designs; mostly Dimas' bits of life-wisdom or observations doled out almost as if for his own self-amusement.

"So, you know," Dimas finally said. He sounded resigned. "How?"

"I found a report. Or rather, someone found it for me. It had your account in it – the one you gave to the man on Jacques Cousteau's ship."

Dimas nodded. He didn't ask how or why Easton came by this information, he seemed to just accept it. He grunted. "Hmph. I never set foot on a boat again after that. I swore to keep both feet on solid ground until I die. That's how I became a stonemason, but I never told my family, not even my Eva, what happened. I didn't come to the United States until I could save enough money to *fly.*" He carefully placed both hands on the stonewall on either side of him, as if drawing emotional support from the contact. "So now you know what I-I-I spent a life to forget. And you bring back my pain. Why?"

Without thinking, Easton placed his hand on the old man's shoulder. Even though Dimas was pushing eighty, the shoulder felt as solid as granite. "I'm sorry, Rambo, I truly am. But I had to bring it up. Because ... well, because it's back."

Dimas jerked his head around and stared at Easton. The glasses made him look comically wide-eyed. "*Back?* What do you mean?"

"Back as in out in the river there. Something, or *someone* has brought it here. Now it's out in the river, killing people. Somehow, I have to find a way to help stop it. I haven't a clue though. That's the only reason I brought this up with you … maybe something useful you might remember?"

Dimas shuddered. "All I remember was fear, and wanting to run like a coward. Shame." He shrugged again. "I-I what would I know about killing such a thing? It's a giant sea monster. Stay away from this thing. It can only bring you pain and misery. And death."

"Yeah, I was afraid of that. But if you think of anything, anything at all, let me know. Can you do that?"

Dimas didn't reply, however; he simply looked off into the distance as if gazing back through time at old faces. And old nightmares.

24. "... ANYTHING LARGER THAN A CARP IN THE WATER, SHOOT IT."

The sea green painted room located on the third floor of the Philipseburg Memorial Inpatient Psychiatric Unit had a scenic view of the Hudson and the old Victorian 'Vandersteen' house at the edge of the hospital grounds, with its cupola and widow's walk. The room was essentially a calm plain envelope with nothing more than a bed, and IV and monitor, with a side table, two chairs, and a wall-mounted television that was never on. The side table had an assortment of family photos, a G.I. Joe 'Retaliation Roadblock' figure, and a baseball. For the past year, the rooms' one full-time occupant was the now eleven-year-old Curtis Jackson, who had been a comatose state since witnessing the traumatic deaths of his two friends at Raadsel Point.

He wasn't without visitors during that time – his parents were there at least twice a week along with his two sisters, and from time to time, classmates from Washington Irving Middle School would drop by for a visit, though those visits had been tapering off over the course of the year. And there was nothing on this particular Friday morning to suggest it would be any different from the 395 days preceding it.

And yet at 11:21 a.m., all of that abruptly changed.

Curtis was sitting in the adjustable bed, propped up by pillows, his skin looking slightly flushed from the physical therapist's visit an hour earlier. Then, just as the second hand on the wall clock ticked onto the twelve o'clock position, his eyes abruptly opened.

In the black hole that had enveloped, then swallowed up his conscious thoughts since that fateful day, an image had taken form moments before. To his eleven-year-old brain, it didn't make a whole lot of sense; an old disheveled-looking Indian, with rumpled clothes that looked like they hadn't been washed in weeks and wearing a face that was kind but possessed a weathered sadness about it. At first, he seemed to materialize out of the formless void. Then the Indian opened his mouth, enough for Curtis to observe his even, still-white teeth.

"Wake up," the old Indian said.

And Curtis did.

For a disorientating moment after his eyes opened, he could still see the Indian at the foot of his bed, bathed in an iridescent/silvery light. Then as the Indian dissolved, a flood of nightmare images bubbled up from Curtis's subconscious like noxious gasses released from a bog; whipping tentacles, a spray of blood … the *pop!* of snapping bones … and that hideous squishing sound of something expanding… awakening…

Even as the monitors erupted in a cacophony of beeps and alerts, Curtis began to scream.

It took a moment for his dry and flaccid vocal chords to get their act together, then they found the found they had pretty good memory as well.

It was just after 2 p.m. and Chief Hendricks was standing in the waiting room, talking with Lieutenant Sanchez and Detective Eckhart. Curtis Jackson's family was still over in the room with him, still coming to grips with the shock of getting their son back after so long. Although the kid was now sedated, Hendricks had sent in Eckhart as soon as the doctors permitted to get a much awaited statement.

What Curtis Jackson told her wasn't sitting that well with the police chief. In fact, the details Eckhart was now relaying to him – combined with everything else that had been going on – was giving him what he used to call a good case of the 'Heebie Jeebies.'

"He said tentacles came out of the crate and killed his two friends?"

Eckhart, looking sharp as ever in her pressed uniform, stood with her arms crossed and looked up at Hendricks intently.

"That's what he said. In excruciating detail. I don't think he's making this up. It fits with all the evidence of what's been happening here recently, which he couldn't have known about. Even if he had overheard someone talking about it, there were key bits we didn't leak out to the press."

I was afraid you were going to say that, Hendricks thought. Thumbs hooked in his belt, aloud he said, "So let me get this straight. Last year, three kids stumbled onto an antique crate that's washed up on the Point, a crate that contains some sort of dormant giant sea creature that wakes up, eats two of the kids, then smashes its way out and into the river. Is that about the cut of it?"

"It gets better, Chief," Sanchez cut in. "The kid distinctly remembers seeing the name '*Edmund G. Wood*' on the side of the crate. If you remember, Captain Fowler verified that ship foundered and sank near World's End back in 1904. Even stranger, someone dug up a monograph on it recently at the Historical Society."

Hendricks looked back and forth between his two officers with a look that implied he was really hoping he could make them tell a whole other story by sheer force of his will. One that sounded a lot less *crazier*.

Sanchez must have picked up on this as he raised his hands up in a placatory gesture. "We're not making this up, Chief. It's what we're getting."

Hendricks gaze zeroed in on the lieutenant. "I'm aware of that. What about that Reinhardt kid over at the NOAA? Has he been able to shed any more light on what we're dealing with?"

"He's still convinced it's the real deal. He's out there scanning the river right now using the inflatable rescue launch. But it's a lot of area to cover. Still, he'll let us know the minute he has anything. Plus, as you requested, Fowler is out patrolling the river on the police boat with four of our best sharpshooters on board. And we've notified the departments up and down the river that an 'undetermined threat' maybe in the area that's being investigated. The local fishermen weren't too pleased and we have a bunch of police departments scratching their heads, but it's enough due diligence to cover our butts if it anything else happens and vague enough to cover it if it doesn't. Also, I've set up spotters at the locations you specified along the shore. I'm not sure what else we can do at this point, unless you want to get the Coast Guard involved."

Hendricks gaze relented and he put a hand on Sanchez' shoulder as he steered them toward the exit. "We'll leave them out of it for the moment. Their district commander and I locked horns a few times in the past, so I won't make that call unless it's completely necessary." They paused as they came up on the nurse's station.

"So what's your next move, Chief?" Sanchez asked.

Hendricks rubbed the bridge if his nose with his thumb and forefinger. "We just have to hold tight for the moment. But I'll tell Fowler that if he spots anything larger than a carp in the water, shoot it."

25. "YOU LOOK LIKE THAT CRAZY GUY ON TV ..."

"Mom, listen to me ... I said I was sorry ... *fifteen* times already! Okay, fourteen. I told you something came up. I know Sherrie is your favorite niece ... the wedding will survive without me, I'm sure. Of course I'm not ashamed of being Albanian! I love being Albanian! It's the first thing I tell everyone I meet, yes I changed my name, but look at me, I'm an Albanian and proud of it! Why do you keep saying that? Yes ... I know I'll miss my cousins from Milwaukee ... look Mom, I'm driving a car ... I have to call you back ... yes, oh shit there's a cop ... I ... arggghhhh!" Guillamo Del Tesler rolled his eyes and tossed the phone to the passenger seat of the rental car. For a moment, a garbled shrieking voice came out of it, then Del Tesler grabbed it again and turned it off.

It had been the third call from his mother since leaving the city. The first one had come while sitting in a massive traffic jam just off the Triborough Bridge, which despite being renamed the 'Robert Kennedy Bridge' six years previous was *always* going to be the Triborough in his mind. There was nothing remotely 'Kennedy' about the bridge (or *bridges* – there were actually three); it all but announced itself as a blue-collar, Depression-era project where function was the focus, not form.

Del Tesler had been dreading going to his cousin's wedding out in Long Island, knowing from experience his mother would be parading him shamelessly before friends and family like he was a circus act, ("My son, the celebrity! He's on television *you know*! He's very famous!") while his father would sit in the background, no doubt muttering, "Yeah, but when is he going to get a God-damned real job?" under his breath. Just before leaving before rush hour on Thursday, he'd phoned his parents and in a rare stroke of luck got their answering machine where he'd left his regretful sounding message, or at least one as regretful as he could make it.

Then the phone calls began.

Followed by the text messages.

They were all variations on the same theme: *Why would you do this to us? Where did we go wrong with you? Why do you hate us so?* And the classic: *Why are you so ashamed of your heritage? You should be proud of it!"*

None of which was really true, he told himself, well, *almost* not really. It wasn't his heritage he was ashamed of, it was the embarrassing way his mother shoved him in front of everyone's faces. Because the real reason she was going ballistic this fine September afternoon had nothing to do with the aforementioned accusations but everything to do with his mother's ego and incessant need to prove herself better than anyone else around her. Which was one of the key reasons Ron Schmensky had become Guillamo Del Tesler.

The phone buzzed again just as Del Tesler turned the Hyundai Sonata he'd rented into the small parking lot of 'The Horseman' diner in Sleepy Hollow. It was the one place he remembered from a road trip years ago and he figured he'd better grab a late lunch before heading all the way up to Wyvern Falls.

He was expecting the call to be Guilt Tirade Installment #4 from his mother but was surprised to see it was an overseas number. He backed into a parking spot and answered it.

"Hello?"

"Guillamo? It's Otto," said his mentor in his thick German accent. "Where are you?"

"Stopping for lunch. I'll be in Wyvern Falls shortly. I'm picking up the crew in the morning but figured I'd have a look around first. Did you get the pictures?" Del Tesler had sent digital photos of the rocks he'd received via FedEx the day before, along with a .pdf of the 2003 report of the hi-resolution sonar scan conducted by the State of New York of the Hudson River bottom, which had revealed some interesting things in the area around Wyvern Falls and Raadsel Point. Otto Wierling was visiting relatives over in Switzerland, five hours ahead of him.

"Yes yes, very excellent. I think we have enough material for another documentary. Maybe even two, *ja*?"

"Definitely," Del Tesler answered enthusiastically. "The evidence is better than I thought. I'm pretty sure they're submerged runways. And the Indian artifacts ... it all fits! I'm pretty sure we—" His voice was interrupted by a call-waiting beep. "Mom" came up on the caller screen.

"... Otto, did you (BEEP) get that?" Del Tesler tried to pick up his conversation

"Huh? I did not catch that, Guillamo. What did you say?"

"Well, it's very suggestive, isn't it? The fact that (BEEP) clearly shows that ... Otto? Otto?" Del Tesler, for all his tech-savvy skills, still had a tendency to get derailed by the combination of call-waiting/hypersensitive touch screen functions on his phone. He jabbed his finger at the screen. "Hello? Hello?"

"– HOW DARE YOU –?" screamed his mother's voice.

"Well perhaps –" said Otto.

"-NEVER FORGIVE –"

"Hello? Are yo –?"

Exasperated, Del Tesler jabbed at his phone angrily another few seconds, eyes blinking rapidly, before giving up and tossing it aside. He got out of the car and slammed the door shut, fuming. His head was a white riot of emotions. Here he was, a grown man, 32 years old, a man who had been seen across the world on television, interviewed in Newsweek and counted 75,000 followers on his Twitter profile and over 160,000 likes on his Facebook page. And yet with a few quick pokes at his emotional buttons by his mother, he felt instantly reduced to a foot-stomping, temper-tantrum-throwing two year old who wanted nothing more to scream at the top of his lungs and hammer his fists onto something, anything.

Instead, he kicked the tire of the Hyundai.

"Ouch!" he said, toe smarting.

Del Tesler stood there a few minutes in the parking lot, moussed-up hair waving gently in the light breeze, nostrils flaring. Before him, Route 9 sloped down and curved out of sight. Towards the bottom where it curved north again was the real Sleepy Hollow – the one the Irving had written about at least – with its Old Dutch Church and cemetery and Pocantico River – though the covered bridge was long since gone. And further north, where it became Route 9B, lay Wyvern Falls and Raadsel Point and a beckoning opportunity to reboot his career.

As he slid into the booth by the windows, an eager-faced waitress who didn't look a day out of high school brought a menu and a glass of water. It was at least a step up from his last visit years ago when he had been served by a tired-looking middle-aged woman who smelled of clove cigarettes and was wearing cut-off shorts. A quick glance at the menu revealed they had his two favorite items, mac & cheese and chamomile tea, the two things he ate and drank obsessively. The diner was predictably decked out in all things Horseman, including a framed poster from the 1999 Burton movie and a plastic model of horse-mounted Christopher Walken's diabolical Prussian displayed on a shelf.

He had just placed his order when a moment later, a weathered-faced old man who might be a truck driver or contractor leaned over from the next booth over and with a leering eye said, "Hey, you look like that crazy guy on TV."

Del Tesler, who never shied at being recognized better or for worse, smiled and cupped his hands in front of him. "So I've been told."

The man studied him, eyes squinting. "Hmmm. Well, you *kind* of look like him … almost, but no cigar," he said, then turned back to the local paper he had been reading.

Indignant, Del Tesler was about to respond when he was distracted by another person coming up to his table. He looked up to see a pretty Goth/Emo dressed girl with low-hipped jeans, a torn T-shirt, and an assortment of piercings. Her dyed black hair was a tough contender to his for mousse consumption and was swirled around her head like a frozen storm.

"Guillamo?" she asked, just to be polite.

Del Tesler's face brightened. "Ah. You must be Jennie. Pull up a seat!"

To his surprise, she bent over and kissed him on the cheek, just a bit longer than was just being friendly. Del Tesler blushed. All thoughts of his mother went right by the board.

The day was suddenly looking up.

26. HUDSON RIVER, 3:08PM

The afternoon was turning into a breezy one out on the river with a stiff wind coming up out of the southeast, chasing cat's paws up the river while picturesque mountains of cumulus clouds rolled dramatically overhead.

Ben Reinhardt sat in the front of the launch, arms resting on his knees, looking down and trying to fight off motion sickness. In his hands was what looked like a large iPad tablet in a waterproof housing, which was picking up a data feed from the 'Phase Differencing Bathymetric Sonar Unit' on board through the sled being towed five meters behind the boat. The amazing part of the device wasn't just the 5 mm resolution of the 3-dimensional river bottom and the schools of fish above it, but the fact that it updated in real-time in whatever direction he pointed the tablet, provided it was downward. The problem was that, combined with the choppy water and the motion of the boat, it was difficult to stare at the screen for any length of time without getting seriously motion sick. Despite the fact that Reinhardt had never been seasick a day in his life.

Always a first time, his instructor had once told him.

Well fuck-me very much, he thought to himself as he looked up at the horizon again to steady his vision.

He had spent the previous day jumping through all sorts of administrative hoops but finally negotiated getting the phase differencing bathymetric sonar unit sent up. It had arrived just that morning and Reinhardt had been all but exploding with excitement. He was certain this wasn't any hoax; whatever was lurking in the river was going to turn the field of marine biology on its head and he was going to be the right man at the right time to do it … a once in a lifetime opportunity. And if he could play his cards right, maybe even make a fortune in the process. Or at least pay off his student loan in a hundred instead of six hundred years. The trick of course would be figuring out how one or both of the creatures could be captured. Without someone else claiming the credit. Reinhardt had been brainstorming various scenarios on that plan and had even called his old roommate Chad Metz at Columbia who specialized in whale biology. Chad, who was just wrapping up his graduate thesis, said he'd get back to him later that day with a few options.

In the meantime, the first step was for Reinhardt to capture some hard evidence.

It was a monotonous task, running the boat back and forth across the river in a standard 'mowing the lawn' pattern that was necessary ensure a comprehensive data capture – the sonar unit was steadily building a detailed point cloud of what was below independent of the handheld tablet – the tablets purpose was mainly as an interactive viewer, though it could also record stills or movies. The downside – like all cutting-edge technologies – was that it still had a lot of bugs. Every so often the tablet would just lock up and the only solution would be to do a cold reboot – shutting it down and letting it sit long enough for the memory cache to clear itself out. Typically, that would happen at a critical moment – such as the start of a live demonstration with key officials and/or the press standing about – as if the unit was cursed by malicious nano-gremlins. Which Reinhardt was increasingly convinced it was.

Still, it was the best thing available that he could get his hands on.

At the back of the launch were the two police officers Captain Fowler had assigned him for that day. The pilot was a ruddy-faced young man named Liam Healey who looked fresh out of the academy – though his youthfulness was deceiving; his family had been working the river for three generations and Healey had all but grown up on a boat. Despite a disability, his father still worked part-time as a river pilot on the maintenance tug for the Tappan Zee Bridge.

Next to him was a police academy graduate from Healey's class – a muscular young black officer named Reggie Ducat. The two had been mortal enemies back in their high-school football days; now, they were all-but-inseparable best friends.

The launch had just completed its last circuit and was coming about near the western shore when Ducat spotted something floating in the water about sixty yards away. Ducat snatched up his binoculars to confirm what he already saw, a half-conscious man in a life vest adrift in the middle of the river. He immediately pointed and shouted at Healey to change course when the tablet in Reinhardt's hands began to emit a series of beeps that sounded like an angry bird.

Reinhardt aimed the tablet and was alarmed by the large blur zooming up from the south like some sort of whale on hyperdrive. Whatever it was, it was too large and fast for the microprocessors to handle. The screen froze. Any further speculation was rendered moot by what happened next.

The water around the man erupted as a massive reptilian head broke the surface, swallowing him nearly whole in gaping jaws lined with wicked-looking teeth. The force and momentum of the creature were terrifying. None of the three men had ever seen anything like it outside of a television documentary, and nothing approaching this scale: sixteen tons of sea dinosaur breaching the surface.

The momentum carried the thing nearly half out of the water, enough for the three slack-jawed men in the boat to see its fish-white underbelly and huge front fins. For one hideously majestic moment, it seemed to hang in the air, cascades of water streaming down its head and sides, one quivering human leg sticking out from its jaws. Then, with a heart-stopping snap, the jaws closed and gravity reasserted itself. The monster came back down and hit the water sideways with a thunderous clap that seemed to shake the whole river.

Unknowingly, they had just watched Jerome Burke meet his death.

Reinhardt sat mesmerized in the bow, unable to process what he had just witnessed. Though for one terrifying second, he would have sworn the things' basilisk gaze had locked onto him, as if to say, 'You're next on the menu.' He heard one of the policemen yelling, 'Holy fucking shit!' and then realized, with a very bad feeling in his guts, that the creature in the water had landed *toward* them.

He glanced down at the now useless hi-tech tablet in his hands and thought, *I'd trade every penny of the $290,000 price tag of this damned thing for an AK-47 right now. Hell, even a wood club. Anything to give me a fighting chance.*

Then he almost flipped backward as Healey gunned the throttle and the launch shot out obliquely from where the monster had just gone under. Healey may have been a seasoned river man beyond his years, but this was completely outside his scope.

He panicked.

Partly, it was the instant realization that despite the fiberglass hull, the rest of the boat was essentially just an inflatable raft, part of it was seeing how easily the creature had just swallowed an entire full-grown human being in a single bite. His only thought was to get the hell out of there immediately.

The launch veered wide and then began to swing back toward the Wyvern Falls Marina. Ducat was screaming into his handset, trying to raise Captain Fowler and his crew who were presently just north of Raadsel Point. But between the wind, the roar of the engine, and the constant *thwumping* of the boat impacting the waves, little if anything was getting through.

Reinhardt crouched in the front of the launch, terrified.

He didn't think the creature could catch them at this point – not unless its evolution included high-speed turbojets – but it was obvious they were approaching the docks way too fast. In other circumstances, he might have considered jumping off the boat, but there was no way he was going to take his chances with that thing in the water, no way at all, thank-you very much. Instead, he hunkered down as low as possible and prayed.

Healey did cut the throttles as they came up on the boat launch, but by then, it was already a matter of too little too late. The launch actually shot out of the water and up the ramp twenty or so feet before it slid and snagged on the low rock wall running alongside the launch. Then the boat flipped end over end.

Oddly, Reinhardt was spared the worst. He was slammed into the ground hard enough to get knocked out cold, but aside from some abrasions and bruises would walk away intact. The two policemen weren't quite so lucky, though they would at least both live. Healey cartwheeled into a park bench and broke both his legs and five ribs; Ducat tumbled into a 9-11 memorial sculpture and suffered a broken arm and fractured skull.

Later, both men would count themselves lucky.

The phase differencing bathymetric sonar unit snapped its securing straps and flew out of the boat after Ducat, missing him by a few feet but slamming full force into the same sculpture and smashing itself to pieces.

Not long after that the sirens began to wail.

27. THE MAYOR CUTS A DEAL ...

"Are you trying to ruin me?" the mayor hissed into the phone.

"Take it or leave it," Igor Gorimov fired back. "You want problem fixed? I fix it. But it'll cost you. Ten grand. Cash."

"Five grand, cash up front. Five after you deliver."

"Deal," Gorimov replied and hung up.

Mayor Santos had been carrying on with the Russian for ten minutes, negotiating up and down, forward and backwards in a whirlwind that would have left most men so dazed, confused, and confounded they probably wouldn't be able to remember their own mother's name for an hour or two.

Santos leaned back in his chair, his fingers playing with his moustache as he stifled a grin. *Crazy Russians*, he mused, *thinking they could out-negotiate the son of Alicia Santos – aka 'The General' – the five-foot-tall dynamo who was the terror of every merchant and retailer up and down the Hudson Valley.*

He'd just sealed the deal at half the price he told the promoters it was going to cost.

A hefty, immaculately groomed man with an impressive pompadour (which contrary to what many on the gossip mill asserted was completely natural, custom hair sculpting products aside), Santos had honed the open-armed, 'just a big teddy bear' charm to a science. In most ways, he was the consummate politician; charming, positive-minded, effusively tactful and photogenic on the outside, while inside operated a shrewd, merciless wheeler and dealer who almost always got what he wanted and would inevitably be deftly out of the picture should the chips fall on the wrong side.

His office on the second floor of the Wyvern Falls Municipal Building – that stalwart federal-style edifice on upper Main Street – was the sort of room Howard Taft or Teddy Roosevelt would have looked perfectly at home with, puffing on a cigar while fingering a watch fob hung across a bulging waistcoat.

Santos had made a few upgrades to the modern era, including a laptop and cordless phone system, but the aging wood panels and plaster detailing still evoked that stuffier, bygone age when slogans like 'Remember the Maine!' and 'Speak softly and carry a big stick' still echoed off its walls. Santos had also added a few personal touches, including many nods to his extended Mexican family (photos, kid's drawings, tchotchke's) as well as carefully creating a calculated amount of mess on his massive desk to convey to any visitor just the right mix of an over-worked but getting-to-it bureaucrat.

At the moment, though, he had his feet kicked up as he leaned back in the high-backed antique leather banker's chair and considered whether he should step outside for a cigar to celebrate.

It had been a panicked call to Tommy Falcon two days previous that had ultimately led to his hooking up with the Russians. Falcon, a local pawn shop owner with rumored ties to the mob and other less-than-legal connections, had deferred him to a contact down in the Brighton Beach section of Brooklyn who could secure the services he needed: someone to capture whatever was terrorizing the waters off Raadsel Point and sell it to the highest bidder, as well as saving the lucrative GreenWaters Festival in the bargain.

The trick was expediency. To do such a thing through normal channels would have required months of petitions, filings, etc., along with circumventing marine animal activist groups, etc., etc.

The deal had worked out even better than his wildest expectations.

Igor Gorimov, it turned out, had a lengthy track-record procuring large sea animals – mostly killer whales – by any (often illegal) means for a variety of clients. Primarily, however, he procured them for 'Atlantis Marine World,' a chief competitor to the SeaWorld amusement parks. Atlantis Marine World had recently had privately contracted Gorimov and his associates to broker a deal with Kamogawa Sea World in Japan which involved a group of Japanese fishermen from Iki Island creating an illegal 'drive fishery' of whales and dolphins that Atlantis subsequently 'rescued,' ensuring a win-win deal for all those involved. Except the whales and dolphins, of course.

When Santos had explained he needed two 'rare' giant and previously thought to be extinct marine creatures captured and turned over for a substantial profit, Gorimov had answered, "No problem. In fact, I think Atlantis would pay you quite well, after my cut of course."

"Of course," Santos had agreed, practically jumping out of his chair in delight.

"Of course," Gorimov repeated to himself after he hung up the phone in his messy office over in Sheepshead Bay. A heavy-set man in his 50s with a shaved head, a goatee, and a gold earring, he had no intention of honoring any deal with what he told his colleagues was some 'Taco Monkey politician' up the river – he was already setting up a deal with the Japanese to buy the creatures (based on Mayor Santos' descriptions) that was triple what Atlantis was offering up front. After hustling all parties involved it was Gorimov's intention to high-tail it to some remote location and retire once and for all from this business, which was drawing increasingly lower returns anyway.

Gorimov grabbed the pack of Marlboros on his desk and shaking one out, lit it. *How about Sao Paolo, with all those hot Brazilian women … or maybe some place like Antigua,* he said to himself, blowing smoke up at the ceiling, *I heard there's some nice real estate available after that billionaire went to jail …*

28. DINNER ... A FIGHT, AND A KISS.

Sarah knocked on his door just before 4pm.

It was one of those slightly cool September afternoons when one becomes keenly aware summer is drawing to a close and autumn is gathering itself in the shadows. From somewhere out in the yard came the reedy back-and-forth calls of a pair of cardinals, and in the distance, the forlorn horn blast of a Metro North train heading up the Hudson line. The sun seemed to be hesitating amongst a bank of low clouds just above the cliffs on the opposite shore.

Sarah stood on his front porch in a pair of faded jeans and a black chamois shirt. She was wearing her hair loose and had a fresh look to her as if she'd just stepped out of one of those shampoo ads, such as one with mountain lakes, pine trees, and panoramic skies in the background. Easton stood in the open doorway marveling – not for the first time in the past few days – at how life could swerve into such unexpected courses. Such as whatever one resulted in this very striking and attractive woman standing at his doorstep. For a split second, he had an odd, aching thought; he wished every time he opened his front door he could find her standing there, waiting for him.

"Hi," she said, breaking out in a smile.

Easton was about to respond when he was shoved aside roughly as Rovsky pushed past him to greet their visitor. The dog sat down obediently in front of her and did the slight twist of his massive head and imploring eyes look, the one that instantly produced dog biscuits from pockets at the local dog run.

"I'm pretty sure he's starting to like you," Easton said.

"Or maybe he knows this native woman bears gifts," Sarah answered. "Paw." She said to the dog, extending her left hand. A large log-like foreleg shot up in response. She produced a bagged up dried pig's ear from her purse and held it out. With surprising delicacy, Rovsky took it in his jaws with a definitive 'clack' and pushed his way back into the house. Sarah stepped up and gave Easton a probing look.

Standing with his hands in his back pockets, he shook his head. "You're spoiling him," he said finally.

She moved in closer and brushed his lips with hers. "Maybe I need a little spoiling too," she teased.

Easton slid his hands around her waist and pulled her in close. Once more, he was aware of her body scent – it made him think of cedar and oranges. "That can be arranged," he said. "Come in and I'll see what I can do."

"How is it?" Easton asked.

The two of them were sitting at the dining room table having tea with a tray of English tea cookies that Easton's mother still insisted on sending him every month. Sarah was puzzled at the whole fuss Easton made over it and aghast at the amount of milk and sugar he mixed in – she always drank hers black – particularly after he'd explained he only used loose Earl Grey tea leaves ordered bulk from Twinings in London. ("It's still the same tiny shop on the Strand that tea was being sold out of 300 years ago," he'd told her as he was making it)

Sarah took a long sip of the tea, her eyes widening. "Hmmm … it's stronger than anything I've ever had before. It makes me want to stand up straighter." She wasn't particularly sold on the cookies, which seemed a hard and stale for her taste, but was too polite to say so. Such a thing would have been considered extremely bad form in Indian culture regardless.

Easton was nothing if observant, noting the abandoned tea cookie on her plate with a tiny bite taken out of it. He looked at her over the rim of his cup. "I reckon that's why we drown it in so much sugar and milk. Christ, you ought to see what we do to our meat and vegetables." He set the cup down and leaned back. "Don't worry about the cookies, though. Actually, I think they're dreadful myself. It's just tradition. And a nod of respect to my mum."

Sarah held her cup in both hands and looked at him right back. "I don't see anything wrong with that."

Easton took a long sip of his tea, then took a desultory bite out of one of the cookies. "Quite a day out on the river, I heard. Two policemen are in the hospital and a young man from the Oceanographic Institute got knocked around pretty good. Apparently, this creature everyone is now calling 'Ossie' popped out of the river next to them and they took off in a panic, driving the police launch up on shore and flipping it."

"*Ossie?*" Sarah said stifling a laugh. Then she grew serious. "They were lucky they didn't get killed. What were they hoping to accomplish?"

"I think they were trying to get a better handle on what they're dealing with. I guess they figured out it's a little more than they *can* handle."

Sarah raised a brow. "A *lot* more than they can handle apparently. There was quite a ruckus out at the Point. Fowler came by and told me I can go back tomorrow morning to tie up any loose ends, but otherwise the Point is off-limits until further notice. Either they're doing a lousy cover-up or they can't get their stories straight. One version I heard has it one of the shore observers saw a right whale jump breach near the police launch, scaring the hell out of them, another says it was a giant mutant alligator."

"What do you think it is?"

"I think it's something we should just leave alone and hope it's here for another reason that doesn't involve us. In fact, more and more I think that is the case."

"Well, there's certainly something to be said for that," Easton answered. "But if this thing is some sort of surviving dinosaur, I would think there would be all sorts of things to be gained by capturing it."

"And then what? Put it in a zoo? A sea-land theme park for people to ogle over? What a horrible thing to do to any living creature. Better to kill it instead."

The two of them sat quietly a moment, then Sarah pulled a slim bundle wrapped in cloth and placed it between them.

"This is for you."

Easton cocked his head, puzzled. "What's this?"

"It's something I want you to hold onto."

When he unwrapped it, he saw that it was the large bone-handled Bowie knife he'd seen on her hip that very first day he'd met her out at the Point. Which now seemed like years ago. The sheath was of stiff hand-tooled leather with tassels and an Eagle's head embossed on it. The patina on the rivets and discolored stitching suggested it was quite old.

"It belonged to my grandfather," she explained.

Easton unhooked the thong that secured the knife in position and eased the blade out. There was minor pitting on it, but the blade gleamed and looked wickedly sharp.

"Sarah, this is an amazing piece. But I can't accept this. It's a family heirloom."

She placed her hand on his arm. "You have to. And you have to promise you keep it close to you this weekend. I can't explain why, actually, you just have to." Her grip tightened and she locked eyes with him. "Promise."

"I promise."

She studied him carefully, as if to gauge his sincerity. After a few seconds, she asked, "What time do we have to be at your friends for dinner?"

"Seven. Give or take," Easton replied.

"That gives us plenty of time for my next surprise."

"It does?"

In response, her hand dropped to his lap and gave another place a little squeeze. "Yes," she said, her voice taking on a husky quality. "But you'll have to take me upstairs to find out what it is."

Easton leaned in and raised an eyebrow. "I'm pretty sure that can be arranged too."

Jim Franks and his fiancé Karen Evershaw shared an 1880s Second Empire Victorian with a wrap-around porch on the high side of Crichton Avenue. The slate roof was original, though most of the details such as the wood finials had been replaced with meticulously accurate reproductions by a local carpenter Franks had hired. When he had first purchased the property five years previous, it had been in shambles and had been borderline derelict, having been vacant for years. After three years of eating up most of Franks' savings, it had been turned around into neighborhood showpiece worthy of any 'This Old House' feature. It had since been featured in *Westchester Magazine* twice.

After a giving Sarah a quick tour of the place, Easton and Franks wound up in the grotto-like backyard with its flagstone terrace and canopy of tall trees, while Karen had kidnapped Sarah, hustling her off into the kitchen to sample a new cocktail she had been working on.

Easton liked Franks' backyard almost to the point of envy. On more than one occasion, he had joked about moving into it during the summer. The back of Franks' property was cut into a hill that rose steeply up towards the properties up on Lincoln Place parallel to Crichton and had been landscaped into terraces combining lush vegetation, walkways with accent lights, and hanging Chinese lanterns. It managed to look neat as a pin yet slightly wild at the same time. Immediately behind the house was an area large enough to accommodate an oblong teak outdoor dining table and chairs and a stainless-steel gas grill that looked like it cost a fortune.

Easton was sitting cross-legged with a glass of Carhude, a Speyside single malt Franks kept around especially for him. Franks was nursing a bottle of Negra Modelo with a sliver of lime wedged in the neck. A plate with Spanish olives, fig-infused cheese, and baguette slices that Karen had brought out earlier was on the table between them. Franks had been plying Easton with questions about everything including sea monsters and alluring American Indian archaeologists. From the nearby kitchen screen door came Karen's musical laughter and snatches of animated conversation between the two women. Easton figured Sarah was getting the third degree, but from the sounds of it, not in a bad way. He took a long pull off his scotch, followed by a couple of olives, tossing the pits into a small bowl.

"So they decided to close down the GreenWaters Festival this weekend," Franks was saying, "I heard your pal Chief Hendricks announced it around noon today. I bet that went over really well. Good thing he's not an elected official."

"Well, it was a smart idea," Easton replied. "Given what's happening."

Franks glanced towards the kitchen, then back at Easton. "Just what the hell *is* happening, John? I heard there was another attack out on the river today."

Easton wasn't sure if Franks was inquiring about the river or his love life. "That's an excellent question my friend, and a question I would certainly enjoy answering ... next question please?"

Franks threw him an amused look. "You've been hanging around too many politicians, bud," he said, then he shook his head. "Now everyone in town has their skirts all up in bunches over 'Ossie'? Whelma Fitzpatrick has become an overnight celebrity. I heard she's getting calls from National Enquirer and the Star."

Easton nodded. "Well, that's probably for the better. It's when the legitimate media starts taking her seriously that you should be concerned."

"So it's true? We've got some kind of monster on our hands out there in the river?"

Easton thought it over a moment. "Between you and me – and *just* between you and me, I'm convinced we have do have a serious problem. Two of them in fact."

"What do you mean, *two*?"

"Two as in *two monsters* out there in the river. One may have broken loose from an old shipwreck – don't ask how it could have survived so long because I have no idea ..." Easton went on to briefly describe the two accounts that had been deliberately left for him at the Historical Society, along with what Sarah had discovered at the Point and 'Rambo' Dimas' involvement.

Franks didn't say anything for a few minutes, only taking a few pulls off his beer and nodding to himself as he tried to get his head around the whole story. Anybody else would have dismissed it all as nonsense. But not Franks. He and Easton, along with the town librarian Tucker Brooks and a local antique collector named Will Simpson had gone face to face with things right out of one's worst nightmares. But he still wasn't really sure which was better; living in a world where such things were possible or one where they weren't. He decided he was leaning towards the former, by not by much.

"I guess this means I should probably cancel my river fishing plans for the next few weeks," he finally said.

Easton let out a small laugh. As far as he knew, Franks had never fished in his entire life. "Yeah, you might want to do that," he replied.

"So what's your plan?" Franks asked.

"Right now? Enjoy a good dinner and seeing if I can get you to pour another glass of that fine scotch."

"You gotta talk first, bud. Seriously, I mean someone or *something* is handing you clues – practically knocking you over the head with them it sounds – so they must want you involved directly for a reason ... no?"

Easton smiled grimly. "Well ... they may need to drop another or two. I have absolutely no idea how to do anything about this situation."

Franks considered this. "I don't know, isn't the police chief supposed to call in a group of well-meaning but woefully underprepared scientists to try and capture this thing, no doubt fucking it all up in the process? Or at least an unscrupulous opportunist who claims he has some unconventional-yet-unproven technology to save the day, which nearly gets our hero and most definitely at least one key person killed in the process? That's how it usually works in the movies anyway."

Easton laughed. "Yeah, that always works in the movies, mate."

Franks let that sit a moment. Then after glancing towards the screen door at the back of the house he tipped his beer towards Easton. "So what's the scoop with Doctor Pocahontas in there? Word around town is that you've been keeping her fireplace warm out on the Point there."

"Where did you hear that?"

"A little birdy told me," Franks replied with a wink.

"Was your little birdy a six-foot-plus black guy, about 230 pounds and with a genius IQ?" Easton asked, bullet-pointing the head librarian. Tucker Brooks had a reputation for knowing everything about everybody, though he was usually discreet about it.

"That sounds like one really big little birdy," Franks said, not giving in.

"With elephant-sized ears, apparently." Easton glanced up as something above caught his eye; a glimpse of the white head and broad wingspan of a bald eagle coasting over just above the treetops. *Damn thing looks like a low flying airplane*, he thought.

"On the other hand, that is one *serious* birdy," Franks added, following his friends gaze. "Actually, we've had a pair of them working the neighborhood lately. Kind of makes you wonder about some of those missing animal posters in the area. You know, like the ones with a little white dog that say something like, 'Have you seen my Fifi?' I'd be willing to bet Fifi wound up as eagle chow."

Easton was about to comment when the back door opened and Sarah and Karen came out bearing a new concoction Karen had cooked up called 'Blond Martini's.' From the way they were walking a little erratically, Easton decided they may have sampled a couple already.

Franks bit his tongue, and saying nothing, got up to fire up the grill.

Half an hour later, they were set up around the table. Franks had grilled up some salmon fillets along with sliced zucchini, and Karen had thrown together a fried rice dish with mushrooms and scallions. As a side, she'd also sliced up some of the last tomatoes from their garden and laced them with fresh basil, balsamic cream and olive oil. To wash it all down, Easton had brought a couple bottles of wine – in tonight's case a Vouvray and a White Bordeaux.

"Can't say I've ever had anything like it," Easton commented between mouthfuls. "What on earth did you put into this fish?"

"Yes, it's really quite delicious," Sarah added.

Franks grinned. "Actually, it's something I just improvised. Fresh lime juice, *sake*, sweet garlic, and truffle-infused olive oil. The rosemary and thyme are from our little herb garden over there. The trick is not to marinade it for more than half an hour. And the fresh herbs really put the spin on it."

"Something you 'just improvised'?" Easton said disbelievingly. He'd enjoyed quite a few of Franks backyard cookouts over the years, but this new gourmet twist was news to him.

"Well, you can thank Miss Evershaw over there. She's become something of a cooking channel junkie in her free time. She was starting to make me look bad in the kitchen, so I had to start boning up on my culinary skills."

"He's a little competitive, if you hadn't noticed," Karen chimed in. She turned to Sarah. "So, you said earlier that you work for the Museum of Natural History? Do you spend most of your time out in the field?"

Sarah took a sip of her wine. "As much as possible. I don't care much for sitting around offices."

"Well, some of us don't have a choice," Karen responded.

"You *always* have choice," Sarah shot back. "You just have to stand up and make it."

Karen bristled slightly at that, so Easton interjected, "Karen teaches English at the local high school. When she's not inventing cocktails or giving Jim here a run for his money in the kitchen." His aim was to put a little humor in the conversation but instead found his words falling flat.

"That's nice," Sarah said noncommittally.

Undaunted, Easton continued, "And Jim runs his own digital design company out of Irvington – Kinetic Media Associates. High-end stuff. He cut his teeth in the New York Advertising market but managed to reach escape velocity and move up here a few years ago."

Franks leaned forward a focused his charm towards Sarah. "Yeah, well ... Manhattan is great when you're young and angry and trying to prove yourself, but at some point, I decided I wanted a driveway to pull my car in and not have to deal with people packed in above, below and every side of me. Plus, there's a lot more oxygen up here, and a whole bunch of these green things they call trees. But some days I do miss the concrete canyons of Madison Avenue." He smiled wistfully and refilled his wine. "So what do you think of our little town so far?" he asked Sarah.

Sarah put her knife and fork down, wiped her mouth carefully with her napkin and took a long sip of her wine. Something in the deliberateness of her movements made Easton feel uneasy. The expression on his face grew wary.

"It's unique," Sarah continued, "I'll say that. And beautiful. That's why my ancestors settled in the area. Things went pretty well for them here for ten thousand years or so, until the Europeans showed up." She carefully set her glass down and looked Franks in the eye. "Of course, you know what happened after that."

An awkward silence descended over the table. It was Franks who spoke first, sitting back and calmly placing his hands on the table. "Quite honestly, I actually don't. At least not the specifics of what happened here in the Hudson Valley."

Sarah gave him a hard look. "So you live here, you enjoy this place and talk about how great it is, with no understanding of its history or the terrible price that was paid." She drained her glass in a gulp and placed in firmly in front of her. For one horrified moment, Easton had thought she was going to throw it over her shoulder.

Franks looked stung, while Karen's eyes narrowed, her wine glass halted in mid-air. Easton was alarmed, thrown by the sudden turn in conversation that threatened to get ugly between his closest friends and the woman he was enamored with. *Hadn't Karen and Sarah been acting like a couple of chummy schoolgirls just minutes before?* "Look, Sarah—" he started to say but Franks cut him off with a raised hand.

"It's okay, John." For one of the few times in their friendship, his face took on a dead serious look, with no hint of mischievousness. His green eyes seemed to go a shade darker. "I opened this door, so I'll accept whatever's coming through it." He didn't take his eyes off Sarah. "No offence intended," he said to her evenly, "but I guess you could say I deserved that. Still, in fairness not all of us are history experts like yourself. Everybody always loves the tale of how Manhattan was sold to the Dutch for twenty-four dollars or something, and yes I was guilty of watching 'The Last of the Mohicans' and enjoying it like a lot of popcorn-gobbling moviegoers, but I've never really heard what really happened around here before the Dutch showed up. So tell us."

Sarah glared at him for a moment, nostrils flaring, "Ignorance isn't an *excuse*," she snapped. Then, after a pause, she seemed to back off a degree or two. "It's a touchy subject. And that story everyone tells about Manhattan being sold for twenty-four dollars is a myth. No deed has ever been found and the title that's up in the New York Archives in Albany that scholars used to refer to is a fake, probably made in 1677. And the individuals who sold the island it were never specifically identified as 'Manhattans' though they did live in and around the area. The first document that supports that appears in the 1650's, 25 years later and after they were long gone. It's just another example of how false history gets to be accepted over time as fact. You just need enough people to repeat it often enough."

Sarah took a breath, her fingers straightening an imaginary object on the teak tabletop. Easton was aware how she had a self-contained calmness about her when she fell into the rhythm of telling a story, though her eyes took on a look that managed to seem fierce and sad at the same time. There was also something bold and immutable about her as well, a quality that said once she was rolling she wouldn't stop until she was finished, even if the building was burning down around her.

She glanced at Easton and looking back at Franks resumed, "So you wanted to know what happened here? First, you have to understand *who* was here. The Indians on this side of the river were sub-tribes of the Delaware-Munsee and spoke Algonquin. All were part of the Algonquin Confederacy. From Yonkers up past Tarrytown were the Weckquaesgeck, then the Kitchawank, Sint-Sinck, Wappinger, and further to the north, the Mahicans. On the west bank and northern New Jersey, you had the Lenape – and moving north their sub-tribes; Tappan, and Esopus. Even further north were the Mohawks, who were actually the eastern-most tribe of the Iroquois Confederacy. They were the enemies of the Hudson River Indians. Also, there was the small tribe known as the

Sestaqua out on Raadsel Point. When Henry Hudson first arrived in 1609, there were tens of thousands of Indians settled in on both sides of the river. By the 1640s, the majority were gone."

Easton spoke up, "Really? That far back?"

Sarah sat back and folded her arms, "Yes, that far back. A lot of it was due to disease the Europeans brought – smallpox, measles, typhoid … and plenty more. They decimated the Indian populations up and down the river, wiping out whole villages. It had been an uneasy clash of cultures from the start; but the Europeans had the technological advantage; guns and alcohol. There were occasional violent outbreaks on both sides, sometimes brutal murders, but the worst was 'Kieft's War' in 1643. The director of the colony – it was *New Netherland* then – Willem Kieft, was really something, all right. In addition to being incompetent, corrupt, and a coward, he was always blaming others for his failings. In an effort to shore up the colony's mismanaged finances, he first tried to force local Indian tribes to pay him a tribute. When that failed after a series of incidents (starting with one where it was claimed a bunch of pigs were stolen and a Swiss Taverns keeper was slain by Indians), he launched an all-out war, sending his soldiers to indiscriminately slaughter natives in the region. History books are filled with accounts of how savage the Indians were. Well, to give you an idea how savage the Europeans were, when Kieft's soldiers went after a village in what is now Jersey City, one witness reported, quote; 'Infants were torn from their mother's breasts, and hacked to pieces in the presence of their parents, and pieces thrown into the fire and in the water, and other suckling's, being bound to small boards, were cut, stuck, and pierced, and miserably massacred in a manner to move a heart of stone. Some were thrown into the river, and when the fathers and mothers endeavored to save them, the soldiers would not let them come on land but made both parents and children drown,' unquote.

"And Kieft rewarded those soldiers afterwards. The Indians in the region fought back, slaughtering settlers in return, but they were no match for Dutch weapons. There was another war in the 1650s – it started with an uprising with the Esopus Indians across the river – and that was the final one that broke the remaining power of the local tribes. The British moved in and took over in 1673. For a short while, they honored previous treaties, but once they saw that local Indian tribes lacked any strength, they dropped any pretense and just took what they wanted and threw the Indians out. The final straw was what was called 'King Philips' War' – the last major revolt by Indians in the area, though that was really about the Wampanoag Confederacy in Connecticut. After that, the remaining tribes broke up and most began to move west, though some went to Stockbridge in western Massachusetts. That was followed by the many years of lies, broken promises, and treaties as the U.S. Government and its people systematically stole lands and broke the will of us until most the descendants wound up in either Oklahoma or Wisconsin. Fragments of a once great and proud people laid waste by European greed and treachery. Not a very nice story I'm afraid. But there you have it – that's the end of that one."

It seemed a pall of gloom and despair has settled over the evening. For a space, no one said a word. Easton looked shocked, Franks depressed, and Karen somewhere between very uneasy and about to break out in tears.

The silence dragged out.

Finally, Sarah stood up, dropped her napkin on her plate and without a word turned and left.

After taking another pull off his beer, Franks looked over at Easton and letting out a whistle, said, "Wow. I can only imagine how much fun she is at Thanksgiving."

"Balls," Easton said, standing up. "I'm really sorry about this."

Easton caught up with her by the front sidewalk. "Sarah, wait!"

She paused under the shadows of a chestnut tree, the outlines of part of her face accented by a nearby streetlight. Although lights were on in the old houses up and down the street it was a quiet evening in the neighborhood.

Sarah looked him but didn't say anything. Easton was upset, but he was also confused, frustrated and sad and … angry? *Why the hell did Franks have to 'open the door' as he'd put it and wreck the whole evening? And why did Sarah have to bring down the whole evening with such a depressing tale, on the first opportunity to meet his closest friends?* And in spite of that part of him wanted to …

He tried to read her expression, but she was all cool, aloof, and enigmatic. But he also sensed her arm trembling underneath his hand.

"I can walk back to the cabin," she said finally, starting to pull away from him.

Easton didn't let go. "Sarah!" he said more forcefully.

Nothing.

Part of him – the one that occasionally slipped the locks on its cage and capered about with its horns and cape in rage and fury – wanted him to just turn his back and *say fuck it … fuck all of this.* And for a moment he almost, *almost* did just that. And if he had, things might have turned out completely different for both of them.

But he didn't.

Instead, Easton, over-riding that scampering devil, took a deep breath and said in a firm voice, "Come on, take a walk with me."

The Lowgate Bridge was one of the most scenic locations in the village. A steel and stonework truss arch-style built at the turn of the last century, the bridge spanned the Wyvern Falls Creek right where it cascaded into a steep-sided gorge that wound its way down to Raadsel Bay. Below the bridge nestled into the north wall of the gorge was an old mill dating back to the 1790s, provided the finishing iconic touch of an image that had been sketched, painted, and photographed countless times over the centuries. The bridge featured pedestrian walkways on both sides of it with ironwork railings, benches, and lampposts that evoked its Victorian origins.

Easton and Sarah walked out to the center of the span where it gave a tantalizing view of the bay and the river beyond. For a moment, the two of the simply stood there, each absorbed in their own thoughts. A cool breeze plucked at their clothes and ruffled their hair. The lights of a passing barge twinkled out on the river.

Easton, who hadn't smoked in years, was struck by an almost overwhelming urge to have a cigarette. Instead, he stood by the rail and took in the view. He was keenly aware of Sarah standing next to him, both close and yet distant. She surprised him by speaking first.

"I'm sorry, John. I shouldn't have told the story that way. I made a wreck of the evening, and I know they're your friends. It's just ... I can't escape the past. It's part of who I am."

Easton nodded, his hands resting on the rail. "Yeah, that's something I can relate to," he said, thinking about a thing or two in his own past that had come back to haunt him these last few years.

Such as *psychic ability*.

He mentally cringed at the words.

Then she placed her cool hand over his. "It's more than that, John. I'm terrified. Not just about us, but that something terrible is about to happen ... I've been having dreams. Bad ones."

Easton continued leaning on the railing, turning this over in his head. *So it isn't just me*, he realized. Within the last few days, he'd felt an underlying sense of dread creeping into his thoughts, even while awake. A vague sense of impending doom, like he was rushing toward some yawning precipice or terrible event. At first, he'd dismissed it as a subconscious reaction to this whirlwind situation with Sarah – his natural pessimism thinking, 'If it's going too good, it has to self-destruct' kicking in. And, of course, there was all this business with these 'sea monsters' in the water, though the solution to that was fairly obvious – he intended to keep both feet firmly planted on *terra firma* until this matter was resolved.

But since this morning, he wasn't so sure. He was getting the sense that the threat was external, not internal ... as if lurking in the atmosphere.

Or water.

"So what is it you want to do?" he asked, not quite sure if he was addressing her or himself. "Pack your stuff up and run back to New York? Take off to Antarctica and hang out chatting with penguins until this whole thing blows over?"

"No," she said. "I learned long ago you can't run, or turn away from your fate. Any more than you can make your own heart stop beating or the sun to stop setting in the evening." Her hand tightened around his. "You asked me what *I* want?"

Easton straightened up and faced her. The sense of a rapidly approaching precipice was more acute than ever, along with something else ... an instant hyper-awareness of every detail in his existence resolving itself with alarming clarity: the two of them, lovers, facing each other on the bridge, the as-yet-unwritten abyss of possibilities that entailed. The cool caress of the September breeze that teased her hair ... and her hair's lustrous jet-black color ... the bold lines of her face and the glint of starlight in her dark eyes as she stared at him ... the naked emotion revealed in them. He saw her lips were parted just enough to reveal a hint of teeth and felt the subtle current (of what? Life? Heartbeats?) flowing through where his hand held hers and marveled at what forces of existence enabled such a sense of intense intimacy even if for just a fleeting moment.

The impersonal glow of the titanic heavens revolving above at a seemingly glacial pace, the glitter of lights on the water, the vague smell of wood smoke, water, and from nearby the scent of a sugar maple, the steady hammer of his heart beating in his chest – all of this registered in his consciousness in an instant and he knew, with a certainty that was frightening, that he loved this woman and would never forget this moment for his remaining days on earth.

There was something else in her look; surprise.

She was reading his thoughts ... and he realized he could hear hers.

[I want ... *you*]

[… To what? Kiss you? Do cartwheels? Run for President?]

[… Just holding me would be a good start, smartass …]

[… yeah? Show me …]

She dropped his hand and grasping him by the back of his neck pulled him in close until their noses were touching. His hands slid around her waist.

And they kissed.

For a long time.

29. "LOVERS EVER RUN BEFORE THE CLOCK..."

To Easton, it felt like an eternity, an eternity part of him wished he could drop into and never have to leave. But such being the human condition the field of time and space reasserted itself; it was getting late, Sarah was shivering slightly from the chill in the air, back at his house was a very large dog waiting to be walked.

[… Did we really talk with our thoughts?]

[… it's strange … I've never done this before … I'm getting cold though …]

They half-turned and Easton paused, taking a deep breath and taking in the vista from the bridge, and aloud said, "Lovers ever run before the clock …"

"What's that?" she asked, her arm around his waist. He decided it felt pretty good there. He was also glad the evening was veering back from the precipice of disaster.

"William Shakespeare. Just popped into my head."

"Time flies when you're having fun?"

"Something like that. Come on, I'll take you home. You're not supposed to be out on the Point until tomorrow anyhow." He took her free hand and turning it palm up said, "I see a couple glasses of wine, a sheepskin rug, a fire in the fireplace, and a tall handsome stranger in your immediate future."

"Can I pass on the tall handsome stranger and get a certain tall handsome detective in his place?"

Easton touched his fingers to his temples like a swami consulting some higher powers and said, "I believe … the fates say … *yes*!"

That got him a quick smile and another kiss.

A mile and a half away, Crazy Jack lay awake in his bed, having snapped out of his doze by what sounded like someone speaking directly in his ear; "Lovers ever run before the clock...."

He had no idea what that meant or why. Connected to the dream he had been having? He didn't think so. In the dream, he had been soaring, like an eagle, through the flattened blur of time/space and then became aware he had transformed into a young version of himself, standing by what seemed like a tall thick wall built of trees set as posts in built up of intertwined branches. It was a palisade, of course, like the one that once walled in the compound out on Raadsel Point. Correction; it *was* Raadsel

Point. The way it was long before first contact with the white men and their big ships.

This Indian fort – or *castle* as they came to be called later, was large; a rough oval shape perhaps a hundred yards across at its widest. The walls were set atop a low earthen *burm*, a built-up ridge of dirt perhaps a foot and a half high. The center area was dominated by a large fire pit ringed with field stones while there was only one average-sized wigwam built of poles and sheets of tree bark, a single deerskin flap covering its entrance. A lazy whorl of smoke drifted out of the opening in the top.

The rest of the compound was set up with planting areas, though it was clear to him the primary purpose of the castle was ceremonial – there were no other living structures other than the one.

The people around him were tall – both the men and women were broad shouldered with narrow hips, beautifully featured with skin ranging from tawny to pale white. The men all wore leather breechcloths with belts – some with leggings and boots, here and there could be seen a wolf or lynx fur draped around a shoulder. Their appearance was even more varied. Some men had shaved the sides of their heads, their straight black hair long in the back and jutting out at spikey angles on the top and front; others simply wore it long. Eagle feathers were prominent and facial markings were wildly different; red pigments were favored, though black, yellow, bright blues abounded. Some had a series of black dots or stylized shapes. All wore some form of wampum on their person, the pearly white or bruised purple beads made from the Quahog shell. The woman all wore doeskin wraps that covered the right shoulder, some had leggings as well. They also wore wampum as well as bracelets made of stiff woven hair dyed red. Many wore their hair braided though like the men, some wore it loose though, sometimes with bangs cut in the front.

They were by and large an attractive tribe, fine featured with snow-white teeth and even in his dream child-self, Crazy Jack knew they were his ancestors – the Sestaqua, *the People of the Falls*.

The ones who had vanished all those years ago.

Some sort of ceremony was being organized. Pots and woven grass platters of food were everywhere, and there was a ring of cooking fires with clay stewpots hung over them. The complex aromas of wood smoke, cooking meat, and bear fat filled his nostrils. *What sort of dream is this*, he asked himself, *where I can smell things?*

His dream-self wasn't concerned with such issues, however. He was more aware of a sense of agitation amongst the people around him and with that the realization that there weren't many males – something terrible had happened … a war? That seemed right. Many of the men he did see bore scars and recent injuries.

His perspective shifted above and with the speed of thought he zoomed/faded north where hundreds of war canoes filled with warriors were coming, fierce-looking men armed with bows, spears and axes … Mohawks? Mohicans? He couldn't tell. It didn't matter. Whatever tribe they were, they were on a mission to wipe out the Sestaqua once and for all.

Another disquieting perspective shift: Crazy Jack found himself in the compound again … before a ceremonial stand of interlocking elk antlers. On top was the Last Horn of the Witch Buffalo … a gift from the Wyandot countless generations back when the Sestaqua were migrating across the Ohio Valley towards what would be their final destination in the Hudson Valley. The gift of that horn was a story itself now lost in the veils of time – something about a *W'axkook* or horned river monster the Sestaqua saved the Wyandot from …

Behind the stand were seven elders. At first, Crazy Jack thought they were some of the twelve sachems but the more he looked at them, the less he was even sure they were even Indians – they had a vaguely silvery, iridescent quality to them, as if they were just a shimmering approximation of an Indian male. Their faces were devoid of expression and their hair long and grey, so long it fell almost to the backs of their knees. The wampum that trimmed their clothing gave off pulsing light, as if electrified.

Who are you? his dream-self asked them.

We are — (?) they replied in unison, without moving their lips. It's a nonsensical word they call themselves, one that his brain is unable to process. Then as one, they gestured towards the horn, which he realized he was now holding in his arms. Crazy Jack was confused. *Where are the twelve ancestors? Or are the twelve simply emanations of the seven?*

He turned and before him was the entrance of the compound and with it the path that cuts down through the hill and leads toward the water – it's the same path that exists even today in the real world. Outlined at the entrance is a woman, her back to him, appearing to glow in the morning light. When she turned around he saw that she was the sachem's daughter, *Kiishooxkw*, a woman his dream/ancestor-self was in love with and hoped to marry. He recognized her – he has seen her since … but those thoughts became lost as the seven elders spoke in his head, instructing him on what he must do next.

This is not the first time the summoning has been performed, they tell him – the mythical battle of the rivers monsters a few millennia in the past was the first – *but this will be the last.*

In his dream, his heart whimpered, though outwardly his face betrayed nothing ... he is now cursed with understanding; the horn must be taken to the water and used to summon the ancient water monster and the thunder beings to defeat the northern warriors who will arrive by nightfall. There is a price; *Kíishooxkw* must sacrifice herself to the river as an offering ...

Which was when Crazy Jack awoke in his bed.

Outside, a few hardier crickets maintained their songs as if in defiance to the cool evening, while upstairs in the attic a squirrel scratched and nibbled at something. Crazy Jack studied the shifting pattern reflected up on the ceiling by moonlight through the torn curtains, and realized tears were running out of his eyes leaving icy trails past his temples.

Now he remembered ... and understood.

It's her, isn't it? he asks in his head. *You took from me the one thing I loved ... and now she is here again, and again you would take ... why? What thing have I done that is so terrible you would cause me such pain and heartache?*

It was a fruitless question, he knew. *As if I was the only one who could cry pain and heartache.* And what happened that day so many hundreds of years back was nothing compared to the unguessed at pain and suffering that was yet to come; yes, the northern Indians had been defeated that day, their war canoes caught in a terrible storm as the Thunder Gods shot their bolts of lightning at them and the monster chewed up canoe and man alike. The river was red for days. But the real doom was still to come, first arriving in the form of a single ship with a captain named Henry Hudson.

So now what? Crazy Jack asked, thinking about the seven beings he thought of as the 'Sky People.' *Were they real? Or a recurring aspect of his dreams? Messengers for the Great Creator?* And on the heels of that: *Who can tell? Dream and reality ... reality and dream? Which is which?* He sighed, his gnarled hands folded across his chest. *I'm just a tired old man, who's seen too many friends and loved ones pass ... why can't you just let me join them? Haven't I done enough?"*

"– No."

The seven voices spoke as one, aloud, startling him.

The light through the windows and reflecting off the walls with their peeling strips of old wallpaper took on a silvery sheen. The strips seemed to coalesce into seven elongated and roughly humanoid shapes like a shimmering sketch that, with a sudden *pop* winked into full dimensional existence.

In what might have been a dream within a dream, he was told what he must do next and wearily, he listened.

While Crazy Jack lay in his bed listening to one voice made of seven from creatures that had half-materialized out of the wallpaper, over in the village Guillamo Del Tesler slept in his room on the top floor of the American Hotel, snoring softly. The bed sheets still exuded the faint smell of sex and sweat from his wild tryst earlier with a certain 22-year-old archaeology student, who had just left an hour before. On the nightstand next to him was a bottle of mineral water and a dog-eared copy of Erich von Däniken's 'The Gods Were Astronauts,' along with two discarded Trojan packets.

Blocks away, John Easton had been dreaming about being trapped in an underwater tunnel in the Hudson while a giant creature with tentacles tore at his legs when he was half awakened by Sarah Ramhorne running her hand across his brow. She'd been having a nightmare herself, one where she was wading out into the roiling waters off Raadsel Point, powerless to stop herself from heading to what she knew would be her certain death, when Easton's moans woke her. Neither spoke for a few minutes; she lay in his arms, stroking his hair, savoring the warmth of their intertwined bodies that was like a low-banked fire between the sheets. A slow kiss, then both drifted off into sleep again while at the foot of the bed Rovsky stretched out his huge log-like legs (and equally huge toes) briefly, then began to snore.

Over at Hudson Terrace Apartments, Lieutenant Ray Sanchez lay in a deep slumber next to Detective Eckhart, who lay on her side with her hands tucked under her pillow, eyes wide open. Eckhart had been dreaming about her grandmother who had died of complications from emphysema some twenty years previous. She hadn't thought or dreamt of her grandmother in years, though she had loved her dearly. It had been a beautiful, almost melancholy dream where it had been a bright sunny morning in the breakfast nook of her grandmother's kitchen – the house was long gone now – and they had been making those big soft ginger snap cookies like when Eckhart was a little girl. She'd always loved the 50s' style kitchen at her grandmother's, with its knotty pine cabinets and chrome trimmed table with white Formica. Her grandmother had just patted the seat next her and said, oddly, 'Come, my little Katarina, it is time for you to join us!' when looking down she saw with horror her grandmother's hands elongate into black, vicious-looking tentacles with hooked teeth on the ends, her eyes enlarging into saucers and her mouth into a cilia-lined beak while her head took on a shovel-shaped, insectoid quality. "I've mished you sho mush!" her grandmother said, her voice degenerating into a watery, *squishy* gurgle. Then there came the hideous scrape of those chitinous hooks across the tabletop accompanied by that hideous smell, the rank odor of dead fish and seawater ...

It would hours before she would get to sleep again.

Down towards the Tappan Zee Bridge aboard the *Thomas Jefferson*, Ben Reinhardt lay in his bunk, staring up at the ceiling and wondering whether his career was already finished. The light bamboo paneled stateroom was spartan and stripped down, leaving little for his eyes to settle on. He felt like a tractor trailer had backed over him a few times and still had a splitting headache from the concussion, but knew he'd gotten off light compared to the two cops.

He'd been released from the hospital earlier that day after having his statement taken and had been expecting some sort of attention or buzz – certainly this had been a watershed moment in any scientist's career – observing a *bona fide* extinct marine dinosaur alive and in its element. Instead, nothing. No eager news reporters looking for the scoop on what had happened out on the river, no major stations knocking on his door or clogging up his smartphone with requests.

Zilch.

Well, not zilch. Instead, he found himself in a shit-storm of trouble for having destroyed a one-of-a-kind experimental unit – a very *expensive* experimental unit – never mind that it hadn't been his fault. He was ordered confined to quarters pending a full investigation into what happened and they had even confiscated his phone, though not before he'd gotten one call off to a friend of his down at Columbia.

Aside from being in a lot of physical pain, Reinhardt was mentally stung, hurt, and utterly demoralized. Though he'd been through his fair shares of ups and downs in life, never anything approaching this. Part of him was still in shock. It seemed incredible how quickly things had gotten royally fucked up. No one was interested in the amazing creature he had witnessed out there on the river, let alone following up on it. Instead, he had been dressed down for violating every protocol in the book, for not going through proper channels or procedure in the using a highly sensitive piece of oceanographic equipment, then having it destroyed on his watch.

Instead of reaping kudos, he was facing possible dismissal from the program, and the ship commander had assured him all this was going to impact his permanent record.

What the fuck!? he asked the blank expanse of ceiling. The worst thing would be telling his parents back in Boston. They weren't particularly well off and had scrambled to help put him through college, even borrowing against the house. They'd banked everything on him, without complaint or even a hint of pressure. "Show them what you've got,' his father had said, a man who dropped out of high school to work as a bricklayer.

And now he'd blown it.

It was a long while before Reinhardt too would find sleep that night.

On the river, the black surface of the water was almost preternaturally smooth, a cool cloudless evening with the moon, stars, and cliffs glimmering with mirror-like clarity in its reflections. Somewhere in the murky depths off Raadsel Point, a leviathan-sized creature appeared to be in a half doze, slowly gliding above the rippled dunes of the river bottom past the oyster beds and the rotting remains of a British frigate that had been scuttled back at the end of the Revolutionary War.

Further north amongst the submerged canyons of World's End, another creature also quietly lurked, its dinner-plate-sized eyes observing a group of river sturgeon idly swimming overhead. It too went into a semi-stasis, conserving its energy for what part of its alien nervous system may have sensed would be an eventful day …

30. THE DARKNESS THAT CAME AFTER DAWN.

When morning first arrived on Saturday, all initial indications were that it was going to be a brilliant start to the first official weekend of fall. The weather report, according to the *Wyvern Falls Patch* appearing in local email boxes by 6 a.m. called for mixed clouds and sunshine, with temperatures in the high 60s. On the shore opposite the village, the Palisades Cliffs picked up the early rays of light beautifully, bathed in a slight mist that suggested it was probably going to be just another sleepy day along this section of the Hudson River. One with little to report, except that a barge was leisurely working its way north and perhaps a sailboat or two. A handful of gulls drifted casually around the air over the harbor while a slight breeze plucked at the feathers of those who idled along the shore, ruffling the open expanse of bluish green water in broad patches that obscured whatever currents – or creatures – moved below.

Along the Metro North platform, a handful of desultory weekend commuters waited for the local train whisk them down to the city, some with cups of hot coffee and some a muffin or bagel, others just standing empty-handed while gazing up at the sky and probably cursing whatever machinations of fate was steering them to work on what was shaping up to be a fine day.

Over at the sprawling 1930s Cape Cod on Van Cort Lane, Roy Hendricks was puttering around downstairs in his basement workshop, putting the finishing touches on a model of the HMS Rose, an 18th-century frigate 'plank-on-frame' 1/75 scale kit he had been working on and off for the past two years. Getting all of the details absolutely correct had been a side obsession of Hendricks, to the point of obtaining original documents from the National Maritime Museum in Greenwich, so that he could properly hand carve all the blocks and tackles (after finding out the ones with the kit were all wrong). The partitioned-off workshop was also where he kept hidden his other hobby, his collection of Carole Landis pictures. Since being a kid, he had been secretly enamored of the tragic 1940s Hollywood starlet and had quietly amassed a collection (some even signed by her) over the years, unbeknownst to his two daughters or late wife. It had never crossed over into the overly perverse such as bizarre masturbation fantasies – but just sort of simmered along as a quirky hobby of his. He might or might not have been amused to discover that what he thought of as a 'sort of naughty indulgence' would have been considered laughably mundane by his daughters.

Lastly, the workshop was the one room and last bastion inside the house where he occasionally indulged his other past time: smoking his pipe. His daughters hated the damn thing but allowed him this last holdover from his past. Provided he kept the cellar window open of course.

He had just finished touching up the gold leaf on the quarter gallery of the ship and was tamping down some fresh cherry tobacco into his pipe when the phone rang. The phone – one of those corded wall units that was a refugee from the 1970s – rang three times before he reluctantly picked it up.

"Hello?"

"Hello, Chief." It was Lieutenant Sanchez. "Sorry to bother you, but we have a developing situation you should be apprised of."

Hendricks jaw tightened as he set the pipe down. "What's the situation?"

There was the sound of some commotion in the background, voices shouting and yelling. "Um, a few minutes ago, a large group of people over-ran our checkpoint at the entrance to Raadsel Point."

At the same time, Easton was out at the Point in the cave helping Sarah cover up the bottom of the petroglyphs. He'd swung by Franks' house earlier to apologize but there was no one home and the Land Rover was gone. He finally got through to Karen's cell and found out they were over at Home Depot arguing over paint colors for the second-floor bathroom they were remodeling. "Well, it was certainly *interesting* meeting your friend last night," she said distractedly, "but let me have Jim call you back. He's suddenly gotten some crazy ideas about color schemes that's about to get a bucket of 'Behr Premium Plus Egg-shell' dumped over his head. Bye."

Easton had gotten Fowler to let them past the checkpoint blocking the only access road out to Raadsel Point to pick-up Sarah's belongings and tie up a few loose ends – in this case, putting the cave back to rights. Fowler hadn't been too happy about it but agreed to let them pass. "Just get your stuff and get the hell back here. And if you see anything odd, especially in the water, you run like hell? Got it?"

"Got it," Easton had agreed.

Then Sarah reminded him about the cave. "We have to make sure we cover the bottom of the petroglyphs – we can't take any chances of anyone finding this for the moment."

"Why?" he'd asked.

Sarah had looked him in the eye, "Because it's *my* discovery – probably the most significant thing in my career so far. But I don't want this getting out until it's properly documented and photographed. I can't screw this up. Okay?"

The day had turned unseasonably warm and humid and even the breeze wafting through the cave felt oppressive, tinged with brine. They had just finished kicking the gravel and sand back into shape when Easton paused, head cocked. From outside, there came a commotion with sounds of water splashing. For a split second, he had a horrible feeling the next thing he would see would be a series of black tentacles whipping around the corner.

Instead, there was a series of yells and muffled curses, and the next thing he knew, a bunch of people were clambering into the narrow space with them, led by a man with the strangest looking hairdo the detective had ever laid eyes on.

"Who the hell are you?" Easton asked.

The man, who was wearing a pair of cargo pants and hiking boots that were soaked, gave him a big wide grin.

"Guillamo Del Tesler, *Ancient Astronaut Theorist*, at your service!"

31. CLEARLY EVIDENCE OF ANCIENT ALIEN ASTRONAUTS ...

Along with Del Tesler was a small camera crew and an assistant with curly red hair in pigtails and red converse sneakers.

"Um, you can't come in here, this is an archaeology—"

"Great!" Del Tesler said, ignoring Easton and marching right past him, boots squelching. "Ahhh … a classic pre-contact petroglyph!" He whirled around, grinning at Sarah. "So, is this where they found the stones?"

Sarah stood hands on hips and looked at Del Tesler like he was a member of a bizarre (and not very pleasant) species that had just slithered out from under a rock. "Excuse me, can I help you?" she asked, evenly.

Before he could answer, they were interrupted by another person entering the cave.

"Oh … I thought there wasn't supposed to be anyone here!" Jennie Roderick said, stepping carefully into the now crowded space. Dressed in Doc Martens, a way-oversized sweatshirt and grey-black jeans that looked airbrushed on, she looked like she had just rolled out of bed. Or from the look of her hair, out of the middle of a tornado.

When she saw Sarah, she immediately looked away, then flicked her hair out of her face with one hand as if suddenly sure what to do next.

"Jennie Roderick? What are you doing here?" Sarah asked, eyes narrowing.

Jennie glanced up, then away again. "I … .um, like, you know."

"No I don't *know*," Sarah snapped back. "And who the hell is this guy?" she added, at no one in particular.

Del Tesler straightened up, grinning. "Hi! I already told you, I'm Guillamo Del Tesler, Ancient Astronaut Theorist." He put his open hands out like a game show host welcoming a new contestant. "And this is totally amazing, clearly a visitation site!" he added enthusiastically. One thing Easton decided was that, nutty fruitcake or not, it was hard to resist the man's boyish charm. On the other hand, it was obvious Sarah didn't have that problem.

"You're interfering with an archaeological dig site," she said. "Not to mention this entire area has been declared off-limits to the public by order of the police department. You have to leave. *Now*."

Del Tesler didn't seem to hear her, though Jennie did her best to shrink behind the camera crew. Instead, he stepped right over to the petroglyph and began tracing his fingers over it like it was a kind of holy relic. In what at seemed like less than a minute, the fill lights were up and the camera was rolling with Del Tesler jumping in like the whole thing had been scripted. Standing strategically to one side, he pointed up and down at the artwork. "As you can see, combined with evidence of submerged landings strips along this area of the Hudson – from areas that haven't been above sea level in 3,000 years - this Indian drawing from centuries ago *clearly* indicates ancient alien astronauts visited here." He framed his hands around the upper part of the petroglyph. "The seven symbols here align *exactly* with the stars in Orion, giving us an excellent indication as to the origins of these alien visitors. There's no question, ancient aliens have visited this area of the Hudson in the past. In my mind, absolutely no question at all." Like a seasoned pro, he held his pose a moment longer for the camera, then slapped his sides triumphantly and added, "Is it a take?"

"Fabulous. You fucking crushed it!" the cameraman said. "But let's do it again just in case." Suddenly, he found the camera lifted out of his hands.

"How about *not*?" Easton said.

The cameraman, a blond-haired kid who was dressed in an expensive hipster get-up that suggested he had just stepped out of an Apple Store said, "Hey, dude, you can't do that!"

Easton let his jacket open just enough to reveal the shoulder holster and the butt of the Beretta sticking out of it. "I just did, mate," he said, staring at the kid until he looked down. Then he flicked the power switch to 'off.' He turned around and addressed Del Tesler, "Pack your stuff and get the hell out of here, or I'll ring up the police chief and have you all arrested for trespassing."

Easton had no idea whether they would believe him. In fact, Del Tesler looked completely unfazed.

"Really? I think the police will have their hands full with all the other trespassers!" Del Tesler said, flashing his enthusiastic grin as if this was all some sort of big prank.

That was when Easton realized he could hear music from outside. Lots of music actually – from an *assortment* of bands.

"What in the bloody hell!?"

Easton was standing with Sarah at the top of the bluff not far from the cave. What they were seeing was almost too bizarre for words.

A motley assortment of boats had drawn up in and around the Point like the strangest amphibious invasion ever attempted. Rowboats, Sunfish, Cabin Cruisers, beat-up day sailors – an oddball fleet of whatever the festival goers owned or cold lay their hands on were everywhere. The scale of it was staggering.

From the campgrounds nearby came music and the sounds of large crowds. Just off the point was the river sloop GreenWater with a deck full of people and further out what looked to be an old, antique-covered barge.

Apparently, the GreenWater Festival was underway after all.

By the gate, Lieutenant Sanchez and Detective Eckhart had stood helplessly next to their Police SUV along with two WFPD officers, hands on belts, not sure what would happen next. If it was one, two, even a dozen people, they wouldn't have hesitated. Instead, *hundreds* of people showed up at once in what was without a doubt an intentional – if sloppily executed – strategy that instantly overwhelmed the police checkpoint. Streams of people by-passed them on both sides; old hippies, young-looking protesters, students, whole families. They carried coolers, backpacks, pulled wagons of food, and supplies. Some arrived on motorcycles, some on bikes, some on ATV's. The road out to the point was quickly clogged with vehicles, becoming a snarl of minivans, SUVs and hybrids.

Mostly they ignored the checkpoint as if it wasn't even there, though occasionally there was the derisive shouts like "Nice morning, Piggies!", "We're taking back our festival, fascists!" and the charming, "Out of the way, meat-eating Nazis!" One little girl with frizzy hair being tugged along by her grandmother stopped next to Detective Eckhart and looking up with a serious expression had asked, "Hi, Miss Policeperson, have you considered reducing your carbon footprint?"

Hendricks had told Sanchez to stay calm and just let them pass until he could get up there with reinforcements. Fowler had been deployed back out onto the river to assess the situation, but for the moment, it was obvious little could be done to stop the festival from happening.

Ten minutes later, Hendricks and every remaining available policemen on the force – nearly forty in total – found themselves hopelessly mired on the roadway way back by the Raadsel Bay Condominiums. Not accidentally, many vehicles had been abandoned haphazardly to ensure maximum disruption, including many old trucks and even a nearly derelict school bus.

How the hell did they even manage to drive half these things out here? Hendricks wondered. Inwardly, he was kicking himself for having absurdly underestimated the festivals organizers and follower's determination. *I was a damned fool for thinking they would cave in that easily,* he'd said to himself on the drive down from the police station. *I just didn't think the sons-a-bitches were that well organized.*

'Oh, a lot of them are Luddites," Hendricks' daughter had told him earlier when he was leaving the house. "But they really know how to use social networking, Dad. You need to get with it."

Then he had gotten ahold of Carrie O'Donnell from the village clerk's office. Aside from being a reliable source of any doings of village officials, she also happened to be his late wife's second cousin. One of her *favorite* second cousins as it were. What she'd told him almost sent him ballistic; *The word is the mayor had a secret meeting with Joe Depeyster yesterday and suggested there might be a way or two to move forward with the festival. Though you'll probably never be able to prove it ... you know the mayor.*

He knew the mayor alright. Ray Santos was a tricky customer when it came down getting nailed down on anything. And Joe Depeyster, who was not only one of the directors of the GreenWater Committee but owned the trucking company that delivered all the equipment for the festival, would certainly have been all ears for anything the mayor might suggest in that regard.

All that would have to wait for the finger-pointing fuck-fest afterwards.

Right now, he had to figure a way to close the whole thing down before someone got seriously hurt.

Or killed.

Easton and Sarah walked into the festival unchallenged. In previous years, a hefty admission had been charged at the gate, but apparently whoever had re-organized the festival had opted to turn it into a sort of free-for-all. Later, it would come out they'd pressed people for donations during the frenzied last minute meet-ups that had enabled the whole even to still happen.

Although Easton had never attended the festival in the past, standing along the vendor's fairway it was as if Hendricks cancellation speech had never occurred.

The festival was *jammed*.

The three separate sound stages and vendor's areas had been set up days before, so the logistics hadn't been overly difficult – the main issue had been getting enough people together and coordinating their timing so as to render any police resistance pointless. The result had exceeded the organizers wildest expectations.

In fact, the turnout had been *triple* what they'd originally anticipated.

Easton was taken aback at the scale and over-the-top merchandising of the whole thing. In the few years of living in Wyvern Falls, he had somehow developed a vague assumption that it would be a sort of loose, badly organized hippy carnival. Instead, he found the two of them strolling past booths selling everything from Kai-Kai sandals to Swatches. And the festival itself was branded and merchandised to the hilt: custom GreenWater iPhone protectors, coffee mugs, calendars, even bio-degradable ash urns embedded with a tree seed so your deceased beloved could contribute to the well-being of the planet.

The food venders had prices that would make even a hard-core New Yorker blink. Tofu shakes, soy-burgers, carrot juice, herbal power-boosters, and gluten-free vegan dishes were selling at rates any Starbucks would envy.

There was, predictably, the tie-dye and bead jewelry vendors wedged in amongst solar panel contractors, organic farm produce (*Ten dollars for a bag of carrots?* Easton wondered, *maybe I'm in the wrong profession!*) and no shortage of mediocre artwork booths, including one artist who created sculptures from 'found' objects. Which while conceptually interesting to the detective, still had him wonder if perhaps the artist should have focused on finding some talent first.

The most surreal moment, however, was when Easton found himself at an apparent 'New Age Indian' vendor run by a handsome elderly woman decked out in what he could only describe as 'Aging Native Hippy.' The booth had the usual assortment of dream catchers, incense, turtle rattles, and drums. Easton was looking over the collection of spear tips and arrowheads when the woman drifted up to them, and after an appraising glance at Sarah said to him, "Has she told you yet?"

Nonplussed, Easton decided to play along. "About ...?"

The woman, whose ruddy complexion hinted she might have Native blood, had the iciest blue eyes he had ever seen. They took on a sideways, crafty look as she nodded at Sarah and said quietly in Easton's ear, "How we arrived here of course."

"Through the Bering Strait?" he ventured.

"Of course not. We came in ships. From the stars."

"Oh right, I think I did hear that somewhere ..." Easton deadpanned. Sarah put a hand to her mouth and turned away, stifling a giggle.

The woman pretended not to notice. "She's forgotten," she said, with a knowing nod at Sarah, "About all the technology that was lost."

"Er, technology?"

"Yes, the *technology*. When Atlantis sank beneath the waves. Before then, we Indians knew how to fly … oh did we ever. But too many … like her … have forgotten. But there are still some of us, amongst you."

"Hmmm, I've always suspected …" Easton replied.

The woman fixed him with her ice-blue stare, the gaze of a fanatic. "Oh, yes we are! Hiding in plain sight!"

"I see."

A gnarled hand clasped his arm and she leaned in conspiratorially. "Perhaps you do. But she doesn't. Tell her we shall be waiting for her … but she has to remember!"

"Rest assured, I will," Easton promised.

Two booths down, Sarah turned to him and asked, "Did she try and sell you a sacred Indian charm bracelet?"

"No, I was only asked to remind you of your Ancient Atlantean origins and the aliens that brought you here. I really had no idea." Easton found himself looking at a teenage kid walking by who was wearing a T-shirt with a pseudo-symbol mosasaur chasing a swimming human symbol. The type above it read, *Ossie Loves People: They Taste Just Like Chicken!*

"I couldn't tell you *everything* up front," Sarah said, giving him an amused look.

"That's okay," Easton said, taking her hand in his, "I forgot to tell you I'm actually from the galaxy Andromeda." He was about to say something else when he saw something out in the water he didn't like.

It looked like a commotion on board the sloop GreenWater. And further down river what looked like a pair of large fishing trawlers charging towards them. And then beyond that, something else; a dark squall line of clouds rolling down from the northeast.

On the nearest stage to where Easton and Sarah were standing was an aging folk activist by the name of Myra Simmons, an old stalwart from the early sixties who despite being fifty pounds overweight still sang with the same mournfully rich, crystal voice that had drawn a legion of devoted followers. With her signature long black hair now turned silver, she was in the middle of her set with one of her more popular anti-war ballads – 'Setting Sun on Silent Guns' – when she found herself getting drowned out by a young blues guitar player named Jay Cropper, who was laying down a smoking lead that would have given Buddy Guy a hard run for his money.

Cropper, a gaunt 20 year old with scraggly brown hair, an old denim jacket, and a battered Fender Telecaster was the latest sensation amongst the 16-25 set, a guitar prodigy who tended to take off into his own orbit while playing with an ease and recklessness that made even accomplished guitarists seriously consider quitting for good on the spot. Cropper had just launched into the ripping solo of his breakout hit 'Five Fathoms Down' when the first signs of trouble started.

At first, it sounded like the group clustered around the deck of the sloop was excited about something. Then the screaming began.

Jim Franks was in his backyard repairing the wooden compost bin he'd built the year before up against the low fieldstone wall that defined the back property line. It had been a relatively quiet morning aside from the nearly disastrous excursion to the Home Depot over in Hawthorne. For a few precarious minutes, it looked like Karen and him were going to get into a smack-down drag-out fight (the young bald-headed man working the paint counter had been looking back and forth at them like he was watching a ping-pong match, one hand on the store phone ready to hit the security speed-dial).

Then Franks had simply thrown up his hands and said to her, 'You know what? You pick. Whatever you want. I'm heading over to the gardening center. Find a huge bag of stinking mulch and bury my head in it." And just like that, the fight was over. Karen's hand flew to her mouth and there was a perilous moment where she started to snort, giggle, and yell at the same time, which precipitated a laugh that began to rumble in Franks' gut until it erupted in a series of guffaws.

'The Great Paint War' finally ended with both parties acceding to Karen's original choice and Franks had wound up buying supplies for three other household projects he hadn't really thought about, until that is he found himself caught in the hypnotic spell of the Depot's endless home improvement possibilities.

Now, despite having sworn to himself earlier he was going to kick off and do absolutely nothing this weekend, he found himself rebuilding the compost bin, having just trimmed and pruned the trees out in front.

He was crouching by the bin, hammer in hand, and a couple galvanized nails in his other when he became aware that someone was standing on top of the wall about a yard to his right. Which was strange as he hadn't heard or seen anyone approach.

Looking up he saw a short, withered old Indian standing with his hands at his sides. The man's clothes looked so old and lived in, Franks suspected that if the man stepped out of them, they would simply remain there, upright, holding their shape until their owner came back. The old Indian looked at Franks calmly, as if he could take all day or even week if necessary to say what was on his mind.

"Can I help you?" Franks asked. He'd never seen this particular man before, though he felt like he knew him.

"You'll have to hurry," the old man answered.

Franks held up the hammer and nails. "With this? I didn't think it was *that* much of an emergency."

The old man shook his head. "No. To the waterfront. You have to hurry if you want to save your friend's life."

All humor dropped off Franks' face. "What the hell are you talking about? What *friend*?"

"Your friend, John Easton. If you don't hurry, he will die."

Even as the old man turned to leave, Franks had dropped everything and was running toward the Range Rover in the driveway.

32. THE NIGHTMARE FROM WORLD'S END

It was exactly 11:17 a.m. when everything went to hell, at least by Easton's wrist watch.

He checked it just out of reflex – after years of police work, any time an incident resembling a noteworthy situation arose, he automatically noted the time, and for that reason, he always insisted on a dependable watch. In this case, it was a classic Rolex, and the second hand was just sweeping the six o'clock position when the screaming began out on the river.

Even as he grabbed Sarah's hand and began to run towards the water, the sloop came to a lurching halt as a spray of tentacles erupted out of the water and slithered around the hull like some sort of B movie. Only this wasn't some blue-screened stop-action Harryhausen special effect. Even from a couple hundred yards away, Easton could hear timbers groaning and snapping, as if the very ship itself was crying out.

At first, no one seemed to be paying attention – there seemed to be more interest in the brawl that had begun to break out between Myra Simmons' and Jay Croppers' respective fans (surprisingly the younger Cropper fans were getting the worst of it), then one woman holding her two children said, 'Oh my God,' and began to cry. That triggered a ripple effect as the crowd turned its attention to the horror that was unfolding out on the water.

Gabriella Powers never wanted to go out on the water that day.

A beanpole of a girl, thirteen years old with a café-au-lait complexion and an afro usually tied back loosely with a hair clip, she had been shipped up from Yonkers for the weekend by her mother to visit her aunt who, by her own observation, was a complete whack-job. Aunt Flo was many things; Avant-Garde musician, folk art painter, veteran actress of countless community plays. She had also been high as a kite as she and a group of her friends clambered aboard the 100-foot sloop GreenWater to celebrate their triumphant victory over the 'forces of tyranny' that had attempted to shut down their yearly festival.

The ship itself was a reasonably accurate replica of the Dutch river sloops of the 18th and 19th centuries, a wide-beamed, shallow-bottomed boat with a single large mast, specifically designed for ferrying cargo up and down the Hudson as safely as possible. Given the large number of visitors on board on this particular day, however, the crew was sailing her as close to the wind as possible to keep the deck level

Gabriella, who was terrified of deep water, had been dragged along (practically in tears) on this outing and quickly positioned herself on what she felt was the safest position on the boat: sitting on the main hatch cover just aft of the main mast. Her strategy was fairly simple – close her eyes, grip her knees, and count the minutes until it was all over.

Thirty-five of those minutes had been counted when she was disturbed out of her safe place by a middle-aged woman who had banged her head on the main boom and started complaining loudly to one of the sloop's crew: a stocky kid who might have passed for a younger version of 'Slash' from Guns-n-Roses. The woman, who looked to Gabriella like one of those upper east-siders one would be more likely to see at an Elizabeth Arden beauty salon than stuck on an outing with a bunch of half-zonked graying hippies and activists, was laying into the kid about how everything was a safety hazard on board the ship and should be clearly marked with appropriate warning signage. To his credit the kid, who stood blinking with incomprehension, said nothing.

Gabriella made the unfortunate mistake of making eye contact with the woman, who immediately included her as a silent ally in her rant as she went on about how lawyers would be summoned and lawsuits filed as soon as they were back in cell phone signal range.

The woman was cut-off as the ship suddenly lurched to a stop.

This time, she definitely made her own point as her head hit the massive boom with a crack, hard enough to make Gabriella wince. Anybody who was standing on the crowded decks at that moment stumbled (two people actually fell over the rail and into the river) or fell to the deck. Gabriella was able to put her hands up and check her forward momentum by placing her palms on the main mast as the kid instinctively grabbed one of the mainstays. The woman, blood already ribboning down her forehead, swayed but miraculously stayed upright. She tried to focus again on Gabriella and was in the process of trying to say something when from behind and above her head appeared a glistening black tentacle thick as a full-grown python. Gabriella was able to note the splay of chitinous hooks at the end of the swaying appendage before the woman, even in her state of dumb shock, sensed something was amiss and half turned her head just as the thing struck.

Gabriella wanted to close her eyes, clamp shut more than anything else in the world, but her eyelids refused to obey. There was a hideous *ripping/smacking* sound and the woman spun back around in a ghastly pirouette, half her face torn off. Then, to Gabriella's horror, the woman collapsed on top of her, spraying her with blood and gore.

Within moments, everything went to hell.

The undulating tentacle was joined by a dozen others. Rigging, hull and human bodies were quickly clutched, torn, and ripped to pieces. Lines snapped, splinters flew, blood splattered. Those able to jumped overboard.

Gabriella shrieked and tried to bury herself on the deck as the ship groaned and began to list heavily to port. The coppery smell of blood mixed with seawater and an overpowering rotten fish smell permeated her lungs. There was a splintering snap as the main mast let go and tumbled over followed by the sluice and bubble of water as the hull began to collapse under the titanic grip of the monster attacking it.

Gabriella's eyes finally got with the program and she squeezed them shut, repeating 'ohGodohGodohGod' non-stop as she readied herself to die.

Something slithered past her and the deck jumped as the hulls cross-supports broke, then Gabriella found herself being hauled up from under the armpits. At first, she thought it was whatever nightmare was attacking the vessel and she screamed, only to realize it was the young crewman from earlier, now blood-streaked and the front of his chest slashed open. Still, for whatever reason – perhaps she was the only person left who appeared savable – he grabbed her and dashing/half dragging her the five steps to the starboard gunwale, leapt overboard.

The icy waters of the Hudson were a shock.

Putting his arm around her chest in a classic life-saving hold, despite his terrible injuries, the kid managed a powerful side-stroke away from the carnage.

It was difficult to believe such a large and ruggedly built ship could be destroyed so quickly. In less than seven minutes, the entire vessel had been reduced to scraps, the bulk of its destroyed hull let go to drift down through the murk to the Hudson's silty bottom. Debris, flotsam, and mutilated bodies were everywhere. Those still capable screamed and cried for help, though one by one, their numbers quickly diminished as *Typhon*, the nightmare from World's End, continued to feast.

Then the Russians arrived.

Easton never thought twice about what he did next. Plunging into the water, he half-waded, half-bounded to the closest boat which was an old classic 17-foot Star Craft with a brand-new outboard motor. Soaked, he clambered on board and lent a hand to Sarah who was right behind him –

yet even as he did so, he had a strangely simultaneous moment of premonition/déjà vu that this was going to have bad consequences for both of them … yet paradoxically had *already* happened. He had time to think, *I'm going out on the water and I swore I wouldn't*, and then he was in action. From the screams and cries, it was clear people were still alive out there – some of them were kids for Christ sakes – and he could no more stop himself from doing everything in his power to try and save them than he could re-write his own DNA code. And from the looks of things, he and Sarah looked like the only two people doing anything.

Except … what were those two fishing trawlers doing?

Fortunately, whoever owned the boat had done him the favor of leaving the keys in the ignition. Easton jumped into the small pilot's seat in the cockpit behind the aluminum-framed windshield and fired her up.

The engine was still warm and turned over with a rumble, sending a few large puffs of blue-black exhaust floating backwards. "Stay in the back – get ready to start pulling them out of the water!" he yelled at Sarah. Then he rammed the throttle forward and the boat took off.

As they headed out into the river, Easton noted a bunch of things simultaneously; directly ahead about two hundred yards out was the debris from the GreenWater with its survivors thrashing about in the waves, then there was the monster – Typhon (as he had begun to think of it since reading the account) – in the midst of it, just under the surface and picking off the unlucky ones. Further out in the middle of the river was the refurbished antique *Freedom Barge* with a small crew aboard, being pulled about by what seemed to be a small, 1940s vintage tugboat. The pilot seemed indecisive about what to do. It wasn't hard for Easton to imagine why – an entire 100' long ship had just been completely destroyed before everyone's very eyes.

And whatever had done it was still there in the water.

To the south of all were the two fishing trawlers, erratically charging their way towards them.

The other thing Easton noticed was wind picking up as the storm front rolled in closer from the northeast. *From the Dunderberg Imp's territory*, he thought, *Damn his soul*. He wasn't sure which way the tide was moving but opted to head downwind to start picking up survivors, praying the boat was agile enough to scoot them out of danger if Typhon decided to add them to the carnage. At the moment, all he could see was the occasional tentacle flailing out of the water and the roiling water indicating where it was lurking just under the surface.

As they came upon the first survivor, a stern-looking woman in her 50's who was clutching the remains of one of the hatch covers, Easton looked back and noted Sarah's face; terrified but determined. She didn't hesitate as the boat slowed to a stop, but reached over the side and grabbed onto their first rescue. A moment later, with Easton's help, the woman was safely on board, battered but alive.

Keeping a wary eye on the water, Easton eased them toward the next victim.

Hendricks got the call from Fowler just as he walked past the gate with his officers, having dispatched three men to locate the festivals power generators and shut them off. Fowler and his team aboard the WFPD's sleek police launch *Themis* had been in the bay proper ticketing boaters when the GreenWater was attacked. With his view blocked by the southern headland of the Point, he didn't see anything, and it was a matter of wasted minutes before he could sort out the sudden onslaught of calls from his spotters along the river that a serious disaster was unfolding just out of sight.

Ordering his men to ready their weapons, he gunned the *Themis*'s throttles and the twin Volvo-Penta D12-650 diesel engines roared to life, sending up a double rooster-tail as the 44' Fast Patrol Boat shot out of the bay.

As he rounded the point, he became aware of multiple things at once – the GreenWater was gone, only one small boat was out trying to pick up survivors, and the weather was about to turn nasty.

Grabbing the binoculars kept on hand by the pilot's seat, he scanned the area and called Hendricks.

"Chief, the sloop is *gone*."

Over by the festival gate, Hendricks pulled up short. "What the hell do you mean *gone*?"

"Gone as in *destroyed* gone. Something just … just pulverized it. There's debris all over the water. It looks like we're turning this into a rescue operation – we're going to need help." He was about to say something else when to the south he saw the two large trawlers heading at him apparently being hauled at a high rate of speed by something underwater. Whatever it was, it was huge and moving fast. One of his officers, who was looking at the Cyrillic writing on the bow of the nearest trawler – an ungainly looking sixty-footer – yelled out half-jokingly, "Holy shit! It's the Russians! *The Russians are coming!*"

"Got to go—" was all Fowler said before the sharpshooters on his boat began firing. Then abruptly, the nearest trawler slewed sideways … and slammed into the *Themis*.

Hendricks looked at his radio, alarmed, as he registered his captain's words and heard the shots himself. "Jesus, we have to—" he started to say to his two senior officers but Sanchez and Eckhart were already sprinting toward the water.

Igor Gorimov's day was going to shit.

It had started out well enough – just north of the Tappan Zee Bridge construction zone, they had picked up the creature on the radar and immediately he ordered the nets slung between the two boats – the *Pravda* and the *Svetlana* – as they moved into parallel position at full throttle. Whatever it was, it was fast, but even so, the two trawlers shortly began to gain on it.

Gorimov was standing on the high bridge of the *Pravda* with his skipper, a tough old Ukrainian named Piotr with a bushy red beard. At the bow of each ship were two marksmen, one armed with a tranquilizer gun and the other with a semi-automatic AK-47 in case the former didn't work. Each vessel also had a special cannon manned by a crewman at the bow, both set to fire a broad, weighted net simultaneously that was secured to both ships.

The ships were actually U.S. built deep-sea fishing trawlers that had been originally picked up from the fishing fleet out at Montauk at the height of the Recession from a couple of desperate local owners. Battered and banged-up and smelling of decades of hauling fish, Gorimov's only major concern was that they did what they need to do, which in fairness they had. Up to that day.

The trouble started right after they closed in range and fired the forward net. Gorimov and his crews had been estimating they were after something in the magnitude and strength of a powerful whale, such as a humpback or sperm.

It quickly became apparent they were way off the mark.

The cannons went off, firing the net forty yards forward and down into the water, then a minute later, the creature shot forward like a locomotive, dragging the two ships like they were nothing more than logs.

The sharpshooters weren't having any luck either – as if aware of their purpose the creature was keeping too far below the surface for them to get a good shot. With its constantly swerving course, the deck movement was too much for them to get an accurate aim regardless.

"What the fucking hell have we netted!?" Piotr had yelled above the roar of the engines.

"Neptune's balls and a lot of fucking money, that's what!" Igor had yelled back. "Don't worry, it'll tire soon enough, just you watch!"

Only it hadn't worked out that way.

By the time they had been dragged to the area of Raadsel Point, the creature had yet to show *any* signs of slowing down and both ships were beginning to take on water, their steel-plated hulls buckling from the strain. Gorimov was beginning to wonder whether they might have to seriously consider cutting the damned thing loose when they came up on the disaster unfolding of the Point.

Standing on the bridge, Gorimov, by all accounts a brutal man who had seen plenty of horrors (and committed more than a few himself) was shocked to witness the last few moments of the GreenWater.

"Holy shit!" he said, watching one human being arc through the air after being torn into two pieces by a pair of undulating tentacles. This was nothing like drive fishing a pod of killer whales or dolphins; this was being pulled into a slaughterhouse. He actually had gotten as far as starting to yell at the crew on the foredeck to cut the lines when suddenly – impossibly – the creature plunged down and sideways underneath his vessel.

He had time to look down and see they were being dragged into a police boat that he hadn't even noticed, before snapping his head around just in time to see the *Svetlana* slam into them.

The last thing he saw before tumbling to the deck below was the head of the creature shooting out of the water twenty yards away, having chewed its way out of the nets like they were made of cheap string instead of high-tensile fiber.

Around the same time, Ben Reinhardt was startled in his cot by a furious pounding on the stateroom's door. He had spent part of the morning packing his few meager belongings into his backpack, having been told earlier they were kicking him off the ship and sending him back to Columbia for disciplinary action, then essentially had spent the last hour contemplating the ceiling again when the interruption came.

"Hold your horses," he grumbled, dropping down and rubbing his eyes. He was exhausted, overtired, and depressed. And not much in the mood for monkey business.

He threw open the door and was surprised to see Lieutenant Walker, a young man from Delaware, whose features hinted he might have some Kennedy blood in the family tree somewhere. He looked like he was born into the creased and immaculately pressed uniform he was wearing.

Reinhardt hated him. But he was surprised to see Walker accompanied by two crew officers from security detail.

"Get your stuff," the lieutenant said without any preamble. "You're being transferred."

"I'm being … *what*?" Reinhardt responded, scratching his head. His curly hair was standing up in tufts.

"Transferred," Walker repeated in a curt tone. He looked peeved.

"Transferred? Where?" Reinhardt echoed, not understanding.

"To the *Okeanos Explorer*. She's alongside us right now. Now hop to it, wonder-boy."

"The … the what?" He knew the ship alright. But what the hell was it doing here?

Walker focused on a point somewhere past Reinhardt's shoulder. "Just hurry up, will you?"

Ten minutes later, a disheveled and wits-addled Reinhardt found himself on the 'mission deck' of the Okeanos, standing next to the secured rescue boat when out of the ROV garage stepped a man he probably idolized more than anyone in the world.

For one of the few times ever in his entire life, Ben Reinhardt was in a complete state of shock.

"Hey, welcome aboard, Ben!" Bob Ballard said, extending his hand. "I hear you've been finding some very interesting things up here in the river."

Peeling out of his driveway in his Land Rover in reverse, Jim Franks almost didn't see the man standing there and very nearly ran him over regardless. After screeching to a stop and displacing a good amount of loose dirt and gravel, Franks rolled down his window and sticking his head out started to say, "Jesus Chri—" before checking himself.

No one was there.

Then came a tap at the passenger window.

Framed in the glass was a face he knew very well. Franks leaned over and rolled that window down as well. "I'm kinda in a rush," he said loudly, exasperated. "What can I do you for?"

Rambo appeared unruffled. Franks might as well have yelled at a slab of rock. "I'm coming with you," the old man said in his thick accent. It wasn't a question.

Sanchez and Eckhart along with a younger officer named Doyle jumped into the most readily available boat they could find: an aluminum

15–footer with an Evinrude outboard engine. A minute later, with Sanchez manning the outboard, they were high-tailing it out of the bay.

Aboard the *Themis*, the two sharpshooters broke off their fire as Fowler veered the boat, just as the trawler slammed into them. There was a sickening crack as the hulls impacted in a glancing blow, but Fowler's deft maneuvering spared them the worst. He saw the creature breach the surface (*damned if it wasn't some kind of extinct sea dinosaur!* Fowler thought) before it plunged under in the direction of where the GreenWater had broken up, leaving them with a sinuous flick of its long serpentine tail.

"We definitely put a few rounds into it," one of the officers, an ex-marine named Dan Taylor, said. He pointed to the traces of blood floating on the surface. "But whether it did a damn bit of good is anyone's guess."

Fowler nodded, turning the boat about in pursuit. "One of you stay in the bow and fire only when you are absolutely sure you have a clear shot, and one of you get your ass below and check out the damage," he yelled above the rumble of the engines. "The rest of you start pulling people out of the water as we get up to them!"

To the west of them, Easton and Sarah had pulled three more victims out of the water (one already dead) when they eased up alongside two more, a half-numb Gabriella Powers and the young crewman – Dave Crane – who had rescued her. Gabriella was suffering from the early stages of hypothermia and shock, but otherwise was unscathed. Crane's lips, however, were blue, and as Sarah and Easton manhandled him onto the boat, the extent of his injuries looked serious. To Easton, it looked like something had raked half a dozen two-inch fishhooks across the kid's chest.

But there wasn't time to dwell on it as Typhon veered its course toward them. *Christ, the damn thing is fucking faster than I thought,* Easton said to himself, pulse racing as he jumped back into the pilot's seat. He was just pushing the throttle forward when the first tentacles seized the boat.

Easton glanced back as Sarah screamed and saw a terrible sight – the creature's head breaking the surface as it snatched at the back of the hull. For a moment, he was simultaneously mesmerized and repelled; the upper part was nothing like a squid at all – it was some sort of mutated nightmare union of giant sea insect and cephalopod. The head/upper carapace was broad and flat and consisted of wide overlapping plates. Large dinner-plate-sized eyes dominated either side, but a line of decreasingly smaller sub-eyes trailed in towards a series of mandibles and a mouth that resembles a distorted, upside down parrot's beak. From under the massive carapace trailed a series of tentacles that were small up front but elongated in size towards the bottom. The body and tentacles were largely a blackish-green, with a spotted pattern towards the edges while what he could see of the underbelly was the pale pinkish-silvery hue of a dead perch. The creature had somehow latched onto the stern of the boat with its mandibles and was swinging its body around to bring its longer tentacles to bear and finish the job.

Fiberglass snapped and splintered as one cable-sized tentacle lashed towards Sarah. In one fluid motion, Easton drew his Beretta and fired, once, twice. The appendage snapped back, but the mandibles redoubled their attack, splintering the back end of the boat. Compared to the GreenWater, the Starcraft would be short work for it. He fired again and again at the thing's head until the magazine was empty, but it just seemed to infuriate the thing further.

Easton was considering how he could get Sarah and their five rescues to jump off the bow and take their chances overboard when he saw something even more incredible: a giant shape just under the water zoom in behind Typhon, like a massive torpedo. He almost tumbled off the boat as creature and craft were suddenly rammed forward. The buzzing/chittering sound coming out of Typhon's head reached a screaming crescendo, then the boat gave a second sickening lurch as it was released.

For the next minute or so, Easton and everyone in the immediate area found themselves witnesses to the strangest sea battle ever fought.

The *Mosasaurus*, or 'Ossie' as some had come to call it, was a good 50-feet in length head to tail, or about as long as a semi-tractor trailer. Its head alone was roughly six and a half feet long, large enough (as Captain Fowler and his officers could readily testify) to devour a human being in one bite. Weighing around sixteen tons, its flippers and whipping tail were powerful enough to propel it at incredible speeds of up to 30 miles-per-hour.

The creature known as Typhon – actually the last of a hitherto completely unknown species – measured roughly twenty-five feet long with its head and body, though its longest tentacles extended as long as thirty feet beyond that.

The mosasaur clamped Typhon in its massive jaws and immediately found itself wrapped in a writhing net of tentacles. Wrenching itself around, the giant sea reptile actually thrust itself half out of the water, executing a spinning flip while giving out a muffled hissing roar that struck an atavistic chord of terror in those nearby, a primal rumble that bellowed swift and terrible death from a lost aeon.

It felt as though the entire river shook with the concussion of those two titanic bodies hitting the water; a ten-foot sheet of water sluiced the air and the impact wave that rippled out nearly swamped the already crippled Starcraft. Almost simultaneously came a brilliant flash as lightning lanced across the sky, followed by a thunderclap that stunned the ears.

Thirty yards to the east, Fowler kept the police launch zig-zagging back and forth as long as possible, having picked up as many survivors as they could while the sharpshooter in the bow kept his assault rifle trained on the unfolding battle, pulling off an occasional shot when the angle was clear. He'd quickly discovered, however, that the hull was damaged and they were slowly taking on water, so after five minutes or so, he was forced to turn back towards the marina.

Behind him, the two Russian vessels were locked together and listing, not quite sinking but drifting with the current and as far as he could tell out of commission.

Meanwhile, aboard the Starcraft, Easton was trying to nurse the damaged engines to life, at the same time seeing with growing alarm that they were beginning to sink. The mangled stern of the boat was only an inch above water and was already beginning to submerge even as he watched. With that came even worse news – there were only three life jackets on board.

If that wasn't enough, more lightning ripped through the sky and the first rain squall hit.

33. THE CLASH OF THE LEVIATHANS.

The *Mosasaurus* was mortally wounded.

It was vaguely aware of the fact in its primitive reptilian brain that something was wrong, that one of its front flippers was no longer working and that the lung on the left side wasn't functioning much as it filled up with blood from where two bullets had torn through the parallel trachea that fed it. And the long haul up the river pulling the two trawlers had sapped its energy. But it was first and foremost a prehistoric killing machine, its species an unmatched predator and top of the food chain in its time. Even as its strength began to ebb, its jaws continued to thrash and chomp with terrific force, severing tentacle and fracturing carapace.

It had come to the area not by choice, but answering to the sonic call it had been hard-wired to respond to, the peculiar frequency of a distressed mate that it was unable to resist. A call it hadn't heard in decades which resonated with its sort of limited version of loneliness, a desire to see its own kind.

Then it had arrived in these restrictive waters and swum about in confusion, sensing only the presence of another large predator in the area, an alien enemy it had never encountered before, though its scent and vibrations hinted at one of the mosasaur's favorite diet, the giant squid it occasionally encountered out in the ocean.

So it had loitered about, feeding off the larger river sturgeon and striped bass in the deeper waters, though not particularly liking the taste.

Until today, when it picked up on the chemicals being released by the other; announcing hunger, agitation, feeding.

So it had circled around in a diminishing circuit, zeroing in on its prey.

Then had come the taste of blood and the small thing floating on the surface that it had gobbled up.

Followed by the stinging pain of hard objects piercing its body from seemingly nowhere.

And then, the *other*, close by. Preoccupied.

It struck.

Now it was dying.

The Typhon was seriously injured as well.

It had grown flush and strong since it had been jangled out of its long hibernation the year previous. It had its own peculiar alien logic that drove it to attack and devour anything living and any large object in its habitat – including boats on the surface – drew it like a magnet. There was something in the frequency of the motors that was highly agitating to its nervous system.

And it had developed a taste for human beings.

Now it found itself fighting for its life.

The armored carapace had spared its internal organs the worst of the attacks, but now those were shattering and caving in to the enormous pressure of its attacker's jaws, and a good third of its feeding and attacking tentacles had been severed or damaged beyond use.

Its mandible tore and scratched at the thick scales around the attackers head, the parrot-like beak elongating and tearing out chunks of flesh from the from the softer underside of its enemy's lower jaw. Its thrashing tentacles squeezed and tore.

Crunch.

Snap.

Smack.

The two monsters broke the surface three more times, then, locked in their vice-like death embrace, began to sink towards the bottom of the river.

Jim Franks didn't bother trying to get out to Raadsel Point. He had already gotten a call that morning that the festival was still on and from previous experience, knew that at best, the road out would be jammed. His band 'The Vapors' had been scheduled to play originally, though when one of the GreenWater promoter's asked if he'd still be interested he'd declined.

Instead, he drove right through the parking lot of the Raadsel Bay Yacht Club and tore through the front lawn right past the flag pole one unfortunate kite-surfer had married recently, tearing out huge divots of the perfectly manicured grass which had just been replaced that morning.

A minute later, he was dragging Rambo out onto the docks, checking out the few remaining powerboats still moored there.

The first one he spotted was Chester Billingsworth's classic cigar boat, a beautifully crafted triple cockpit Hacker-Craft runabout, all gleaming brass trim on acres of varnished wood. Chester, a 58-year-old commercial developer with white hair and a twenty-thousand-dollar smile, was himself fussing around the cockpit. Like a lot of local people,

Franks wasn't exactly a card-carrying member of the Chester Billingsworth fan club, having born witness to the man's questionable practice of buying up historic buildings and flipping them over into cheap developments. And not to mention tail-gaiting everyone in town with his deep green classic Jaguar convertible, usually punctuated with aggressive hits of the horn. Franks had almost gotten in a couple road rage incidents with Billingsworth in the past few years, but this time, he was on a mission.

"Hey, you can't come aboard my—" Billingsworth said as Franks jumped down into the cockpit, shoving him aside.

"I'm taking your boat," Franks announced distractedly, looking around for the starter switch.

"But it's mine, you can't have—" Billingsworth snarled as he grabbed at Franks, who wasn't in the mood for lengthy explanations. Before he could finish his sentence, he found himself tossed overboard into the oily water alongside. Franks got the engine turned over just as Rambo carefully clambered in next to him.

A minute later, that twin engines of the Hacker-Craft let out a throaty burble as Franks eased her out of the marina, then split into a roar as he rammed the throttles forward and sped out into the bay.

Over in the cave at the north side of the point, Del Tesler, along with Jennie Roderick and his film crew, were have an entertaining lunch after reshooting several scenes. Each take had improved on the previous and by the last Del Tesler was claiming, " … the sunken walls indicate a definite sort of landing strip or buried city and the Ossie is most certainly a sort of guardian placed by aliens to protect them … those structures are clearly, CLEARLY evidence of ancient astronauts." Then adding after a significant pause, "That is a *fact*."

The two 24' pontoon boats he'd rented that morning were safely anchored nearby. Someone had set up their iPod Touch with a portable speaker dock and had cranked up the current playlist which included Prince, Beyoncé, and Lady Gaga. His assistant had laid out food for everyone on a small folding table; mixed wraps and chips (and plenty of Del Tesler's favorite orange soda) courtesy of Wyvern Falls' Main Street Deli.

With the storm coming in, Del Tesler had opted to weather it out in a safe, dry place while regaling his crew with tales of his adventures with Otto Wierling and the wondrous evidence of ancient aliens they'd uncovered over the years, as well as a few of his mentor's philosophies.

"The lost technologies of ancient Egypt were *astounding*," Del Tesler was saying through a mouthful of chicken Caesar. "The precision alignment of the pyramids? The evidence is right there in front of you. And think about it, why would the Egyptians, if they were so intelligent, spend forty years and all that money and resources building a gihumongous monument just to stick one body in it? Of course they wouldn't – that's nuts! And if you look at that bust of Nefertiti with her beautifully elongated skull, exactly, *exactly* like the elongated skulls from those ancient tombs in Peru?" He leaned forward and gestured with his free hand. "There simply is no other explanation. Ancient Aliens ..."

Next to him, Jennie was nodding thoughtfully, all but brimming with excitement about finding herself hooked up with this crew ... and of course Del Tesler. She was screwing a bona fide *celebrity*. A steady stream of uploads had been going to her Facebook and Twitter accounts since the day before with predictable responses from her small group of friends like, "OMG, that's sooo cool!", "I'm like so jealous!" and "UR my idol!"

Of John Barringer, she'd heard nothing, even though she hadn't *unfriended* him yet, which annoyed her somewhat. *He should have appreciated me more*, she thought with a slight pang, followed by: *whatever, I always knew I was destined for bigger things ...*

Meanwhile, Barringer was moaning in pain in the cabin of the *Themis*, having been rescued earlier, minus half of his left leg. Despite the shock and loss of blood, the tourniquet one of the officers had applied was holding and there was a chance he might even make it.

Lieutenant Sanchez veered their boat just pass the *Themis* and picked up two survivors when the rain began. Eckhart was sitting with them, not able to do much except offer some soothing words of encouragement. One of the survivors – Gabriella Powers' Aunt Flo, didn't look like she was going to live much longer but the other one, a teenage kid, looked like he was going to be fine.

Looking about, he decided, with the storm kicking up, that the best option would be to make for the *Freedom Barge*, which had already altered its course to assist with Easton aboard the sinking Starcraft. For one moment, as he sat in the stern and twisted the throttle on the Evinrude, his eye fell on Eckhart and he marveled, not for the first time, at what an exceptional woman she was. Her level of empathy was inspiring. Despite not having children of her own, she had a certain calm, motherly demeanor that grew even stronger in emergency situations.

He sometimes wondered why she hadn't become a nurse or doctor instead.

It doesn't really matter, he thought. *I love her all the same.*

Down the river, the Okeanos Explorer was moving full speed ahead and was just coming up on the scene of the disaster. Ben Reinhardt found himself in the pilothouse with Ballard, Commander Mitchell, and his officers, feeling like he'd just been snatched from the gates of purgatory and dropped into a surreal fantasy.

An hour previous, he was convinced his marine scientist career was either over or seriously derailed for an extended length of time; now here he was, standing on the bridge of his dream ship with the head of the Oceanographic Institute himself.

The pilothouse was crowded with personnel at the extensive command console at its front. Ballard had guided Reinhardt to the front port corner by the forward slanting windows. The front thirty or so feet above the water was impressive – an imperious position that made him feel like they were in command of the river itself.

"Something major is going on upriver," Ballard was saying. "That may involve something both you and I have seen recently."

Reinhardt blinked. His brain felt scrambled. "Uh, really?" was all that came out. He felt like a complete dope.

Ballard nodded. "Yes, really. A *Mosasaurus* or *Tylosaurus proriger*, it appears."

That got through. "I don't understand," Reinhardt answered. "You've seen this thing too? Where?"

"It passed us on the way up here apparently," the director replied. "Now we're on our way to hopefully find out why. If we're not too late."

"Grab the line!" the bearded guy by the side of the barge was yelling.

Easton was trying to take in the bizarreness of the situation and was only partially succeeding. The vessel was what appeared to be a covered 19th century 'Hudson Valley Railroad Barge' that had been turned into a sort of floating museum/education center. The hull was a rusted iron hulk, shaped like a traditional barge, but on top was a heavy-timbered superstructure that was reminiscent of an old-fashioned rail car, though much broader and flatter. On the side was hung a large black canvas sign with large white black letters spelling out *Freedom Barge*.

The tug captain had veered the barge as close to Easton's sinking vessel as he dared, when the crewman (dressed in a traditional striped shirt and canvas pants) had appeared in the sliding side door with a heavy-looking hemp rope.

Easton got a hold of the line and hauled them up alongside the barge, even as the Starcraft began to submerge. Someone produced a rope ladder, and after a chaotic interval of screams, shouts, and grasping hands, the survivors were pulled one by one up onto the barge, and none too soon. Even as Easton's dripping foot left the tilting bow, the Starcraft began to roll, and with a sluice and gurgle, slid beneath the waves.

The thunderstorm was passing over.

Standing in the open side door of the barge, his arm around Sarah – a blanket had been produced somewhere and she'd wrapped herself in it, shivering – he was wondering if it was truly over. With the adrenaline dissipating in his system, he was beginning to feel that familiar bone-weary exhaustion, though it came with a certain grim satisfaction of having narrowly escaped disaster. He pulled her in close and kissed the top of her head, noting the briny aroma of her damp hair. Overhead, the clouds were breaking up into cavernous stacks punctuated by more subdued flashes while more boats began to arrive on the scene.

Aboard the *Themis*, Fowler was starting to circle back toward the marina where Hendricks had already made sure several ambulances were waiting on standby. Stretched out on one of the benches in the sleek-but-utilitarian cabin, John Barringer slipped in and out of consciousness, moaning in agony.

Easton turned as someone inside the poorly lit structure of the barge asked if he'd like some hot coffee. The interior was all aged timbers and an assortment of antique barge accessories including coiled ropes, pikes, gaffs, life preservers, and oil lanterns, even a battered-looking cast-iron stove stuck dead center with a protective metal railing around it. Two small skylights banished some of the shadows to the corners, but overall the atmosphere was of persistent gloom, dampness, and old timbers.

Exhibit tables were set up around the perimeter, and in one corner, a refreshment stand offering hot and cold drinks, cheese and crackers and such. Framed antique photos of Wyvern Falls and rail men from yesteryear hung along the walls, along with a collection of vintage signage probably worth a fortune.

Easton took a few steps in and gratefully accepted the two (recycled) paper coffee cups of steaming black coffee from a woman he thought he recognized from the coffee house on Main.

He didn't see the cigar boat arcing out around the Point at a hefty 35 knots, correcting its course to head straight at them.

Twenty or so feet away aboard the aluminum fishing boat, a thoroughly soaked Lieutenant Sanchez eased them towards a body in the water at Eckhart's urging. As they drew close, he could see it was a thin-looking woman with long, curly brown hair floating on her side. Eckhart, dressed in her WFPD blues (though also soaked to the skin), leaned over trying to snag the woman's arm. As she did, it was quickly apparent the woman was dead – the corpse half-rolled revealing a gaping chest cavity and missing arm, the knob of the clavicle gleaming.

Eckhart choked, and covering her mouth with her forearm, half-turned back towards Sanchez, and that was when he saw something terrible rise up to the surface beyond her.

"Katrina!" he yelled.

There was an agonizing moment as he saw her register alarm from his expression, then just as she half-turned back towards the water, two ropelike tentacles whipped out of the water and snatched her out of the boat. With a muffled 'ungh!' she was yanked underneath the waves.

Sanchez instinctively jumped up and had taken two bounding steps towards the bow to jump in after her when the front of the boat was hit with enough force to flip it up in the air, as if flicked away by the wounded leviathan in front of it.

For Sanchez, the result was instantaneous: the metal bow cap connected with his forehead as the boat flipped over, and by the time he landed in water, he was knocked out cold.

Easton had just turned around at the commotion outside, a cup in each hand, when he saw the tentacles rising up in the air behind Sarah, who was silhouetted in the doorway. Even as he released the cups and leaped forward, the barge made a sickening lurch that sent people and objects flying every which way.

He distinctly heard her call his name "John?" in a frightened plea as she grabbed the doorframe for dear life. Even as the deck began to tilt, Easton leap-frogged forward and managed to grab her wrist.

One tentacle coiled around her torso and squeezed. Bones snapped.

Sarah screamed.

34. DAMN YOU TO HELL AND BACK ...

It was unquestionably the most horrible moment he had ever experienced in his life. A person he had completely surrendered his heart to being destroyed in front of his eyes. Sarah's eyes bulged with terror and pain as the tentacle tightened even more, her scream turned into a muffled gurgle as her rib cage collapsed; blood erupted from her mouth and the hand gripping Easton's spasmodically dug its nails in, gouging his skin.

Inexorably, she was being dragged down into the water, pulling Easton with her. Below, the mangled head and carapace of Typhon appeared just below the surface, the feeding mandibles quivering in anticipation

Even as he cried out in his own physical and mental pain – it felt as if his very soul had been caught on a ragged fish hook and was being ripped out of him – he heard her voice in his head say what at first sounded nonsensical; *kuh-tah-hoh-lull* ... *puh-nuh-nee* ... before the patterns of sounds resolved themselves (at the blink of thought) into '*Ktaholël* ... *punëni* ..."

[I love you ... let me go.]

He hung on a moment longer, his face a rictus of agony. Then released her.

Sarah was immediately yanked below the waves.

What happened next was a blur. It was as if a red sheet of fury enveloped him – a berserker rage as it were, and even as he hung half over the water unaware of several hands trying to grab his feet, his arm came down and his fingers brushed something attached to his belt at his hip, something he had no recollection of putting on when he'd left that morning.

Sarah's knife.

As he plunged into the water, he tore the thing out of its sheath, snapping the securing thong, and with a swift kick, pushed away from the barge and toward the frothing waters.

Half a dozen tentacles immediately seized him, though he noticed with distracted satisfaction that half of them were barely functional and the two others that feebly grasped toward him were no more than severed stumps. The air seemed filled with a buzzing chittering sound as he was yanked in toward the monster's mouth, the upside down parrot beak extending and snapping. Nearby underwater, he could see Sarah's hair floating and the pale glimmer of her skin.

Easton wasn't even afraid. He had been transformed into a bestial, snarling animal with only a single purpose in mind – *kill*.

Claws tore at his skin, two tentacles seized him and pulled him towards that hideously snapping mouth, and then he found himself for a split second within mere feet away from the things left eye, which seemed to glare at him with alien menace as if contemplating this strange violent creature it was about to eat. There was a brilliant flash of lightning, and for a fleeting moment, even his primal rage, Easton swore he saw reflected in that giant orb the faces of the thunder beings in the sky overhead; angry and vindictive.

"Damn you to hell and back!" he hissed.

The creature hesitated, its bizarre iris dilating, and that was its undoing.

Easton's hand, gripping eight inches of wickedly sharp steel plunged straight into it, almost to the shoulder, then slashed and cut at whatever brain and tissues were in reach.

Typhon died screaming its alien, buzzing scream.

Consciously, it was over within moments, the brain blinking out in an explosion of pain even as its giant body convulsed. The tentacles gripping Easton reflexively snapped him away, breaking his arm at the elbow as he was tossed aside like a rag doll. Bits of gore and a hideous black ichor encased his sleeve and hand, which still gripped the knife so hard the knuckles were white.

Even as Easton felt himself sliding into the fuzzy grey lined blackness, he heard the creak and groan of the barge as it began to tilt even further, snagged by the spasming death throes of Typhon as the creature's nervous system exploded in dying, chaotic signals.

"Sarah …" Easton had time to think.

Then nothing.

35. ONE FOR ANOTHER.

Franks witnessed the whole thing, knowing full well he was never going to make it in time to save John Easton.

Still, he had to try.

He cut the throttles as the cigar boat came up alongside the tilting barge, close to the deck that was tilting perilously close to the waterline. The monster had latched onto the barge in its final death grip, its sheer weight causing a massive imbalance and, if not actually capable of sinking it, was well on its way to capsizing it.

It was Rambo who saved the day.

Even as they banged into the hull of the barge, he barked something at the terrified crew in the doorway and clapped his gnarled, powerful hands together. It took a few tries then someone got it.

A second later, a large axe was thrust at him handle first.

In any other circumstances, Franks would have marveled at the veracity of the old man as he began to swing and chop at the tentacles with the fury of a deranged woodsman half his age. Instead, Franks was focused on finding Easton. He finally spotted him a few yards away, floating face down. Not far from him floated Sarah's corpse.

Tears streaming down his face, Franks jumped into the water.

Half a mile away at the base of the Point, Crazy Jack stood near the edge of the water, a silent witness to what had just happened out in the river.

His face was a portrait of age and sadness, the seamed lines of his leathery skin deeper and more defined than ever as if he had put on ten years in as many minutes.

He, too, had seen the flashing faces of the Thunder Beings in the clouds, as if announcing themselves in this final act, and as he stood there he felt all the tremendous weight, desire and bittersweet reality of the human condition; pain and loss, the fleeting bonds then separation, of old friends and loved ones continually fading, receding into the mists of time.

There were the good things too, of course. Too many to count. The sublime beauty of a particularly pleasant day, an eagle soaring over the thermals or just the eager chirping of a newly born chick … the anticipation of a slice of one's favorite bread before the first bite and the lingering caress of a lover's touch.

Even just the simple joy and anticipation of taking a good solid dump on the toilet.

He'd lived so much – far longer than he should have. But he was tired. And this was too much; it had to end.

And there was *her*, dying all over again. The cycle of pain, anguish, sacrifice.

He murmured an old Indian prayer under his breath, then looking out at the broad expanse of the Hudson River, breathtaking even with the carnage and destruction this day, and sighed. He sensed they were about to arrive even before the figures popped into existence behind him.

"Take me instead," he said, not looking back. "One spirit for another – a fair bargain."

He felt, as well as heard the seven-voices-as-one in his head: [*A balanced energy exchange then ... an agreement ... action and reaction ... harmony ...*]

Although the correct terminology wasn't in his vocabulary, all at once Crazy Jack understood something else; these beings weren't extra-terrestrial, they were *interdimensional*.

The air around him seemed to grow very still for a moment, as if even the rocks were listening.

A moment later, he fell to his knees, teeth clenched as his chest began to collapse.

But like his ancestors before him, he never cried out once as he died.

At the remains of the fort above him, the same frizzy-haired young girl who had inquired about Detective Eckhart's carbon footprint earlier looked down at where the old Indian stood where the rocks trailed into the water.

Her eyes went wide as she saw the seven figures pop into existence, tall humanoids with slightly silvery, iridescent skin and eyes. They wore clothes that vaguely suggested men's shirts and pants, without being specific. One actually half-turned and looked up at her, but she didn't sense danger or malice, only curious indifference.

"Look, Grandma, it's the silver men!" she said excitedly.

Her grandmother, emotionally overwrought and fixated on the horrible tableau out in the river, didn't even look down.

"Nonsense, child, we haven't seen Mister Silverman in years. He's in Florida."

Seconds later, they popped out of existence.

36. ONE WEEK LATER ...

Easton was sitting in the hospital chair, legs crossed and in a half-doze when she woke up.

It wasn't anything dramatic, just a fluttering of the eyelids, a twitch of the fingers resting on top of the blanket. He had positioned his chair right alongside the hospital bed so that he could hold her other hand with his left, his right arm being in a cast.

The I.V. drip continued its methodical delivery of prescribed nutrients and the heart monitor its dutiful acknowledgment of a steady heartbeat.

Then just like that, she woke up.

Sarah Ramhorne had been in coma for exactly a week. In that time, she had also entered in Philipseburg Memorial's records, and folklore, as a *bona fide* medical miracle. Her body had been recovered by Franks with the assistance of the first civilian rescue boat to pull alongside the barge, hoisting her limp body onto the cigar boat Franks had 'requisitioned' along with four other victims. Franks would never forget the sound of her broken chest bones cracking as they did, nor the horrible angle of his friend's arm as he lay propped in the corner of the boat's cockpit. He had motored back toward the marina with tears streaming down his face, numb with shock.

The first EMT's to examine her at the emergency treatment area that had been hastily set up in front of the yacht club had pronounced her dead.

Franks had been sitting by a still unconscious Easton when Karen Evershaw had come running up, nearly in hysterics (she'd seen her fiancée peel out of the driveway but had no idea what was happening until after she'd jumped into her Saab and followed the sirens and commotion down to the waterfront). Her first order of business, of course, was Franks, which after establishing he was intact turned her to Easton, whose arm the EMT's had rigged with a temporary sling along with taped compresses to staunch the worst of the ragged wounds inflicted by Typhon.

Franks had been holding up fairly well, until Karen asked about Sarah and he'd pointed to the still form lying in the grass nearby, a blanket half-covering her soaked body. It was Karen who had gone over to her, shocked that this person she had last seen as a living, breathing (if upset) human being was the same as this waxy-looking, blue-lipped caricature with a horribly distorted chest, and had sat with her a moment, pulling aside the loose strands of wet hair out of Sarah's face when she suddenly noticed a twitch in one the eyelids. The EMT who had rushed back over, an older, white-haired volunteer named Jake had been surprised, then relieved; "My God, she is alive. She definitely had no pulse when they brought her in … I-I … yes, it's barely there, but she's alive alright!"

Easton had awoken a short while later in the ambulance next to her and had let out a heavily sedated sob when he was informed by the attendant that Sarah Ramhorne – in spite of extreme physical trauma – was still amongst the living.

The doctors at Philipseburg had insisted on keeping Easton for three nights straight on intravenous antibiotics to knock out any potential infection in his system, since they had no clear understanding about the nature of the thing that had mauled him other than the tests indicated it had transmitted levels of bacteria beyond any animal (or fish) bite they had ever encountered. After that, Easton had spent every available hour at the hospital, heading home only to walk Rovsky and catch a little sleep.

On the first day at the hospital, Franks had appeared in Easton's room with the news about Sarah; "The doctors are stumped, pal," he'd said. "They were going to perform some surgery to put her rib-cage back into proper shape, but apparently it *repaired itself*. I know that sounds utterly 'X-Files,' but that's what happened. But it gets even weirder. The attending physician who was examining her blood samples claimed he observed some kind of sub-cell nano-bytes repairing the cell structures, but when he brought his colleagues over to verify it, they began to disappear – 'winked out of existence' was how he described it. They did a bone biopsy afterward and were even more shocked – they're saying something had somehow gone in and 'systematically rebuilt the bone scaffolding'."

When Easton had questioned his doctor about it later that day, her response had been evasive. "Well," Doctor Rosenberg, a no-nonsense woman in her 50's with sculpted thick brown hair had said while tapping her pen on his chart, "that was what Doctor Riley *claimed* he saw, but he was under a lot of stress with all the disaster victims coming in. When we finally got her x-rays, everything seemed normal. But now that things are settling down, he's taken some much overdue leave."

As she'd turned to leave, he'd asked, "Is there such a nano-technology – any sort of development at the NIH or such?"

"No," had been Dr. Rosenberg's perfunctory response. "That kind of technology doesn't exist yet. May *never* exist yet for all we know."

The next morning, a tall man had shown up in Easton's room. If the Genesee County Sheriff's uniform wasn't a tip off, the unmistakable family resemblance certainly was. He'd stood in the doorway for a minute, studying Easton with hard eyes and a completely expressionless face. Easton simply stared at him back. He had no idea which direction this might go. After a moment, the man looked away and walked over to the window and gazed out at the panoramic river below, his thumbs hooked in his belt. The gun at his hip looked massive.

"So you're John Easton," he'd said finally.

"Yes, I am."

After another lengthy pause, the officer had turned and looked at him again for a long time. It wasn't clear whether he liked or didn't like what he saw. Then he said, "I'll come back in a few days to check on my sister." And left.

If he did, Easton didn't know about it.

Once off his IV, Easton spent hours at her bedside, holding her hand. It was on the second day of this that he noticed the dull ache in his fractured radius and ulna had disappeared and his fingertips where he touched her skin would develop a warm tingling sensation after the contact had lasted awhile.

Then a week later, she woke up.

The fingers entwined in his gave a light squeeze.

"John," she whispered. Despite continual dabs of the water and towel, her lips were still chapped.

Easton swam back into consciousness, a smile creeping across his face.

"*Chich ntàpi*," she said hoarsely. It sounded like *cheech nn-tuh-pee*.

Easton shook his head.

"I'm back," she announced, managing a smile. Despite being pale, her whole face seemed to warm up.

The first thing he did was to prop her head up and give her a few sips of water. Then she'd whispered one request, almost like a little child; '*Hug.*'

Easton felt his ears watering as he carefully took her up in his arms. They stayed like that a bit then she pulled away, running her hands over his face as if to verify he was really there. Then after a soft kiss on his lips, she laid back. Easton stayed leaning over, holding her hand to his cheek.

"I had a dream ... it was terrible. There was a *Maxa'xak* ... a river monster. It didn't have horns but ... it was like a giant sea insect or something. It was killing me. The pain was awful. And I saw you ... with the knife. Coming to save me … and then I was carried away, pulled in some sort of invisible current. There was light … not like sunlight, but a sort of … I can't describe it. Partly, it was a light of knowledge and understanding, that everything made perfect sense, everything I had ever done and would ever do in my life … this seems to go on forever. Then I heard you call my name."

"I did?" Easton didn't remember – not out loud anyhow – but he had definitely talked to her in his own troubled dreams. The night before he had awoken at 3 a.m. from a lucid dream where they were having sex in his childhood bedroom …

"John?"

He shook his head and looked back at her. "Yes?"

"Do you still love me?"

It was an odd question. He didn't think he'd said so a first time. *But it didn't really matter*, he thought, *did it?*

"Yes. I still love you," he said, squeezing her hand.

That got a bigger smile. "Good. Then get me some food," she said. "I'm so hungry I could eat a horse."

"That's good to hear," he answered, "because from my own first-hand experience, I'm pretty sure that's what they've been passing off as meat on the menu here."

The next morning, he took her home to recuperate. The Natural History Museum was giving her three weeks paid sick leave. The Doctors at Philipseburg Memorial were utterly confounded, but further blood tests had revealed nothing unusual in her system. And her ribcage had healed itself completely. To make matters stranger, Easton's arm had all but healed up as well.

"I don't know what the heck the two of you have been eating and drinking," Doctor Rosenberg had said as they were leaving, "but if you have any leftovers, I'd love to have a shot at them!"

They were having coffee in the kitchen a short while later when Sarah asked if it was okay with Easton for her brother to visit. When he told her about his first encounter, she laughed.

"That sounds like my brother. He's always been very protective of our family, especially since our father died. He's a good guy once you get to know him – he was just sniffing you out probably. His full name is William Jay Ramhorne by the way, but I call him Billy."

Easton took a long sip from his mug. After a week of the watery mud they passed off as such at the hospital, it was almost a religious experience to be drinking his beloved Sumatra again. Heck, it was a joy just to be relaxing back in his house. When he'd first walked through the door, it'd felt like he'd stumbled into someone else's place. Except for the dog, of course. Rovsky had stared at him with his massive head tilted as if to say, *where in the hell have you been?*

"That sounds like a strong name, William Jay," he said.

"It is, isn't it? My mother named him after William Sampson, the Indian actor. She was a big fan of his, even though he was Muscogee. He was a big, tall, and powerful man. I think the name rubbed off on my brother some."

"Well, he's welcome here anytime. Any of your family is." Easton caught himself. Was he saying what he thought he was saying? Sarah studied him from over the top of the mug cupped in her hands as if reading his mind. Which, unnerving as it was, was very possible. "But there's one other thing. *Two* actually."

When she didn't respond, he continued, "I don't know what really happened out there. I mean, how it is that you're still alive. I mean, to hell with the doctors, I was there, I saw that monster killing you … well … I don't understand." The words felt tangled up in his mouth, but he kept going, "I mean, look at my arm. It should have taken six weeks to heal. None of this makes any sense."

Sarah set her mug down and placed her hand over his. Something in her expression suggested to him that she had an idea, or at least an intuition, but wasn't willing to give it away just yet. "You let go," she said instead.

Easton was perplexed. "Yes, but …"

She squeezed his hand. "No. You *let go*, and that's important. Only those things you can truly let go can come back to you."

"Sarah, that doesn't make a shred of sense …"

A smile crept at the corners of her mouth. "Well, maybe it does, maybe it doesn't. But I'm here. You slew the river monster. And that's the end of that."

Easton chuckled. "Yeah, I guess I did. But I'm in no hurry to try that again. I think I can scratch that one off the bucket list." He glanced over at the counter where the Bowie knife was laid out next to the drying leather sheath after an intense cleaning. The doctor in charge of emergency had joked they'd had to practically break his fingers to get it out of his grip when they'd first brought him in.

He realized Sarah was still looking him steadily in the eye. Clearing his throat, Easton said, "And the other thing … I … well I, er …"

"– Yes," She answered, cutting him off.

"Yes?"

"The answer is *yes*. You were going to ask if I would want to live here. With you. And your scary monster dog."

Easton felt a little off his stride. "Look … I mean, you're not obligated to –" She stood up carefully and pulled his head to her stomach. As he looked up, she put a finger to his lips. "Let's go upstairs," she said quietly. "I'm still healing, so you'll have to be very gentle …"

37. ONE HELL OF A FUCKING MESS ...

In the end, it could have been worse.

The final tally, in the report that landed on Chief Hendricks desk that following Monday, was thirty-seven dead and forty-nine injured or hospitalized. The police department was in shock at the loss of Detective Eckhart and Lieutenant Sanchez was completely devastated – Hendricks had offered him a month of paid leave and all the support he needed. They'd had a long talk later that day, Sanchez with fifteen stitches across his forehead and sobbing uncontrollably – he'd made it clear he held himself personally responsible and that his clumsy actions had resulted in her death. Hendricks was having none of that though, and after a half hour of alternately laying into him and share his own grief-stricken history, Sanchez stepped out of the police chief's office with his face still tear-stained, but with his back a little straighter.

But to compound matters, her body hadn't been recovered yet, along with at least ten others, though the coroners were still sorting out the remains in the stomach of the creature recovered by the barge with the help from the Okeanos Explorer crew.

They held a funeral for her three days later.

Eckhart had been well-liked by both the force and the community, and the turnout had been one of the largest for a fallen police officer in the village's history.

The organizers of the GreenWater Festival were all up on a caseload of various charges, though they'd brought in a team of high-powered attorneys and Hendricks had a bad feeling the whole lot of them would get off with a slap on the wrist. Hendricks was furious, however, and made no bones about it. The mayor was hiding in his office (under his desk for all the police chief knew) and if by some chance they attempted to hold another one the following year, Hendricks was going to see to it every permit was denied.

Then, there was the cover-up.

Hendricks and Fowler had cooked it up the day before, first bringing in Jim Franks and quizzing him on all that 'computer magic' and '3D special effects technology stuff.' Then the mayor was hauled in for an intense meeting that lasted hours.

This time, Hendricks nailed Santos to the spot and wasn't giving him any wiggle room. "I know about the Russians, Ray – they seriously damaged our launch by the way – and the deal you cut with the

GreenWater folks. So unless you want to find yourself in a serious fucking shit-storm, not to mention criminal charges, this is how this is going to play: with Mister Franks help here, we're going to put out an announcement that the disaster at Raadsel point was due to human error – the sloop and barge collided, resulting in serious loss of life."

"But there were witnesses … smartphones … pictures … we can't cover up something this big!" the mayor had argued.

"No, not completely," agreed Hendricks, "but we can put enough of a spin on it to throw off the worst of the media fall-out. With a little help from Mister Franks here and his digital design studio."

The mayor, who had been worrying his manicured nails, had looked at Jim Franks like he was a used car salesman. "Him? How?"

"By the wonders of technology," Fowler chipped in. "Kinetic Media is going to issue a PR blurb tomorrow about how the monsters showing up on everyone's smartphones was a … what did he say it was?"

"A viral 'Augmented Reality' app we were testing out as a publicity stunt," Franks answered. "Photorealistic 3D creatures we generated using 3DS Max and After Effects and such, exploiting a forced client-side download via a security loophole the NSA actually created with all handhelds."

Fowler nodded and pointed at the mayor. "*Exactly.*"

The mayor made an unconvinced face. "You think anyone will believe that? What about all the regular cameras? This all sounds crazy …"

"Oh, it'll be enough to keep them guessing," Hendricks cut in. "We have to. I mean, do you really want even *more* crackpots over-running the 'Falls after this? The regular cameras won't be an issue I think – there weren't that many and we confiscated them as we served summonses to every single person involved out there. They'll get them back after any incriminating images have been deleted. And which story do you think the public will believe; a bunch of battling sea monsters witnessed by a bunch of people most of who were half-zonked on pot or a sly deployment of the latest and coolest 3D technology?"

The mayor didn't have an answer for that one.

Chester Billingsworth got his boat back, and at first tried to press all sorts of charges against Jim Franks, until it was made clear Franks had acted only in the interest of saving lives, and within a week, Billingsworth had reworked his version of events. To anyone sitting with him at the Yacht Club bar, he would explain (usually after his third or fourth martini) how he'd actually called Franks over to his boat and offered to help with the rescue effort, and that the only thing that had prevented him from doing so had been a fluke accident when he'd stumbled just as the boat was taking off and fallen overboard. But by God, his boat had helped saved the day!

Guillamo Del Tesler held a press conference the following day after the disaster announcing his amazing finds out at Raadsel Point and the successful filming of what was going to be the premier episode of a new season of Ancient Alien documentaries on the History Channel. He also introduced his new personal assistant, Jennie Roderick, who had been instrumental in bringing many 'illuminating facts' to his attention that would no doubt require further investigations of what was *clearly* evidence of Ancient Aliens visiting the Hudson Valley in the past.

When Miss Roderick had stopped by to clean out her desk at the Historical Society, Captain Fowler had been a little less than cordial.

"So what do you have to say for yourself?" he'd said, hands hooked in his belt and leaning against the doorway of the main office.

Jennie had been hastily boxing up her few personal effects and refused to do more than glance at the police captain. "Not much," she'd mumbled.

"*Not much*?" Fowler had growled. "Young lady, you took irreplaceable Indian artifacts that belonged to our society, damaged them permanently, perpetrated a hoax, and then shipped them to a so-called 'Ancient Alien Theorist'?"

Jennie shrugged. "I don't know, I guess. I didn't really think about it."

Fowler had just stood there shaking his head. Part of him wanted to shake her by the neck, another throw any legal charge he could at her. In the end, he'd done neither. "You *didn't know*," he echoed disbelievingly. "What a waste."

As Jennie headed for the door, he'd called her name once more. "Jennifer?"

"Yeah?"

"I will have to let the school know what you did. You'll be blacklisted from working in any archeological field again."

She shrugged. "Whatever." Then left.

At the same moment, the Okeanos Explorer was navigating past the construction barges for the new Tappan Zee Bridge. Down in the mess hall, Bob Ballard had just sat down for a short talk with Ben Reinhardt after introducing him to his new crewmates. First, they were going to drop off the remains of Typhon for a thorough examination by the marine biologists at Woods Hole in Rhode Island before heading back to wrap up the U-boat investigation off the east coast. Ballard had been disappointed they hadn't been able to recover the mosasaur – despite a thorough search – but had told the team earlier, "Well, that's how it works. We lost one thing and found something else just as interesting."

Reinhardt had confessed his thoughts on losing the sea reptile and what a loss, both financially and moral-wise it had been. Ballard just sat back and crossed his hands on his stomach. "Well, win some, lose some. But I'm glad we got you as part of the team, Ben." With his boyish grin and cap tilted back on his head, he looked like a little kid instead of a seventy-one year old. "I don't have to tell you that it's not always about fame and fortune and all that stuff. Sometimes we just work on things because, well, because they're just *cool*. And this next assignment off of Africa is going to be *really cool* ..."

"Next assignment?' Reinhardt had asked, perking up.

"Oh yeah, after this U-boat thing is in the bag, we're heading to the West African coast to see if we can't find another mosasaur. According to this book someone gave me, they supposedly encountered one in the 1950s there. Oh, and it'll be a joint expedition with the Musée Océanographique de Monaco ... have you ever been to Monaco?"

"No!" Reinhardt said, brightening up.

"Ah, well you will after this trip ..."

38. OCTOBER 2ND, THURSDAY, 7:10PM.

"Well, that was certainly one fuckfest of a month," Jim Franks said, taking another pull of his bottle of Palmer's Harvest Ale at the far end of Mooney's Bar. Next to him, John Easton sat with a glass of single malt, this one a 15-year-old Aberlour Pat Mooney had been stocking recently. October had arrived blustery and rainy. Easton had pulled out one of his military-style sweaters, while on the back of his barstool hung a black leather double-breasted jacket. The one that evoked the days of early aviators. By contrast, Franks looked all 'Urban Outfitter' with his dark gray turtleneck and down skier's vest.

"Yeah, you can say that again," Easton agreed, flexing his hand. His right arm had been out of the cast for two days but still felt stiff.

"Well, that was certainly …" Franks started in again then trailed off, distracted by a face on the flatscreen TV mounted near the ceiling at the bar. "Hey, is isn't that … Pat, can you turn the sound up a minute?"

In front of a cosmic backdrop was a square-faced man who looked like his face had been carved from a block of granite. His equally chunky hands were making aggressive chopping motions in the air. On one corner of the screen was the History Channel logo. The caption to the left identified the man as 'Otto Wierling: Author, Filmmaker. *Ancient Astronaut Theorist.*'

Mooney grabbed the remote and started tapping the volume control.

" … Ossie was unquestionably placed there by Ancient Astronauts as a kind of guardian, a guardian which, in our infinite foolishness, we have lost. But we continue to strive for answers," he continued in his thick German accent, truncating each word as if his mouth was an industrial-strength chopper, "embracing ze *Sturm* and *Drang* of free expression and destroying the conventions of modern rationalist thought! This, the Ancient Astronauts understood …"

"Okay, that'll do," Franks cut in, then turning to Easton added. "Where in the hell do they find these nuts? On the History Channel?"

It was a moderately busy night at Mooney's Pub. A handful of the dubiously called 'Mooney's Regular's' were manning their well-worn stools at the far end of the bar. A group of staff from a local dentist's office were celebrating someone's birthday in the back dining room where the booths were and a bunch of twenty-something's were keeping the main bar area lively. One couple was standing at the far corner opposite the bar, checking out the enigmatic (and infamous) Wurlitzer

Jukebox. No sooner did Pat Mooney cut the TV sound than the Wurlitzer kicked in again.

There was a shocking moment when a female voice belted out 'I nearly died' before Mooney got the volume under control from behind the bar and the song resolved itself into hypnotic sling-shot guitar riff of Garbage's 'Vow,' with Shirley Manson managing to sound both seductive and otherworldly at the same time. Easton had often wondered what constituted that curious quality between bands that *tried* to be cool versus those that simply *defined* cool and once again came up empty handed. He only knew that Garbage was one of the groups that were unquestionably the latter.

But the apropos-ness of the line as well as the volume of its initial delivery brought another matter to mind that needed to be addressed.

"Jim, there's something I need to tell you ..." Easton said, contemplating his scotch.

Franks shot him a wary look, "What? That you're not going through with sex change after all? What will you do with all the bras and panties? And just what is it with you British guys and women's clothes?"

Easton let out a laugh that was half a choke. "Er, no. Nothing as drastic as all that. It just that, I never thanked you."

"Thanked me for what?"

"For saving my life that day. On the river."

"Yeah well ..." Franks was uncharacteristically at a loss for words. He looked at the floor as if he might find something very interesting down there. There were only a couple of leaves he'd probably tracked in and a dirty cocktail napkin. He almost told Easton about the Indian showing up in his garden but decided against it.

"Either way, I owe you one," Easton said.

"What, are you kidding?" he replied. "I only pulled your ass out of the water to keep things from getting boring around here." He looked over as the front door to the bar swung open and Karen and Sarah walked in, bring with them a fresh gust of heady autumn air. "Well ... almost boring," he amended.

The two women sidled up to them at the bar. Karen was in a camel-hair coat, zip-front cardigan, and English riding boots while under her doeskin jacket Sarah was wearing jeans and a heavy white Cable-Knit commandeered out of Easton's dresser. Karen had taken Sarah out shopping for winter clothes earlier, and while not acting like best buddies, there at least seemed to be a tacit friendliness between them. There had been an awkward moment two nights before when Sarah had dropped by Frank's house unannounced and had offered an apology – one of the few she'd ever made in her life – and then she'd wound up spending a couple hours sampling some of Karen's more adventurous cocktails. Easton didn't get any particulars when she'd gotten home much later other than one or two things had gotten ironed out.

"Aren't you two ladies a sight for sore eyes?" Pat Mooney said, materializing at their end of the bar, the ever-present white towel folded over his shoulder.

"Flattery will only get you so far," Karen replied, flashing him one of her more charming smiles. "But if you're lucky maybe even a fair kiss."

"Oh we'd be doing more than kissing," Pat responded. "If it weren't for your fine man here and twenty less birthdays on my poor aching bones, I'd be rolling you over in the clover and back again for a week. Or my name is Maggie Thatcher. Now what can I get you?"

"Well then, Miss Thatcher, how about a bottle of your Harvest Moon Pumpkin Ale and ..." She turned to Sarah, who shrugged, "Make that two."

Pat shook his head and fixed Franks with a mischievous eye. "In my day, a woman would never taunt a barkeep in such a fashion."

Franks tipped his beer towards him. "Pat, in your day, they hadn't invented bars yet. Christ, the mastodons were still fighting mammoths over watering holes."

"Ooof," Pat said with a chuckle as he went to retrieve their drinks.

After Franks had raised a toast, he asked Easton, "So did you ever figure out who was behind the whole books and 'Witch Buffalo' horn business?"

"No, not exactly," Easton answered. "Fowler said he had a lead on a suspect – Crazy Jack, that Indian guy we used to see around here every so often. Apparently, he was a patient at the now abandoned Mohansic State Hospital – something about a murder a long time ago – but as long as he'd been showing up around Wyvern Falls, he'd been essentially a harmless, if eccentric, character. But they'll probably never know for sure."

"How's that?"

"He's dead. They found his body near the water at the tip of Raadsel Point. It was bizarre. They assumed from the nature of his chest trauma he was another one of Typhon's victims, but he hadn't been in the water – his shirt was dry. And intact. It should have been torn to shreds. But there it is."

Standing close to Easton, Sarah suddenly took on a sad, faraway look. Then she shuddered.

"What is it?" Easton said, sensing something amiss.

Nothing ... something, she said in his thoughts, *for a moment, I thought that ...*

Easton had a fleeting glimpse of images like tatters of memories – a palisade ... seven silvery figures ... a youthful Indian male standing by a river while a sachem's daughter was sacrificed ... then it passed.

Franks was looking rapidly back and forth between Sarah and Easton, not sure exactly what he was witnessing. "You two need to lay off the spooky shit."

Sarah smiled wistfully. "We should say a toast, and a prayer for him, to honor his memory. And his sacrifice."

"Here-here," Franks said, "to Crazy Jack."

As a Richard Butler came on the Jukebox and broke into the first raspy lines of 'Little Fist,' the three bottles and a glass clinked.

39. "IT'S ALWAYS BETTER ..."

That Saturday, John Easton was out walking Rovsky when he spotted Rambo sitting on the low wall in front of his house, and after the usual exchange of greetings ("Evening, sir.", "*Alo.*") sat down beside him.

Rambo, hands on knees, was looking off into the distance, his magnified eyes swimming in his thick-rimmed glasses. "You know," he said after a bit, in his heavy accent, "the secret to happiness is to stop looking ..." – here he nodded toward the neighbor's yard – "... over there. Over there, it's always better. Better yard. Better yard. Better wife. Better job." He shrugged and made sound that sounded like 'sheesh.' "Just look at what you already have ... and appreciate it. That's all."

Easton chuckled. He loved the old man, with his professional shrugs and his occasional no-nonsense observations on life, even when he kept repeating things.

A minute later, they were joined by a tall man in a red flannel shirt, jeans, and cowboy boots who had also been strolling around the neighborhood, Billy Ramhorne. Sarah's brother had taken some days off upstate and returned to stay with them a few days. He hadn't been overly friendly with Easton, but he had shaken hands with him this time when he'd shown up, and after a long talk with Sarah, thawed out a couple degrees at least. Things had improved even further when Easton took him up to the local firing range at Blue Mountain and they'd spent an afternoon burning up some ammo.

"It's a good place, this neighborhood," Ramhorne said after a spell. "Though the town is haunted by many, many spirits of angry warriors."

"Is it?" Easton said.

Ramhorne showed his teeth in the growing twilight. "Nah. I just made that up. But there *is* something spooky about this area, that's for sure. There's a *thinness* between worlds here. Things can get through. You look out for my sister."

It was the most words Easton had heard him speak to him since he'd arrived. "That's the plan," he said.

The three men sat for a while watching the sunset.

Rovsky sighed.

EPILOGUE

Iki Island, Nagasaki Prefecture, off the South West Coast of Japan.

Standing along the edge of the dock, the four Japanese businessmen stood with identical hands-clasped stances, frowning. Alongside the dock was secured a large 15-meter tank filled with sea water.

On the other side of the tank were two brand-new looking fishing trawlers.

It was a typically warm and humid day at the island. After weeks of 'Yellow Sand' events – storms originating from the increasingly abused Gobi desert in China – the skies had finally dawned clear and inviting. The marina – in the crowded harbor of Katsumoto Port – was jammed mostly with leisure boats these days, since the negative press about the islands fishing practices had all but killed off the fishing fleets.

The eldest of the businessmen, a thickset man in a very expensively tailored suit, said nothing. Next to him, however, his young assistant was borderline hysterical.

"What is this!?" he demanded, pointing down into the tank.

Floating in the tank was a fiberglass model of a *Tylosaurus*, roughly forty feet long. Someone apparently sawed off the jaw and tail, then jury-rigged them with a motor so they flapped mechanically back and forth. On one flipper was a nameplate, the writing which someone had attempted to badly sand off. It had once read, "Property of Hastings Museum, Hastings, Nebraska."

"Are you crazy!? This is not what you promised to deliver us! This … is, is a ridiculous fake!"

The heavy-set man in front of them shrugged and turned around. Igor Gorimov flashed them a big smile with a gold tooth in it.

"Hey, you asked for a dinosaur, I deliver you a dinosaur. No problem…"

AFTERWORD AND NOTES FOR THE CURIOUS ...

Ahhh, well here we are again, at that afterthought part of the manuscript where I get to dole out credit where it's do and shed a little light on one or more things you may have picked up in this grisly little tale.

First and foremost, I have to thank my wife Tomiko for providing – unintentionally – the whole idea for this novel. One fine summer day were enjoying lunch along the Ossining waterfront when somewhere out in the river a large fish leapt out of the water, probably (I hope that's what it was!) a river sturgeon or carp and I said, "Hey, was that a river monster?" to which she immediately replied without hesitation, "No ... that's our 'Ossie' ..."

And thus a legend – in my mind at least – was born.

It didn't help that sometime later while on a visit to New Orleans she picked me up a T-shirt as a surprise that sported a street sign graphic with an alligator chasing a terrified backpacker with the caption, 'Alligators love people – they taste just like chicken!' and rubbing my hands together while grinning I thought, *I bet Ossie loves people too – because they taste just like chicken!'*

The rest as they say, is history.

Next, I have to thank you, Dear Reader, for your support and for sticking it out and reading this whole mess, thus enabling me to continue what I love doing most – telling stories. I really, really appreciate it.

As always, I have a wild time delving into and discovering what ultimately becomes the backstory for these tales, along with inevitable surprises and by-roads that get discovered in the process.

In this case, a lot of this began one day while biking along the river and taking a break to soak up the view it sort of struck me; just 400 years ago there was a completely different culture and race of people on this spot – how strange is that? I decided then and there I wanted to find out as much as I could about the indigenous natives of this area I live in, along with what happened to them.

That turned out to be much harder than I thought.

Growing up in the Finger Lakes region of New York State, I knew plenty about the Iroquois & the League of Nations and of course labored my way through James Fenmore Cooper's 'The Last of The Mohicans' (my God what a convoluted tale ... who is the hero again? Hawkeye? Deerslayer? Natty Bumppo?) but of the lower Hudson River Indians, zilch. Oh, we're all told that story about the Manhattan Indians and selling the island to the Dutch for twenty-four dollars, but that's based more on myth than fact, just as it's relayed in this story.

Suffice to say, there is plenty out there on Hudson Indians, provided you're willing to do a little digging. A good primary source for historic descriptions of local Indians is 'A Description of New Netherland' by Adriaen van der Donck, originally published in 1655. As an astute observer and also a law enforcement officer for the Dutch patroonship of Rensselaerswick, van der Donck was in the unique position of meeting 'first contact' Natives and knew it. He made laborious notes detailing clothing, customs, etc. of local Indians before they became too altered by exposure to European goods and customs. I also read 'Indian Tribes of Hudson's River' by E.M. Ruttenber, which contains exhaustive details on local Indians about everything from diet to clothes, although I have to warn potential readers to take much of this with a grain of salt; Ruttenber's history was written in the 1870s long after the people he was writing about were gone, and I'm told on good authority that some parts of it are outright fabrication, a common practice by historians of that period. A more thorough (if academic) source I tapped was 'The Munsee Indians: A History' by Robert S. Grumet and 'Picture Rocks, American Indian Rock Art in the Northwest Woodlands' by Edward J. Lenik. Though neither may prove to be an ice-breaker at parties, both will certainly improve your knowledge.

I would sincerely like to thank Laura Redish of Native Languages of the Americas for providing me with several translations and insights for my queries on Munsee/Lenape words and phrases, some which no doubt seemed bizarre. An invaluable resource if you wish to *hear* how Lenape is spoken, go to www.talk-lenape.org, which has a huge database of recordings of native speakers including Laura Thompson Dean, one of the last speakers of the Lenape *'Unami'* dialect and a master storyteller. Her Lenape name *'Wenjipahkeehlehkwe'* translates as 'Touching Leaves Woman.' Also, I have to thank John Phillips, Scott Horecky, and all the members of the Lower Hudson Chapter of the NYS Archaeological Association for their insights on local Indians, local legends, Fort Kitchawank, as well as those fascinating lectures held at the Nature Center out at Croton Point. It was John who tipped me off about the load of Indian local artifacts the Ossining Historical Society is in possession of (which despite being an OHSM trustee, I was completely unaware of); it was really something – and humbling – to hold in my hands relics and weapons crafted by unknown natives going back thousands of years in the area.

Strange things continued to arise in the course of writing this story; I came up with the concept of a local character named 'Crazy Jack' over three and a half years ago as a semi-otherworldly being and thought even then it was a pretty stupid & cliché name for an Indian character. I even had Sarah Ramhorne saying as much in this story until, much to my surprise, I discovered this past summer while writing 'Nightmare' that 'Crazy Jack' is in fact a well-known mythical character in Lenape/Delaware folklore, usually described as a trickster; I ended up having to completely re-write Sarah's dismissal.

I also spent a fair amount of time visiting various locations that inspired the story, from the *burms* marking the site of that infamous Kitchawank fort (where apparently 12 sachems were buried, two of whom are still there) to sitting atop the 'middens' of oyster shells left by those original Americans over the centuries.

The tragic and disastrous clash of European and American Indian cultures is unquestionably a terrible, and oft overlooked, chapter in (local) American History. Personally, it's not my intention to judge it one way or another, but simply to bring some attention to who lived here and some understanding as to what happened. If you're looking for an excellent visual as well as historically accurate look at Indians in America, including the NE, nothing tops the PBS series 'We Shall Remain.' You can see it online.

Sea monsters continue to be an endless source of fascination for me, dating back to those Saturday afternoon monster movies like 'Beast from 20,000 Fathoms' and 'It Came from Beneath the Sea,' tapping that primal fear of giant deadly things lurking just out of sight in the murky depths waiting to gobble you up. Every time as a kid we got on a ferry or boat out onto deep water I knew, *I just knew* something huge was waiting underneath the waves, biding its time ...

Last, apologies to fans of Ancient Astronaut Theorists – I actually do think the world is a far more interesting place with these people in it (Come on, who would you really rather party with, Giorgio Tsoukalos or James Randi? Be honest!). Do I believe in aliens? Let's just say, I think assuming we're the only advanced life-forms in a universe consisting of billions and billions of galaxies (and that's only what we can detect from out little corner of it) is beyond arrogant. But at the same time, I'm often shocked at the level so many in this current era of ours vastly underestimate the technical and engineering capabilities of ancient civilizations and just assume they couldn't create such things as the Pyramids or the Nazca lines without 'Alien Intervention.' For those people, I point you to the old chestnut about what the word 'assume' makes.

A few more final things. I did do a fair amount of research on Jacques Cousteau (really out of curiosity; like many of my generation, I grew up fascinated by those weekly episodes of 'the Undersea World') and the events described certainly could have occurred in the context of that time period, though of course as far as I know, no mosasaurs have been sighted off the coast of Africa. Yet. However, if you ever do find yourself in Monaco and looking to get a little exercise, I highly recommend hiking up to the Musée Océanographique with its fantastic cliff-top views of the Mediterranean and its basement exhibits that look like a set out of '20,000 Leagues under the Sea.' Also, I can't say enough about Bob Ballard and his tireless efforts with the National Oceanic and Atmospheric Administration (NOAA). What he does in regard to ocean exploration and bringing attention to both the dire need to protect it as well as what incredible opportunities it offers is nothing short of fantastic. At the risk of a little soapboxing, I'm going to include a little quote from the man himself:

"One of the biggest issues facing the oceans is a lack of awareness. You can't see what goes on in the ocean the same way you see what happens in a forest or in an African savanna. So people don't know that we waste 54 billion pounds of fish every year while 8 million people die of starvation. They don't know that every single fishery will have entirely collapsed by 2048. Or that 90 percent of all large predators in the oceans are gone. And if people could see that. If people could see the amount of waste and destruction in the oceans, they wouldn't stand for it for a second."

You should support the NOAA in any way you can. I was surprised to find out what NASA spends in a year on Space Exploration could fund the NOAA for 1600 years. Give that some thought.

Well, that about wraps it up, Dear Reader. Again, I hope you enjoyed reading this little story half as much as I did writing it, and if you think of it, drop me a line on Twitter or my blog and let me know your thoughts...

Oh, and stay tuned, the next Wyvern Falls adventure is already underway, something about an odd place in town called the Roderick Estate ...

Robert Stava, Ossining
11/21/13

Robert Stava is a writer, art director & musician currently living along  the Hudson River, not far apparently, from that strange village of Wyvern Falls where so many of his tales are set. His wife Tomiko Magario is a professional ballet dancer & teacher in NYC. An ex "Mad Man" and NYC musician, Stava is also an avid mountain biker and holds a 2nd Degree Black Belt in Karate. When it comes to writing, his firm belief in "nothing beats hands-on experience" has landed him in the ER several times over the years, much to his wife's chagrin. These days when not holed up in his attic overlooking the river while knocking out horror stories, he can be found poking around old ruins and cemeteries in the area.

His short horror stories have appeared in various anthologies in the U.S and U.K. "The Nightmare from World's End" is his fourth novel set in Wyvern Falls. His first book, "Combat Recon" – a pictorial history of his great uncle's experiences as a 5th Air Force combat photographer in the SW Pacific during WWII – was published as hardcover in 2007.

CHECK OUT OTHER GREAT DEEP SEA THRILLERS

MEGATOOTH
by Viktor Zarkov

When the death rate of sperm whales rises dramatically, a well-respected environmental activist puts together a ragtag team to hit the high seas to investigate the matter. They suspect that the deaths are due to poachers and they are all driven by a need for justice.

Elsewhere, an experimental government vessel is enhancing deep sea mining equipment. They see one of these dead whales up close and personal...and are fairly certain that it wasn't poachers that killed it.

Both of these teams are about to discover that poachers are the least of their worries. There is something hunting the whales...

Something big
Something prehistoric.
Something terrifying.
MEGATOOTH!

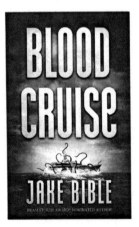

BLOOD CRUISE
by Jake Bible

Ben Clow's plans are set. Drop off kids, pick up girlfriend, head to the marina, and hop on best friend's cruiser for a weekend of fun at sea. But Ben's happy plans are about to be changed by a tentacled horror that lurks beneath the waves.

International crime lords! Deep cover black ops agents! A ravenous, bloodsucking monster! A storm of evil and danger conspire to turn Ben Clow's vacation from a fun ocean getaway into a nightmare of a Blood Cruise!

CHECK OUT OTHER GREAT DEEP SEA THRILLERS

SEA RAPTOR
by John J. Rust

From terrorist hunter to monster hunter! Jack Rastun was a decorated U.S. Army Ranger, until an unfortunate incident forced him out of the service. He is soon hired by the Foundation for Undocumented Biological Investigation and given a new mission, to search for cryptids, creatures whose existence has not been proven by mainstream science. Teaming up with the daring and beautiful wildlife photographer Karen Thatcher, they must stop a sea monster's deadly rampage along the Jersey Shore. But that's not the only danger Rastun faces. A group of murderous animal smugglers also want the creature. Rastun must utilize every skill learned from years of fighting, otherwise, his first mission for the FUBI might very well be his last.

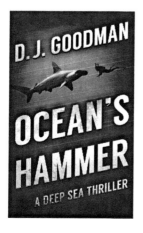

OCEAN'S HAMMER
by D.J. Goodman

Something strange is happening in the Sea of Cortez. Whales are beaching for no apparent reason and the local hammerhead shark population, previously believed to be fished to extinction, has suddenly reappeared. Marine biologists Maria Quintero and Kevin Hoyt have come to investigate with a television producer in tow, hoping to get footage that will land them a reality TV show. The plan is to have a stand-off against a notorious illegal shark-fishing captain and then go home.

Things are not going according to plan.

There is something new in the waters of the Sea of Cortez. Something smart. Something huge. Something that has its own plans for Quintero and Hoyt.

CHECK OUT OTHER GREAT
DEEP SEA THRILLERS

THEY RISE
by Hunter Shea

Some call them ghost sharks, the oldest and strangest looking creatures in the sea.

Marine biologist Brad Whitley has studied chimaera fish all his life. He thought he knew everything about them. He was wrong. Warming ocean temperatures free legions of prehistoric chimaera fish from their methane ice suspended animation. Now, in a corner of the Bermuda Triangle, the ocean waters run red. The 400 million year old massive killing machines know no mercy, destroying everything in their path. It will take Whitley, his climatologist ex-wife and the entire US Navy to stop them in the bloodiest battle ever seen on the high seas.

SERPENTINE
by Barry Napier

Clarkton Lake is a picturesque vacation spot located in rural Virginia, great for fishing, skiing, and wasting summer days away.

But this summer, something is different. When butchered bodies are discovered in the water and along the muddy banks of Clarkton Lake, what starts out as a typical summer on the lake quickly turns into a nightmare.

This summer, something new lives in the lake...something that was born in the darkest depths of the ocean and accidentally brought to these typically peaceful waters.

It's getting bigger, it's getting smarter...and it's always hungry.

CPSIA information can be obtained
at www.ICGtesting.com
Printed in the USA
LVOW10s1616160517
534727LV00004B/840/P